D0712955

ESSEX
DOGS

DAN JONES

ESSEX DOGS

VIKING

VIKING
An imprint of Penguin Random House LLC
penguinrandomhouse.com

First published in hardcover in Great Britain by Aries, an imprint of
Head of Zeus Ltd., a part of Bloomsbury Publishing Plc, London, in 2022
First United States edition published by Viking, 2023

Map design by Jamie Whyte

ISBN 9780593653784 (hardcover)
ISBN 9780593511756 (ebook)

Printed in the United States of America
1   3   5   7   9   10   8   6   4   2

This book is a work of fiction. Apart from the historical figures,
any resemblance between fictional characters created by the author and
actual persons, living or dead, is purely coincidental.

For Violet

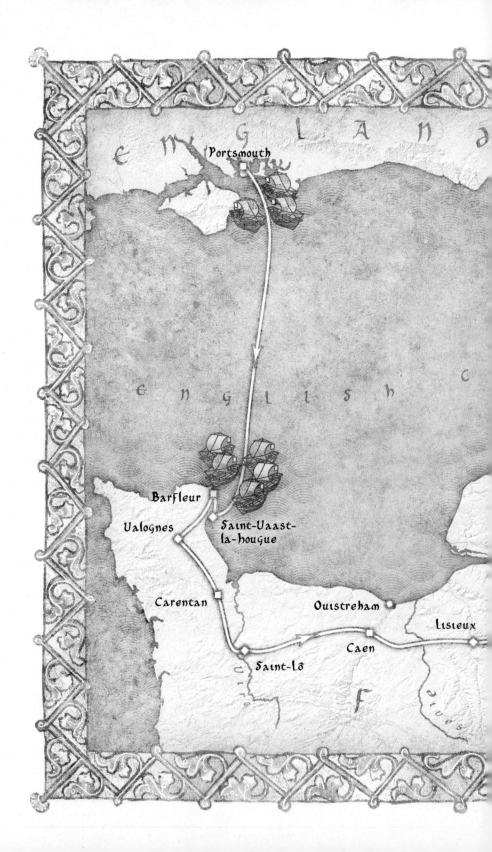

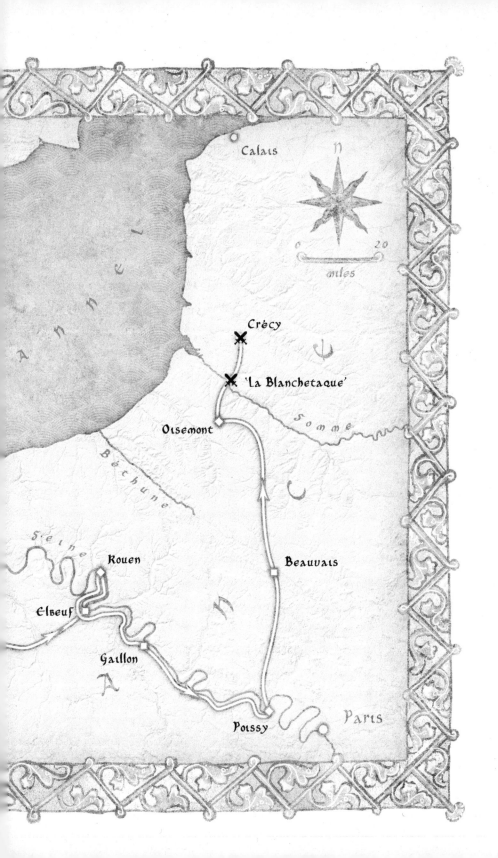

... and nothing was left unburnt.

The Chronicle of Geoffrey le Baker

PART 1

WATER

12–19 JULY 1346

I

This is to let you know that on 12 July we landed safely at a port in Normandy called La Hougue, near Barfleur... many men at arms at once landed... On a number of occasions our handful of men defeated large numbers of the enemy...
Letter from the chancellor of St Paul's to friends in London

'**C**hrist's bones, wake up!'

'Loveday' FitzTalbot jerked his head up. Father had dug him in the ribs with a sharp elbow. Despite the cold saltwater spray that whipped his face, the rocking of the landing craft had lulled him into a moment of sleep.

He had dreamed he was at home.

But now his eyes were open again, he saw that he was not. They were still here. Out at sea. As far from home as they had ever been. Getting further from it every second.

There were ten of them crammed into the little pinnace: himself at the steerboard, Millstone, Scotsman and Pismire further forwards, the priest they called Father beside him at the stern and the archers Tebbe, Romford and Thorp in between them.

Two more archers, Welsh brothers who had been added to the company on the eve of their departure from Portsmouth aboard the cog *Saintmarie*, were pulling the oars.

Loveday scanned the horizon. Normandy. France. As far as he could recall, only he and the Scot had ever been out of English waters. And neither of them knew the coast that loomed half a mile distant, darkest grey in the dawn. What was more, their orders aboard the *Saintmarie*, handed down from Sir Robert le Straunge, were troublingly vague. They had only, Sir Robert had said, to storm up the beach and cut the hairy bollocks off any Frenchman who stood in their way.

When Loveday had asked what Sir Robert – and the great lords and the king above him – knew as to how many Frenchmen might be minding the beach, with crossbows cocked and lances couched and their bollocks unsevered and hoping to keep them so, Sir Robert had waved airily at him and told him there would be plenty enough to make good sport. He said he had this directly from the Marshal of the Army, Lord Warwick, who had it from King Edward himself.

Noble men. Knightly men. Men who knew best.

If I had wanted good sport, thought Loveday, I would have stayed home in Essex, playing dice in the inn near Colchester and paying a penny to lay my head of a night between the thighs of Gilda, the alewife's girl.

But he had held his peace with Sir Robert. The man was a fool, but he was the fool who had recruited them for this campaign. Who would pay their wages for the next forty days. The Dogs hired their sword- and bow-arms to anyone who paid – in any sort of activity where brute force and sharp steel were needed. That summer the business was war. Sir Robert's recruiting agents had promised he was a man who paid on time, and who did not interfere too much. Long experience told Loveday other paymasters were not so easy-going.

So here was he: forty-three summers old, still fit and strong, but grey at his temples, with fat settling around his middle and age creeping into his bones. And here was his company: the Essex Dogs, men called them. Some of them being from Essex. All of them having sharp teeth. Packed into a tiny pinnace, heading towards a French beach at dawn.

The king's great invasion of France – a thousand ships and fifteen thousand fighting men aboard them – was starting.

The Essex Dogs were at the front of it. And Loveday had one wish. The same as every time.

To come home with everyone alive and paid.

At the prow of the boat, the thick-necked stonemason Gilbert 'Millstone' Attecliffe was spewing into the sea. Seasickness, rather than apprehension, thought Loveday, for Millstone had little fear in him – too little, at times. He had known Millstone seven years. Seven years since the heavy-handed, softly spoken Kentishman had cracked the skull of a foreman on the floor of Rochester Cathedral to settle a dispute about the construction of the new spire, and quit masonry for freebooting and fighting.

In that time he had never known Millstone use an intemperate word; nor had he ever seen him take a backward step – an attitude that scared Loveday sometimes.

But this was the least of his worries now. As the Welshmen hauled the oars and Loveday tried to position the bow of the landing craft to ride the tide in to the beach, he could feel a strong current was pulling them hard north, towards the highest point on the bluff.

If I were organizing the defence, that's where I'd put the crossbowmen.

Loveday called to his men to keep their heads low and their eyes on the shore. At the same time, he tried to read the waves breaking ahead, that he might sense when the water would be shallow enough for them to leap overboard, and drag the pinnace up the sands. In the half-dozen other landing craft that were struggling nearby with the same current, he guessed other captains were wondering the same thing.

Loveday's mouth was dry.

He looked behind him, back to the pregnant hulk of the *Saintmarie* and the scores of other cogs that had thrown down their anchors around it. In their bellies, horses kept tethered for two days and nights would now be stamping and snorting. Knights and men-at-arms turning on their straw mattresses. Archers and infantry lying cold and aching on the damp deck.

Loveday pulled the stopper from his leather canteen and took a long tug of ale. It was heavily spiced and already close to spoiling. He belched and tasted sage. He passed the canteen to Father and, summoning more courage than he felt he possessed, he shouted to the Dogs the war cry he had heard from the Spaniard he met drinking a campaign's pay away in London many years before, a swarthy man who had fought the Saracens and bore a long scar from his hairline to chin to prove it.

'*Desperta ferro!*'

Awake, iron!

Scarcely had the words left his mouth than a volley of crossbow bolts sheared the air. A bonfire went up on the bluff to their right. And Loveday heard the cries of Frenchmen above them. Then they appeared – perhaps two companies, maybe more, waving crossbows and hooting. One was baring his arse in their direction, in the Scottish style.

Now the boat was barely a hundred feet from the sands. Loveday roared to the Welshmen to pull for their lives.

The bigger of the two nodded, muttering something in his own language, and they bent their backs. The boat lurched in the water, then sprang forwards like a mastiff unleashed.

As his crew scrambled for iron helms and leather caps, to his left Loveday heard sharp yells of fear and distress. The nearest craft to them had run into a rock, hidden somewhere below the surface. The company – a mixture of men-at-arms and archers – was leaping into the water. He saw a dozen men dive from the boat, which sank like a porpoise diving for squid. Only four surfaced – all archers, who beat the water with their arms, thrashing for the shore. The rest, Loveday guessed, had never learned to swim, or else had been pinned to the seabed by the weight of their packs and armour.

As that craft and its crew foundered, a volley of huge stones came flying down from the clifftop. Millstone yelled from the prow: 'Catapults!' Before the word was out of his mouth, the Dogs saw one of the archers struggling in the water hit directly by a lump of stone the size of an anvil. His skull collapsed. The seawater around him turned dark.

More crossbow shot flew across them – two bolts cracked into the side of the pinnace and another fizzed so close to Loveday's nose that he felt the air move. He tried to calm his breath. Remind himself he had been under bombardment before and lived. But even in the cold, he could feel sweat trickling down his spine.

In front of him, Tebbe, Romford and Thorp were trying to stand and nock arrows to shoot back. Loveday bellowed at them to stay low. Tebbe ducked down again, and the Scot leapt back, putting his giant hands on Romford and Thorp's shoulders and forcing them prone.

Still the Welshmen at the oars pulled and pulled, and then,

at last, the boat rose high on a breaking wave and fell with a thump on to hard sand. The impact half winded Loveday, but he heard Pismire shouting from the bow, screaming at the Dogs to get out and drag the boat up the beach.

Then, as if lifted by the hand of the Lord, Loveday was up, grabbing his sword and heaving himself over the side of the pinnace, into the saltwater, losing his breath for a second time as the cold hit him and his clothes became heavy. Freezing wool clinging to his thighs. His leather overshirt like a coat of mail. But he found his feet, and started bawling orders. Millstone and Scot were behind the pinnace, pushing from the stern as the three archers dragged at the bow – all five of them heaving in unison, dropping to the shallows as each new wave of bolts and stones rained down from the clifftop above.

Fifty yards, away at the foot of the steepest part of the bluff, lay the overturned and rotting shell of an old fishing boat, its broken ribs glistening like a whale carcass.

'Cover – get to the wreck!' Loveday shouted to Pismire and Father. The three of them bolted up the beach, their heads hunkered low into their shoulders. The priest's rough grey cassock was soaked and dragged in the sand as he ran. They slid behind the stinking planks of the dead boat and lay on the sand, panting. They were so tight now to the bluff that the missiles from above were flying over their heads and the other boats making the same landing.

Loveday turned on to his elbows. He took a moment to wipe seawater from his stinging eyes. He spat out blood, and ran his tongue around his mouth, feeling for his teeth. They were all there. He reckoned he must have bitten his cheek.

He returned his focus to the beach.

Despite his earlier misgivings, he saw the current had

dragged them so far along the sands that they had ended up with the shortest run to cover once they landed. The three archers, helped by Millstone and the Scot, had beached the pinnace and were sheltered behind it, waiting to time their run to the cliffside. The Welshmen were behind a small outcrop of rocks a short distance away. Loveday nodded at the taller, blond one, whose name was Lyntyn.

The nod was returned.

One by one, Millstone, Scot, Tebbe, Romford and Thorp all scampered – half running, half crawling, apewise – from the pinnace to the wreck. Loveday checked them all in. The mantra he had learned from their old leader, the man they had called the Captain, had stuck with him: *Bury your dead. Leave no living man behind.*

The Dogs were all there. They spat and cursed and checked themselves for damage. Loveday watched a man-at-arms from some other company running up the beach. He was hit with two bolts – one in his side and another through his neck. Blood spurted and the man fell to his knees, eyes wide and disbelieving, before a third bolt from some sharp shot above them flew into his face through his right cheek. He fell sideways, lay on the sand and did not get up.

'Christ spare his soul,' said Tebbe, tall and spare, the lankiest of the three English archers, who wore his hair long at the neck, woven in a tight plait that reached his mid-back.

'Christ will know his own,' said Father. He swigged deeply from Loveday's flask, which he had carried from the landing craft. He craned his neck and looked towards the top of the cliff, where the crossbows and catapults were embedded. Took another swig. Wiped his mouth with his hand.

'Let's get up there and kill those fucking Frenchmen.'

★ ★ ★

They lay on their fronts and surveyed the land's lie. Loveday scrambled next to Millstone, Pismire and the Scot, his three most experienced men.

Pismire pointed out a steep path cut into the bluff, a hundred paces from the wreck. 'The way up's there,' he said, pointing to the clifftop.

Not for the first time, Loveday was grateful for Pismire's sharp eye amid the frenzy of a fight. He nodded. 'Aye. How shall we play this?'

'Keep it simple,' said Pismire. 'We creep behind them, cut their throats, and stick their crossbows up their arses, stirrup-end first.'

Loveday looked at the other two. The Scot nodded. Millstone shrugged. On the other side of him, Father was jabbing his dagger into the dirty sand in excitement.

From the beach came a thunderous crash. Another torrent of rocks hurled from the clifftop hit a boat being hauled out of the surf, scattering the archers dragging it. One lad, no more than fifteen summers on him, had his leg shattered. He collapsed, screeching. White blades of bone poked through his pink flesh. The lad writhed and cursed. His fellows hid behind their half-beached boat and trembled.

Loveday took a deep breath. He gripped Pismire by the arm and spoke to him clearly.

'Very well,' he said. 'We do it. But let's see what's up there first. Go with Scotsman. Take Tebbe and Thorp. See how many are there. If you can make them hop a little, do it. But if not, send one man back and call for support. Then wait for the rest of us.'

Pismire nodded assent. Loveday looked around the company. Made a calculation. 'Take Father, too.'

Father took one last swig of Loveday's flask and tossed it back. He grinned, all brown teeth and bloodlust.

Pismire raised an eyebrow to Loveday. He had trusted Father, once. In recent years his faith had waned. He looked at the old priest. 'You gawp like the hell-mouth,' he said.

'To mind you of your sins,' said Father.

Tebbe and Thorp checked their arrow bags. The youngest archer, Romford, tugged Loveday's sleeve. 'I'll go too,' he said.

'You stay here, boy,' Loveday told him. 'I need you. The French may come at us down the beach. We need at least one bowman for cover.'

Romford pouted, peevish. But he did not complain.

On the beach, the lad with the shattered leg was still screaming.

Loveday turned away from the sound and nodded at Pismire. 'Godspeed,' he said. 'And be sure you all come back. Remember what the Captain—'

Pismire rolled his eyes. He did not care to be reminded of the Captain any more than he cared to look after Father. 'Let's go,' he said to Scotsman, Father, Tebbe and Thorp. The five men waited for a gap in the barrage from the clifftop; then they set out at a low sprint along the foot of the bluff towards the little path.

Loveday, Millstone and Romford watched them go. Loveday ran his hand over his head, squeezing water out of his thin, straggly hair. He did the same for his beard. He looked over to the rocks where the Welshmen had been taking cover.

The brothers were no longer anywhere to be seen.

★ ★ ★

Pismire led the group up the steep path. They crawled on their bellies like snakes, using the cover of the long grass. For Pismire, it was easy to stay concealed. Short, compact and wiry, with dark hair cropped close to his head, he was the smallest of the Dogs, having barely grown in height since his twelfth nameday.

The children in the village had given him his nickname after their word for the tiny, biting ants which used to plague them when they played in the long fields on saints' days. In temper and size he was just like the tiny creatures: you would scarcely notice him – until he sunk his sharp jaws into you.

They neared the top of the path. It became clear that Pismire's guess was right. The sandy, scrubby track had carried them around to the top of the bluff. They stayed low. But by raising their heads a little, they were able to survey the land as it stretched out all around them.

Yet when they took it all in, they found it hard to believe what they saw. Pismire had been sure from the barrage of missiles and bolts which the first wave of landing craft had suffered that there would be a large encampment of defenders wearing King Philippe of France's livery of bright blue and gold fleurs-de-lis: knights couching their lances, men-at-arms brandishing swords and ranks of crossbowmen positioned to shoot down whoever was foolish enough to do as they had and pop their heads above the rise.

But mostly what they spied was empty fields. The only defenders visible were the company at the high point, some three hundred paces to their right, who were operating three small catapults and a score of crossbows. They were lightly armoured: not one of them wearing thick metal plate.

They were dressed almost exactly like the Dogs: in coats of hardwearing cloth or leather padded with horsehair, and, here and there, a few pieces of mail. A couple of crossbowmen wore simple, open-faced helmets.

They had the advantage of position, realized Pismire. But there were barely two dozen of them, all poorly prepared to fight at anything but long range.

Pismire looked at the Scot. The Scot looked back at him. They had fought together long enough to know that they were thinking the same thing.

'Let's make them dance,' said the Scot. They glanced behind them. Father was giggling to himself and thrusting his hips into the coarse sand of the pathway. Tebbe and Thorp were awaiting instructions.

Pismire silently motioned them forwards, spotting a route between clumps of thorny bushes covered in tiny yellow flowers, which protected deep undulations in the clifftop. He sent the archers right, hugging the line of the cliff. Then he, the Scot and Father crept left, inland, to the path along which the Frenchmen had arrived; where the grass lay flattened from the tramp of feet and the drag of the trebuchets.

They hunkered in a hollow. Pismire watched Tebbe and Thorp slip into their own position. He paused a few moments, counting his breaths. Shrieks rose from the beach below – men's cries sounding like angry gulls.

The lightest of rains had started to fall. After the scouring spray of the sea it felt warm and refreshing. The tiny droplets scattered the rising sun's light, creating pinpricks of bright colour in the air.

Pismire waved to the archers. Then he watched in satisfaction as they began to shoot.

Tebbe and Thorp had grown up in villages on Foulness Island off the Essex coast, where mists and sea-raids and biting easterly winds bred men tough and where every boy grew up with a bow in his hand.

Now, protected by the landscape and their position, they were in their element. Turn by turn they stood, nocked, drew, sighted and shot – smoothly and at ghostly speed.

They aimed first for the men hauling the catapults. Tebbe shot first, and his arrow sailed a handspan high, whistling above the Frenchman's head. But as he flattened himself Thorp was sighting, using Tebbe's missed shot as a marker. He sent his first arrow straight into the man's chest. The man flew backwards as though he had been kicked in the heart by a mule. He lay on the ground, his legs twitching helplessly.

Thorp ducked, and Tebbe stood, nocked and shot again. The French company were staring around them in panic, trying to locate the shooters' position, but the Essexmen were too fast. Tebbe took a second catapult-operator, the arrow bursting his eyeball and burying itself deep inside his head.

Two down, thought Pismire. Now the dance begins.

By the time Thorp and Tebbe had taken their next two shots, missing twice before both hitting the same crossbowman in the thigh and gut, the French were in a frenzy. Their beachward barrage of bolts and stones had ceased and they were scrambling for cover.

One crossbowman took cover behind a trebuchet. Tebbe watched him load his bow, then waited patiently for him to peer around the wooden frame to line up a shot. In the brief moment that he steadied himself and aimed, Tebbe shot two arrows in quick succession. The second split the man's breastbone, and he went down with a moan.

Thorp stood straight away and also shot twice. He took one Frenchman through the throat as the man flailed around looking for cover. The second arrow glanced off another crossbowman's helmet.

The French were screaming at one another.

Pismire, the Scot and Father exchanged smiles.

Any moment now—

The first to break and run was a young crossbowman with lank hair and a few patches of downy fluff here and there on his cheeks. He hurtled away from the cliff-edge, throwing his weapon away in terror as he ran.

Pismire tapped the Scot on the shoulder.

The boy hurtled towards them. The huge Scotsman drew his legs beneath his body, crouched and coiled like a dog baiting a bear.

The boy never saw him coming. As he ran past, the Scot sprang, transferring all his weight through his right shoulder and into the boy's ribs. He knocked him sideways, and in one clean motion, rose, turned the boy face down on the ground, knelt on his back, crooked his arm around the boy's face and leaned back.

The boy's neck snapped. His body jerked and flapped like a fish. The Scot stood up, no thought now for cover, and roared.

Three more Frenchman, also running from Tebbe and Thorp's arrows, paused. They looked at the Scot, then at one another, then scattered in three directions, running pell-mell across the clifftop and trying to escape the vast bulk of the flame-haired monster before them.

Pismire leapt up and gave chase. He careered across the uneven sandy grassland, gaining steadily on a middle-aged man. The man half turned with a hand out to try and fend Pismire off, but Pismire jumped at him, wrestled him to the ground, pulled his dagger and stabbed the man four or five times in the chest. He stood, sucking for air, and looked around. The Scot was clubbing another Frenchman in the face with his fists.

Further off, Father had found the body of a crossbowman felled by an arrow through the stomach. He was bending the arrow backwards and forwards, and laughing maniacally at the man's screams.

Tebbe and Thorp were continuing to shoot. Thorp sent one man skittering across the hilltop with an arrowhead planted in his buttocks. Tebbe lodged an arrow in another man's spine, and watched, impressed, as he went down, his legs suddenly useless beneath him.

Pismire noticed too that arrows were flying at the Frenchmen from another direction. At the top of the path, the Welsh brothers who had rowed them to shore had reappeared. They stood side by side, silently loosing arrows at the French as they fled, impassive as if they were shooting ducks on a millpond.

Pismire sank to his haunches and allowed himself a smile. The archers could finish this job. He felt the heavy tramp of the Scot's feet as the big man approached.

'Five men against two dozen,' said the Scot. 'When did we ever have it this easy?'

Pismire nodded. 'But where are the rest?' he said.

The Scotsman shrugged. He had blood smeared on his face, and some of it was dripping, mixed pink with rainwater and sweat, from the tips of his ginger beard.

'Maybe there is no rest,' he said.

Leaving the archers and Father to their sport, the two men walked back to the top of the path that led up from the beach.

As they looked across the sand, they saw Loveday, Millstone and Romford gathering driftwood for a fire.

Half a mile out to sea, the English flotilla was swelling: a huge, creaking mass of cogs, hulks, horse-transports and smaller vessels.

A rainbow of heraldic flags and pennons fluttered above them, brightening the flat grey of the morning sky. And from their direction, a galley pulled by twelve sets of oars was now sharking towards the shore, the royal arms of lions and fleurs-de-lis quartered fluttering above it.

The Dogs stood and watched it, breathing heavily, steam rising from their heads.

'King Edward's boat,' said Pismire. 'Our king has missed all the fun.'

2

When [the English fleet] was drawn up and anchored on the shore, the king came off his ship. But as his foot touched the ground, he stumbled and fell so heavily that the blood gushed from his nose… [He said:] 'It's a very good sign for me. It shows that this land is longing to embrace me.'

Chronicles of Jean Froissart

The Dogs made camp on the beach. Loveday watched his men work. The three English archers and the Scot were unloading the landing craft while Millstone and Father put up a makeshift windbreak of oilskins and oars. Once it was up, they sat in its lee, stretching their legs around a driftwood fire and trying to dry their sodden clothes. The silent Welshmen made their own fire a few yards away. The flames from both fires gave off a pleasant, salty smoke. It tickled the back of Loveday's throat.

Settled for a moment, Loveday pulled from his pack the tiny figure he was carving from a piece of oxbone. It was a craft he'd learned as a child, and he liked to practise it for good fortune, and to keep up his blade skills. Over the years he had made hundreds of these figures. He usually gave them away.

He noticed the youngest archer, Romford, watching him work.

'Who is it?' Romford said.

Loveday smiled: the lad had a true archer's eyesight. The carving was no bigger than his thumb, yet through the fire-smoke the boy had seen it was a figure.

'It's a saint,' he said. 'A woman. I think. Maybe St Martha.'

'Who's she?'

Loveday shrugged. 'She did something for Christ. I can't remember what. I just like to carve. It's a habit.'

Romford nodded, as though he understood.

The tide was now a long way out. The receding waters exposed ridged sand and shallow pools, which gleamed like polished glass in the afternoon sun. Where men had fallen on their fight to take the beach, there were now dark patches. The bodies had been hauled away, feet first, to be blessed by priests and buried by their fellow soldiers. Loveday remembered the Dogs he had put in the ground over the years. 'No-Arms' Peter with his shock of white hair. Garvie. Wiseman the Jew.

And he remembered the one who had gone unburied. The Captain.

He shook the thoughts and the faces out of his mind. He knew the other Dogs considered it unlucky to speak of their dead. He turned his attention back to the beach.

Out at sea, hundreds of little craft were ferrying back and forth between the sand and the cogs. Rowers heaved in the surf. They unloaded seasick troops – knights and men-at-arms, Welsh archers and northern spearmen, and crowds of ordinary footsoldiers – peasants carrying weapons of all sorts: short swords and daggers, mallets and clubs, axes and mowing scythes. On the horizon more large transports were coming into view. The whole of England seemed to be decamping to the long, muddy sands. Hour by hour the beach was filling up with curved longbows made of ash, hazel, elm and yew, crates of arrows and spare pieces of armour, long coils of rope and iron chain, barrels of grain, flour, pork, salt fish and ale. Hundreds of horses, released from their days at sea, whinnied and cantered around. Herdsmen and kitchen porters brought live beasts ashore for the royal and noble kitchens: inside wooden cages chickens cackled and geese honked. Pigs tried to flee the boys minding them, who swore and beat their hairy flanks with sticks.

Most of all though, the beach was filling up with men. Hundreds, thousands of men, with accents and dialects from every corner of England and Wales. Some dragged packs; others travelled empty-handed as though they had just left their village in search of a lost sheep. Some were fresh-faced and full of wonder at the unimaginable fact of setting foot in another kingdom. Far more wore the rough, hard-bitten expressions of travelling, brawling men. Men like the Dogs, who made their way in life with their fists, wits and weapons. Sometimes robbing, sometimes fighting kings' wars.

Always looking for a job. Always spoiling for a fight.

'They're having a damn sight easier time landing than we did,' said Pismire, following Loveday's gaze around the beach, and prodding the fire's glowing coals with a stick.

'Ah, shut up – you enjoyed it,' said the Scot, running his fingers through his hair and beard and teasing out little scabs of congealed filth.

Pismire grunted. 'Maybe I did. I'm not bellyaching. In fact, if this is how it's going to be, it's fine with me,' he said. 'After tonight we're getting paid to be here for thirty-eight more days. I'd rather spend them winning easy fights than hard ones.' No one among the Dogs was more exact about counting down the days of a contract than Pismire.

Father leered. 'The French fuckers don't want to stand and fight. They've scuttled off to hide their coin and their daughters,' he said. 'Let them try. We'll sniff them out.' He put two fingers to his lips. Stuck his tongue out between them.

Loveday caught Millstone's eye. Millstone shook his head and stared into the flames. He disliked this kind of talk. Loveday understood: he knew Father was becoming a menace. There was a time when the wayward priest had been one of their best men. Fifteen summers ago, when he had abandoned a parish ruined by famine and corrupt bishops, and taken to a life of ministering to the Essex Dogs and occasionally helping with their work, he had been tough, clever and alert. Recently though, age and ale had got into his heart and gnarled it. Now he often seemed dangerous to anyone around him, friends and enemies alike.

Yet he was one of them. And to Loveday, that mattered above all other things.

Feeling the mood tighten, Loveday changed the subject and spoke to the whole crew. 'Anyway. At least we didn't fall on our faces in the sand.'

Earlier in the day the Dogs had watched King Edward and his commanders go through their own beaching ritual. The galley that brought ashore the king and his eldest son, the Prince of Wales, had been sleek and fast, rowed by thickset oarsmen in royal livery. But there had been a moment of farce when Edward tried to wade through the shallows on to the land he claimed.

A large breaker had swelled behind him, and the king had lost his footing in the shingle, falling in a heap. Royal knights had quickly hauled him up. The prince had stood back, as if amused. It had been the talk of the beach ever since.

'Can you believe the silly fucker came up with a bloody nose?' the Scot muttered. 'Feels like an omen, you ask me.'

'Thank Christ nobody did ask you,' flashed Pismire. 'Not in the king's earshot, anyhow. I'd stay as far away from him as you can. He'll take one look at your ginger beard and have you strung up.'

'For what?'

'For being a thick fucking dirty Scot who hasn't washed his hair since William Wallace was alive, that's what. Most of your lot fight with the French. Which makes you the enemy, first time you open your mouth.'

Loveday grinned. Pismire and the Scot could do this all day. They often did.

'What about his son, though?'

That was Romford. Loveday looked again at the youngest member of the Dogs. Sixteen years old, Romford was a streak of lean muscle and bone – his white teeth still strong and all there, and his yellow beard soft and wispy, emerging in odd patches below his prominent cheekbones. He could be shy and awkward, but Loveday was yet to see him panic or fret. Romford sat beside Millstone, and the two of them made an odd couple: the grizzled stonemason, his skin as dark as a Saracen's and wiry black hair in tight, springy curls. Next to him Romford looked like an angel.

'The prince was born the same summer as you, wasn't he?' Loveday said to the boy.

'Aye,' said Romford proudly. 'And now he's a knight. Dubbed on the beach on his first campaign: *Sir* Edward, Prince of Wales.'

'And what does that make you?' asked Father.

'Me? I'm the Prince of *Wails*.' Romford mimed drawing a

bow and loosing it. An imaginary arrow flew straight through Father's heart.

Father covered a nostril and blew a lump of glutinous brown snot into the sand. He wiped his nose with his sleeve. 'You dream of shooting me, boy, I'll strangle you while you sleep,' he said.

Romford smiled, but said nothing. Tebbe and Thorp sniggered. Father glared.

Along the beach, from somewhere near the king's pavilions, a short blast of trumpets sounded. Loveday hauled himself to his feet. He put the little figure of St Martha back into his pack, sheathed his knife and nodded to Millstone. 'Time for us to take our orders,' he said. 'We'd better go and find Sir Robert.'

It took them a long time to find Sir Robert's pavilion, for the beach was at least two miles long, and packed with bodies. The drizzle of the afternoon had blown away and the sun now warmed the sands. As some men continued to land and unload, many of the first companies to arrive had settled down to drinking and singing, celebrating their safe delivery from the seas. Boasting of what adventures they would have, and what terrors they would visit on the French.

Loveday and Millstone weaved between these groups. They stepped over small streams of piss running down from the dunes at the back of the beach towards the sea and ducked away from royal officers looking to press idle men into carrying boxes.

They missed Sir Robert's tent at first, and had to double back to find it. When they arrived, they found the briefing had begun. They slid in quietly at the back of the group of two dozen men gathered around the portly Essex knight whose offer of wages for fit, experienced fighting men all of them had answered, back in the exciting months of the early spring, when the king's invasion plans had been announced.

Sir Robert's voice was a drone. 'What I must stress to you most of all,' he was saying, his face purple at the cheeks, his nose grossly distorted by drink and his piggish eyes blinking fast, 'is that by royal ordinance there shall be no looting or ill treatment of the ordinary folk of this land. Your forty days' pay depends on this.

'The king has come to claim his right to the French crown, illegally usurped by his false cousin Philippe. That means the people of this land are the king's subjects, and we are here to liberate them, not to distress them. The king is most particular on that matter. So what that means is, is, is...'

Loveday took a deep breath. He looked around the group. From what he could see of the other men's faces, all were bored and restless.

Next to Millstone, someone spoke up. It was a lanky, thin-limbed man perhaps ten years younger than Loveday, with sandy-coloured hair and brows, and a long face, on which he had trimmed his bristles into a moustache. There was an arrogance in his eyes. 'Is this a war or isn't it?' he said. 'Have we come here to fight? Or to hear the people confess their sins, wipe their arses and offer to bring in the harvest?' He had a broad accent. Somewhere further up the coast from Essex. East Anglia, somewhere. 'At dawn this morning you were telling us to ram our spears up their holes and cut their women's tits off.'

The rest of the group shuffled their feet in the sand. Sir Robert's cheeks deepened in colour, from purple to midnight his forehead, took a step forwards so that he was also facing Millstone.

No one else in the group moved.

'Men, I must implore you—' said Sir Robert.

Then Millstone spoke. Calm and measured. 'I'm trying to listen to Sir Robert,' he said. 'I was hoping you could keep quiet.'

The East Anglian bent down, and put his face right in Millstone's. Their noses nearly touched. He spoke with a sneer. 'And I was hoping you could come to my campfire later and suck each of my men's pintles,' he said. 'Put a pretty frock on when you do it.'

Millstone smiled. 'I'm a little old for you, I think,' he said.

Loveday held his breath. A look passed over the East Anglian's face. And Loveday saw what he was about to do. The man stepped his right foot back and withdrew his head a fraction.

Millstone saw it too. As the East Anglian went to drive his forehead forwards and butt Millstone in the bridge of his nose, the stocky stonemason, deceptively light on his feet, pivoted on the ball of his own left foot, swinging sideways and stepping out of the East Anglian's way.

When the man piled his head forwards and downwards, Millstone's face was no longer there. Instead, the momentum of his headbutt took him forwards, and he crashed face first into the sand. The rest of the men in the group roared with laughter and clapped.

The East Anglian's companion, the one with the brand on his face, moved his hand to his belt. Loveday stepped quickly forwards and put a hand on the man's chest. 'No.'

The tall East Anglian sat up in the sand, a look of pure rage his face. There was blood trickling out of his nose. It turned moustache red.

blue. 'The king is most particular,' he repeated. 'Most par
These are—'

Millstone was staring directly at the lanky East Ang

'His subjects,' the East Anglian continued. '/
ordinances. We heard you. I'll tell my men to use their p
for firewood and start gathering wildflowers for posi‹

Sir Robert did his best to ignore the insolence. '
remain on the beach until the ships are unloaded. '
the king will headquarter in La Hougue. There is a f
there, which will suit his purposes.' Sir Robert gest
in the direction of the headland where the Dogs had
the catapult men to ground. 'I myself expect to be
attendance on him, being of course one of his n
trusted advisors.'

Millstone was still staring at the East Ang
Unflinching.

There was no way the East Anglian could not se‹
a few seconds he swivelled around to face Millst
almost a head taller than the round-shouldered
He glared down at him. 'The fuck are you lookii

Millstone did not move. Did not blink. Did i
kept staring.

Sir Robert's blustering trailed off as he real
was occurring in the group. 'Men, I – really,
you—'

No one took any notice. The East Anglian r
Slowly. With a snarl. 'Fuck,' he said, 'are you l

Millstone's eyes did not flicker. Loveday,
tensed. His knife was in his pack. His short
by the campfire. He balled his fists slowly
other East Anglian, with a scar in the sha

Millstone smiled at him. 'First the king,' he said. 'And now you.'

Sir Robert, squawking, had by now pushed his fat frame through the group, followed by one of his men-at-arms. The man-at-arms wore only a padded gambeson, with no armour on top. But he was a commanding enough presence that Millstone and Loveday took two paces back, the East Anglian with the branded face slunk away, and the tall one sat up on the sand and did not attempt to continue the fight.

'Shaw,' said Sir Robert, his face now white with fury. 'What is this?'

Shaw glowered, sullenly, at Millstone. 'Nothing, Sir Robert,' he said.

Sir Robert breathed hard through his nose. 'Quite so. Nothing.' He turned to Millstone and Loveday. 'And you Essex men—'

Millstone held up his hands in apology.

'We meant no trouble, sir,' said Loveday. He reached out a hand towards Shaw, to help him from the beach. Shaw just looked at it. He spat a ball of bloody phlegm, which caught in the sand and shrivelled. Loveday withdrew his hand.

Sir Robert looked around the whole group. 'This sort of brutality will not be tolerated, or repeated.' He cleared his throat and brushed a few grains of sand from the arms of his quilted tunic. He returned as best he could to his briefing.

'La Hougue is at this minute being secured and the royal headquarters prepared. There will be ale and pork supplied to you all before sundown. I am told it is of the finest quality.'

There were a few muted laughs.

'In the meantime, we make camp,' said Sir Robert. 'Remember: we are here to protect the king's loyal subjects.

May God bless you, men. We meet here again in two days, by my pavilion, after the morning's Mass. For now, I bid you goodnight.'

Sir Robert left the group and swept back towards his pavilion. Millstone and Loveday backed away from the group; then they weaved away once more through the crowd, towards where the Dogs had made their fire.

'What was that?' asked Loveday. Millstone was staring straight ahead and did not meet his eye. Loveday nudged him. 'Well?'

Millstone shrugged. Shook his head slightly. 'I don't know. There was something I didn't like about him.'

'What? Why? Who is he?'

'I don't know,' said Millstone. 'Maybe I'm wrong. It was just a feeling. Nothing more. But now we know.'

'Know what?'

'What to expect.'

The Dogs saw the first flames flickering from the high ground at dusk.

Scotsman was tending the cooking pots, heating dried beans and herbs in ale to form a thick stew, and blackening the skin of the leathery piece of salted pork Tebbe and Thorp had brought back from the quartermaster's station on the far end of the beach. The Welshmen had caught crabs by the rocks and were boiling them alive in seawater.

All around the beach other small companies were making similar meals. On the shoreline, knights were exercising cramped horses, cantering along the sand. It was a warm, pleasant night, with a light breeze coming off the sea, which kept the air fresh, and blew away the stink of so many men and beasts.

But over the hills, houses had started to burn. There were three, perhaps four sources of smoke, which rose in greasy black gouts. Burning thatch, coughing up months of grime that caked the roof-straw.

Loveday looked west, into the sunset, to see the fires. 'Not everyone got the king's message,' he said.

Pismire stood next to him, shielding his eyes against the late-afternoon's glare with his forearm. 'I'm sure they got the message,' he said. 'They just don't give a damn.'

By the time they sat down to eat, darkness had almost fallen, and the torches were lit. Now the Dogs were quieter. Loveday could feel the tension in the group, even before it was spoken. They had tasted blood and felt the prickle of excitement at the closeness of death. Some of them wanted more. Father was drawing five-pointed stars in the sand with his dagger-tip. Millstone and the Scot were staring intently at their wooden cups of beans. Pismire was gazing steadily into the cooking pit, and Romford was looking uncertainly from one older man to the other.

Loveday spoke first so that no one else had to. 'We camp here tonight,' he said. 'Those aren't the king's orders or Sir Robert's. They're mine. We camp tonight. There's a long road ahead of us to Paris. There'll be more than enough along it for us all.'

Father jabbed his dagger hard into the sand. He pulled away from the group to where he had scraped out a sleeping-pit, and wrapped his blanket around his shoulders. He muttered something to himself.

Loveday ignored him. 'The French may come again tonight,'

he said. 'Probably they won't, but we should be ready. And it isn't just the French.' He glanced at Millstone, but he said nothing more about Shaw and the East Anglians. He just made arrangements for the watch. 'First shift is Millstone and Romford. Second, Tebbe and Thorp. Third, Pismire and Father. Pismire, rouse me before dawn.'

Then he repeated it, as if it needed saying. 'We camp here tonight.'

The sleepers turned in to their sand-beds. Soon most of them were snoring. Romford and Millstone sat together by the fire, Millstone telling the boy some old story in his soft and gentle voice. But two of the Dogs were missing.

The Welsh brothers were gone. Where they had been sitting was now just a pile of broken crab-shells.

Just before dawn, Pismire shook Loveday awake from a dream.

He was glad to be dragged out of it. He had been attending a funeral at the king's court, standing among the mourners as a bier was carried: a small coffin set on the shoulders of six weeping women.

The king had presided over the court, eyes black and hollow, with blood dripping from his nose. That had been terrifying. Worse, he knew the woman in the coffin was the mother of the six women. And that she was also someone he loved.

Someone he did not want to think about. Whose name he no longer spoke.

Not here, not now. Not ever.

So Loveday sat up, patted Pismire gratefully on the arm, stretched his back, stiff from the hours on the ground, and looked about him. Pismire settled into his own sleeping-hole. Father, who had been on the previous watch with him, was already snoring quietly.

When he had his bearings, Loveday wandered over to the fire, which was down to its embers. He blew gently on the glowing fragments to check there was still heat in them, then started towards the back of the beach, looking to scavenge anything that might serve as kindling to restart the fire in readiness for the morning's cooking.

But before he had gone more than a few paces, he saw six or seven bound faggots of chopped sticks, stacked alongside the Dogs' kit.

He stared at them for a moment.

He had not heard that the royal quartermasters were yet giving out firewood. He had been told that the troops were expected to scavenge the beach for their fires. He glanced at Pismire and Father, both as deep in sleep as though it was their first rest of the night.

Then he looked inland across the countryside. Little curls of drifting smoke were all that marked the houses which had been alight the previous evening. Loveday considered where the bundles of sticks might have come from – whose hands had chopped and tied them – and whose hands had brought them to the Essex Dogs' beachside camp while he lay and dreamed of undead women in coffins.

Someone had disobeyed his orders. Anger surged briefly in his gut. He ought to throw the firewood in the sea.

But he did not. The morning air had a bite to it, and Loveday knew that soon enough he would be cold, and hungry. He picked up one of the kindling packets, and used his knife to slice through the twine that bound it. It was good – chopped from well-seasoned logs, and split down to thin, even lengths. No bark. Nothing wet. Nothing rotten.

Loveday made a small pyramid of sticks over the night's coals, knelt low beside it and blew gently until the fire licked up and the new fuel began to catch. He kept blowing – a gentle stream of air that steadily gave new life to the blaze. Then, little by little, he added more sticks. Soon the wood was crackling. Loveday hauled two of the timbers the Dogs had salvaged from the wreck that had sheltered them when they took the beach. In no time at all, he had the campfire blazing.

Loveday crossed his legs and sat close to it. He pulled his blanket round his shoulders and looked around the group of sleeping Englishmen – and the two Welshmen, who had returned. He studied them as they slept, and decided, with a pang of relief, that it must have been they who stole the firewood.

That conclusion set his mind at ease. They had not understood his orders. They had acted for what they thought was the good of the group. He pulled out his figure of St Martha and started to scratch away at her side, trying to form her right hand.

As he carved and scraped, he thought back to his first campaign. The wild lowlands of Scotland. They'd stormed a beach then, too, at the inlet of that place called Kinghorn. It had been a much smaller affair, Loveday recalled. Himself among the footsoldiers who pounded screaming out of the sea under the cover of longbow shot.

He looked at the Scot, lying now on the other side of the campfire, breathing softly into the dirty nest of his beard. They had fought on opposing sides that day, although he hadn't known it until much later. Loveday let the memory wash briefly over him. The vast numbers of men all pressed together in one place. The stench of the pre-battle, as hardened warriors pissed and shat where they stood, their nerves overtaking any last pretence of modesty. Then the surge forwards as the clarions blasted. The press of the melee. The deathly whistle of the longbow shot above. The whinnying of horses, pierced all over until they looked like hedgehogs. The push and sway as the two armies closed ranks. The impossibility for most of even swinging a sword or club. But the animal energy that kept every man there pressing in the direction of what seemed to be the front line – the crazed lust to connect weapon with flesh. To strip away life. To kill. And to live. The horrible last stages of the fight, when the Scottish knights began to fall on one another, horses crushing prone men inside their armour.

It had been Loveday's first battle. He had not landed a single blow on anyone. But he had come away from it in a state of ecstasy.

Loveday had seen many more battles since that one. All were different, yet all were also versions of the same one. And all were preceded by what lay ahead now. The march. The long stretches of boredom. Cooking, building fires. Robbing towns. Hurting civilians. Stealing food. Taking orders from idiots like Sir Robert, the latest of a long line of Essex knights of that name, whose whole purpose was paying lesser men to work their estates and risk their lives in wars, in the hope that the Le Straunges might earn the favour of greater lords and kings.

The campfire crackled. One of the beams Loveday had dragged on to it broke apart. The flames leapt. Loveday took a piece of kindling and leaned forwards, rearranging the fuel to keep the blaze burning steady. Dawn had now broken. The first light had a clear, clean sheen to it, and the heat rising from the campfire made it shimmer. Loveday looked through the wobbling air at the prone figures of his comrades. Romford, motionless with his mouth slightly open. Millstone murmuring gently to himself. And Father, who rolled on to his side as though he felt the force of Loveday's gaze bearing on to him.

Who opened both his eyes and stared back.

Who cracked a black smile. Flashed Loveday a wink.

3

The English, eager to make war on the enemy, ranged across various parts of the country... Several reached the town of Barfleur, where they found an abundance of hidden riches...

The Acts of War of Edward III

The Dogs spent the day kitting themselves out at the supply tents that now lined the beach. By splitting up and joining long queues they amassed much of what they lacked from the landing craft and their packs. They fetched bowstrings and sheaves of arrows, spare arrowheads, small sacks of flour, dried beans and heads of garlic, several flitches of bacon and a round, sour-smelling cheese, a couple of shovels and small hewing axes – since those being issued by the king's officers were new with stout handles of ash-wood and those the Dogs carried were old and battered – and three coiled lengths of rope of various thicknesses. Father insisted on selecting these. He said he would hang a Frenchman before the summer was out.

They laid claim to a solid, four-wheeled cart, not new but in excellent repair with its axles recently replaced, the moving parts greased and a taciturn, long-eared donkey supplied to haul it. They also secured six fit horses from a large corral set up on the furthest end of the sands.

The Welshmen, Darys and Lyntyn, took the foremost interest

in selecting the mounts. They communicated with the animals on a silent, instinctive level, calming them with their touch and reading in their eyes a character that was hidden from the rest of the men. Loveday had watched them murmur to the beasts and to one another as they selected the six allotted to the Dogs' company. He had never seen anything like it.

That afternoon they idled. Loveday explored the sandy flats above the beach, where the trebuchets had been. When he came down, they found Tebbe, Thorp and Romford had joined a group of Kentish archers who had set up butts against the dunes for target practice. They had stuffed straw into the bloody doublets and overshirts of the French trebuchetmen the Dogs had killed on landing. Now they killed them again.

Loveday admired the strength and grace with which the archers drew their longbows. He had never been able to shoot one well. As the archers practised, a young pigherd sauntered over with a grin on his face, urged on by a group of his laughing friends. Loveday watched him ask one of the Kentishmen for a turn on the bow. He saw the lad nock an arrow, but struggle to draw back the bowstring even halfway. When he loosed the arrow, the tough, waxed hemp string raked hard along the inside of his left arm. He yelped, and the arrow flew off sideways, missing all the targets by yards. His friends exploded in laughter and the boy trudged back to them, shaking his head.

Loveday smiled to himself. Any fool or child – even a woman – could pull the trigger on a crossbow. But the longbow took massive power through the shoulders and back, a keen eye, mastery of the breath, a steady hand and years of training. Which was why it was one of the deadliest weapons in the world.

That was why King Edward had spent a year recruiting so many thousands of archers, loading them on to ships and bringing them to this faraway beach, so they might help him be the master of two kingdoms instead of one.

The following morning, after another night on the sands, Loveday and Millstone returned to Sir Robert's pavilion, which they found more easily since there were now several large banners flying around it. The flags bore Sir Robert's colours – an ugly mess of pink, grey, green and gold. When the round knight rolled out to meet his men, he was dressed in the same hues: diagonal stripes slashed across a thick woollen cloak, which he wore over a long, padded gambeson half covered by a sleeveless coat of mail. The clothes looked expensive, but were far too warm. The day was hot, and sweat trickled from Sir Robert's temples down to his jowls as he addressed them.

Loveday wondered how he could bear to be so uncomfortable. He also glanced around the group, looking for the East Anglians. They were there: Shaw was standing on the far side of the group from the two Dogs – a plug of dirty brown linen stuffed in his left nostril. He glared at Loveday when he arrived, but held his peace, avoided Millstone's eyes entirely, and did not interrupt Sir Robert once as he outlined what was to take place that afternoon.

First, Sir Robert explained the organization of the king's army. There were, he said, to be three divisions. 'King Edward will lead the middle,' he said, 'and that division will consist mostly of his household men. The rearguard will be led by the Bishop of Durham.'

Loveday had already seen the bishop on the beach, galloping

his horses and slapping the backs of his personal retainers. He carried a mace and swore loudly and often. After Father, it was hard to imagine a less likely man of God.

'The vanguard is to be commanded by the Prince of Wales,' Sir Robert continued. 'In light of his youth, the prince will be assisted by the most worshipful Constable and Marshal, the Earls of Northampton and Warwick. We will be among this division.' Genuine excitement rippled around the group. Even Shaw looked impressed. To ride in the vanguard meant danger. And danger meant reward.

'There are fifteen thousand men here,' said Loveday. 'The cogs are still unloading, with every tide. How much longer will it take us to form up into these divisions?'

Sir Robert smiled. 'Two days? Perhaps three. But we will not be waiting for the villagers and the rabble to wake up and work out which direction they should be walking in. As I have told you, we are among the vanguard. When we march out that will be our place. But today there is another task. Our duty is to ride out and clear the area to the north of our camp, so that the divisions may go out unmolested by land or sea.'

With a finely shod foot, Sir Robert smoothed a patch of sand in front of the small group, and sketched out a simple map of the nearby terrain.

'We are here... And this is the headland... And here,' said Sir Robert, 'is a pleasant city known as Barfleur. As I speak to you, English ships are heading there. And French ships are sitting in Barfleur's harbour.

'Our task today, if God will grant us the strength to complete it, is to go there, and make sure those ships never sail again.'

★ ★ ★

The donkey that pulled the Dogs' cart brayed noisily when Romford and Thorp tried to hitch it to the wooden shafts. The men were preparing to fall out beside a track at the top of the bluff. The morning had grown extremely hot. All the cool and damp of the rain that had greeted them when they landed seemed to have been seared from the air. Flies buzzed and bit, annoying the men and the animals. The donkey dipped its head and stamped. It snapped its yellow teeth at Thorp.

The Welshmen looked on impassively as Thorp stalked off in fury, aiming to cut a switch with which to beat the beast. But after he left, Lyntyn, the taller of the pair, stepped up to the cart. He put a calming hand on the donkey's nose, leaned in and murmured to it: words that sounded like a song.

The donkey's eyes narrowed, and it snorted. But then it submitted. It stood calmly while Darys helped Romford fix the shafts to its leather harness, and attach a collar around its breast. Once this was done, Lyntyn motioned to Romford to sit at the front of the cart. Out of instinct the lad looked at Millstone, who nodded. He hopped up. As he did so, Thorp returned with a long, thin, freshly cut whip of hazel.

Romford grinned. 'I'll take that.'

Thorp stared at the placid donkey and puffed in exasperation. But his mood quickly passed. He slung his sleek yew bow across his body, and checked the arrow-bag that hung by his side. Then he re-counted the bundles of extra arrows that were loaded on to the cart. 'Ready,' he said, to no one in particular.

Sir Robert had told Loveday that Barfleur was six miles distant, north from the beach and headland, at the tip of the peninsula where the English had landed. The three English archers and Father would take turns driving the cart and walking beside it. Millstone, Pismire, Loveday and the Scot were tacking up their horses. Although they had been hired as footsoldiers, all the Dogs could ride – and would if they possibly could.

The Welshmen were already in the saddle. Darys was checking the draw on his bow. He called in Welsh to Lyntyn, who laughed. They had been hired as mounted archers by royal recruiting agents who worked their wild mountain country and spoke their tongue. Deadly in broken combat, a mounted archer could control a horse with one hand – or none. Shooting from the saddle, Saracen-style, they could put an arrow through your heart and another through your eye from a hundred paces and be gone before you knew it. This took even more training and physical strength than ordinary bowmanship: only with phenomenal power in the belly and thighs could one control a moving horse while sighting a bow. For a campaign into unknown territory, Loveday was pleased to have them in his company.

A trumpet blast came from somewhere further down the line. Loveday turned in his saddle to see the source. A smart and well-formed group of heavily armoured knights and mounted men-at-arms, perhaps twenty of them in total, were trotting briskly along the coastal path, sending up a cloud of sandy dust. In the centre was a tall man in his early thirties, under whose command Loveday had fought many times before.

Thomas Beauchamp, Earl of Warwick and Marshal of the Army, rode a huge, dappled-grey destrier, draped in red cloth stitched all over with golden crosses. He wore fine plate armour on his upper body, although below his thighs his legs were unprotected. A long sword hung by his side. He was not wearing his helmet, but at the back of his group of attendants, Loveday saw a squire of about Romford's age, who carried it ceremonially on the front of his saddle. It was huge: a beautiful item polished so hard that it gleamed in the sun. It tapered to a conical point at the crown, and was fitted with a hinged visor with a grille.

As the earl rode along past the small companies like Loveday's, which formed his vanguard, he called out greetings. 'Hello, boys! Hungry today? Who feels like sinking a ship?'

Loveday thought back to when he had first seen Warwick nine summers earlier, on campaign in Scotland. The earl had served then as captain of the whole army, aged just twenty-four. Now he was its marshal – third in command, behind only the constable, Northampton, and King Edward himself. Yet a man who had remained at ease among archers and footsoldiers like the Dogs.

Loveday called around the group. 'Look to yourselves! Warwick is coming.' The Dogs stopped and watched the nobleman trot past. The Scot removed the battered iron hat he had been adjusting over his enormous head. Millstone shielded his eyes with a stout forearm and nodded respectfully. Pismire spat, but also nodded. Father sneered. But he was on the other side of the cart from the path, and no one but Loveday saw – or cared. Warwick and his retinue rumbled past, the earl's voice still calling clear over the clatter of hooves.

'To Barfleur, boys!' he shouted. 'Let's show these French devils who we are!

The rough road to Barfleur hugged the coast, which rose steadily as they moved north. After a couple of miles they were walking with a succession of cliffs and small coves on their right-hand side. The surf pounded and roared against the rock and sand. At times the drop down to the sea was no more than a dozen yards from the roadside. And in the water, beyond the breakers, sharked a detachment of the English fleet, most with their sails furled and long oars working steadily from the sides.

'Can you see the *Saintmarie*?' Romford turned his head and shouted to Millstone, who rode just behind the cart.

'Not a chance,' called Millstone. 'The cogs can't come this close to shore.'

'Reckon you could hurl a stone in the sea from here?' Tebbe asked Romford with a grin. He bent and picked up a small rock from the side of the rutted path, and handed it up to him. Romford swivelled on his perch behind the donkey, and launched it. He had a powerful arm, and the Dogs watched as the stone followed a shallow arc through the air, and disappeared over the cliffside.

'Easy,' said Romford. 'We should have wagered for it.'

Father scowled at him. 'You don't know it landed in the water,' he said.

'Where else would it have landed?' Romford asked. 'The moon?'

Father grumbled at the ground, and the Dogs trudged on.

Each cluster of houses they came to along the road was empty, and several of them had been burned out.

Ahead of them in the long, snaking line of the vanguard was Shaw's company of East Anglians. None of them was mounted. They called back and forth to one another as they marched and occasionally broke into snatches of song in their distinctive, drawling accent. Whenever they passed an abandoned settlement, two or three of the East Anglians would break ranks and run inside the dwellings, occasionally coming out with some prize the previous looters had missed.

Loveday saw Millstone gazing at Shaw. Still trying to place him. There was something about him that troubled the stonemason. Loveday felt it too. So did the other Dogs. As Shaw's company broke into another song, Scotsman growled, 'Romford, reckon you can break one of their skulls if I pick the rock for you?'

Romford grinned. 'I can try.'

Scotsman handed him a pebble. Romford looked carefully at the East Anglians, gauging their distance. Then he whipped his arm and tossed the pebble high, so that it arced towards the sun, before descending, as if dropped by a seabird, a few paces behind Shaw.

While the pebble flew, Romford dropped both hands to the donkey's reins and assumed his most innocent expression, fixing his eyes on the road ahead, as if checking for ruts that could break their cart-wheels. When the pebble landed, Shaw jumped. He looked up, but saw no bird. Then he turned around to glare at the Dogs. All he saw was Millstone and Scotsman eyeballing him. Shaw thought for a moment, then touched his hand to his swollen nose, and turned away.

Loveday saw Romford's shoulders shaking as he held in his giggles.

After they had been on the cliff road for more than two hours Barfleur finally came into view. It was a large town, with a band of low stone wall running around its outside. This was only to mark a boundary, rather than keep out enemies, for nowhere was it higher than a man's shoulder. Loveday counted just two or three thick towers on their side of the wall. But on their crenellated battlements there was little sign of activity, or even life.

'No flags,' said Pismire. 'Do you think there's anyone at home?'

Loveday edged his horse to the front of the company to try and get a better look. 'They must have known we were coming,' he said. 'It hasn't exactly been a surprise attack.'

The Scot growled. 'I'm taking no chances.' He pulled up a battered, rounded kettle hat, with a crown and brim of iron, which he had strung round his neck on a length of thin brown leather, and set it on his tangled auburn hair.

Yet deep down, they all knew Barfleur had been abandoned hours, or even days ago.

They drew to a halt with the rest of the raiding party, taking care to move away from the East Anglians. 'Let's wait to see what orders come,' Loveday called to his men.

Pismire snorted. 'What do we need to wait for? They've shat it and run. You know what's coming. We'll be going in on foot, grabbing what we can, burning what won't move. Am I wrong?'

Loveday shrugged. They all knew Pismire was right. 'So be it,' he said. 'Let's get down and hobble the horses.' He looked at the archers. 'You cover us when we move in. Watch the towers. You'll see nothing. But watch them all the same.' He motioned to the Welshmen to do the same, hoping that his sign language made sense. Then he turned to Romford. 'You stay with the cart.'

Romford looked crestfallen. But he stayed on the cart all the same.

The rest of the Dogs readied themselves for the order to advance. They finally all pulled on helmets and leather caps, and grabbed weapons and sacks. Millstone dug around in the cart for his favourite tool: a heavy hammer with a thick, square iron head and a stout wooden handle the length of his arm. He swung it around, and tossed it from hand to hand.

Finally, from ahead of them, three sharp trumpet blasts cut the humid midday air. Loveday did not need to say any more. The archers nocked their bows and took aim at the tower-tops. The rest of the Dogs looked at each other, then put their heads down and set off, at a steady pace, towards the open gates of Barfleur.

As Loveday had predicted, the town had been abandoned in a hurry. After the Dogs had funnelled through the stone gatehouse, they found themselves in a warren of cramped streets, with timbered buildings of mostly two storeys leaning inwards towards one another.

Most had already been scavenged hard. As they passed one house, Loveday used his short sword to push open an unbarred door, which swung on its hinges as though its owner had just gone to fetch a nail. He looked inside: a dingy room, bare of anything except a cooking pot abandoned on the floor. The air stank. Something sour. Loveday turned back to the street. He saw the source of the smell: a wine cask, broken some time ago, and left to drain and pool.

A few groups of English troops were already on a pillage, although by the looks of things they had not found a lot left behind. Loveday and Millstone rode side by side at the head of the Dogs, and laughed as they saw two men trying to struggle out of a house carrying a straw-filled mattress.

'Not much left to steal,' said Millstone.

Loveday nodded. He gazed around the sorry town, more

doors hanging open everywhere. He could feel his men's disappointment at the apparent lack of loot. 'We could at least take a look,' he said. Around him, the Dogs smiled. Then they spread out to see what they could find.

Loveday watched them go. Millstone stayed beside him. 'Which direction?' he asked. Loveday considered it for a moment.

'Let's get down to the waterside,' he said.

At the harbour, the Earl of Warwick was directing operations from horseback, pointing around the docks with a huge, leather-gloved hand, and directing the movements of hundreds of troops with the ease of a shepherd whistling instructions to a sheepdog. Beside the earl, Loveday saw another richly dressed lord, also sitting on a big horse. He wore a smirk on his face and his left leg was withered: the foot turned inwards at an awkward angle in the stirrup. Loveday did not know who he was.

Ahead of them, the tide was low. In the water Loveday counted around two dozen vessels, all unguarded. Furthest out, anchored in deep water, were four large galleys, with the raised fighting platforms men called castles at the fore and aft. English ships were already surrounding them, sailors throwing out lines with hooks and barbs at the ends, pulling the bows of their vessels adjacent, then leaping daringly from deck to deck.

Closer to the harbourside, tied alongside short wooden piers, were five smaller ships of a similar design. There were also two large fishing boats, flat-bottomed and curved along the bows, and many more smaller boats too. Warwick had men running from the streets to the docks. They were dragging anything flammable from the land, and piling it inside the vessels.

Pismire and Scotsman wandered up to join Loveday and Millstone. There was no sign of Father or the archers.

'What are the rest doing?' asked Loveday.

Pismire batted the air with a dismissive hand. 'Still robbing,' he said. 'What else?'

Loveday nodded. As he did so, the Earl of Warwick turned on his horse and spotted the Dogs.

'You men,' he called. 'Lay hands on anything that will burn! We'll have a bonfire today! Go!' He pointed towards the harbourside houses.

'You heard him,' Loveday said to the others, and he led them to the nearest building: an open-fronted workshop with a low roof covering a timber frame. The roof's poorly maintained thatch extended almost to the ground. Loveday grabbed at it with both hands and pulled. A huge chunk came away so easily he almost fell down on his arse. He laughed. 'Christ's teeth,' he said. 'The damned place is begging to be burned.'

The Dogs piled in, all hauling at the thatch. They coughed as the straw came away in clumps, releasing clouds of dry dust. Then, with their arms piled high with fuel, they staggered back towards Warwick and his companion. The lords turned to them and smiled. 'Pick whichever you choose,' Warwick said to Loveday. 'They all have to burn.' The other nobleman laughed loudly, with a high-pitched voice. There was something cold in it.

The Dogs took their piles of thatch to one of the fishing boats. The Scot jumped down from the harbourside on to its deck, and they set up a line, passing straw across to him, then running back to the town to grab more armfuls. After the first run, Tebbe and Thorp arrived. They were each carrying a pair of large metal candlesticks, which they showed off proudly.

Loveday set them to work, and with their extra hands, it was not long until the fishing boat was full of tinder-dry straw. The Dogs moved on to another, smaller boat. Then another. Finally, they helped a larger group of men pack stick and straw into one of the warships. A few of these were East Anglians from Shaw's crew. They were all slightly mangy: fleabitten, like stray cats. One was the man with the brand on his face – looking again, Loveday could see it was the letter 'M'. Another was missing both his ears. They said nothing to the Dogs, but shot furtive glances their way from time to time.

When they were finished, the Dogs stood back. Warwick's men-at-arms had set up a water butt in the centre of the harbour, and the Dogs walked over to fill their flasks. As they drank, the earl approached, on foot now. 'Fine work,' he said. 'Are you the same Essex men who saw off the defenders on the beach?'

'We are, my lord,' Loveday replied.

'Fine work,' said Warwick again.

'Thank you, my lord,' said Loveday. He wiped his brow, coming away with a streak of wet black grime on the back of his hand. Warwick looked spotlessly clean, and Loveday was suddenly aware of how filthy and ramshackle he must appear.

Warwick smiled. He raised an arm, protected above and below the elbow with a combination of mail and plate armour, and pointed out of the harbour. The English sailors were now unhooking their chains from the lonely French ships, preparing to fire them, then move off. Warwick watched awhile in satisfaction. Then he spoke up. 'Do you see that rock?' he asked Loveday, picking out a small, dark hump that stuck out of the water near the harbour mouth. The waves threw up small licks of foam around it.

Loveday nodded.

'That was the rock where all this began,' Warwick said. 'My friend – Sir Godefroi – tells me that many generations ago a ship struck that rock and all aboard, but for a butcher, drowned.'

Not knowing how to respond to this, Loveday just listened.

'A king's son died on that ship,' said Warwick. 'A young man as fine and strong as our own prince. Drowned in the night, along with many other young men and women. A tragedy.' He looked Loveday straight in the eye. 'What is your name?'

'FitzTalbot, sire,' said Loveday. 'Men call me Loveday.'

'Well, FitzTalbot,' continued Warwick, 'the death of a prince on that ship brought disaster to England. Civil war. Misery and destruction. They said in those days the angels slept. And, so my friend Sir Godefroi says, it also ensured that there would be war between our realm and the French forever. Had that prince lived, this land would now be England.'

He sighed. 'But he did not. So it is not. And here we are. At war for that ancient right. A war that may last for a year. Ten years. One hundred years.'

Warwick waved at the buildings around Barfleur's harbour, almost all of which now stood stripped of their thatch and in many cases half their timber. Hot and dirty soldiers lounged in the shade. 'In these towns, FitzTalbot,' he said, 'the English army grinds its teeth. That is why the French have already fled. They flee or they die. At our hands.'

Warwick smiled, teeth white and eyes dancing. Then he took a deep breath, savouring the air, full of salt and dust and now the smell of warm pitch, heating somewhere close by. Loveday also looked around the harbour. The rest of the Dogs were standing together in a huddle. Father had rejoined them, wearing a large gold crucifix on a thick chain around his neck. Loveday turned back to Warwick. 'What now, my lord?' he asked.

The earl drew his shoulders back, then puffed out his cheeks. 'Now? Let's burn the ships!' He waved an arm towards his men-at-arms, who produced torches and moved forwards to the waterside. Warwick gave a small, theatrical bow to Loveday and walked off to supervise. Most of the English troops around the harbour also drew near to watch.

Yet as they did so, Loveday heard a noise. It was faint over the hubbub of the crowd and crackle of the torches and the dry thatch on the boats.

Yet it was distinct. And Loveday recognized it.

A cry. A voice.

Romford's.

Loveday turned away from the harbour, where black-and-orange flames were beginning to leap higher than men's heads from the water. He threaded his way urgently back through the crowd, and when he was clear of the throng he broke into a run, pounding through the crooked streets back towards the gate.

In no time he was back where they had entered the city. And when he reached the gatehouse he saw that his ears had not failed him.

It was Romford. And there, pinning him against the sunbleached stone of the gatehouse wall, was Shaw. The East Anglian had a hand gripped around his throat. Both were red in the face.

Loveday ran towards them, his hand going to his belt to unsheathe his short sword. But as he was a dozen yards away, there was a blur to his right, and Scotsman overtook him. The

Scot covered the distance to Shaw in two bounds. He stretched out his right hand and grabbed Shaw by the shoulder, tearing him away from Romford and spinning him roughly around.

Loveday pulled up, panting. The backs of his legs were cramping, and his lungs were burning. But the Scot had hold of Shaw, and the East Anglian was wincing in pain as the big man's fingers, each as wide as two of most men's, crushed the muscle and sinew of his shoulder joint. He had blown the plug of linen out of his bloody nose. It lay on the dusty ground between their feet.

The Scot growled in his face. A wordless, animal threat.

Behind Loveday, Pismire and Millstone now appeared. Loveday glanced round. The rest of the Dogs were following. Pismire strode up to Romford, who was still standing with his back pressed into the gatehouse's dusty white stone.

'What in the name of Christ is this? You were supposed to be minding the cart.'

Romford was pale. 'I'm sorry,' he said. 'He – I didn't mean—'

Shaw sneered through the pain in his shoulder. 'Your puppy here needs to be put on a leash.'

Loveday looked from one to the other. 'Well?' he said to Romford.

There was something strange in Romford's eyes. He looked at Shaw with fear, but another feeling besides. A deep hatred, as though he knew the man of old. Or knew of his kind. Romford looked at Loveday as though he wanted to explain. 'He was…' But then the look in his eye changed, and he said no more, but just looked at the floor.

Shaw flushed slightly. 'If he throws another fucking stone at me, I'll slit his throat.' Then he grimaced as the Scot tightened his grip.

'We'll decide what he throws, who he throws it at, and how hard he fucking throws it,' the Scot snarled, his face close to Shaw's. 'Got that?'

Shaw said nothing. He stared sullenly until the Scot eased his grip, then pushed him hard to the left, so Shaw stumbled and nearly lost his footing. The East Anglian loped off without looking back.

Pismire rounded on Romford once more. 'When we tell you to mind the cart, you fucking mind it,' he said. 'Every man here is a thief or worse. You think we want to spend the next thirty-six days with no cart and no gear?'

Romford shook his head. He looked as if he might cry. Millstone stepped forwards and laid a hand on Pismire's shoulder. 'The boy understands,' he said.

Pismire shook his hand off angrily. 'There's nothing to understand,' he snapped, without looking at Millstone. 'You do as you're fucking told. That's all.'

He stormed off to check on the cart. Scotsman went with him, cracking the knuckles on the hand he'd clamped on Shaw's shoulder. Father and the archers also wandered away.

But Loveday and Millstone remained with Romford a few moments longer. 'What happened?' said Loveday again. 'Was that really all about throwing stones?'

Thick, black smoke was beginning to swirl through the streets of Barfleur, billowing up on the wind and turning the air thick and greasy. Coughing troops were starting to file back out through the gate, some hauling plunder, others clapping one another on the back and making jokes. Loveday ignored it. He raised his eyebrows, inviting Romford to answer him.

In turn, Romford seemed to be searching Loveday's eyes.

Looking for something in them. A sign that he could tell the older man a secret.

But whatever he was seeking, he did not find. 'I'm sorry,' he said after a few moments. 'I meant no harm.' Then he hung his head and said no more. He just went back to the cart, which was standing untouched where they had left it. And though he resumed his place in the driving seat and did his job steering the donkey back along the clifftop path towards the beach camp, he seemed to disappear into himself for the rest of the day.

There was no question Loveday could think to ask him that would draw him back out.

4

The king began his journey into Normandy... By thickly wooded and very narrow roads, the army reached the town of Valognes, a rich and worthy place.

The Acts of War of Edward III

'Haven't seen a French fucker for days.' The Scotsman spat on the road.

The Dogs were riding and walking in file, Millstone out ahead on his own, the rest squeezed tightly together on a track that was barely wide enough for their cart to fit along, and rutted deeply beneath their feet. On either side thick green hedgerows crowded in, tight around them and higher in places than the heads of the mounted men. Blackthorn laced through with brambles and dogrose scratched their arms. Insects darted around, tiny flies getting in their mouths and eyes.

'Shit country,' the Scot continued. 'Shit people. Cowards. Who'd want to conquer a place where they run away at the first sniff of a fight?'

They had been on the move for several hours and all the men were irritable. The sun was hot above them. The air was humid. Loveday was sweating, beads forming on his forehead and dripping down the end of his nose. Even the shade of the hedgerows provided little relief, for the air was still and heavy between them, as sapping to the lungs as steam.

Pismire, riding just behind Loveday, was stripped down to his undershirt yet still as wet from sweat as he had been from seawater when they landed on the beach. He snapped at the Scot. 'Of course we haven't seen any. They've fucked off. And what do you expect? If I saw your ugly neb within a mile of my house, I'd put my wife and daughters on my back and my things in a wheelbarrow and be gone before you could say your paternoster.'

'Which wife and daughters are those?' growled the Scotsman. 'Your chicken-pizzle has seen about as much action in the last twenty years as that lad's.' He looked back to Romford, who was doing his best to keep the donkey pulling their cart over the ruts.

Romford, half hearing and realizing he was being teased, reddened and looked around for support. The boy had come back out of himself in the days since the incident with Shaw at Barfleur. Millstone in particular looked after him, putting his arm around his shoulder when he needed it. Tebbe and Thorp also chivvied him along in their own way, praising him when they could and drawing him into their endless conversations about the finer techniques of bowmanship.

'When was the last time either of you heretics said a paternoster?' called out Father, inserting himself into Pismire and Scotsman's squabble. He still wore the gold crucifix he had stolen in Barfleur. Six days of mottled, grey-flecked stubble lined his face. He had been drinking heavily and his eyes were bloodshot and constantly watery; the lower lids drooped, exposing their pink insides.

Romford, a little shyly, saw this as a chance to join the fun.

'I haven't heard you speaking to Jesus much this week, Father.' He smiled and looked around the group. Tebbe and Thorp, walking at the rear of the cart, chuckled.

Father looked murderous. 'You watch your mouth, boy,' he snarled. 'Or I'll be speaking to Jesus as I'm giving you the last fucking rites.'

Loveday listened to the men bicker. It was best to leave them to it. They were hot, dirty and bored. They needed something to do. Loveday didn't worry much about Father's threats to Romford. The Dogs would look after him until he could look after himself. That was their way. The young lad had wandered from a home he never spoke directly about and asked to join their crew as they idled in dirty taverns, waiting to embark the *Saintmarie* at Portsmouth. Loveday had agreed – but only after Tebbe had quizzed him about the finer points of bowmanship. An extra body would allow the Dogs to make their numbers up to ten, as Sir Robert had requested of his crews. But none of that mattered now. Once he was one of them, he never would not be.

So while his men bickered, Loveday stood in his stirrups to try and see how far ahead the line of the vanguard stretched. The tight lane made it hard to tell, for it followed a long rightward curve, along which Loveday could only see clearly for a few dozen yards.

Yet if he craned his neck and peered to the very top of the hedgerows, Loveday fancied he *could* see somewhere near the front of the line, where the long procession of companies was headed by one of the great lords. At first it was just a flash of colour that caught his eye. But as he watched, he could make out flags in dazzling red, cut with crosses and stripes in gold – the colours the Earl of Warwick wore on his horse and his shield. When he stretched and looked in the other direction, the colours were different: to the rear of the line, he saw brilliant glimpses of flags with red dragons roaring on fields of green. Welsh colours. That told him the young Prince of Wales, Edward, rode there. In theory the prince was in charge, for he was his father's heir – and would one day command whole armies by himself. But plainly he was being eased into leadership gently. Nothing to keep you out of trouble like a couple of thousand men-at-arms and archers between you and the front line, Loveday mused.

He called to Millstone ahead of him, to pass on the thought.

As he did, an arrow cut the air, almost grazing his right shoulder.

Loveday leapt in his saddle and put his hand to his short sword. He looked frantically around him, to see where the shot had come from.

He saw the Welshman Darys smiling.

'Christ's bones, Welshman, mind where you shoot,' Loveday called. Darys raised a hand in apology. Loveday turned and looked at where the arrow had landed. On the small grassy verge a young rabbit was twitching. Darys's arrow had skewered it. As he rode past the rabbit, the Welshman used his bow to hook it from the earth, flip it in the air and catch it. He broke its neck with a practised twist. Then he set about skinning it in the saddle, guiding his horse along the track with just his heels.

Loveday breathed out heavily, his heart pounding. He shook his head at Darys and looked forwards again.

Some distance in front, the column of the vanguard was slowing down. The company in front of them was pulling up, and its leader, a young Midlander, shouted to halt. Millstone and Loveday reined in their horses, and quickly the message was passed back along the line.

'What's the problem?' complained Pismire. 'Has the marshal stopped for a piss in the hedge? Or have we finally got something to do?'

Loveday could see Millstone asking a similar question of one of the Midlanders. But all that came back in return was a shrug. Another fat bead of sweat dripped from the end of Loveday's nose. Butterflies danced in and out of the undergrowth. The Dogs' horses were shuffling their hooves and snorting. Penned in between the hedgerows, the heat of the day was stifling. But the line was at a standstill. There was no way forwards or back.

'Great,' said Scotsman, wiping his brow. 'So now we sit here and roast like swine.'

Behind him Tebbe produced a loud and convincing piggy snort. Thorp and Romford burst out laughing.

'Watch it,' growled the Scot, turning round to look at them. 'You carry on, and that Welsh savage will have you shot, skinned and on a spit.' He nodded at Darys, who was cleaning rabbit-blood from his hands with a rag from his pack.

Darys looked enquiringly at Scotsman, not understanding him.

'Ah, forget it,' said the Scot. He clambered down from his saddle, bent and touched his toes, stretching out his lower back. Shielding his eyes, he looked up at the perfect blue sky, and the sun beating down directly above them. 'We're going to be here for a while,' he said.

The line was still for hours. In the roiling heat men could do nothing but sweat, and either complain or doze. Once the Dogs had exhausted their complaining, most of them chose sleep. Father, drunk and sluggish, crawled under the cart, like a beast into his lair. Scotsman stamped down a long patch of spongy grass in the ditch beside the hedgerow on their left and lay on his back, wriggling occasionally and cursing as ground insects bit him. Millstone simply stretched out in the sun on top of the cart. His Saracen-like complexion seldom burned and he among all the Dogs seemed truly to enjoy the warmth. Tebbe and Thorp involved Romford in building a makeshift sunshade from blankets, knotted with twine to the side of the cart and pegged on the ground with arrows. The three lay head-to-toe beneath it and snored. The others – Pismire and the Welshmen – simply followed the moving shade of the hedgerows around, and flopped on the ground where they could.

Loveday did the same as Pismire and the Welsh, shuffling around after the shade. But he found it hard to sleep. He tried carving a little more on his oxbone saint, but sweat made his hands slippery, and after he had nicked his thumb twice with his knife he gave up. He thought perhaps he might follow Father's lead and drink until he passed out, but knew that was unwise. So he just stared above, watching the occasional tiny clouds scudding across the sky, listening to birds call to one another, and thinking of all the other times he had sat bored and uncomfortable on campaigns. Never had he been in hedgerow country like this. But all the same, he had spent many hours passing the time in discomfort for reasons he never knew or understood.

He had just started to doze off when an odd bird-call caught his attention. Loveday liked birdsong, and he could tell a bird from its warble in almost any part of the world he had visited. Yet this was unlike any he had heard before – high-pitched and melodic, but otherworldly, as though from some creature of heaven. It twittered and trilled, changing its song each time it sounded, but always recognizably the same tone and chirp.

The more Loveday heard it, the more curious he became. For a while he sat still and listened. The noise came and went. Then it stopped for a long time. But just as Loveday was about to give up, it returned. Now it was close by, and he was certain of the direction. It was coming from the hedgerow where Scotsman lay sleeping in the ditch.

Moving slowly and deliberately, Loveday picked his way over to the hedge, taking care not to disturb the slumbering Scot. Again he listened. Again, there was a long period of silence. Then the song came again – now from ten paces along the hedgerow. Loveday tried in vain to imagine what kind of bird was making it. He pictured something small, the size of a wren or sparrow. Yet colourful. Vibrant enough to match the strangeness of the song. He knew no bird like that. So he followed the song, and once more stood still.

It came again – and now it was right in front of him.

Loveday looked hard into the hedge, straining his eyes, trying to see past the infinite shades of green and brown that made up the thick mass of foliage. He pushed his head forwards, despite the thorns that pricked the skin of his cheeks, where his beard began, and listened as hard as he could.

When he was sure he knew where the bird was, he moved his hands very slowly into the hedge, parting the leaves and sharp spiny branches. But suddenly he gave a cry and almost fell backwards on his arse.

For from the other side a pair of eyes met his.

Human eyes.

A child's eyes.

Then, very nimbly, a small pair of hands pulled apart the hedgerow branches on the other side, so that for a brief moment Loveday saw a thin, grubby face, covered in freckles, and ringed by a wild shock of brown hair. The face grinned. Then it stuck out a tongue, blew a loud farting sound and disappeared. Loveday heard the patter of light footsteps running away, and a defiant birdsong sound.

He stepped back in surprise, then burst out laughing. 'Christ take us all,' he said.

Beside him, Scotsman sat up in the ditch. 'Christ take us fucking where?' he said. 'What's happened?'

'I'll tell you if you do something for me,' Loveday said. 'Grab a sword and help me get through this hedge. There's someone on the other side of it.'

Scotsman leapt to his feet, fighting instinct kicking in. The other Dogs started waking too.

'Relax,' said Loveday. 'It's a Frenchman. But not one I think will cause us any trouble.'

He took his short sword and started hacking at the hedge. Scotsman joined in. Then Pismire and the archers. After just a few minutes they had made a small, rough hole just wide enough to crawl through.

'Who wants to stick their head into the trap?' said Scotsman.

'There's no trap,' said Loveday. Sucking in his gut and crouching, he pushed through the hole, thorns and brambles scratching him as he did. And when he was through, he gasped once more.

There was no sign of the child who had made the birdsongs.

But in a small field, no more than three-quarters of an acre in size, was a large round pool, shaded by trees and fed by a stream that ran into and out of it.

'Saints strike me down,' said Scotsman, cramming his broad shoulders through the hedge and seeing what Loveday saw. 'We've been sweating our bollocks off all afternoon over there, while right here...'

Now Pismire was through the hedge too. He finished Scotsman's sentence for him. '... is fucking paradise.'

The field seemed to have been grazed recently, though whatever animals were there had been driven away, presumably, Loveday thought, by the child who had teased him with the birdsong. The grass was stubbly and low. The pool was the most inviting thing they had seen in weeks. Pismire went first. He pulled off his boots, then set out at a run towards the pool, throwing away his clothes as he went. The other Dogs started doing the same.

After a moment's hesitation, Loveday joined them, although he jogged rather than running to the water, conscious that his gut wobbled when he moved a good deal more than it once had. The grass felt wonderful beneath his sweaty, stinking feet. And when he waded naked into the cool water after Pismire and the other Dogs, it was like leaving his body and returning to another place in the world. In his life. He waded until he was waist-deep then sank in a squat so the water came up to his neck.

At that moment everything seemed to leave him – the ache, the sweat, the itch and the filth of life on the beach and the road. He slapped his hands against the surface of the water and laughed aloud, ducked his head below the surface and when he came up, swept his thin hair back over his scalp.

He looked at the other Dogs. All of them but Father and the Welshmen were in the water. Father, he presumed, was still passed out under the cart. He could see the Welshmen, sitting at a distance, watching impassively as they always did. Loveday let them do as they pleased.

Romford and Millstone were laughing with one another. Tebbe and Thorp lay and kicked water in one another's faces like children.

From somewhere beyond the trees he heard a trill of the human birdsong that had lured him there.

He knew then that it had come from an angel.

It took until the late afternoon for the column to get going again. By then, the Dogs were in much better humour – clean, cooled and entertained. After their plunge in the pool, they moved about their cart with great energy, checking their gear and making sure it was stacked properly and easy to bring to hand. Father had crawled out from his pit, and was sipping ale to revive himself. They were ready for the line to move, and glad when it finally did.

Once they had moved a little further along the cramped lane, Loveday understood what had stalled them. After just half a mile, the road turned sharply left and the close hedgerows widened out, then ended. The landscape opened into the flatter, wetter marshland, where finally a breeze tempered the heat of the summer sun.

A stream – fast-running and too deep to ford – cut across the road. Loveday assumed it was the same stream that had fed their pool. An ancient wooden footbridge, which would have been barely wide enough for a single footman to cross, had been broken on the far side. Beams sagged forlornly into the water. English engineers – compact men wearing royal livery of red, blue and gold, had spent the afternoon building a new crossing.

Although the delay had been uncomfortable, they had done fine work. A double-width footbridge now spanned the water, level and sturdy enough to carry two footsoldiers abreast – or a single knight on horseback, with a squire at his side. A cart could roll easily across the wooden beams – as the Dogs' cart did when their turn came.

As they passed over the water Millstone pointed out to Romford how thick supporting posts had been driven into the bankside, bearing the load of the horizontal beams. Romford nodded, eager to learn.

Pismire sniped, 'It's a bridge, Millstone. The boy has seen one before.'

'But I wager he hasn't made one,' replied Millstone, his voice calm as usual. 'And I'll say you haven't either, Pismire.'

The Scot grunted. 'Pismire and I are better at burning things down than putting them up.'

Millstone just nodded. 'As we know,' he said.

But the moment passed, for the Dogs were clean and happy to be moving. When they crossed the bridge, Loveday felt like cheering.

And at that moment, a herald came riding down the line, in the opposite direction to the slow forwards rumble of the troops. He drew up his horse in front of Loveday. 'Essex Company?' he asked.

Loveday nodded. 'Aye,' he said. 'That's us. We're under Sir Robert le Straunge.'

The herald made a face at the mention of Sir Robert. 'My lord Warwick commands you to move up the line,' he said. 'Follow me.'

'May I ask why?' said Loveday.

The herald pretended not to hear. He cast a disapproving

eye around the Dogs, seeming particularly appalled by Father, who was swigging deeply from his flask. 'At once, if it please you, gentlemen,' the messenger said.

Loveday shrugged and looked around in his turn. 'I suppose this means we're in favour,' he said. 'Come on boys, we're on our way.'

The road had widened sufficiently for them to move up the line towards Warwick's position at the front. The few men who grumbled at being overtaken soon fell silent when the Scot shot a hard stare their way. As they picked their way forwards, the herald, plump and pink-cheeked, and wearing a bright red tabard embroidered with a golden bear roaring, kept up a monologue about the lordly flags that could be seen along the line, and the aristocrats they identified.

'Quarterly gules and or, my lord of Oxford,' he said. 'Lion rampant double queued, Sir Bartholomew Burghersh...'

The patter did not cease as they advanced, nor did it change pace or tone. Half the words meant nothing to Loveday. He was not sure if the speech was directed at him at all, or the herald was simply practising his art. Eventually, though, it ceased, and the young man delivered the Dogs to Warwick.

The earl still wore a grin on his face as large as the one he had at Barfleur, but he also had several fresh grazes around his left eye, and a muddy purple bruise in his eyebrow.

Loveday dismounted and bowed as formally as he knew, in a show of respect. He felt a little more confident before the lord now that he was clean – even though he realized his clothes were still threadbare and filthy.

Warwick seemed to sense it. 'The Dogs of Essex!' he cried,

striding forwards and thumping Loveday on the shoulder. 'We meet again! I asked Sir Robert if he would mind my borrowing you for a little more fun today. It will of course be reflected in your pay at the end of the forty days. What say you?'

Loveday nodded around the company and raised his eyebrows expectantly. The men needed no prompting. With the exception of Father and the Welshmen, each looked excited by the promise of more action. And the chance of increasing their stipend when their six weeks of service were up was always welcome. There was a murmur of assent.

'We await your command, my lord,' said Loveday, and Warwick's grin grew even bigger than before.

'Wonderful,' he said. 'Two miles along this road lies a rich and worthy town called Valognes. My scouts tell me it has been largely abandoned.'

'Largely?' asked Loveday.

'Indeed,' said Warwick. 'Largely, but not fully. And this is our concern. We believe a small handful of rebellious subjects remain, defiant, inside their houses. They do not seem yet to appreciate how lucky they are to be restored to the happy station of trueborn Englishmen.'

From behind Loveday came a loud belch. Father. Warwick paused, and looked towards the group, quizzical for a second. But his enthusiasm immediately flooded back.

'We must – or rather, my dear Loveday, you must – convince these rebels of their mistake. Show them the light.'

Loveday nodded. Now that he squinted to the south-west he could make out the town Warwick was talking about. Valognes. A church spire and the low roofs of what seemed to be substantial houses on the outskirts. A stone tower – maybe suggesting a castle, although not a large one. Through the haze of the afternoon Loveday could not see much more.

He looked respectfully at Warwick. 'What methods does my lord favour?' he asked.

Warwick also now looked off towards Valognes. 'I leave that entirely to you,' he said. 'There are ways and ways to do most things. But let me tell you something that may help focus your minds.

'The night after you and I met in Barfleur, my men made headquarters in an inn. A rather pleasant place – and quite abandoned. As you may recall, Loveday, we believed we had rooted out and put to flight every trueborn English subject in Barfleur.'

He turned his head and fixed Loveday with a stare. 'However,' he continued, 'a small number of these rebels returned. They had been, I think, living a few days in the woods. Waiting for us. They crept up in the dark. They murdered one of my best knights. Slunk up and cut his throat as he was shitting by a tree.'

Warwick pursed his lips. Loveday swallowed hard.

'By God's mercy, the poor man managed to scream as he died,' Warwick continued. 'By God's even greater mercy we heard him and drew our swords. Of course, it became clear these woodland fools had no more training in the fine arts of combat than your friend there' – he nodded his head towards Father – 'appears to have in the art of keeping his flatulence sealed up in his guts.'

Father stood glassy-eyed and oblivious, picking his nose.

Warwick breathed hard. Something dark passed across his face. But then, just as abruptly as he had lost his humour, he suddenly brightened. He smiled.

'What happened?' asked Loveday, with a little trepidation.

'What happened?' Warwick repeated, now quite full of his usual bonhomie once more. He pounded Loveday yet again on his shoulder. 'What happened, man? By St Peter's grey-plumed ballsack, what do you think happened? We fought them, and we ran them through – every one of them!'

He patted the hilt of the large sword than hung by his left side. 'I myself slew three. Young Weston over there opened the belly of a man so fat the floor was covered in his guts as if it were a plague of worms!'

Warwick grinned. 'Our swords tasted their blood and our tongues tasted the wine we found in the cellars. In fact, there was only one sweet taste our evening lacked. There wasn't a woman among them, more's the pity!'

The earl roared with laughter, directing his mirth at the Dogs for their approval. They all joined in – Millstone, Pismire, Scotsman, Tebbe and Thorp out of deference; Romford, younger than the rest, genuinely heartened by the talk of blood and guts and women. Father gurgled lazily, realizing something was funny, but unsure what it was. Only the Welshmen remained blank-faced. They seemed to have no idea what was being said, and took no special interest in Warwick.

When the laughter died down Warwick put his arm around Loveday's shoulder, more gently than before. He cleared his throat. 'My point, good FitzTalbot, is this,' he said. 'Valognes must be cleared of the king's new subjects before the king arrives. It must, by my faith! I believe Edward will be here at dusk. I do not want any surprises. I do not want a second swollen eyebrow. I do not want any more of my knights killed with their hose around their ankles.

'My advice to you, therefore, is to get into the town and clear it by the fastest methods you know. King Edward has promised the good people of this land their lives. But as you know, the king's peace does not extend, and never will extend, to rebels, felons and evildoers. If I were you, I would offer every man, woman and child left in that town a simple choice. Die today. Try to flee, and die tomorrow. Or get out on to the road, fall to their knees and beg the king for their lives.

'But as I say, it is up to you. There is just one thing, my dear Loveday...'

'My lord?'

'Don't give them long to think about it.'

5

We moved towards Valognes, and took the castle and town.

Letter of Edward III

The road wound through the marshes for a little over half a mile, entering Valognes from the north-east. It was a poor track. Some patches were cobbled with stone and pieces of building rubble; but in most places it was just parallel ruts through sandy soil and long grass. The Dogs left their cart with the baggage train, which was beginning to catch up with Warwick's vanguard.

They spread out on the sides of the road, walking half-crouched, slowly and carefully, each man with two or three arm-spans between him and the next. Loveday went slightly ahead. The archers positioned themselves on the wings, bows readied but not drawn. The Welshmen were to the left, Tebbe, Thorp and Romford on the right.

In the distance Loveday saw Shaw's company advancing from another angle.

Warwick's scouts had reported no substantial force in the town. But Loveday preferred to see for himself. So he had told the Dogs to be wary. They carried weapons: Millstone his hammer, the archers their bows, Father a short club and the rest of them short swords. Loveday had his whittling knife tucked in his belt. The men had donned what armour they owned: Tebbe and Thorp in short-sleeved coats stuffed with horsehair at the chest and back; Millstone, Pismire and Scotsman in longer coats of a similar style and their battered metal hats; Romford with just a cap; Father and the Welshman without even that. Loveday was dressed in his own hair-stuffed coat, trimmed with leather at the shoulders and sleeves. He had once owned an old mail vest, made some time in the reign of the king's grandfather when, like now, there was war almost every summer. It had seen him through campaigns many times in his life, and saved his life more than once. But he had sold it several years ago to a pedlar in Southwark, for it had been starting to rust and lose links at the fringes – and more to the point, it no longer fit over his belly.

There was no time to rue that now. He focused on the situation ahead of him. He could see no movement between the houses on the outskirts of the town. But he could also identify plenty of danger points.

To the Dogs' left, two hundred yards distant, stood an ancient, broken-down cluster of stone-and-mortar buildings Loveday guessed must have been a bathing house, built many centuries ago during the days of the Roman emperors. That might provide cover for an ambush.

Then, just behind the first clutch of houses, inside the town proper, the spired church offered a perfect position for any sniper with a crossbow.

Farther on still, in the heart of the town, there was a small tower. A half-decent marksman embedded there could pick an approaching company off before any of them knew what was happening.

There was plenty to think about. And no single approach that Loveday considered completely safe.

They would have to split up.

Loveday turned to his right. He gave a low whistle to Pismire and the Scotsman. He pointed to the ruined bathing house. The two nodded silently and peeled off from the company, arcing back and round, to survey the complex of half-tumbledown stones from a wider vantage point.

The Welshmen closed up the gap they left.

Next, Loveday considered the church. He looked around. He had Father to his right. The filthy priest was soberer than before, but he was still sweating and grey-faced. Once upon a time Loveday would have had no qualms about sending Father to the church – alone, if needs be. He might even have seen the funny side of sending the murderous priest to a house of God.

Those days were long gone. So, passing him over, Loveday caught Millstone's eye. He pointed to him, and to Romford, and to the church. Millstone nodded. Gripped his hammer. Romford set his face as sternly as he could. Loveday smiled to himself. The boy was eager to impress. They would make something of him yet.

Millstone touched Romford softly on the shoulder, and they too split away, heading off on an arc of their own. Loveday read Millstone's intent. He was planning to flank the church. Come at it from the west, with the sun behind them – use that to dazzle any potential shooters below the spire.

Pismire and the Scot were good. Millstone was good. Romford followed him willingly and would learn fast. And by splitting his crew and sending the four off on their own path, Loveday had now reduced his exposure to the two most dangerous hazards on the approach to Valognes.

He still had four lethal archers with him.

But he was personally partnered with Father. He could watch Father's back. But could Father mind his?

The Captain had always been insistent: men should only work in pairs when they trusted each other to the death.

He shook his head. He had trusted the Captain to the death once. But then the Captain had vanished, abandoning them without a word. There had been many rumours about where he had gone and what had happened to him. Some said he had been killed in Paris. Others that he had been taken out and buried in the marshland of the Thames Estuary. Others that he had absconded with the daughter of a wealthy Flemish merchant, and was living in blissful retirement somewhere their faces were not known.

All Loveday knew for certain was that the Captain had left them, and that the grief for a friend who had walked away was ten times worse than for a friend who had been killed. That was why the other Dogs would not speak of him, and why he himself tried to put the Captain out of his mind whenever he appeared there.

Attempting to do just that, Loveday scanned the lie of the land ahead. He slowed the pace of his group, giving the others time to find their way to the bath-houses and the church.

The breeze was picking up over the marshes. It blew through a stink of rotting vegetation and stagnant water.

Loveday whispered a silent prayer to himself. He looked at the pairs of archers on either side of him, and Father loping a few steps behind. Then, still half crouched to the ground, he quickened his pace towards Valognes. He thought to himself: Awake iron.

Desperta ferro.

★ ★ ★

The small stone gatehouse at the side of the road was un-guarded. The low town gates were open. Loveday led Father and the four archers through them cautiously, scanning the streets ahead. The gates opened into a small square, from which several small streets ran away towards the rest of the town. One went directly towards the small tower, the others fanned out through quarters made up of close-pressed houses and shops.

The archers covered all sides of the square, bowstrings now drawn halfway.

To his left, Loveday heard a scuffle of feet on dirt. A small pack of underfed mongrels lolloped into view. They were snapping at each other lazily. Sniffing the streets for anything to gnaw. From the corner of his eye Loveday saw Lyntyn take aim with an arrow at one of the larger animals. He hissed at the Welshman through his front teeth. Shook his head.

Lyntyn shrugged and lowered his bow.

Loveday looked at the three streets leading off the square. He motioned Tebbe over to him.

The archer moved to Loveday's side, creeping sideways, with his bow still readied and his eyes still flicking around the square.

'Tebbe,' said Loveday in a low voice, 'you and Thorp. The road to the right. See what you can find. Work your way round and meet me at the tower.'

Tebbe nodded. He flicked his thin grey plait over his shoulder. Loveday placed a hand lightly on Tebbe's upper arm. Felt the muscles taut where the archer held his bow steady. Looked at the small tear-shaped ring he wore on his right thumb to protect the pad from the chafing of his bowstring. It was made of some hardwood. Walnut perhaps. Worn smooth and shiny with age and deadly use.

'Don't kill anyone,' said Loveday. 'Unless you must.' For a split second Tebbe took his eyes off the square and glanced left to meet Loveday's gaze. He nodded his head a fraction of an inch. Then he sidled away, whistled to Thorp, and the two set off towards the far corner of the square.

Now Loveday turned to the Welshmen. They were already on the move towards the left street. As usual, they did as they pleased.

Loveday let them go. He took a deep breath. Then he set off towards the middle street, with his hand on the hilt of his short sword, motioning for Father to follow him. A little colour seemed to have returned to Father's cheeks. He cleared his throat and coughed phlegm into the dirt.

Loveday tried to enthuse Father for the task by speaking to him in his own language. 'Let's root the bastards out,' he said. Father just snorted and chewed more phlegm.

The street that led towards the tower was lined with buildings of one or two storeys, which cast long shadows in front of the two men. Loveday peered through a pair of window shutters left hanging open. He heard no sound nor saw any sign of life. He stepped over a rough waste gutters cut at the roadside, crusted with old slops and shit baked hard by several days in the heat.

Loveday sidled as quietly as he could into the doorway of the house nearest him, pushing it open with the tip of his short sword. The lower level seemed to be a leatherworker's shop. His footsteps squeaked as he walked over offcuts of tough fabric and bent buckle pins scattered on the floor. He ran his left hand over empty clothes-rails. There were no finished goods hanging on them.

He recalled Pismire's words that morning.

They've fucked off. And what do you expect?

He stood a moment in the leatherworker's shop, inhaling the smoky, musky scent of the leather. Every town he had ever been to had a tanners' quarter and a leatherworkers' lane. He had never been able to pass either by without thinking about what leather really was: dead skin rubbed with warm shit.

He backed out of the small shop-room. As he did, he bumped into Father. Gentle as the impact was, it made him jump. He looked round and found Father's face a bare few inches away from his own.

'Surprise,' leered Father, and he moved back a couple of paces, and coughed again, leaving a brown globule of throat matter on the reeds of the floor.

Loveday turned away and walked slowly back out into the humid street. The leatherworker's shop was empty. Now, he thought, for the rest of it.

They made their way slowly down the street from building to building. Each shop on it was similar: shoemakers, beltmakers, and a couple of small tailors' premises. Father put out a hand and pushed a window shutter, green paint peeling and hanging off its hinges. It squeaked noisily – a sound exaggerated by the echo of the empty street. They carried on, pushing open each door they passed and peering inside. There was no one to see and nothing to steal. The buildings contained scraps and offcuts of materials – ragged strips of pale undyed cloth and raw, unworked leather – or tools not worth saving.

The whole town seemed to have been swept clean by inhabitants who knew they would be away for a long time.

As they moved, the afternoon sun's rays reflected up from the ground and in from the whitewashed walls, and made the job even more tense and uncomfortable than it already was. Loveday's skin prickled inside his padded coat. His back ached. His lips were cracked and salty. He wanted to lie down. But he pressed on.

When they neared the end of the street, Father began to complain. He had completely sweated through the ale he had drunk so freely earlier that afternoon. Now his flask was empty. He was becoming hungover.

'We've picked the wrong fucking street,' he groused. 'Why couldn't we have searched the brewers' or the vintners' quarter?'

Loveday puffed out his cheeks and tried to ignore Father's moaning. But the priest whined on.

'There's no one here. We're wasting our time, and I feel like shit. That jumped-up prick Warwick is trying to torment us. Nobles. Every one of them's the same. I bet he's sitting in his tent getting his pole greased by one of his squires. He's probably laughing at us. And here we are chasing after nobody.'

On and on he went. 'Mouth's drier than a nun's cunny. My head's pounding like a Spanish donkey's arsehole at Christmastide. I've got worse pains in my guts than the old king's fuck—'

Eventually Loveday snapped. He sheathed his sword in his belt and rounded on Father. 'Will you quit your complaining?' he demanded. 'You think I want to be here? You think any of us wouldn't rather be happily pissing our lives away in some cool dark inn back at home? I know it's hot! I know you're hungover! I want to fill my guts with French wine as much as you do, but we've got a job to do. We stay alive. We stay together. We get paid our forty days. We go home. So are you going to help me? Or are you—'

He advanced on Father, prodding him in the chest. But as he did, Loveday heard a small creak. Then, from above their heads, something flew down and hit Father hard in his right temple.

Father's legs collapsed under him. He crumpled to the earth like a child's doll. Blood started spreading from his head.

Loveday stood, frozen, for what felt like an age.

He heard his heart thudding.

He heard the mongrels in the square yapping.

Somewhere high in the rooftops he heard a songthrush sing.

And he heard Pismire's voice, as clear as if it were beside him.

What do you expect?

Then, with his whole body feeling as though it was pricked by tiny, hot needles, he came back to his senses. They were under attack from somewhere – a rooftop or a window. Somewhere they had missed. Someone with a good aim – possibly a crossbowman.

But he quickly realized there was no crossbowman. Rather, a few feet from Father's prone body lay a broken lump of rooftile. A few of Father's grey hairs curled from one corner, glued there by a spot of blood.

It had been a lucky shot.

Relieved, but still on high alert, Loveday dropped low, slid towards Father, and pushed his arms beneath the older man's armpits. Taking the weight of the priest's body, he rolled him sideways, so he was briefly lying on his back with Father on top of him.

Then Loveday bent his knees, dug his elbows into the street

and threw all his strength and weight into his heels, until he was crouched on his feet. He hauled Father backwards towards the gutter on the shaded side of the street.

It was like dragging a dead animal. The priest's body was completely limp. Loveday moved him quickly to the wall of a shoemaker's shop and propped him up beside the doorway. Father's head lolled to one side. But he was breathing.

That done, Loveday backed himself against the same wall, making himself as small as he could. He adjusted his helmet, pushing the brim back and looking back and forth at the windows on the upper storey of the buildings on the opposite side of the street. He forced his breathing to slow, and felt his heartbeat follow. He spelled out the situation to himself.

There could not be many attackers. Possibly just one.

That was good.

What was not good was that the attacker could be anywhere on the street. He could be moving between buildings. He could be armed with more than just tiles.

He could probably see Loveday.

And Loveday could not see him.

So Loveday did the only thing he could do. As he always did when in doubt. He waited. He listened. He controlled his breath. And he kept his eyes open.

He stayed still so long that in his crouch the muscles in his lower legs began to cramp. He wiggled his toes inside his boots to try and keep them from going numb. He gritted his teeth.

And eventually his patience was rewarded.

Briefly, right on the edge of his vision, he saw something move.

It was barely anything. A tiny impression of motion, and a flash – light catching metal or glass. Loveday turned his head towards the source. He saw nothing. But he could feel where the movement had been.

Instinct told him.

If Loveday had learned anything his long career fighting and staying alive, it was to trust instinct. He knew where to go. The upper storey of the leatherworker's shop. It had to be.

No, it didn't have to be.

It was.

Loveday looked left and right down the street. He counted to five with his breath. He drew his sword again. Then, moving softly but quickly, he crossed the street diagonally and re-entered the leatherworker's shop.

As he pushed the door open, he cursed himself. In the darkest corner of the shop a wooden ladder led up to a gap in the ground-floor ceiling. Either it had not been there when he and Father had first looked in the shop, or he had missed it. Either way, he had given no thought to what lay above the beams of the low ceiling.

He should have looked more closely. A lot more closely. The man had been above his and Father's head the whole time. Somehow – distracted by their quarrel, or just exhausted by the heat – they had walked right underneath him.

Loveday was certain that the man was still there now.

He stepped around the edge of the room as quietly as he could. He listened for noises above. All he could hear was the sound of blood rushing in his ears. He made his way to the foot of the ladder and stopped. If he climbed the ladder, he was at risk of having something far larger dropped on his head than the tile that had knocked out Father.

If he didn't, there was no way he could get to whoever was up there.

For a few moments, Loveday considered pulling away the ladder and setting fire to the shop – which would probably mean burning the whole street and maybe others around it. He thought better of it. True, Warwick had told him to deal with insurgents any way he saw fit. But he had a feeling the earl would not be impressed to find a fire ripping through an entire quarter of the city the king and his son meant to occupy that night.

So Loveday took a big gulp of air, and did what he knew was the most direct, but also the stupidest, thing he could. He inched his way towards the ladder. Then, tucking his sword under his arm, he put both hands on the ladder's sides, and started to climb.

One rung. Two.

There were only a dozen or so wide-spaced rungs before the ladder disappeared through a gap in the boards of the ceiling. Climbing was awkward with his left arm pressing in to his ribs to stop his sword from falling. But he continued, creeping slowly upwards until the top of his helmet was just below the gap.

Then he steadied himself. He moved his feet up another rung but kept his hands where they were, so that he was in a compact crouch on the ladder.

By now his heart was hammering. His thighs burned as he held his position. He ignored the pain, and quietly moved his sword back into his right hand, so that he was holding on to the ladder with just his left.

Then, summoning every scrap of energy in his body, he pushed through his feet, thrust his hands up to catch the edges of the ceiling-hole and flew upwards.

He burst into a low room, lit by the afternoon light streaming through three sets of small windows facing out towards the street.

And without thinking of anything else but avoiding the blow he was sure would be coming, he dropped and rolled. He rolled low. He aimed for the side of the room. Then he tucked his legs under him again, and crouched, sword out in front of him, back pressed against the steep slope of the eaves. He looked frantically around the room ready to fight.

There was no one there.

The shutters to the windows hung open. Dust was dancing madly in the sunbeams, where he had disturbed it leaping into the roof-space. A spider dropped down from somewhere high in the roof, and began to swing on its line of gossamer.

Otherwise the room was empty of life.

'Christ on the holy tree,' Loveday breathed to himself. His hands were shaking. He wiped sweat from his palms on to his thighs. He had been certain that the man who had hit Father was there.

He had been wrong.

Unless—

Slowly Loveday eased himself out of the eaves, and peered into the gloom at the far end of the room. A few wooden crates were stacked there, leaning against one another, standing on their ends. He stared at them. Something in their arrangement struck him as odd.

If the man was small, it was just possible that he was hunkered behind them.

Loveday thought hard.

His first instinct was wait. To sit tight until the man behind the crates gave himself away. Yet he was not sure there was even anyone there. And in the street, Father lay bleeding in the sun. He would need attention if he was to survive.

So for the second time, Loveday took the more direct – and stupider – option. He eased himself out of the eaves.

He dropped silently to his hands and knees. Again he tucked his short sword under his left arm and clamped it to his ribs. And slowly, like a hound stalking a squirrel in the woods, he started to crawl towards the crates. There were probably fifteen paces to cover. He moved as slowly as he possibly could.

He tried to put only the barest pressure on the rough, dusty floorboards, knowing that one loud squeak of the beams below would give him away.

He crawled closer.

And closer.

As he neared, he knew he had been right. He could smell another person. A familiar stink of human hair-grease and filth told him they were unwashed. Probably for many days.

Whether the man had smelled him, he did not know. If he did, he was waiting for Loveday to make the first move.

Which was good. Because that was exactly what Loveday had decided to do.

When he was no more than two armspans away from the crates, he pushed his weight on to his hands and pulled his knees forwards, so that he was balanced on the balls of his feet and the fingertips of his left hand.

He held his sword in his right.

He exhaled silently, then took one last, deep breath, drew back his sword and steadied himself to sweep at the crates.

Then he swung.

With a crash, the crates scattered, splinters of wood flying in the air. Loveday braced to fight.

Then his heart nearly exploded, as from behind him a hand tapped his right shoulder.

Loveday let out a yell and spun around, using his left forearm to shield his face from whatever strike might come.

But none did. For standing in front of him was a young woman, perhaps twenty summers old.

Her face was streaked with dust. Her hair, a mass of light blonde curls, was laced with cobwebs. Her face was soft and quizzical, but there was something hard and victorious in her eyes. She wore a long, shapeless shift, which hung on bony shoulders, cut short to expose her upper arms and long to cover her legs, finishing somewhere around her ankles.

Loveday took a step back, but she made no move towards or away from him. She showed him her hands. They were empty.

Loveday stared, nonplussed. The woman stared back at him. Then she raised her right hand, and waved. As though they were standing half a mile apart.

She smiled, though the triumphant look did not leave her eyes.

For a moment, Loveday said nothing. He breathed hard. He dropped his sword to his side. 'Saints and fucking devils,' he said. 'What in God's name is this?'

The woman did not answer his question, though he knew she understood it, because she spoke to him in English.

'You should go down the ladder,' she said. 'I think your friend is waking up.'

6

The inhabitants of the town came out and threw themselves
at the king's feet, asking him only to spare their lives.

The Acts of War of Edward III

Pismire and Scotsman had picked their way carefully around
the ancient bathing-house. They found nothing and no one.
The walls, which had been plundered for stone over the years
by the townsfolk, sprouted with weeds bearing tiny white and
blue flowers. Sunbleached grass heavy with seed grew in sunk
sections of the floor, which had once served as washing pools.

Between clumps of undergrowth, Pismire noticed tiny tiles
the colour of bone and rust arranged in mosaic, depicting fish
and mermaids. The arm of some old god, knotted with muscle,
thrust a trident from the deep.

'This party's over,' Pismire said to the Scot.

The big man grunted agreement. 'Looks like the party was
over a thousand years ago,' he said. 'I'll say it was fun in its
day, though. Let's go and see if Loveday has found anything.
Or if he's at least managed to sober Father up.'

'Father?' snorted Pismire. 'I doubt it.'

The two men set off towards the city gates. They entered
the square and looked around them. Like the bathing-house, it
seemed completely devoid of life.

'God's holy fucking shinbone,' said Pismire. 'Thirty-four days left. Are we ever going to see any more action?'

But this time the Scot raised his arm to hush Pismire. 'Quiet,' he said, cocking his head to one side. 'I hear something.'

He pointed at the street just ahead of them, leading to the quarter where the tailors' and the leatherworkers' shops stood. Pismire stood still, and strained his ears. He heard a noise that sounded like a cow calling for its calf. He looked up at the Scot, puzzled.

'I know that sound,' growled the Scot. He pulled his sword, held it in two hands, and started at a jog towards the source of the noise. Pismire followed two paces behind him, his hand on his own blade.

When the Scotsman and Pismire rounded the curve in the street they saw what was making the sound. It was Father. He had come around from his stupor, and crawled from the place where Loveday had left him slumped against a shop wall. But he was in a bad way. He sprawled across the street on his back, groaning and cursing, with the sun beating down on him. His words were half-formed, and slurred. Blood was leaking from his head.

The Scot ran to him, and knelt down over him, shielding him from the sun's direct heat. 'Father,' he said. 'Father, you stupid fucker. It's me: Scotsman.'

Father looked at him, his eyes struggling to focus.

'What happened?' asked the Scot. 'Where's Loveday?'

'Where am I?' slurred Father. 'I want a drink. Fetch me a fucking drink, or you can go to the devil.'

The Scotsman shook Father urgently by the shoulder. Father groaned. 'Where's Loveday?' he asked again.

Father just shut his eyes.

Pismire looked around. 'Loveday!' he called. There was no reply. Pismire looked around the street. 'Tebbe!' he yelled. 'Thorp! Christ,' he said to Scotsman. 'Where are they all?'

As he said it, Tebbe and Thorp appeared around the corner of the street, closely followed by Romford and Millstone. They looked confused.

Then, out of the door of the leatherworker's shop, appeared Loveday. He too had a baffled look on his face. There was dust in his hair and dirty sweat streaks ran down his face.

At his left side stood a small, grubby-faced young woman. Her arms were secured behind her with a strip of raw leather.

'Who the fuck is that?' Pismire asked.

The Dogs were assembled in the street. Father lay breathing unevenly and occasionally whimpering or groaning in pain.

Loveday looked blank. 'She was up there,' he said, pointing to the leatherworker's window, from where the woman had thrown the tile. 'We checked the whole street – but we missed her.'

'Did you miss anyone else?' asked the Scot, looking around at the other windows. 'I'll put my helmet back on if you did.'

'I don't know,' said Loveday. 'I don't think so.'

Pismire looked the woman up and down. She was short – shorter even than he was – and her fair hair was dirty and tangled. Her face was caked in soot and grime. But there was something compelling about her – a defiant spark in her clear, light blue eyes. She did not look at all distressed to have been captured by Loveday, and did not struggle against the binds he had tied around her upper arm, or the light grip he had on the belt between her shoulder blades.

Pismire turned to Loveday. 'Have you asked *her* if anyone else is around?'

Loveday shrugged. He still looked slightly dazed. 'Not yet,' he said. 'I was – I mean—' He looked at Father. 'How is he?'

'He's out cold and he's going to have a fucking headache in the morning,' said the Scotsman. 'Same as most evenings.'

Millstone, who had been standing at the edge of the group, looked doubtful. 'That's a nasty cut on his head,' he said. He looked around the other Dogs. 'I've put holes in skulls like that myself. They don't tend to heal fast.'

Pismire breathed hard through his nose. 'We'll deal with him later,' he said. 'There'll be a doctor in Warwick's retinue. But can we please find out from this woman whether any of the rest of us are going to need healing too?' He walked up to her. 'What's your name?' he said.

The woman just shrugged.

Pismire raised his voice. 'I said: What's – your – name?' he repeated. 'Who – are – you? Is – there – anyone – else – here?'

Again the woman did not reply. Instead, she giggled. She looked over at Father, lying prone on the road. Then, ignoring Pismire completely, she leaned in to Loveday's ear and whispered. 'He has gone back to sleep.'

Then, without saying another word, she let her legs flop beneath her and sat on the ground.

The Dogs looked at one another, nonplussed.

'Lord, give me strength,' muttered Pismire. Then a trumpet blast sounded from behind, in the square.

Millstone glanced back. 'That'll be Warwick,' he said. 'Come to inspect our work. And all we've got to show him is a madwoman, a bunch of empty shops, a pack of stray mongrels and a drunken priest with a hole in his head.' He looked at Loveday. 'You'd better start thinking of a good explanation.'

Warwick rode through the gates flanked by half a dozen of his household knights in their smart scarlet surcoats, emblazoned with golden crosses. Their horses were huge, and although the men were not in full armour, the breastplates and the bracers they wore over their forearms glinted as they caught the late-afternoon sun.

The red-cheeked herald who had escorted Loveday and the Dogs along the line earlier trotted at the rear of the group. A squire with a trumpet rode next to him.

Loveday led the Dogs into the square. Millstone led the woman. The Scotsman carried Father over his left shoulder. The priest was half-conscious. Blood dripped from his hair and left a trail behind the Scotsman's feet.

Warwick sized them up. He looked from the woman to the Scot and back. 'FitzTalbot?' he said.

Loveday cleared his throat. 'My lord,' he began. 'We—'

'Who's she?' asked Warwick, interrupting him.

Loveday cleared his throat again. 'One of the rebels, sire,' he replied. 'We – I – We found her hiding in the upper room of a shop, a few streets away.'

Warwick nodded. 'I see.' He looked at Father. 'What happened to your friend? A drunken fall? Or are these combat wounds I see?'

'A little of both, my lord,' replied Loveday.

Warwick cocked his head to one side. 'And where are the others?' he asked. 'The other rebels, I mean. Where are they?'

Loveday nodded slowly. 'Yes,' he said. 'The others.'

Warwick sighed. 'FitzTalbot,' he said. 'Forgive me if I repeat myself. But the king is coming. I asked you to clear the town of rebels ahead of his arrival, and to waste no time in doing it. And here I see you have brought me a smirking wench and a half-dead drunk. Where are the rebels?'

'Your grace,' Loveday said. 'You see—'

'Don't grace me, FitzTalbot,' snapped Warwick. 'If I wanted my worshipful pipe tugged, I would ask young Thomas back there to do it.' He motioned to the ruddy-faced herald.

The herald looked mutinous. But he kept quiet.

'I am sorry, my lord,' said Loveday lamely.

Warwick nodded. 'I am sure you are,' he said. 'But sorrow does not seem to have conjured any more rebels from these houses. Unless—'

At this point, however, he broke off. For into the square shuffled a bedraggled-looking group of townsfolk. There were seven or eight of them – men and women.

They huddled together, their heads downcast, moving only to steal the occasional glance backwards.

Behind them, mounted bareback on horses that did not belong to them, rode Darys and Lyntyn.

Darys had his bow nocked and drawn.

Loveday saw that one of the men in the group held his right hand in front of him. An arrowhead stuck out from the back of the hand. A broken arrow shaft emerged from the palm.

'Painful,' muttered Pismire.

'Very,' said the Scot.

Darys tilted his head in greeting to Loveday. Then he looked directly at the Earl of Warwick and lowered his bow.

The earl stared from the Welshmen to Loveday and back. He laughed. 'By God,' he said. 'FitzTalbot! I was moments from committing the deadly sin of wrath. But it seems your men have done well after all.'

Holding his reins in one hand and shielding his eyes from the sun with the other, he called across the square to Darys and Lyntyn. 'Archers,' he boomed. 'This is fine work. Please corral your prisoners here in the square. We shall keep them under guard. May I ask you – have you reconnoitred the tower in the centre of town?'

Darys and Lyntyn looked blank. Lyntyn leaned in to Darys and whispered something. They both smirked. Warwick looked at Loveday and raised an eyebrow.

'I believe the central tower was my men's next objective,' he said. 'Your grace.'

Warwick paused, and then grinned at Loveday. 'Very well, FitzTalbot,' he said. 'Then *my grace* suggests you lead your men on. Keep the prisoners here, under guard. The woman can stay here too. Choose three men to stay and watch that they do not escape. And leave your wounded friend. Young Thomas can wait with them and keep him sedated by reciting genealogies.'

Loveday motioned to the Welshmen to take their prisoners to a shaded corner of the square and guard them. He told Romford to take care of the woman. Young Thomas once again glowered.

Warwick guffawed. 'Remove that foolish expression from your face, Thomas. It does not become you.' Then to the Dogs he said, 'Let us go and inspect the tower. The king may wish to lodge in it this evening. My knights and I are at your disposal, FitzTalbot. Lead us on!'

★ ★ ★

When they arrived at the tower, they found Shaw and his gang of scrawny, hard-bitten East Anglians outside it. Sly and wheedling, Shaw briefed Warwick on their achievements. He grinned nastily at Loveday.

He and his company had taken half a dozen prisoners, who were on their way to the square. They had cleared the southern and western quarters of the town. They had sustained no serious injuries.

Even more impressively, they had already examined the tower, and found it abandoned.

Loveday felt a pang of envy. He gritted his teeth. Shaw had been lucky. The Dogs had not. But luck in war could be everything. The difference between living and dying.

Warwick seemed slightly deflated at missing the opportunity for a fight, but he did not dwell on it. He ordered Shaw and his men to return to the square and refresh themselves. He left the Dogs and his knights outside the tower, while he stepped inside to inspect it for himself.

When he finally emerged from the door, which was located on the first storey, accessed by a solid wooden scaffold, he called down orders to his knights. 'It will suffice for the night, men,' he shouted. 'If not for King Edward then for the Prince of Wales. But we need to move quickly. I see from the top that they are on the move. Take the prisoners to the roadside. And bring nooses for all of them.'

Back outside the gates of Valognes, the Dogs mingled with a crowd of other troops arriving at the town. At least one hundred companies of the vanguard milled around, some joking with one another, others more orderly, checking kit and feeding their animals.

Loveday could hear accents and languages from all over – the burr of West Country folk babbling against the estuary bark of Londoners, Kentish and Essexmen. The Welsh and Cornish languages lilted over the drawl of Midlanders. A few Flemish mercenaries grunted gutturally to one another. Men in crews and larger companies, drawn from all over Edward's kingdom and the lands of his allies, thrown together under the leadership of a few great lords and expected to find common cause.

Most seemed relieved that their day of slogging along the poor roads between hedgerows and marsh had led somewhere. A stiff wind had picked up from the north-west. It whipped a salt tang in from the sea.

Romford was looking anxiously at the prisoners, both those the Welshmen had taken and the half-dozen captured by the East Anglians. 'Will he hang them?' he asked.

Pismire squinted at the captives, now surrounded by Warwick's henchmen. 'I hope so,' he answered Romford. 'I like a hanging. It'll give us something to look at before we sleep, any rate.'

Romford looked queasy. Millstone rolled his eyes. Put his arm on the boy's shoulder. 'Ignore him,' he said softly. 'There'll be no hangings tonight. It's all for show.'

Loveday also looked at the captives. He noticed that those Shaw's crew had captured had been badly treated. Most had bruises and cuts around their eyes. Several were nursing broken arms. A boy and a girl, neither older than about ten summers, were weeping softly. Every prisoner had a noose around their neck, tied in strong rope, with a length trailing from the loop around their necks to their hands. They had been stripped to their undershirts and stood barefoot on the hard, dusty road.

The woman who had knocked out Father stood slightly apart from the group. She had the same faraway look on her face that Loveday had seen when he first burst in on her. The rest of the group seemed to want nothing to do with her, nor she with them.

The prisoners switched their noose-ropes from hand to hand and waited. Occasionally one or two of the younger lads from the arriving companies would approach to jeer or swear at them. But they were soon pushed away by Warwick's guards.

After a while no one bothered the prisoners at all.

Loveday could feel Romford's anxiety building. It seemed to rise off him like vapour. He felt it too. He tried to think of something to say to comfort the boy, but nothing came.

Then, from the direction of the hedgerow-road, sounded the low thud of a drum. It beat a steady rhythm, and was soon joined by the squawk of musical instruments. The reedy whine of a shawm carried a portentous melody on the sea breeze.

The crowd of troops parted, falling back off the roadside, and in rode a group of brilliantly dressed warriors in full armour, their surcoats showing the royal arms of blue-and-gold fleurs-de-lis and roaring lions. They formed a sort of box, four men strong at the front and rear, and four on either side. The musicians blowing pipes and beating drums came behind.

In the middle of the squad of knights rode three more figures. One was Sir Godefroi, the French nobleman with the withered leg, who had turned traitor to his own king, and whom Loveday had seen with Warwick at Barfleur. One was the young Edward, Prince of Wales, who rode stiff-backed, his eyes darting around, shaking his head occasionally to flick his hair out of his eyes.

The third was a tall man with a long, rich brown beard. He did not wear armour, but was dressed in a velvet jerkin as blue as midnight and a black moleskin hat. He had a long face – striking, rather than handsome, with his eyes set close together beneath thin brows.

It was the prince's father, King Edward III.

The last time Loveday had seen him was when the Dogs had watched him disembark and trip, face first, on to the sand of the beach at La Hougue.

From a distance, then, it had seemed that he had lost his dignity. Now it was clear he had not. The king radiated something Loveday thought he could feel pulse through his own skin.

Instinctively Loveday lowered his eyes as the royal party rode in his direction. Half raising them he saw some of the troops drop to their knees as the king went past.

Edward took no notice. Instead, he and his knights rode towards the group of prisoners. When they were about twenty yards away from them, the knights reined in their horses.

Those riding before the king moved aside. Warwick's guards prodded the captives with their hands and elbows, forcing them to stand to attention and face the English king. The musicians stopped playing.

The crowd fell silent.

Most of the captives dropped their heads, their chins sinking to their chests. The woman did not. But she did not look at the king either. She stared over the heads of the men all around her, as though looking for a sign in the sky, where the approaching sunset had turned long thin strips of cloud vivid shades of yellow and pink.

King Edward surveyed the little gaggle of barefoot townsfolk with a cool steady gaze. Beside him, Sir Godefroi leaned over and whispered in his ear. The king nodded.

Then King Edward spoke directly to the prisoners, in slow but fluent French. He wore a stern expression.

'*Mon cher peuple*,' he began. '*Vous m'avez déçu.*'

'What's he saying?' whispered Pismire to Loveday.

Loveday scrunched up his face. He knew a little French. But not a lot. 'I think he's pissed off,' he whispered back to Pismire.

The king continued.

'*En Angleterre, on dit que les rebelles méritent de mourir comme des chiens...*'

One of the children let out a little whimper. A guard gave him a shove in the back.

'*Cependant*,' continued Edward, '*le Christ nous a enseigné à être miséricordieux.*'

Pismire, who had edged close to Loveday, kicked him sharply in the ankle. Loveday glanced sideways at him. Pismire raised his eyebrows, questioningly. Loveday shook his head in frustration.

'Something about Jesus,' he said. 'Stop fucking kicking me.'

The king continued. Loveday lost the thread of what he was saying. But as he spoke, those among the crowd who could understand French better than Loveday suddenly let out a cheer. As they did, Warwick's men pushed roughly in front of the prisoners and took the trailing ends of their nooses in their hands.

Holding two or three prisoners each, they turned and dragged them towards the king. Ten yards from him, they halted, turned and shoved the townsfolk to their knees. Many of them were now weeping. Loveday looked at the woman. Her face gave away nothing.

Romford gripped Millstone on the arm. 'He's going to kill them, isn't he?' he said. Millstone did not answer.

Pismire hissed at Romford. 'What's wrong with you? Never seen a man hang before?'

Romford stared at him with an expression Loveday had never seen on the boy before. Something close to rage. Tears were welling in his eyes. Loveday touched Pismire on the arm. 'Leave him be.'

The king's drummer now started up once more. A lone, slow, steady beat. Alongside the king, a herald rode up. In a clear, loud voice he addressed the crowd of troops.

'My lords and fellows of England,' he announced. 'King Edward of England, third of that name, Duke of Normandy and Aquitaine, Lord of Ireland and King of the French, here present to destroy the impertinent claim of the usurper Philippe to hold that title, has carefully considered the case of the rebels of this city of Valognes, who have feloniously held the town in defiance of his grace's right and in breach of the peace.'

'At least this cunt speaks English,' the Scot said. Pismire nodded at him, relieved that someone else seemed to share his concern at last.

'Maybe one day you'll learn to do the same,' said Millstone, staring hard at the Scot. Loveday glared at both of them, and they fell quiet.

The herald continued. 'The sentence for rebellion is death,' he said. 'The king has ordered a gallows built here in his city, and each of these traitors will die there before nightfall.'

At this a great cheer erupted among the troops. Romford looked grey and sick.

The drum kept beating.

'However,' cried the herald. 'However, our king is a great and merciful lord. And at the request of his most beloved friend and ally, Sir Godefroi d'Harcourt, born of this region, he has agreed that if the rebels show contrition here and now, they will not suffer the penalty, but will be set free to warn others of the king's wrath.'

Boos and catcalls rippled around the troops. A few of the bolder men called out insults.

'Hang the French scum!'

'Let's see their tongues burst!'

But the prisoners, latching on to what was expected of them, now fell to the ground, grovelling face first in the dirt. They rolled and bleated, and occasionally rose to their knees to tug at the nooses around their necks, or clasp out their hands in supplication.

The jeers in the crowd went on; the captives grovelled even more pathetically – all except the woman. She simply sat on her heels, staring at the sunset.

The drum kept beating.

Loveday began to feel very uncomfortable indeed. Romford was looking back and forth between him and Millstone. Neither of them could meet his gaze.

The catcalls from the crowd rose in a crescendo. And then the drumbeat stopped. The shouting died down. And the king swung his leg over his horse, and in one fluid action dismounted.

The herald scuttled to him and bowed. The king leaned into his ear and said something quiet. The herald bowed again. The king climbed back on to his horse.

'King Edward has accepted the humble petition of these wretched rebels,' cried the herald. 'And he has ordained that they will live.'

Groans and boos rang out.

'They shall live,' repeated the herald. 'And they shall be given their liberty to tell all the other men and women of this country of their new king's great charity.'

'Long live the king! God save England!'

At this, the Earl of Warwick's men began roughly unlooping the nooses around the captives' necks. One of the guards collected them up – presumably, Loveday thought, so that they could be reused in some future calculated show of mercy. The king's musicians now struck up a triumphant tune and the knights began to fall into formation to ride towards wherever it was the king was lodging that evening.

They began to walk their horses towards the town before pausing. King Edward had raised his hand, and the musicians stopped. The king stood in his stirrups.

Now he spoke in English. His voice was soft, but it was clear.

'Remember, men. I do not wish harm to come to my subjects here in France. We are fierce – but merciful. In all things.'

He nodded around the crowd, most of whom were too far away to hear him. Then a smile flitted across his face. He sat down in his saddle and kicked his horse. The musicians began again. The abrupt restart made a mess of their tune.

The Dogs turned away from the spectacle and looked at each other. Romford's face was a picture of relief. 'That was close,' he said.

Pismire hawked and spat. 'Rubbish,' he said. 'We've been cheated.'

But the Scotsman, who was still looking towards the royal party, cut in. 'Not all of us,' he said.

As the prisoners were being untied and corralled together for escort away from the army, the young prince had broken away from his father and their bodyguard, and trotted his horse over so that he sat directly beside the small group of townsfolk.

He called down an instruction to one of the guards. And instead of taking the noose from around the neck of the woman who had thrown the tile at Father, the guard handed the loose end of the rope up to the prince in his saddle.

The prince looked at the woman hungrily. She gazed back at him with no emotion whatever.

He gave the rope a little jerk. The woman briefly lost her footing, then she was forced to follow a few paces behind the prince's horse, half walking, half running. The prince tossed his hair again and looked around the assembled troops as if seeking their approval.

Then he rode off through the gates of Valognes, the woman stumbling behind him.

7

He went to Valognes, where he stayed the night, and found adequate supplies.

Campaign newsletter by Michael Northburgh

The troops camped in the marshes outside the town. The damp, sandy ground was uncomfortable. Clumps of tough grass stuck in their backs and mites bit their ankles and necks. The Dogs lit a fire and sprawled around it, fidgeting. The fire spat and hissed – green wood gave off damp smoke that stuck in the lungs.

Romford sat and watched the acrid smoke rise. He chewed his nails. Loveday watched him. He knew what he was thinking. The threat of the hangings had scared him. It seemed to have stirred up some terror in his soul. Something in his memory.

In truth, the callous theatre had scared Loveday too.

So had what happened after.

Loveday could still feel the woman's impassive eyes looking through him. When he closed his own eyes, he saw her face. Her shoulders. First he saw her in the eaves of the leatherworker's shop. Then with the noose on her neck. He replayed in his mind her stumble as the prince dragged her off into the town. Her town. Where now the English king and his son were sleeping in homes that were not their own.

Next to him, the Scotsman gave Loveday a shove.

'What's wrong?' he said. 'You've got a face like a eunuch at an orgy.'

Loveday shrugged. 'It's nothing,' he said. 'I'm tired. How's Father?'

The Scotsman craned his neck to where Father lay on the sand, covered in a thin blanket. His chest rose and fell, his breath shallow but steady. Warwick's physicians had bandaged his head with strips of linen, and the bleeding seemed to have stopped. But the right side of Father's face was crumpled and droopy, as though the muscles had been cut from their roots.

The Scotsman cleared his throat. 'I reckon he'll live,' he said. 'He's been through worse. Jesus knows he's done worse. So Christ will decide. I guess the old bastard must have prayed to him at some point in his life.'

He paused.

'That must have been some shot she hit him with.'

Loveday nodded ruefully. 'It was,' he said. 'She was lucky. Or he was unlucky. Or both.'

Darkness was falling, and Loveday suddenly felt exhaustion sweep through him. 'I'm bone tired, Scotsman,' he said. 'Will you organize the watch? We rise and break camp with the light.'

The Scot nodded. He poked at the fire with a stick. 'Leave it to me,' he said. 'Get some rest.'

He whistled to Tebbe, Thorp and Romford. 'You fuckers, first watch,' he growled. 'Pismire, Millstone, second. I'll see in the dawn with...' He looked around for the Welshmen. They were sitting away from the fire with the donkey and cart. Darys was chewing a strip of dried meat. Lyntyn was sharpening a knife.

'Ah, fuck it,' he said. 'I'll see in the dawn on my own.' He went back to prodding the fire.

Beside him, Loveday was already curled up, his blanket pulled up tight around his shoulders. He was drifting off to sleep. In his mind's eye he saw a woman's face. It kept changing. It was the woman from Valognes. Then it was the woman undead in the coffin from his dream on the beach. The woman whom it burned him to speak of.

Whose name was Alis.

Who had been his wife.

Romford sat up with Tebbe and Thorp on the first watch, although as far as he could tell there was little to watch for.

There seemed no danger of ambush, and so far in the march from the sea they had heard nothing of companies thieving from one another. Millstone had told him that usually came later in a campaign, if food grew scarce, or men grew bored and ready to provoke a fight with anyone.

He wondered about the company of East Anglians they had met in Valognes. They had looked mean and hungry. But he shrugged to himself. He had never been in an army before. Millstone seemed to know what he was doing.

Romford liked Millstone. The older man had put his arm around him on the first day he had joined the company. He had asked no questions about what had brought him to the streets of Portsmouth looking for a berth on a ship to war. What had drawn him away from the London streets that had come to pass for his home, and the reasons he had drifted away from everyone he had ever known.

He appreciated the fact that Millstone stepped in when

Father or Pismire sniped at him. Romford liked the feel of the older man's hands when he occasionally placed them on his arm. The fingers hard as horn. The steady way his chest rose and fell as he breathed. Romford had known lots of men in his life. Some had been cruel and violent. Some had hurt him, or tried to. Others had tried to love him more than he wanted. But Millstone was not like that. He reminded him of his father. Before they took his father away. For an argument in a tavern, which had become a fight, a brawl and then a murder.

Out of the corner of his eye Romford watched Millstone sleeping, snoring quietly, a gentle purr from the back of the big stonemason's throat.

I'm safe with him, he thought.

Romford shuffled a little nearer the fire, coughing slightly in the smoke. Since the start of the watch Tebbe and Thorp were taking it in turns to yawn, feed damp wood into the flames, and stand up to stretch their legs. Now Thorp produced a pair of scallop shells he had scavenged on the beach and the two men began a game of cross and pile.

Tebbe spotted him watching them. 'Want to play?' the archer asked.

Romford shrugged. 'I don't know the rules,' he said.

'Christ's knucklebones, any fool can pick this up,' said Thorp.

They explained the game to Romford. Each player took turns to flip the two shells in the air, betting on the combination that would land. They called the brown side of the shell the 'cross' side, and the white the 'pile'.

'You follow?' Thorp asked.

Romford nodded.

They started to play, betting for pebbles and arrowheads.

After six or seven rounds, Romford held all the tokens and Tebbe and Thorp were shaking their heads.

'Luck,' said Romford, sheepishly. But deep down he knew otherwise. He had a knack for games, just as he had for drawing a bow. Even games of pure chance like this. It was as though he could see what the shells and the tokens wanted to do.

How they were destined to land.

They divided up the tokens again, and played another three rounds. Tebbe won the first, but once his streak was broken, Romford took over the shells and again he started winning.

Soon Tebbe became agitated.

Romford did not want to rile him. So he deliberately overwagered, bet against his instinct and lost.

Tebbe swept up the counters, but grumbled to himself as he did. Romford realized the game was over.

'Is our watch done yet?' he asked.

Thorp nodded. 'Wake Pismire and Millstone,' he said.

Romford crept round to Pismire and shook him gently on the shoulder. Pismire blinked his eyes open, and woke Millstone. Romford lay down on the ground, his spot beside Tebbe and Thorp, and pulled his blanket up around his shoulders.

But unlike Tebbe and Thorp he did not sleep.

Instead he stared at the night sky, where black clouds skittered against the deep, star-pricked blue of the eternity beyond. He saw shells turning in the air, the white flashing as it spun in the wan firelight. But most of all he saw the faces of the prisoners. Their scared eyes. The ropes at their necks.

He thought of the day his father had been hanged.

Romford thought of his father's legs – how they had kicked when he choked on the scaffold. Of how women had pushed forwards in pity and yanked his legs to kill him.

He saw his father's face, bloated in death, his bursting eyes boring into Romford's own. He heard his father speak with his swollen tongue. Heard him say: 'Behold, behold, behold.'

'Behold what?' whispered Romford into the dark.

His father's face sagged and the eyes collapsed back into their sockets.

'Behold the end,' he said.

Romford woke up. Sweat was pouring from his body. He was wet all over. Even his shins were damp. He tried to catch his breath. And eventually his heart and lungs slowed their frantic work.

Yet as they did so, Romford felt another unwelcome sensation arising in his body.

An itch.

An itch that had been part of his life for most of the years after they took his father. One that had he knew could not be denied. He peeled his blanket off his shoulders and sat up.

Millstone looked through the fire-smoke at him. 'What you doing, lad?' he asked, in a low voice.

'I need to piss,' Romford replied. 'I'll find a place. I won't be long.'

Millstone nodded.

Romford adjusted his clothing. He felt about next to his blanket for his dagger. Then stood up and walked away from the fire and the camp.

The dark streets of Valognes were lit only by torches and the rays of a bright moon that was nearing full, and which popped frequently from behind the clouds. The town was as busy as on a market day. Romford padded slowly through the gate. He saw men from the army's many companies bustling everywhere in the streets. The torch flicker sent their shadows dancing on the walls like demons.

They pushed in and out of houses, shops and churches. Groups loitered together, leaning on walls, drinking from skins or wine jugs. Some went about purposefully, in pairs or alone, their arms full of bundles: blankets and odd items of clothing.

One young man, lanky and stooped, with the look of a field-boy about him, was hauling a table towards the gates.

Romford made his way among the groups, looking at everything. No one said anything to him, or even seemed to notice him. He passed along a street lined with what looked like good merchants' houses. Several had been taken over by companies. Their doors had been kicked in. In one, where the door hung open, Romford saw a group of men sitting around a table by torchlight, rolling dice and laughing.

He stopped, intrigued by the dice game. A wild thought entered his mind: he should go in and play, and play for money, and win some. He had enjoyed the shell game with Tebbe and Thorp. He knew he could—

Then his blood froze as he recognized the men's voices. They spoke with the same drawl as the tall man with the moustache, who had tried to touch him on the cart outside Barfleur. Who had been angry when Romford told him no, he had to watch the donkey. Who had tried to beat him, then lied when Loveday came, and said he was angry about the pebble Romford had thrown.

Romford started to back away from the doorway. As he did, one of the men glanced up.

Romford knew his face. More than that, he knew his head, for at each side of it the ear had been hacked crudely away – the penalty in England for swindling and stealing money.

The no-eared man snarled at him: 'Fuck off.'

Then all the others turned to look at him.

Romford dropped his face in terror, shielding it with his forearm as though the light of the room were blinding him. But before he did, he saw the thin, spiteful face of the man with the moustache. The man stared straight at him. But Romford was not sure if he recognized him, because his attention was also on someone else.

On the man's lap sat the little girl who had been dragged out of Valognes with the other prisoners and made to kneel in the dirt with her head in a noose. Her small face was still bruised and grimy, and stained with tears.

The man with the moustache had one of his hands clamped on the back of her neck. There was no sign of her brother.

'Fuck off,' growled the no-eared man again, with even more menace than before. Romford turned and hurried away. He ran to the nearest dark spot at the side of the street, and hid himself in a black shadow between pools of torchlight. He just managed not to vomit.

When at last his stomach had stopped cramping and his hands were settled, Romford looked further down the street. What he had seen had terrified him. But it had also made him more anxious than ever for what he sought.

Yet he was still in the wrong part of the town. The houses at the far end had guards posted outside. Flags hung from the windows. He guessed this was where lords like Warwick and Sir Robert had lodged, with their bodyguards and retinues. He turned back.

He went down another street, this one lined with shopfronts. And at the end of it he saw something that made his heart quicken. At the front of one shop, silhouetted against the black of the night, was a small sign, carved in wood, of an apothecary's pestle.

Romford looked around him. He saw no one else on the street. He stayed close to the buildings at the street's side all the same. He spooked himself thinking the no-eared man was following him. He told himself firmly he was not.

Outside the apothecary he stopped and said a small prayer to St Damian. Please, he prayed. Let no one like me have been here already.

He pushed the door. It did not give. He took a couple of steps back and, summoning all his strength, kicked it three times with the sole of his right foot.

On the third kick the door gave, splintering around a weak lock.

Romford shoved it a couple of times more with his shoulder and it opened. It was not the first time he had broken into an apothecary, but the noise made him nervous. He backed once more into the shadows and waited.

Nothing happened. And no one came.

He took a dying torch from one of the walls of the street. It was barely flickering, but it would do. Then, slowly, he stepped back to the broken door, and slipped through it.

Inside, lit by the weak torch and the flickers of moonlight streaming through the open door, the shop looked the same as they always did. Waving the torch around, Romford saw he was standing in the usual small room at the front, where the store-owner met customers, and listened to them describe their ailments. He looked it over, stepping around a stout, heavy, wooden table, where poultices and tinctures were mixed and dispensed.

Then he found what he was looking for. At the back of the shop his torch lit up the entrance to another, smaller room. This was where precious herbs and spices, ground leaves and powders were kept in earthenware jars.

Romford crept towards this second room, opening his eyes wide to make use of the dim, dancing light, finding his way just as much by sense and instinct. His whole body was tingling.

A greasy linen curtain hung across the doorway between the two rooms. Romford pushed it aside and edged past it. It fell behind him and plunged the room into a blackness so deep it seemed to be drowning the torchlight. Romford shivered. He turned around, took hold of the curtain and yanked hard. It came away from the rail holding it, and he threw it to the floor. Then he felt better. The moon's light once more found its way in. He waited for his eyes to adjust, enough that he could make out the subtle patterns of black and grey on the shelves.

He prayed again.

Good St Damian, let them have run away in a hurry.

He got to work on the jars.

Each had a lid of some sort – a wooden stopper or else a piece of earthenware that fitted the mouth of the vessel. One by one, Romford opened the jars, held them to his nose and sniffed.

He was hunting for a smell known only to apothecaries, the very ill and hungry men like himself.

He worked his way through dozens of jars. Not one of them smelled right.

Romford scented aromatic garden herbs. *Head poultices and wounds.*

He shrugged. Put it in his belt-purse. In a war, a remedy like this could be useful. But it was not what he was looking for. He moved on.

Sniffed garlic, celandine and hollowleek. *Stiff joints. Fever.*

He inhaled something he had only smelled very rarely before – a vile, metallic, bloody smell which he thought must come from somewhere deep inside a large animal. *Ox gall? They say it's for the eyes.*

And then, as the prickling in his fingers was becoming unbearable, Romford pulled the tight wooden stopper from a small jar and breathed in a smell that nearly brought tears to his eyes. *Ripe apples. A sharp edge of vinegar. And below it, something musky, like rat piss.*

He laughed out loud.

His eyes dampened.

He licked the tip of his little finger and dipped it into the jar. Felt powder at the bottom. Not much. But enough.

He drew his finger out gently, and rubbed the powder on his gum, above his front teeth.

A bitter taste filled his mouth. Each ingredient in the potion had its own unmistakeable flavour. *Mandrake, hemlock, poppy of the Indies.*

He flicked his tongue over his teeth. It was nicely made. He dipped the tip of his dagger into the jar and brought up a tiny pile of the powder. Put it to his nose. Sniffed sharply, and felt his whole head light up.

Whoever the apothecary in Valognes had been, before he fled, he had been skilled. What was more, he had access to fine suppliers. Which meant that other apothecaries in this country were probably well supplied too.

Romford felt giddy. He dipped his finger once more into the small jar and dabbed a little more powder on to his gum.

The roof of his mouth felt numb. He began to lose the sensation in his upper lip. He sensed his nose was running and rubbed the back of his hand across his face.

His mind started to wander. The itch started to subside. He thought of the dull, careless eyes of every other person like himself who had smelled and tasted this powder. Of the hours he had spent with tens – hundreds – of such people in corners of dark city taverns and dank, uncared-for houses.

Romford took the jar carefully, sealed it tightly with the stopper and edged his way out of the shop. He made his way back through the streets of Valognes like a ghost.

When he got to the camp, he found Pismire and Millstone asleep on their watch. He shook Scotsman awake. 'Your turn,' he whispered.

Then he lay down by the embers of the fire, and hugged himself tightly with both arms. He did not see his father's face any more.

The numbness in his face had filled his whole head with a magical heaviness, and his head in turn warmed his limbs, and made his stomach flutter. Everything seemed beautiful. Everything seemed destined to be well.

St Damian loved him.

Jesus Christ loved him, and all mankind.

Romford felt his whole body become a shifting expression of God's love. Then he passed out.

But he did not have long to sleep.

The first light of the new day was starting to creep up from the horizon.

8

On [Wednesday 19 July], some evildoers... set fire to everything near the road... The English army unharnessed at Saint-Côme-du-Mont. Here they heard rumours that the bridge had been broken down by the retreating enemy.

The Acts of War of Edward III

Dawn broke. Loveday stretched, pathetically thankful for a full night's sleep. A morning haze was already forming. It was going to be hot. Again.

He took a moment to collect himself before standing up. For as far as he could see, little companies were breaking down their camps. Men stamped out night-fires and swilled their reeking mouths with flask dregs. Lines snaked away from the marsh's larger bushes, where temporary jakes had been dug: shallow trenches where troops took turns to squat and shit.

Towards the town, Warwick's knights were armoured and saddled up, moving men out of Valognes's gates. They rode around, grins on their faces, kicking hungover fools who had been awake all night. Bleary-eyed archers and dawn-dazed footsoldiers stumbled about, trying to find their way back to their companies.

Men abandoned loot plundered the night before: now deemed too heavy or worthless to hump along on the march.

Millstone surveyed the debris. Shook his head. 'What a waste,' he said, to no one in particular. 'That was people's lives.'

Scotsman snorted. 'This is war, Millstone,' he said. 'You know how it works. Kings fall out. Their people get fucked. It's not supposed to be pretty.' He rolled up his night-blanket. Stuffed it in his pack, and loaded the pack onto the cart. The donkey was missing. 'Where the fuck are the animals?' he asked, looking around.

'Romford went with the Welsh boys to fetch them,' replied Loveday, motioning with his head to where, a couple of hundred yards distant, the Dogs had tethered their horses and the ass overnight.

'The kid looked half-dead this morning,' said Pismire.

'Romford?' said Millstone.

Pismire nodded.

'He was probably up all night tugging his pintle,' said Scotsman. 'What were you like at that age?'

Pismire ignored the question. 'He needs to hurry up,' he said. 'Anyway. Help me get this worthless priest onto the cart.'

Millstone cleared a space on the back of the cart and padded it with Father's blanket. Then his own, folded double. Scotsman bent down and wriggled one huge arm under Father's shoulders and the other under his knees. He lifted the older man up and laid him out on the rugs.

Father's skin was clammy. He groaned as Scotsman moved him. As he settled he burbled something that sounded like a prayer.

Scotsman peered at his face. He used a finger to gently pull open one of Father's eyelids.

Father's eye rolled down to meet his. 'St Christopher will carry you across the pit,' he said. Then his eye rolled back.

Scotsman shook his head. 'Cunt makes no more sense now than usual.'

'Should we tie him down?' Millstone said. 'If the road's as rough as it was yesterday...'

'Ah, leave him be,' said Pismire. 'Tebbe and Thorp can ride in the back with him and see he doesn't fall out. Unless he wakes up, anyway. Then they'll want to kick him out. That sit right with you, boys?'

Tebbe and Thorp both nodded.

The Welshmen came back with the horses. Behind them lagged Romford, leading the donkey and looking queasy.

Pismire looked at Romford disapprovingly. 'You still asleep, boy?' he asked.

Romford blinked as though he were struggling to remember who he was. 'I'm well,' he said uncertainly. He turned to the donkey, as if asking it to back him up. 'I'm... I feel good.'

Pismire shook his head and glanced sideways at the Scot, who shrugged. He turned back to Romford.

'Well, you'd better do,' he said. 'There's work to do. Hitch that donkey. You're driving the cart.'

Romford smiled, weakly. 'That's good. Where are we going?'

'Excellent fucking question,' said the Scot. 'Loveday, where are we going?'

Loveday scratched his head. He took his horse's reins from Lyntyn.

'Wherever we're told to,' he said.

The last thing Warwick's knights did before they led the vanguard out of Valognes was to set fire to the town with the dying torches that had lit the street by night. They put flames to everything that would take them. Dry roofs and dusty beams lit fast and crackled. Smoke belched a sickly yellow from the town's churches. The wind wafted it north towards the sea.

'They'll smell that back in England,' said Pismire. 'They'll know what we've done.'

'There's more to do yet,' muttered Scotsman.

Romford flicked the donkey with the switch. The Dogs kicked their horses and picked up their heels. And with the rest of the vanguard, they moved out.

But they did not move for long.

Loveday could still smell the smoke from Valognes behind them when the line ground once more to a halt. They had barely gone two miles.

Groans went up and down the line. But the halting nature of the march had now become part of the daily routine. The Dogs' complaints were muted. Once more, they just found patches of shade and settled down to wait. Millstone and the Scot went off for a time and came back with ale barrels, hiked up heavy on their shoulders. All the Dogs drank and filled their flasks.

After a while word came down the line from Warwick's party at the front that they had found another bridge broken ahead. It would take until noon to fix. Maybe longer.

Loveday nodded as he listened to the news spread. Trying to keep spirits up, he made a feeble joke. 'This is life in the king's army, men. You hurry up to get moving, then sit around for hours and scratch your arse.'

Most of the Dogs ignored him. Romford cracked a weak smile.

Loveday gave up. He pulled out his figure of St Martha. Scratched away at her eyes.

After they had sat for a time, a portly figure approached. Sir Robert was walking along the line, stopping here and there to lecture his own companies on what was going on. In the two days since Loveday had last seen him, the knight seemed to have grown fatter.

As usual he was overdressed. He wore a helm, despite the heat. The visor was up, so he could hear and speak, but the leather buckle was done up too tightly. Sir Robert's chins spilled over it.

Loveday straightened his back as the chubby knight approached. 'Good day, sir,' he said.

'A fine day,' said Sir Robert. 'A fine day to be an Englishman at play in a dishonourable land! You may have heard already, FitzTalbot, that we have the French running scared?'

Loveday shook his head. 'All we've heard is that another bridge is broken, and the engineers are working on it.'

Sir Robert smiled slyly, pleased to be able to impart news. He paced around the Dogs' cart, pretending to inspect it. He leaned against one of the wheels. He crossed his arms. Rested them on the swell of his gut.

Loveday gritted his teeth. Sir Robert's smugness rankled with the other Dogs. He could sense their irritation on the air, like a bad smell.

'What would you say, FitzTalbot,' said Sir Robert, 'if I told you that not five leagues hence, the cream of the French nobility is running harum-scarum before us, kicking their horses in desperation to escape with their miserable skins intact and their sides unpierced by our noble English lances and arrows?'

Loveday, feeling unusually defiant, returned to whittling his oxbone saint and said nothing.

'Quite so, FitzTalbot,' went on Sir Robert, seeming oblivious to Loveday's insolence. 'You would be speechless! Your tongue should be paralysed in your mouth at the idea that, so early in our campaign, the enemy is on the run!'

Loveday sighed. He stopped carving. 'Have the French been sighted, sir?'

'Sighted? By the holy backbone of St Boniface, they have indeed,' said Sir Robert. 'I am told – by our noble king's own scouts – that the two lords charged with holding this region – the feeble-hearted Count of Eu and the so-called Green Lion Knight, a fellow named Robert Bertrand – have been spotted fleeing south. They hope that by breaking bridges they can save themselves. Ha!'

Loveday raised his eyebrows. He looked at his men, sprawled around dozing on the ground. 'It does impede us somewhat.'

Sir Robert bridled slightly. 'That may be, Loveday. But it's damnably unchivalrous, wouldn't you say?'

Loveday shrugged.

'When the Saracens surrounded that great French hero Roland at the mountain pass of Roncesvalles in times of old, did he flee?'

Sir Robert rolled the R of Roland and Roncesvalles. Loveday could not remember much about the old songs. He took a guess. 'No?'

'No indeed,' bellowed Sir Robert. 'Why, he blew the great horn and warned his king, then he stood and fought to his glorious end – as a Christian soldier ought. How the Frenchman has forgotten himself since!'

'Didn't Roland get his head mashed in?' Scotsman called from the other side of the cart. Sir Robert flushed.

'You may tell your men, FitzTalbot, that brave Roland died

as a knight should – for love of his faith and his king. It is a pity that such values are waning in our own times.

'To which end we may hold our position here as the engineers do their work. We are headed to famous cities – Carentan, Saint-Lô and Caen – where I have no doubt that we shall earn further reward – and etch once again our names into the chronicles!'

Having found his way to the end of what he seemed to think was a rousing speech, Sir Robert wiped sweat from his face and nodded around to the Dogs. 'Thank you FitzTalbot. As you were.'

Then he rolled off to torment the next company, lounging in the shade of a pair of large pine trees, some way off.

Once he was out of earshot, Loveday looked apologetically around the Dogs. 'Well, there you go,' he said. 'We're off to Carentan, somewhere and Caen. Wherever they are. And whenever we start moving again.'

The Dogs settled back down to wait. As they did so, on the back of the cart, Father suddenly groaned, and propped himself up on his elbows.

He rubbed his head and glared at the departing figure of Sir Robert.

'Who the fuck was that?' he croaked. 'Bastard woke me up.'

It took the engineers much longer to rebuild the bridge ahead than any of them had expected. Morning passed. Midday scorched them, and they drank both barrels of ale, so that Millstone and the Scot had to go and fetch more.

Romford slept in the seat at the front of the wagon. His head lolled back, mouth open, drooling. He disturbed himself

9

The king had [the bridge repaired] and crossed the next day to Carentan... a lot of wine and food was found there, and much of the town was burnt, the king being unable to prevent it.

Campaign newsletter by Michael Northburgh

They still hadn't moved by nightfall, so they made camp around the cart. Tebbe and Thorp played another game of cross and pile. Pismire joined them for a while, lost every round and quit, muttering curses. Romford didn't play. He had stopped scratching himself, and lounged in his seat at the fore of the cart, his eyes glassy and a look of contentment on his face.

As the sun set, Millstone cooked a stew from handfuls of beans and the last of the onions. Scotsman grumbled about supplies. Ale was still available from the royal quartermasters, but they had stopped handing out food. They were expecting to resupply once they reached the next town.

'If we don't move soon, we'll starve,' muttered the Scot.

Millstone stirred the pot, gazing absently into the thickening sludge. 'Don't worry,' he said. 'We'll restock. You know how it works. We arrive, people run away, we load our wagons with their food.'

Father, now awake, seemed to grow more agitated as evening advanced. He would not speak to anyone except Loveday. Yet when Loveday tried to calm him down, Father shrank back, holding his knees and shaking his head. He would say no more about the vision he had seen during his stupor. As though voicing it would conjure it.

Tired of ministering, Loveday gave up. But he kept a nervous watch throughout the night on the old priest, worried that his fear might be spread among the group. Like a plague.

In the morning, at last, the line moved. The engineers had rebridged the river, which the men learned was called the Douve. When they neared it, Loveday understood why it had taken so long to build the crossing.

Although shallow at its edges, in the middle the water was deep, wide and fast-flowing. Once again the wreck of the original bridge stuck out of the water at a hopeless angle. It had been smashed and burned. Black, charred plank-stumps broke the water's surface.

Whoever had broken it had done a thorough job. They had bought themselves time, thought Loveday. But not much.

Behind him the train of restless companies of men stretched back along the road as far as he could see. They were all tough men. Hard men. Killers. Unlike the Dogs, most of them had seen no action since landing on the beach. All they had known was the frustration of marching, camping, sleeping, eating, shitting in the ground. The air was tense.

On the far side of the bridge, the Earl of Warwick sat on horseback, flanked by his friend, the Norman defector Sir Godefroi, and on the other side of him, the young Prince of Wales. There was no sign now of the woman.

Warwick's face was set hard, and he was not booming as jovially as usual.

But as each company passed over his end of the bridge, he barked a line or two of encouragement. The prince and Sir Godefroi called jokes to one another, sniggering at their private quips. The prince had a sly look on his face.

Loveday led the Dogs past the noblemen, and bowed his head to all three in deference. Warwick gave him a nod of recognition.

'FitzTalbot,' he said. 'And the Dogs of Essex, I see, sniffing blood! A mile ahead, now, boys. The town's called Carentan. God speed you there, before there's nothing left for you to feed on!' He looked askance at Father, shivering in the back of the cart.

Loveday led the Dogs as they clattered off the bridge and on to a winding track. The marshland it led through was dry, but sandy. The rumble of so many hooves, feet and cart-wheels sent up a hanging film of dust.

Loveday switched his reins to his right hand and used the crook of his left elbow to cover his mouth and nose. Around him the other Dogs were blinking and coughing, their faces prickling.

Father, sitting with Tebbe and Thorp in the cart, darted his eyes around, scanning the landscape for terrors.

A stone tower and the jumbled buildings of Carentan emerged from the marshland. The companies behind the Dogs were starting to press on their heels. The men ahead were now jogging, or spurring their horses. Shouts went up, and before Loveday could urge caution or restraint on his men, he realized the march was gathering unstoppable pace.

The Dogs were swept along.

From either side of Loveday, the Welshmen appeared, kicking their horses to a canter and heading off on their own towards Carentan. Pismire and Scotsman were also straining to break away from the group. Millstone, like Loveday, was keeping his pace to a trot, but both their horses were twitching under them, hungry to stretch their legs. Loveday and Millstone looked at one another. Millstone's expression said: *Shall we go too?*

Loveday turned to Romford at the front of the cart. No amount of whipping with the switch would persuade the donkey to move faster than its ordinary plod. 'Can you find your way into the town?' Loveday called, above the rising din.

Romford nodded.

'See that he does,' Loveday shouted to Tebbe and Thorp. The archers waved their hands in agreement. 'We'll meet you in the square.'

Then Millstone and Loveday also broke off towards Carentan. Loveday took one final glance back at the cart. The last thing he saw was Father, sitting hunched and haunted, his hands over his ears, rocking gently back and forth, as the cart and the archers trundled slowly forwards.

One winter when Loveday had been young, growing up on the edge of the thick Essex forest, a rich knight called Coggeshall had died of a fever and left his fortune to the church in the next village.

When the spring arrived, craftsmen came, bringing wooden buckets and horsehair brushes, cartloads of interlocking wooden poles and odd tools Loveday had never seen before.

For the whole spring and summer the craftsmen had worked in the church. Loveday had taken every chance to sneak away there, often running the two miles from his father's house once the day's toil was over, so he could loiter and watch these men as they worked until the last light had gone. He loved to peep around the church door at the place where they had stripped back and scaffolded one whole wall of the long nave, then spent their days covering it with wet plaster, on which they painted in bright pigments and dyes.

The craftsmen had worked on small portions of the wall at a time, and although they were always busy – sometimes shouting jokes and lewd taunts at one another, as builders and roofers did, but never slacking off – it took weeks for the scene they were creating to reveal itself.

As it neared completion, Loveday had been both captivated and horrified by what they had created.

The scene was the end of the world. The villagers later nicknamed it the Great Doom. Gleeful demons poked twisted sinners with tridents and spears. Terrified families tried to huddle together, as demented devils yanked them away from one another. Women and men were stripped naked while their judges jeered and pointed. Fires were lit everywhere. Over it all, Christ watched, his face stern and his gaze cold. Those he saved held their hands up to him in pathetic supplication. The damned were herded towards the fiery pit of hell.

Loveday had never forgotten that summer, with its colours and terrors. And he thought of it now, as he rode into Carentan.

The town was a little bigger than Valognes, and much prettier. Although it was not defended, it had not been fully evacuated. Women stood outside their homes, helpless as English troops barged through their doors, leering their demands for food, ale, wine and fodder. Children cowered in tears. Old men stood in front of their families, some holding staves or tools.

Useless weapons, made more so by the trembling hands that gripped them.

Warwick's knights were already on patrol, shouting over and over that there should be no violence against these helpless citizens. But there was no danger of a fight. The townsfolk had more sense than to raise their fists.

So the people of Carentan watched as their homes were robbed. Provisions were pulled from houses, shops and stalls, and carried to a pile in the centre of the town. Between two churches there stood a large covered market – its facade a series of stone arches under which there was cool space for traders to do business. The traders had fled and their long trestles now heaved with produce pilfered from their ordinary customers. This had begun as an orderly process, but as Loveday and Millstone arrived, a surge of troops behind them pressed into the city.

They seemed to bring evil with them, on the air.

It took less than an hour for the knights charged with keeping order to lose control. By that time every building had been stripped, and stripped again. The entire vanguard – some five thousand men – had crushed into the streets, and some of the king's middle division had arrived too.

Companies set up around their carts in the streets to drink and chant war songs. Civilians who had not managed to slip out of the town gates were badgered and groped. Where one or two of the smarter buildings had glass in their windows, this was smashed, to great cheers. The blue-and-gold flags and pennons of the French Crown, along with those of his son, the Duke of Normandy, were torn down from the municipal building and burned.

Meanwhile, hundreds of troops were crowding around the stockpile of food and wine. Warwick's knights were trying to divide it into rations and hand it out. But the knights were not quartermasters. They had no way to keep track of who had been given their share and who had not, or what each company's share ought to be.

A scrum formed, with hands grasping what they could. Loveday spotted Pismire and the Scot fighting their way to the front of the scramble of bodies. He waved as they struggled back through the crowd with what they had grabbed.

Pismire was dragging a half-sack of grain and two wine flasks. The Scot held three dead chickens by their feet. The plucked birds' eyes were closed and their throats roughly slit lengthways. Congealed blood hung in gluey strings from their beaks. Over his shoulder the Scot carried a side and hind leg of some larger animal – a pig, Loveday thought, or perhaps a goat.

Scotsman was red. He was breathing hard as he reached Loveday and Millstone. 'Fucking animals,' he panted. 'Someone else needs to get in there if we want anything else.'

'I'll go,' said Millstone. 'What do we need?'

Pismire looked up at him. 'Grab whatever you can,' he said. 'But if you stand here scratching your arse, there'll be fuck all left.'

Locating the cart amid the thousands of men in the streets was hard. The sun was still high, and most were drinking heavily. Several companies, whose men spoke with northern accents, had formed a large circle and were holding impromptu wrestling bouts.

A bald, barrel-chested miller-type, stripped to the waist, was grappling on the floor with a younger man, also broad and strong. Sweat stood out on their backs; black dirt streaked their faces. They were half laughing, half grimacing as they heaved and tugged at one another. The miller put the young fellow in an arm-lock. It was a skilful move. He wrenched, and Loveday heard a loud pop. The young man yelped in pain.

Loveday winced. It sounded like a dislocated shoulder. That spelled ill for the young man. Loveday prayed he'd never have to go into battle with only one good hand.

The three men continued to push through the crowd. Scotsman edged past a small group of younger men. They were swaying, arms around each others' shoulders, singing a song Loveday kept hearing.

God and right! God and right!
French and Flemish die tonight!
God and right! God and right!
Scuuuuummmmmmmmmmmm!

The drunken chanters swayed backwards into the Scot, barging him into Pismire and off balance. Loveday instinctively took a step away from them. He had seen this sort of thing before. Without dropping the side of meat on his right shoulder, the Scotsman reached out with his massive left hand. He slammed his palm on to the head of the nearest man, and clamped his fingers into his skull. Then, using only the strength in his forearm and wrist, he turned the man around to face him.

But it was not really a man at all.

The reveller could not have been much more than fourteen

years old. His pink cheeks were covered in an oily mix of acne scars and pus-filled cysts, with ripe yellow heads. His eyes were lazy and stupid with drink.

Clenching his fingers into the boy's lank hair, the Scot lifted him a foot off the ground. The lad squealed in pain. His friends shrank back.

'Sing that fucking song again, or nudge me when I'm walking, and I'll pull your fucking ears off,' the Scot growled.

Tears were welling in the boy's eyes. He whimpered.

The Scot gave him a little shake. 'You understand me, boy?' he asked.

The lad squawked an answer. It was more noise than word. Like an animal's call. But it could only have meant yes.

Scotsman dropped him. The boy's knees gave out as he landed, and he curled up in a ball on the floor, holding his head. His friends gawped.

The Scot ignored them. He adjusted the side of meat over his right shoulder, and walked on. Pismire and Loveday exchanged glances. Loveday shrugged half-apologetically at the boys.

Then they followed Scotsman, striding off to find Romford, and the cart.

After a long time searching, they found the cart parked in a quieter part of the town, away from the chanting and laughter of the troops. The buildings that cast pools of cool shade over the street had not struck most of the English as worth pilfering. Loveday looked at their signs. Surgeons. Barbers. Apothecaries.

He shrugged. But when he looked at Romford and Father he thought he understood.

The boy sat calmly on the back of the cart, Father's head in his lap. The old priest's head had been freshly dressed; the old, bloody linen bandages, stained brown and yellow, were balled up on the ground. He lay on his back, his mouth slightly open. Loveday looked at Romford, who smiled shyly back at him.

'Did you change his bandages?'

Romford nodded softly, and put his finger to his lips. 'He's calm,' he said. 'The nightmares have stopped.'

Pismire snorted. 'What did you do to the old goat?' he asked. 'Knock him on the head?'

Romford just smiled. 'Something like that,' he said.

'Well, if he's quiet, let him lie,' said the Scot. 'Better that than his twitching and whimpering.' He looked around. 'Has anyone found anywhere for us to sleep in this godforsaken town? I wouldn't mind a roof over my head for one night on this bloody march.'

Romford looked up, as though he had been sent a divine revelation. 'The barber's shop,' he said. 'I was meant to tell you. Tebbe and Thorp are in there now. They say there's room for us all to sleep before we move again.'

Pismire rolled his eyes. 'Good of you to tell us, lad,' he said. 'Where is this barber's shop? And what are the chances of getting my beard trimmed?'

Romford flushed. 'It's at the end of this street,' he said, pointing to a shop marked by a sign bearing a hand-painted picture of a scalpel.

Loveday nodded. 'Let's go there, then,' he said. 'We can cook and eat, and get some rest. We'll be away again at dawn.'

The Dogs set off down the street. From the other side of town they heard crashes and loud cheers. The familiar smell of thatch-smoke hung on the air. From a few streets away, where the brothels stood, lewd arguments and choruses of ribald male laughter drifted across. Somewhere a lone woman was crying as though the world were at an end.

The Dogs trudged their way towards the barber's shop. Loveday counted his men, and counted them again. He made a vow to God not to lose any of them.

He saw, just for an instant, the Captain's face. Then Alis's. Then that of the woman from Valognes. But he was so tired that they all vanished as quickly as they came. And before dusk fell the Dogs were encamped inside the barber's shop, with a fire lit in the dirty hearth.

Loveday drifted off to sleep listening to round after round of the English army's fighting song echoing around the town's dark streets. He heard frustration in the men's voices: pent-up rage like floodwater trapped, pressing for somewhere to burst free. And time and again he heard the same angry verse, ending with its long, guttural war cry:

God and right! God and right!
French and Flemish die tonight!
God and right! God and right!
Scuuuuummmmmmmmmm!

PART 2

FIRE

22–26 July 1346

IO

The vanguard... climbed to the top of a hill [near Saint-Lô] and drew themselves up in battle array against a possible enemy attack, which they hoped was imminent. Here Henry de Burghersh was knighted by the Prince of Wales.

The Acts of War of Edward III

Three Days Later

The prince was drunk.

The word came down the line as the army moved towards the outskirts of Saint-Lô. When the Dogs drew up with the vanguard on a hillside north of the town, Loveday saw the rumour was true.

The young man rode a beautiful black horse two hands taller than the tired mare Loveday had ridden for the past nine days. But he slouched in the saddle, lurching from side to side. In his right hand he held a silver chalice, which looked as though it had been looted from the vestry of one of the little village churches they had burned the previous day. In his left he held his sword – a long piece of polished steel which gleamed and scattered the sunlight.

He was gesticulating with cup and sword to the knights and nobles who rode around him. His horse's reins sat slack in his lap. He talked loudly, in a voice that still cracked from time to time into a boyish squeak.

He was either a very accomplished rider, thought Loveday, or he had a forgiving saddle. Or he had taken on so much wine he had lost all the stiffness in his body. Whatever the case, he was testing his companions' patience.

The two knights who rode beside him, trying to keep him on the path that snaked up the hill, were grimacing as much as they dared. Warwick rode behind, with the French traitor Sir Godefroi and another high nobleman, whom Loveday recognized as the Constable of the Army: William de Bohun, Earl of Northampton.

Warwick kept turning his head left and right, as if to check the formation of the troops behind him. But from his expression, Loveday guessed he was weary of minding the king's eldest son and could not bear to look at him for long.

As the troops crested the hill, the land dropped away in front of them, and in a green, well-watered valley below, the town of Saint-Lô came into view. The prince stopped. He swilled what remained in his goblet and, without looking, threw it behind him, over his shoulder. It disappeared, rolling soundlessly into long grass on the hillside.

He raised his sword, and the troops who could see him fell quiet.

'Look out,' said the Scotsman, beside Loveday. 'The whelp is going to bark.'

The prince opened his mouth, then shut it again. He did this twice, then let out a high-pitched giggle and slid sideways in his saddle, so that his body was parallel with the ground.

Seeing he was about to fall, the knight riding beside him

shot out an arm and grabbed the prince by his red-and-green tunic.

The prince seemed to find this even funnier. Again he raised his sword, and this time he managed to speak. 'Men! Sir Henry... Sir Henry here is my best knight. He is worth a hundred Frenchmen! Who agrees with me?'

A dutiful cheer went up. Sir Henry squirmed in his saddle.

'Sir Henry! I order you to dismount and kneel.'

Sir Henry looked nonplussed. The prince grimaced. He pointed his sword at the knight. 'Dismount!'

A burble of laughter was now going up, as Sir Henry threw his leg over his horse and climbed down.

'Kneel!'

Sir Henry knelt.

Turning his horse sideways with surprising ease, the prince leaned down from his saddle and tapped the knight on each shoulder with his sword. 'You are such a good knight that I knight you once more. Arise, Sir Henry de Burghersh. My best knight!'

With each of the last three words he struck Sir Henry with the flat of the sword. First his right shoulder, then his left, and finally, a loud crack on the top of Sir Henry's helm, which brought the visor down over his face. Sir Henry raised it. He winced.

'That's a real knight!' the prince cried. He laughed so much tears ran down his face.

Puffing out his cheeks, Sir Henry rose and climbed back on his horse. There was now open laughter around the hillside.

'Daft little bastard thinks he's fucking King Arthur,' muttered the Scotsman.

'Don't,' said Loveday. 'He really will be our king one of these days.'

'He might be your king, but he won't ever be mine. The lads where I come from can hold their drink.'

Up ahead, the prince was trying to reknight other knights.

Loveday looked at the Earl of Warwick. The marshal had a face like thunder. He waved to a group of the prince's squires, carrying sacks of fine cloth dyed red and green and stout wooden poles. They hurried over and started putting up the prince's golden pavilion on a patch of flattish land on the hillside. Soon they were untangling ropes and banging pegs into the hard ground.

It was not a perfect place to pitch a tent, thought Loveday. But the boy was going to need some shade to sleep in.

An hour later, Warwick and Northampton held a briefing. Sir Robert summoned Loveday and Millstone to it, along with the other crew leaders in his company, including the East Anglian Shaw and his no-eared deputy. They kept their distance from the Dogs, and together the men listened as the marshal and constable explained the situation in Saint-Lô.

The earls made an intriguing pair. Northampton was around the same age as Warwick, about thirty-five summers, but he was shorter by half a head and rounder in the shoulders. He wore his long, grey-streaked hair swept back from his face, revealing a thin scar that ran from the middle of his hairline to the centre of his left cheek. His teeth were crooked. His close-cropped beard was turning white even faster than his hair. He was smartly dressed – a livery on his chest of gold lions on a blue background, slashed from shoulder to waist with a white banner bearing red stars. Yet there was something of the earth about him.

Loveday felt a pang of excitement at seeing the constable up close. He had campaigned under Northampton before, in Scotland. Heard the stories of his famous deeds. How he had helped the young king overthrow the usurper when they were barely more than boys the prince's age. How he had killed six enemy knights in one day in the Scottish wars. How he had played hostage for the king's debts to Flemish bankers – then escaped singlehandedly from the toughest prison in Ghent. How he had ruled the captured province of Brittany with an iron fist for a year in the name of the king.

As the briefing came to order, Warwick opened proceedings. 'Gentlemen!' he began, beaming and flashing his white teeth. 'We have been on the road some time. What have we seen of our French friends?'

The assembled men held their peace. Loveday batted at a cloud of tiny flies that circled his head.

'Nothing?' asked Warwick, a smile dancing at the corners of his mouth.

Loveday spoke up. 'We've seen nothing but townsfolk since we beached, my lord,' he said.

He felt the eyes of the group on him.

Warwick nodded. 'Very good, FitzTalbot,' he said. 'I believe your Dogs of Essex have a rare honour in that regard. Few are the men among us who have spilled any French warriors' blood so far.'

He cleared his throat. 'I do not say this to admonish you, men,' he said. 'I know all of you would relish the opportunity to loose your sword arms. We came here to kill. And to take back what is rightfully our king's land. We did not come here to hike miles through marshland and scratch at gadfly bites on our ball-sacks.'

Loveday watched Shaw dig his hand inside his rough woollen breeches. He scratched like a dog. Pulled his fingers out and sniffed them.

'We yearn for the thrill of battle,' continued Warwick. 'And it will come in time. But first we must convince the French to stop running from us. My friend the Lord Northampton will explain more. May I defer to you, my lord?'

Northampton nodded impatiently. 'You may, my lord,' he replied. Throughout Warwick's speech, he had been rocking on his heels and fidgeting with the straps around the waist of his padded gambeson, the knee-length coat over which his armour would fit when battle came. He ran his fingers through his hair. 'That town down there,' he said, in a voice that crunched like boots on gravel, 'is called Saint-Lô. If you want to know who St Lô was, you're asking the wrong fucking man. Sir Godefroi over there could probably tell you.'

Northampton hooked his thumb in the direction of the Norman turncoat, who was standing with a group of Warwick's knights. Sir Godefroi smiled, and began to answer, in English that betrayed only a hint of his own accent.

'Quite so. He was a bishop, a thousand years ago, who—'

'You see?' interrupted Northampton. 'Sir Godefroi knows fucking everything. He must have gone to school more than me, or paid attention, anyhow. Good for him. But personally I couldn't give a hanged man's hard-on who St fucking Lô was and I doubt you lot do either.'

A chuckle rumbled around the group. Sir Godefroi attempted a gracious smile.

The earl went on. 'So fuck St Lô and fuck his halo while

we're at it. Let's talk about his town. Take a good look at it. It's about as big as Leicester. If you haven't been to Leicester, good for you, because it's the arsehole of England. Come to Northampton if you want to see a real town.

'But for now, feast your eyes. It's a big town. They make coins and knives and nice gold jewellery. When we get in there, if there's any gold left, you can help yourselves to it and take it home to your wives. I've heard what you get paid, and I think it's a fucking disgrace. So you can fill your boots.'

Now there was real excitement.

'But that's where it gets interesting,' continued Northampton. 'Getting in there. We've made you men and your fellows slog all the way up this hill in the hot fucking sun. Does anyone want to guess why?'

One of the Midlanders piped up. 'Advantage of position, my lord. We're expecting a fight.'

'Well said, sir,' replied Northampton. 'We're expecting a fucking fight. Or rather, we *were* expecting a fight.'

He looked for a moment down the slope at Saint-Lô. To its western side, on the right, it was bounded by the river they had bridged earlier that day. It was defended by stone walls as thick as a man was tall, and twice as high. At regular points along its length the wall swelled into round guard towers, with arrow slits cut into their sides. The main gateway was approached by a narrow stone bridge across a deep moat. Probably fed by the river, thought Loveday.

Well defended and stocked with food, it looked as though it would be easy to hold, so long as there was a decent garrison of troops.

'Yesterday,' Northampton said, 'that place was crawling with French soldiers. The same fuckers who've been breaking bridges and making us sweat in the heat for the last ten days were holed up in there, waiting for us to arrive, and telling each other how they were going to send us back home or down to the devil. But guess what?'

There was a nervous silence. Northampton savoured it. Then punctured it.

'They've fucking run off again. We have contacts in the town who tell us that last night, their leader, the Green Lion Knight, Robert Bertrand – Marshal of France, no less – heard the rumble of English boots. And like every Frenchman in history, once the game turned from talking to fighting, Bertrand shat in his breeches.

'This old lion smelled the smoke coming from Carentan, and Valognes, and all those other towns whose names we can't pronounce. And, just like always, he's run away.'

Northampton paused, just for a beat. Then he looked over at Warwick, who took over the briefing once more. Northampton went back to rocking on his heels.

'My noble friend has made that all clear, I hope,' Warwick said. 'The enemy has, so far as we can tell, abandoned a rich and prosperous city the size of an English town somewhat inferior to Northampton. So, once more, we will be denied the delights of a battle. But if we penetrate this place, we can enjoy ourselves one last time.

'Tonight we will send units to inspect the defences. These will inform our advance when the sun rises. We will send orders shortly, letting you know your parts in this. Until then, put your companies in order, and await our command.' The earl beamed around the group. 'You may even have time to hear Mass and ask the Lord for forgiveness.'

Warwick cast his gaze across the group once more. 'Any questions?' Everyone shook their heads. Warwick looked satisfied. Northampton looked eager to leave. The constable clapped his hand to his thigh.

'Off you fuck then, lads. Move on our say-so. And don't forget what he said about asking the Lord for his forgiveness. One way or another, you're going to fucking need it.'

Dusk was falling when Sir Robert came to give the Dogs their orders. He made his way slowly around the companies. He came to the Dogs last.

While they waited, Loveday tried to keep his men busy. They unloaded and repacked the cart, checked their weapons and took stock of their food supplies. But they were all weary and uncomfortable, tired now from the exertion of spending more than a week on their feet and out in the open. Loveday could feel one of his toenails working loose inside the leather boots he had barely removed for days. Scotsman's beard was so filthy that it was beginning to form matted locks, which hung roughly from his chin in an inverted V. Most of the men were scratching insect bites.

Father and Romford sat together on the back of the cart, their heads lolling in a doze. Father's animosity towards the lad seemed to have vanished since his accident in Valognes. They now seemed friendly. It was odd, thought Loveday. As if the old priest now looked up to the gentle, cherub-faced boy. Needed him, somehow.

All the Dogs looked up when Sir Robert arrived.

'Good evening, sir,' said Loveday.

Scotsman tugged his beard-strands. 'Please tell us we've got something to do this evening, besides listening to the owls hoot and the foxes fuck,' he said.

Sir Robert smiled slyly. 'As it happens, you have. Somehow or other, news of your prowess with the rude weapons you wield has reached the ear of His Grace the Earl of Northampton. I have come here from the side of the earl himself to request your attendance on his presence. It would seem his grace has an unusual job for you.'

Scotsman narrowed his eyes. 'Unusual?'

'Quite so. Follow me.'

Sir Robert led them through the hillside camp, picking a path between tents and groups of men sitting beside small campfires. The air was acrid with smoke. Loveday recognized the stink. Fuel was running low, and the men were burning bones.

After a while, they arrived at a large blue-and-gold pavilion, pitched a short way from the golden one in which the prince had taken his afternoon's sleep. Two men-at-arms guarded the entrance. Nearby, a commotion was coming from the prince's tent. Male voices, raised but their words indistinct. Interspersed with a woman's shrill sobs.

'I have brought hither FitzTalbot and his friends,' Sir Robert announced. 'At the request of his gentle lordship the earl, who said to me earlier—'

Northampton's voice barked from the tent. 'Is that Sir Robert? Tell him to leave his men and fuck off.'

One of the guards, a man almost as large and wide as the Scot, winked at Sir Robert. 'Would you like me to translate that into cuntish for you? Get lost.'

Sir Robert stormed away.

The big guard nodded amiably. 'In you go,' he said to the Dogs. 'Your luck's in. He's in a good mood tonight.'

The two guards stood aside and let the Dogs file into the pavilion. They found Northampton pacing around, holding a handful of tiny, unripe-looking grapes in one of his hands.

Seated on a large, wooden chair, one leg thrown over the arm, was the Norman knight Sir Godefroi.

'Essex Dogs?' said Northampton.

'Yes, my lord,' said Loveday.

Northampton nodded. 'My friend Lord Warwick tells me you did some fine work on the beach,' he said. 'He also tells me you were less use than a nun's left tit when you got to Valognes. Does that sound about right?'

'It does,' admitted Loveday.

'Right,' said Northampton. 'Well, we'll see which way this one goes.' He threw a grape in the air, caught it in his mouth, chewed and grimaced. He spat a pip onto the floor of the pavilion, which was lined with a greasy, well-trodden rug. From the shadows at the corner of the tent a servant boy scuttled to pick it up.

'Fuck off,' said Northampton. The boy scampered away.

Northampton turned back to the Dogs. 'I'll get to the point. I've got some good fucking tidings for you. You're going to be among the first men we send down there. So far as we know, there's not an enemy soldier in sight. If there is, you'd better kill them. If they kill you, we'll send some more men in behind you to sort it out.

'I don't care what you do when you get there, who you rob, fuck, marry or murder, so long as you come back with one thing. Or rather, with three things. Three things that mean something personal to me. Do you think you can do that?'

Loveday looked around at the other Dogs. Other than the

Welshmen, who were completely uninterested, every man looked eager to hear more.

'We'll do our best, my lord. Just tell us what you need.'

Northampton caught another grape in his mouth. He seemed to like it no more than the first, but he swallowed it. 'Aye. Well. I'll do one better than that. I'll let Sir Godefroi tell you for me.' He turned to the Norman: 'Go on then. I won't dally here with you, if you don't mind. I've got to help my lord Warwick with something.'

With that, Northampton gave the men a curt nod, and disappeared from the tent.

The Dogs turned their attention to Sir Godefroi, who motioned for them to sit on the rug. Then he cleared his throat, and began his tale.

'Gentlemen,' said the Norman knight. 'My name is Sir Godefroi d'Harcourt. Men call me a traitor. I know. But I say this. This land is my home. You are most welcome here.'

He adjusted his position in Northampton's chair. He was a small, compact man, and he sat, thought Loveday, with an elegance that seemed to come from somewhere deep within.

His long, blond hair hung loose at his shoulders. His grey eyes flickered in the pavilion's torchlight. The only imperfection was his withered left foot, which turned unnaturally inwards. Sir Godefroi tried to disguise his disfigurement by crossing his left leg over his right, or hanging it over the side of the chair as he sat. It must hurt him, Loveday thought. Either through pain or shame.

'There are many ancient families here in Normandy,' continued Sir Godefroi. 'Mine was one of these. For generations we had honour. We had land. We had a beautiful home. I tell you these things in the order they are important to a knight. A land and home. But honour above all.'

He looked gravely around the group.

'But my honour has been taken. Three years ago, I fell in love. The most beautiful woman I had ever seen. Jeanne. Chaste and modest, but with the spirit of a true Norman. Such women you see only seldom in life. Perhaps you have heard as the famous Italian poet says? "She makes me tremble with the chill of love."'

Sir Godefroi looked around the Dogs. He saw only blank faces.

'We are not much for poetry, sir,' Loveday said.

Sir Godefroi sighed sadly. 'Yes. Well, for a year I woo my Jeanne. I speak with her father. We agree a marriage. Then, as I make the preparations, the false king Philippe visits Normandy. He decides to give my Jeanne to another man. To the man who now leads his armies in running away. His name is Bertrand.

'But it does not matter who he is. This is wrong. Disgraceful. So I do as a good knight must do. I gather my friends. We ride to this man's house. We burn it, and kill his peasants.'

'Did you get her back?' asked Pismire.

Sir Godefroi shook his head briskly. 'No. She is killed. A shame. But no matter. Honour is restored.'

Loveday's head was spinning. 'But if she's dead, Sir Godefroi—' he began.

'Please,' said Sir Godefroi, holding up a hand to quiet Loveday. 'I will come soon to the point. All men have their pride. And the false French king, when he hears I have restored mine, feels he has lost his own.

'So he sends his army to this land, to do to me as I have

done to his. He arrests my friends, takes them to Paris, and puts them on trial outside the royal *palais*. They are bound and their tongues slit in half so they may not defend themselves. Then they are beheaded. Their bodies hung up by their heels for the birds to peck. Their heads sent here to my country, and nailed above the gates of a town that we all loved.

'That town, gentlemen, is Saint-Lô, before whose walls we now assemble. My friends' heads are still there. They were great men who died in a noble cause. But so long as their skulls hang over that gate, they cannot have a Christian burial. And I cannot have peace.

'My lords the Earls of Warwick and Northampton tell me you are the Dogs of Essex. I do not know you, or what you fight for – whether it is gold, or women, or adventure, or love, or fear. Or any of these things.'

Loveday interrupted. 'We fight for each other, Sir Godefroi.'

Sir Godefroi considered this briefly. But he did not respond directly.

Instead, he said: 'Deliver my friends' heads to me, and you will ride in honour with me at the front of this great army all the way to Paris. I will make you rich men.' He had tears in his eyes. He leaned forwards, over his bent left leg. 'Do this for me, I ask you on my honour. It does not become a knight to beg.'

Loveday opened his mouth to answer. But as he did, a crashing and a volley of cursing at the back of the pavilion announced the return of the Earl of Northampton. The earl stormed into the tent, dragging behind him a boy, who squealed and thrashed as the earl manhandled him.

Northampton gave the boy a kick, and looked furiously around the tent. 'What the fuck are these fools still doing here?' he demanded, glaring at Sir Godefroi.

He rounded on Loveday. 'Hasn't the cunt given you your fucking orders? You're not here to lounge around. Get out there and fetch those stinking heads so this moody bastard can stick them in the ground and the rest of us can get on with burning his fucking country!'

The Dogs jumped to their feet. Sir Godefroi rolled his eyes.

Loveday burbled an apology. 'My lord, we—'

'Fuck off!' bellowed Northampton, his eyes blazing. The boy he was holding started thrashing again. The earl drew him up by the hair and with the back of his right hand slapped him hard across the face.

Loveday gasped. It was the prince.

Once more Northampton fixed the Dogs with a look that promised murder. 'Did I not just tell you to fuck off?' he said, with low menace.

Loveday nodded, and started backing away slowly. As a safe distance opened up between himself and the earl, he gave a small bow, turned and ran. The rest of the Dogs almost fell over one another scrambling after him.

As they went, they heard a screeching erupt from within the tent.

'You didn't see this!' screamed Northampton, as they tumbled out into the night.

II

The King of England went to Saint-Lô... [to retrieve] the
heads of three knights, who for their crimes were killed in
Paris...

Les Grandes Chroniques de France

The moon was well risen, the skies had cleared, and the stars
cast a thin light on to the walls of Saint-Lô.

The Dogs picked their way on foot down from the vanguard's
camp, following the slope of the hill towards a point where the
northern wall of the town ran up to the riverbank. A point
where they could start their search of the walls for the three
knights' rotted heads.

The road into Saint-Lô was less than half a mile to their
left. Loveday had decided against advancing directly along
it. He thought how the Captain would have assessed it.
Exposed. Vulnerable. Obvious. That was how he assessed it
too. So he had led the Dogs on a more indirect approach,
crisscrossing ancient shepherd's trails that wound down the
hillside.

For the nimbler Dogs – Pismire and the archers - it was easy
going. But the bigger men, like Millstone and the Scot, found
their brawn working against them. They puffed and grunted as
the dry earth crumbled and their feet slipped. Loveday went in

the middle of the group, scrambling gingerly, hoping he would not turn an ankle.

Father and Romford brought up the rear. The old priest reached occasionally for the lad's arm. Romford whispered instructions and warnings to Father, helping him avoid falls. As if he were helping a blind man. Father issued his thanks in wet coughs, and spat on the ground every dozen steps.

Scotsman, as usual, was grumbling. 'Whatever that crippled Norman fucker's planning on giving us for this fool's errand, it had better be good. I'm getting too old for games.'

Pismire, ignoring his friend for once, fell back alongside Loveday and spoke to him in a low voice. 'You think they've left a garrison?'

Loveday shrugged. 'I would have. If they only withdrew yesterday, the town will be full of civilians. Can't leave them to fend for themselves.' He paused. 'On the other hand, if they've decided to let it fall, maybe they wouldn't have wasted the troops.'

Pismire was quiet for a moment. Then he said: 'So what you're saying is, we don't know.'

'I know as much as you do,' Loveday replied. 'Which is that there might be defenders behind those walls. Or there might just be a lot of frightened women and children. We've been told to get our arses down here, which means we'll be the first to find out.'

Pismire moved forwards again. Loveday saw him passing the message along to Scotsman. Heard the Scot puff. Loveday looked along the line of the town walls, screwing up his eyes as he sought silhouettes of defenders moving along the ramparts. He saw no one. Heard nothing but the gentle swish of breeze in the grass.

ditch via a wooden bridge. Large gates blocked the way into the city, flanked by two stone watchtowers. The gates were shut tight. But the towers, like every other tower, were deserted.

Nausea began to win the battle in Loveday's stomach.

But it was not only the stink of muck and decay that sickened him. He was now certain that there was no garrison in the city.

They had gone. And left the people to their fate. He had seen what that meant many times before. Too many times.

The Dogs crossed the road and followed the ditch and walls on the eastern side of the city for no more than a few hundred paces. Then the wall bent sharply round again. And there, grey in the starlight, Loveday saw what the Dogs had been looking for.

A fat barbican, built of stone. Approached by an arched stone crossing over the ditch. Hung with flags, which flapped lazily against the stonework in the light breeze.

It was blocked by thick gates, on one side of which hung a gibbet. And there, on the other side, driven into the masonry, Loveday could see five or six iron spikes sticking out of the wall.

Three of them were set with rounded objects which could only be severed heads.

Loveday could also see a small group of men standing outside the barbican on the stone bridge, looking up to the top of one of its towers. They were pointing and jeering up to a pair of figures standing there. Loveday recognized the tall silhouette and East Anglian drawl of the company leader.

It was Shaw.

He was baiting whoever stood behind the crenellated top of the barbican tower.

As the Dogs crept closer, Loveday heard voices calling back

to Shaw, in French. They were young voices. Not much more than boys, thought Loveday. The East Anglians whooped and jeered, picking up stones and hurling them up towards the tower-tops. Defiant cries came back.

Shaw's crew were so busy with their taunts they did not hear the Dogs approach. In fact, they were completely oblivious until Pismire walked up behind Shaw and prodded him in the back.

The tall East Anglian jumped and spun around. 'Virgin's fuc—' he exclaimed.

Pismire smiled grimly at him. 'Good job the garrison's gone, mate,' he said. 'Or you'd be a dead man by now.'

The rest of the East Anglians turned to face the Dogs. There were seven of them. They were all spare and scrawny, their faces covered with straggling beards. The group included the man missing both his ears, and the one with a branded scar on the middle of his head. Up close Loveday saw it was a rough letter M for *Murder*.

Shaw ignored Pismire and leered at Loveday.

'City's being guarded by women and lads,' he said. 'All the men have gone with the army.' He sneered. 'Fucking cowards.'

Loveday nodded. 'And you're negotiating with them to open the gates, are you?' he asked.

Shaw looked sour. 'We're just letting them know how fucked they're going to be when we bring the battering rams down at dawn.'

From the battlements a fresh volley of French curses rang out. Shaw half turned. 'Tell that to your mother when she's—'

Loveday spun him back around. Shaw took a step away from him. 'Don't touch me, you fucking lout,' he snarled.

Loveday bridled. 'Or what?' He felt the Scot step to his

shoulder. The rust-haired giant was the only one of the Dogs who could look down on the lanky Shaw.

Shaw backed off, looking warily at the Scotsman. 'Or you'll be sorry,' he said lamely. Then his meanness reasserted itself. 'What do you limp-cocked Essex bastards want here anyway?' he said. 'Sir Robert sent us to examine the defences. The Midlanders are further down the wall. We don't need you lot, fucking things up for us.'

The Scotsman growled: 'What does that mean?'

Shaw screwed up his face in contempt. 'Everyone in the vanguard knows you lot got lucky on the beaches. And since then you've done nothing. Minding the horses is about your level.'

Loveday could feel the Dogs bristling.

Romford piped up first. 'And what's your level?' he asked, looking calmly at Shaw. 'Minding the children?'

'Shut up, boy,' said Loveday, without turning to look at Romford.

Shaw spoke past him. 'You want to find out?' he snarled.

'You've tried once,' said Romford.

'Shut up, boy,' said Loveday, again.

Shaw took a step forwards. Then Romford took a step forwards. Then the Scotsman took a step forwards. And all at once, Shaw's crew's hands went to the daggers on their belts.

The Welshmen, Tebbe and Thorp nocked their bows.

Loveday swallowed hard.

Then Millstone spoke, his voice hard, but calm. 'We've come here on the orders of Lord Northampton. Not to fight you. Not to get in your way. Not to stop you telling children how they're going to die. To fetch something the earl and his friend Sir Godefroi want, and take it to them.

'Let us do that, and we'll be on our way. But if you try to stop us, we'll kill you. All of you. It'll be a messy fight. But we'll win. We'll dump your bodies in the ditch like dead cats. And we'll take what we wanted anyway. Then we'll see what our level is, and what yours is.'

No one from the East Anglian crew spoke. Shaw glowered, but Loveday could see him calculating his chances. He remembered Millstone from the first briefing with Sir Robert on the beach. He remembered the Scot from Barfleur.

Millstone tilted his head, just a fraction. And Shaw cracked. He sneered, and laughed, hollowly.

'Well, we don't want to get in the Earl of Northampton's way, do we, boys?' He glanced at his crew and then back to Loveday. 'What is it you want?'

Loveday pointed over Shaw's shoulder. 'Those heads,' he said.

Shaw looked incredulous, then disgusted. 'Fine,' he said. 'Take them. But mind those little bastards up there. One of them pissed on Carter's head earlier.'

He motioned to his crew, and together the East Anglians slunk off.

When Shaw's men were gone, the Dogs stood and looked up at the heads beside the gate. Even at a distance they were grisly things. Barely recognizable as human parts at all. Patches of white skull caught the moonlight.

What was more, they were high up. So high, thought Loveday, that even if they had three of the Scotsman, all standing on one another's shoulders, it would still have been hard to retrieve them.

From the battlements one of the boys shouted an insult in rapid French.

'What did he say?' asked Millstone.

'Christ knows,' said the Scot. 'But if he pisses on me, I'm going to climb the walls and start the pillage myself.'

Pismire tutted. 'How do we do this? Scotsman, if you can climb the wall that easily—'

'Fuck off,' snapped the Scot. 'You know what I meant. There's no way any of us are climbing the wall. Look at it – smooth as fucking butter. There's nothing to grab. And if you fell...'

All the Dogs peered down at the ditch. The stench of filth and dead things wafted up.

'Anyone falls in that, they'll either break their neck or drown in shit,' said Thorp. 'Or both.'

They stood in silence for a while. Even the boys on the battlements were quiet. Then Tebbe spoke. 'Romford. Reckon you could knock those heads down with a stone?'

Romford nodded. He looked the wall up and down a couple of times.

Then he smiled, and Loveday felt the smile spread around the whole group.

'I'd bet my life on it,' Romford said.

They all set to work gathering stones for Romford to aim. There were plenty of every possible size lying about. The archers backed Romford to do the job with a pebble. Loveday thought it required a bigger block. He scraped his knuckles pulling a hard cobble out of the rutted path beyond the bridge. He sucked the scratch. Tasted blood and dirt.

Before long, they had a pile of several dozen missiles, and Romford was picking his throwing spot. He stood about fifteen good paces along the bridge from the barbican gates and took his time assessing the angle of the throw. After a while he called to Loveday. 'Ready,' he said.

Yet even as Loveday acknowledged Romford, he was worried. Knocking the heads down was one thing; but the position in which the spikes had been driven into the wall meant that they would most likely fall not on to the bridge that approached the gates, but down into the ditch. 'Someone is going to have to lean over and catch them,' he said.

The Dogs all looked at each other.

No one stepped forwards to volunteer. Romford was moving the first stone back and forth in his hands, ready to take his first shot.

'Anyone?' said Loveday. The Dogs stayed quiet. The men all tried to avoid his gaze. 'Ah, Christ's whiskers,' he said at last. 'I'll do it.'

He walked to the edge of the bridge, and tested the wooden handrail that ran along the side. It was wobbly. He could feel the Dogs watching him. He wondered how they would judge him if he failed.

All now were nervous. Pismire stepped forwards and handed Loveday a large sack. Rather than opening it at the neck, Loveday held it at either end, to make a sort of cradle into which he hoped the heads would fall.

If Romford managed to knock them anywhere near him.

Which was by no means certain.

He turned to Pismire. 'Hold me,' he said. Pismire grabbed a handful of his rough padded coat. Loveday looked up at the battlements, training his eye on the heads. He saw that the French boys were there. They too were watching him.

One of them called down a few words, which he thought he understood.

'*Bonne chance*,' said the boy. '*Idiots d'anglais*.'

The first stone Romford threw narrowly missed the heads. It clattered into the stone of the wall and bounced off at a sharp angle, falling on the far side of the bridge. Loveday, who was pressing his gut as heavily as he dared into the wooden handrail and leaning as far as he could over the ditch, with the sack stretched out and his eyes fixed on the heads, jumped at the noise. As he moved, he felt Pismire's grip slip on his coat. 'Christ, fellow, hold me tight,' he said. Pismire muttered an apology, and set himself again.

Romford threw another stone. This time he hit one of the heads, but did not dislodge it. As the stone landed, Loveday had flinched, ready to move to catch the head. But nothing fell. He felt sweat dribble down the middle of his back. It was pooling just above the crack of his arse.

The Dogs standing behind Romford were quiet, though Loveday could hear Tebbe and Thorp muttering tips about strategy to the lad. He could also hear Father jabbering nonsense to himself. Strange riddles about black doors and the devil.

Then they all fell quiet, and Loveday braced again. His shoulders were now burning from holding the sack out. Behind him, he felt Pismire wriggling, adjusting his footing to keep hold of him. Absurdly, he wondered why he had asked the smallest of the Dogs to hold him instead of one of the bigger men.

He wondered if he was losing his brain as well as his stomach.

But he did not ponder this too long. For with his third shot, Romford hurled a stone directly into the head nearest to Loveday, catching it on its sunken temple. And, splitting with the impact, it fell.

Loveday stared in a mixture of horror and delight. It took less than two heartbeats to plummet towards him. Yet seemed to take forever, as though it were floating, like a lone feather shed from some bird, blowing lightly on the breeze. And as it drifted, Loveday saw every possibility unfold before him, as though God were showing him all his conceivable futures. As though God were weighing them up, and deciding what he deserved.

He leaned forwards, stretching so far over the handrail that he was up on his toes, and he could feel Pismire using all his strength to cling on to him. More strength than he knew the little man could possibly possess. But it was that strength which stopped him from falling. And that strength which allowed him to hold the sack out tight, directly into the path of the falling head, which bounced up off the taut, springy sack and back over his head where – from the cheers that he heard go up – someone caught it. And then Pismire was hauling him back from the brink, and planting him down on his backside on the bridge. And Tebbe was holding the head up, half in triumph and half in disgust.

It was only when he was sitting on the bridge, safe, that Loveday realized Pismire's sudden burst of power had in fact been Millstone and Scotsman hurtling over to help hang on to him. And that God, for reasons unfathomable, had decided to show him some mercy.

He sat on the ground and let the sweat stream off him. The Dogs were now passing around the first head: a grotesque thing, whose eyes had long ago been eaten away by crows, along with the juicy lips and ears. A foul ball shrunk to the size of a puffed-up pig-bladder of the sort village children kicked around on holidays. A ragged neck and crushed spine suggested it had been hacked off roughly by a worthless headsman with a blunt axe.

'I don't know if I can do that again,' said Loveday to no one in particular.

But it did not matter. For as the Dogs inspected their prize, behind them the Welsh brothers had wandered over and were looking at the two remaining heads. And after conferring with one another for no more than a few seconds, Darys had taken off his shoes and was scaling the sheer front of the castle, finding with his hands and toes gaps and crevices to hold that had been invisible to every other man there.

By the time the Dogs turned around to see what was going on, Darys was hanging with his right hand from the spike the first head had dropped from, and tossing down the other two with his left to Lyntyn, who caught them and grinned. The French boys on the battlements yelled in amusement at the sight. Darys, playing somewhat to his appreciative audience, swung back and forth a few times from the spike, building up enough momentum to launch him clear of the ditch when he jumped. He landed on all fours like a cat.

The Dogs stared at the Welshmen open-mouthed. 'Holy Jesus playing the fucking bagpipes on the Cross,' said Scotsman. 'Why didn't they tell us they could do that in the first place?' But if the Welshmen understood, they did not show it. Lyntyn just motioned for the sack. Pismire held it open so he could drop the heads in there. Then the brothers wandered off, without a backward glance.

★ ★ ★

With the heads secured, the Dogs set off back the way they had come, following the stinking ditch, surer now of the way they were going. The dead of the night was well past and the starlit blackness was giving way to a pale pre-dawn grey. Scotsman carried the head-sack slung over his shoulder. Loveday watched its contents bounce gently against the big man's broad back.

They rounded the curve in the city walls, aiming back towards the steep hillside and the shepherds' trails that led towards the camp.

The camp was halfway gone.

Several of the pavilions at the top of the hill, which had been silhouetted against the sky when they left, had come down. Campfires had been stamped out. And even from the bottom of the hill, in the weak light of the halfway-hours, Loveday could see the vanguard forming up into ranks and streaming away from the camp.

They were not heading down the shepherds' paths. They were moving towards the road. The tramp of feet and murmur of voices was creating a low rumble in the night.

Loveday called the Dogs to a halt. 'No point going any further,' he said.

'Why?' asked Romford innocently.

Pismire snorted. 'Why do you think? That lot aren't off to church for matins. The attack is starting now. The lords don't want anyone in that fucking city to escape. They've decided to show the French king how much mercy we're prepared to show him.'

He turned to Loveday. 'Let's get back to the gate, so we can get in there as soon as they smash it down.'

The nausea rose inside Loveday's stomach. There was nothing he could do but try to swallow it down. 'Pismire's right,' he said, feeling weak. 'No point letting those East Anglian halfwits grab all the gold. Let's get back to the gates – fast. Scotsman, give me the heads.'

The Scot handed him the sack. 'With pleasure. Don't let them clatter together too much, or Sir Godefroi will never know who's who.'

They all set out at a run back towards the barbican on the south side of the city. Before they were halfway there, Warwick and Northampton's mounted knights had overtaken them.

The battering ram was a fat, wicked thing, its shaft as wide as a man's arm-span. It was tipped with iron and swung from chains on a wooden frame. When it hit the gates of Saint-Lô, they made a noise like screaming, as though the agonies of the trees once felled to build ram and doors alike were given voice.

The boys on the top of the barbican had vanished. Loveday wondered what they were doing. Scampering for a cellar to hide in? Or standing out in the street, waiting for the doors to come crashing open? Telling their sisters and mothers they were safe? That God would strengthen their arms?

The ram smashed the gates again. Wood splintered and buckled. The companies were now crowding behind the bridge across the ditch. They cheered. Loveday looked around at the Dogs. Checked they were all there.

They were right at the front of the crowd, held back by Warwick's knights, who had formed a cordon to keep the mob back from the engineers working the ram.

Loveday felt the press of thousands of men behind him. Felt their wicked energy crackle.

The air was thick, like before a thunderstorm.

He clutched the neck of the sack containing the heads. He had tied the top of it, and felt the rough knot press into the skin between his finger and thumb.

Loveday craned his neck around, scanning above the crowd for Northampton's or Sir Godefroi's flag. Although dawn was beginning to break, he could not make them out.

He turned to Scotsman. 'Can you see the earls?'

Scotsman shook his head. But the mood of the crowd had overtaken him now, and his eyes were cold. Loveday knew that look. He'd seen it before every raid and robbery they had carried out together. Before every battle they had charged towards, their blood up.

He knew the state the Scot had entered. Both hearing and not hearing. The other Dogs looked the same.

There would be blood. There would be gold. They could take all they wanted of both.

Only Romford and Father looked different. Romford was whispering in Father's ear – urgently, as though giving him instructions. Father nodded. His lips still moved in recitation.

Loveday knew he himself looked otherwise.

He had stormed dozens of places before now. Cities. Towns. Villages. In the border wars with the Scots he had run wild-eyed through streets, grabbing what he could and cutting down anyone who stood in his way.

It had become the way of the English war machine. The way of the Dogs. Suddenly he was not sure if it was his way any more.

The ram swung on its chains. It slammed the gates. Over

the cheers of the English, Loveday thought he could hear the wails and laments of women. The screams on both sides rose in a crescendo.

Loveday grabbed Millstone by the shoulder. Yelled in his ear. 'I have to go,' he shouted.

Millstone, wrenched from his reverie, looked at Loveday in confusion. 'What?' he shouted back.

'I have to go,' Loveday repeated. He freed his arms, held up the sack of heads. 'I need to take these to Sir Godefroi.'

Millstone looked perplexed. 'Sir Godefroi will be here. Don't you want us to stay together?' Then he shook his head. 'Whatever you think.'

Loveday patted Millstone on his shoulder as the big mason looked back towards the barbican. Then he turned and started to push his way back through the crowd. Shoved and elbowed and glowered at anyone who protested.

He barged his way around the city walls. Towards the rise. Towards the camp. He had no idea if Sir Godefroi would be there, or whether he was now with the rest of the troops.

He did not care, either.

As he blundered onwards, he heard two more crunches of the battering ram. Two more cheers of bloodthirsty glee rang out from the barbican side of the city. And now there was, unmistakeably, a rising howl of terror from inside Saint-Lô.

Loveday reached the shepherd's trails and began to stumble up the slope towards the camp. The smoke from stamped-out fires was drifting down the hill.

Loveday blinked hard and coughed. He realized his face was wet with tears.

The head-bag weighed heavy, making his shoulder muscles ache. He switched it from hand to hand.

He got to the top of the slope. Wiped his face with the back of his sleeve. He looked around to get his bearings, and headed towards Northampton's tent, where he had last seen Sir Godefroi. It was still standing. He recognized it from the pennons fluttering above it, but saw that the torches outside it had burned out.

He powered forwards with his head down.

When he was less than twenty paces from the entrance, a small figure ran out of the shadows and thumped into him.

Loveday was knocked backwards a couple of steps. The figure bounced off him and landed on its back.

He looked down in surprise. He knew the face.

The woman from Valognes who had thrown the tile at Father lay on the ground. She was ragged and beaten up. There were bruises on her arms. But a defiant light still shone in her eyes.

She put her finger to her lips, and scrambled back up to her feet. She looked him up and down.

She knew him too. Loveday opened his mouth to say something, but she got there first.

'It's you,' she said. 'You're back. You have to help me.'

12

Such deeds of arms were done that Roland and Oliver...
might have met their match. Men of worth, bold and
insolent, could be seen there...

Life of the Black Prince by Chandos Herald

Father was leaning heavily on Romford's arm, but the boy
didn't mind.

The old priest had been hostile to him in the first days of the
campaign. But Romford had known plenty of men like him in
his young life.

He was aware that something in his face or his bearing
could upset other men, and though he puzzled over what it
was, he knew just as well that he could not change it.

In any case, Father was different now. The wound on his
head seemed to have let some of the poison out of his soul. He
thought back to Father sprawled in the road in Valognes. He
imagined he had seen the evil vapours drifting away, smokelike,
curling upwards as if from a snuffed candle.

Dispersed on the wind, as though they had never been.

When he had seen Father suffering on the cart, he had
known the head poultice he had stolen from the apothecary
would help him. But the powder would help him more.

And it had.

So he had started feeding him.

Not that it had been painless. Romford had been forced to cut back his own use to accommodate Father's, which meant that the itches and the gnawing, nagging inside were closer than he would have liked.

The priest liked Romford to apply it, too. Romford did not like putting his finger in the older man's mouth. The spit on his gums was stinking and faintly oily, and it lingered on Romford's fingers.

The small moan the man gave when Romford touched his mouth also discomforted him.

He remembered other men doing that, in other places. Before he ran. Before he came here.

But he applied the powder anyway. And he liked to see the dull, warm calm creep over Father's face. To feel the malign spirits that writhed in the priest curl up their tails and stop – for a time.

The trouble was, Romford had run through all the powder he had found in the first apothecary. And the smaller supply he had found in the second – at the place they had slept in Carentan – was now a couple of meagre pinches in the bottom of a little leather pouch.

He had dosed himself and Father before the business of walking around in the dark to find the dead men's heads on the gatepost. But he had been reducing the amount he administered, trying to eke out the supply. Scraping every tiny grain of the powder from where it clung to the dead skin of the purse.

From the grip Father was pressing into his arm, which tightened steadily as the hours passed, and with every loud noise that bothered him, Romford knew it would not be long before the monsters inside Father uncurled their tails again.

He watched the battering ram smash into the gates of Saint-Lô. Looked around the other Dogs. Saw Scotsman's glazed stare. Saw Millstone adjusting his hammer grip. Saw Tebbe and Thorp grinning to themselves, bows slung across their bodies. They had enjoyed watching him knock the head down with a stone; he had revelled in their pleasure.

He watched with mild interest Loveday push away through the crowd, clutching the head-bag.

He wondered how easy it would be to raid an apothecary in the middle of a full-blown city-sack. And whether he could trust Father to come with him and not make too much noise or distraction.

There must be others like him among this bloated, hungry crowd. Most would want to steal gold, wet their yards in crying women. Carry away bolts of cloth or barrels of wine.

But there would be a few who were different. Who would care more for what was inner than outer.

Who needed the calm and quiet of the grey powder that reeked of piss and the Indies.

He needed to find it before they did.

Romford looked around him, wondering where the other fiends might be lurking. But in the dawn light he could not tell. All he could feel was excitement and bloodthirst. Men's crazed lust for doing what was wrong.

The crowd around them heaved and swayed as the ram came closer to fatally puncturing the doors. Father gripped him so tightly he could feel ragged nails digging into his flesh.

He whispered in his ear: 'Touch my mouth, boy. The pain is coming back.'

Romford shook his head very slightly. 'Wait until we're inside.'

Father grunted. Romford knew he would not be able to keep him at peace for very long.

When the gates fell, Romford and Father were swept through the barbican with the crowd. At first the Dogs were near the front, but then they fell further back. Men eager to begin the savaging shouldered past. Father half tripped on broken timbers from the door. Romford hauled him up.

'Touch my mouth, boy,' Father said again.

Trying to stay upright, Romford felt for the leather pouch tucked in the bag that hung at his belt. But when he dipped his finger into it, there was even less left than he remembered.

A few grains, no more.

He pulled Father into the street that opened away from the broken gates. Saw scared townsfolk running pell-mell from the army. Saw a scrawny young archer corner a terrified young woman. Screaming at her, his face contorted. His hands groping between her legs.

Father's greedy mouth hung open. He sucked Romford's barely powdered finger like a newborn searching blindly for its first feed. As he did so, Romford kept them both moving. Ahead, Tebbe and Thorp were bullocking forwards, just behind Scotsman, Pismire and Millstone. The Welsh brothers had broken away towards a side street.

Pismire looked round to check that the company was still together. Romford quickly withdrew his finger from Father's mouth.

Pismire frowned, uncertain what he had seen. He yelled over the din of the press: 'Keep up!'

Pismire pointed ahead. Romford knew they would be heading for the goldsmiths' quarter.

Around them the English army was pouring into every street: kicking in doors, dragging citizens into the street. Interrogating them in English. Demanding their wealth. Slapping and spitting in confused, uncomprehending faces. Outside the door of a small chapel Romford saw an ancient priest holding a wooden cross, defying anyone to enter. A pot-bellied Englishman, hair cropped tight to his skull, snatched the cross, threw it to the ground and stamped on it. Punched the priest as hard as he could in the gut. The priest crumpled, gasping. The Englishman kicked him in the face.

Romford looked away. He scanned the streets around, looking for any signs of an apothecary. He knew he had little time. Father was still agitated, and he too felt a prickly sweat breaking on his back. Around his middle. His lungs were tight.

He could hear Father muttering more strange prayers. Tried briefly to make out what he was saying.

'*I stand at the door and knock,*' said Father to himself. '*I stand at the door and knock.*' Sweat was standing out on his face. The sun was rising and fingering into the streets in thin, slanted rays.

Ahead, Scotsman kicked open the door of a little house and dragged out a citizen. Pismire shouted at the man about gold. He pointed at Millstone, who stood holding his heavy hammer, a few paces back. Pointed to the house, then he mimed counting coins. The citizen trembled in Scotsman's grasp and made apologetic hand gestures. Pismire shook his head in disgust, and Scotsman threw the citizen back through his door.

The Dogs looked at one another urgently. Without Loveday it was not clear whether Millstone, Pismire or Scotsman should take charge. But Romford could not wait for them to debate it. He looked down a long street that stretched away to his left. Saw what he thought was an apothecary's sign hanging near the end of it.

His heart thudded. He made a decision. He shouted in Father's ear: 'I'll find something. You stay with the others.'

Father shook his head violently. 'No, boy,' he said. 'Take me.'

Romford sighed. 'If I must,' he said. And he broke off down the street, pulling Father roughly along.

As they hurried away, Romford looked back at the Dogs. Millstone spotted him and raised his eyebrows. Romford pointed purposefully down the long street, and Millstone shook his head. But Scotsman and Pismire were arguing about where to go, and Millstone turned back to them, distracted.

Romford broke into a half-run, Father staggering behind him.

'It's not far,' Romford panted.

'*I stand at the door and knock,*' Father replied.

Romford's sense for an apothecary, guided by the hand of St Damian, did not fail him. Barely one hundred paces along the street they came to a shop with a scale balance painted carefully on a sign that hung above head height.

The outside of the building was tidy and well kept. The timber of the walls had been lately treated with tar and grease and shone glossy in the morning light. Its window shutters were latched but in good condition.

Access to the shop was via a narrow alley that ran down the side of the building, separating it from a private house next door. Romford led Father cautiously down the alley. But as they crept towards the entrance to the shop, Romford realized with dismay that it was open.

Heard raised voices inside. Crashes. Choked sobs.

'Someone is here,' he said to Father.

Fresh sweat sprang on Father's brow. His hands were shaking. Romford wished he had been able to force him to stay with the Dogs.

He listened carefully to the voices inside the shop. Over the cacophony of the riot, it was hard to make out what was being said. But Romford felt he knew at least one of the voices.

He inched closer to the door. Peered around it.

His heart sank.

In a dingy room lined on three walls with shelves carrying vials and bottles, an apothecary and his wife cowered. Before them were two Englishmen, brandishing weapons.

One of them was rangy, and spoke with a pronounced East Anglian burr.

Shaw.

He was shouting at the couple, demanding money. Yelling English words the couple did not know. 'Strongbox, your fucking strongbox.'

'*Désolé, désolé!*' whimpered the apothecary.

The other was one of Shaw's henchmen – the stringy, underfed man with his ears missing. He stepped forwards and hit the apothecary with the back of his hand. The blow spun the man, but he did not fall.

The man with no ears grabbed the wife by her hair. Yanked back her head. Shaw tried her. His face was breath-close to hers, and he continued to scream: 'We'll kill you! Money! Give us money!'

The apothecary tried to pull at the earless henchman and free his wife. Shaw punched him hard in the side of the head.

This time he went down, and lay motionless on the floor, his head at a peculiar angle.

Shaw turned to his crewmate. 'Turn the place over,' he said. He pulled a knife from a sheath on his belt, and put the point of it to the woman's throat.

Shaw started whispering in the woman's ear. She thrashed her head around as much as she dared. Meanwhile, the man with no ears went to work, pulling jars and clay containers from the shelves. Some he emptied. Others he dashed on the ground.

The room started to fill with dust and the mingled stink of a hundred exotic, expensive powders.

Romford could stand it no longer.

He stepped silently into the room, unnoticed at first. Then the man with no ears caught sight of him, lit by the morning sun flooding in through the doorway behind. He stopped what he was doing. He held in his hands a long, thin container, stopped with a piece of rag.

'Christ's arsehole, who's this?' he asked.

Shaw stood back from the woman. He stared at Romford. Recognized him. 'Fuck you want, boy?' he said. 'You following us?'

'No,' said Romford. 'I want something that's here.'

'Then your luck's out,' said Shaw. 'Fuck off right now – or I'll cut your bollock-sack open and feed what's in it to this French bitch before I kill her.'

'I don't think you should do that,' said Romford. 'And it won't help you find their money.'

Shaw narrowed his eyes, and Romford felt him examining his face closely. Then the East Anglian let out a small laugh.

'I see,' he said. 'This little puppy has come here for some medicine.' He reached behind him and pulled a vial from a shelf. 'This what you looking for, boy?'

Romford said nothing. He tried to stay calm. Felt his hands trembling.

Shaw took the vial and smashed it on the floor. He grinned. 'Was that the one, boy?' He picked up another. 'Or maybe it was this one?' he said. He tossed the vial. It shattered.

'Don't do that,' said Romford, but he heard his voice quiver, and he knew Shaw did too.

Shaw laughed even louder. 'Can't sleep at night, boy?' he leered. 'Guts hurt you if you go too long?'

Shaw's mate was now laughing too. Shaw grinned at him. The showman. Then he turned, and with his knife hand sent a whole shelf-full of potions and powders crashing to the floor.

'Stop it!' Romford shouted, his voice cracking like a girl's. But Shaw just howled even louder. He stepped across the room and swept another shelf.

'It's going to be a long few days, boy!' he cackled. More clouds of dusty medicine puffed into the air.

Romford looked wildly around the room. Fixed on the apothecary's wife. Imploring her to give him a signal.

As though she might understand. Or care.

Shaw saw. He snorted derisively. 'What, think she can help you?'

The woman had turned away from Romford. She was crouched over her husband, trying to revive him. She was wailing. Long and plaintive, like a seabird.

'This bitch wouldn't help us, so what good is she to you?' Shaw smiled.

The apothecary's wife started crying.

Shaw pointed his knife at Romford. He traced it through the air, in a line from Romford's eyes to between his legs. He grinned. But before he could do any more there was a blur of movement in the corner of Romford's eye, and Father sprang into the room.

In two bounds he was across it, and before anyone could react, Father was upon Shaw.

He knocked Shaw away from the woman and on to the ground. He seemed possessed with a strength that Romford had never seen in him.

Father grappled Shaw, wrestling the bigger man so he was on his back. He sat on Shaw's chest, wrapping his legs around Shaw's arms to pin them. With his left hand he gripped Shaw's right wrist and beat the hand on the floor behind him, until Shaw released his knife.

He stared into Shaw's eyes. Then, like a hungry animal, Father threw his head forwards and sank his teeth into Shaw's face.

When Romford was a child of nine or ten summers, after his father was dead, his elder brother had taken him to watch dogs fighting in the docks. He remembered the first bout had gone to the death.

Romford could still see them: two mastiffs in a pit hemmed by wooden boards, a tan bitch and a dark black male, both of them snarling, hackles raised, lips pulled back from their gums, showing yellow, rough-edged teeth. They had fought long and hard, jeered and bullied by the men, Romford's brother among them. Men belching and cursing and calling out bets on the outcome.

Romford had watched. Silent. Afraid. Transfixed, as though his eyes were tied to the sight with fishing line.

He remembered how the black dog had pinned the bitch to the side of the pen, snapping, trying to rip her neck and ears.

He remembered how the bitch had seemed to endure it all, as though she could not fight, and did not even known how. Until with one lunge the black dog, tiring, had missed its mark. And then the bitch had taken her chance, rolling into the dog's side and latching her jaws around his soft throat. He remembered how she had worked through the skin and muscle. And how the men outside the pit had fallen quiet, stunned as if sleeping on their feet.

It had seemed to Romford that that moment of horror and death existed outside time, with no start and no end.

And now, standing in the apothecary, he felt the same thing.

Everyone in the room stood, stunned. Except for Father and Shaw. Father bit and thrashed his head, emitting a growl from deep within him.

Beneath Father, Shaw screeched hysterically, bucking his body and kicking his legs wildly on the ground. But he was pinned. And all the while Father was attached to the front of his head, continuing to gnaw and growl.

The two men were clenched at the face. Like lovers.

Father grunted. Then Romford heard a tearing, splitting sound, like the splintering of a young branch hewn from a tree. And finally Father dragged his face away from Shaw's. He spat something ragged and fleshy to the floor. On all fours, he stared around the room, eyes wild.

Romford looked at Shaw in horror. But he already knew what Father had spat out.

In the middle of Shaw's face there was now an ugly, bloody gaping hole.

His nose lay three feet away from him. Covered in Father's spit. Pointing to the heavens.

Father stood up and continued glaring around the room. Blood dripped from his chin. It was smeared all over his face. Then he grinned. As he bared his teeth, Romford gagged. Father's teeth, usually brown, were now red, with the stains darkest where the tooth surface met the curve of the gum. Scraps of white-flecked flesh hung between them.

From outside the building came the yells and wails of the sack.

Inside, the air hummed with a terrified silence.

Then Shaw started screaming. He rocked left and right on his back. He beat his hands into the ground. He formed no words but screamed as though he would never stop.

Frothed blood bubbled up out of the space where his nose had been.

Shaw's henchman stared in open-mouthed horror at his mutilated leader. Father crouched like an ape, hands low, looking as though he might spring again.

The man with no ears stepped back. Silent. Open-mouthed. Then he turned and fled, abandoning his leader, running into the street, back towards the turmoil of the riot.

Romford was left, staring at Father, now prowling around the shop.

Shaw had fainted, and was briefly quiet.

'Father,' said Romford, holding his palm out towards him. 'Father – what—?'

Father growled and turned his dull gaze on Romford. Romford gulped. Father took two steps towards him.

Then Shaw woke up. The East Anglian started shrieking again. The sound seemed to distract Father, and wake him from his possession.

He sank to his haunches and started screeching too.

Romford felt as if he were in a dream, trapped in the shafts of warm light piercing the precious dust of the room. He looked helplessly from one man to the other. The noise they were making was terrible. Romford felt the prickling and the needles in his guts grow dangerously strong. Bile started to boil in his stomach. He thought he would puke, or shit uncontrollably, or both. But as he turned to the door, to run out and void his belly in the alleyway, the daylight darkened.

Into the shop walked Millstone.

Romford nearly ran straight into the big stonemason. Millstone put out his left hand and placed it firmly in the middle of Romford's chest. He looked over Romford's shoulder, trying to digest what had happened.

He spoke calmly. 'What are you doing here?' he said.

Romford tried to open his mouth to reply, but found no words in his throat. Father and Shaw continued to scream.

Millstone walked around him, approached Father, slapped the priest hard in the face, crossed the room to Shaw, kicked the noseless and bloody East Anglian in the ribs, then stood back, surveying the scene of blood and broken glass and pottery. The shrieks had finally stopped, replaced only by heavy breathing and, from Shaw, an occasional moan.

Millstone fixed Romford with his level gaze once more. 'What have you done?' he asked.

Romford took a deep breath. 'I . . .' he began. 'I came here to find a certain powder. It soothes the sick. I have been giving it to Father.'

Millstone nodded his head very slightly. 'Just to Father?' he asked.

'And to myself,' said Romford.

Millstone said nothing.

'And two of the East Anglians were here,' said Romford limply. 'They – well – they tried to stop me. They started destroying the shop. They hurt the man. I think he's dead... That one was going to hurt the woman.'

Millstone glanced at the woman, then back to Romford. 'This is a war,' he said. 'Do you understand what that means?'

Romford nodded. 'I – Father...' he mumbled.

'Father does not answer to any man,' said Millstone. 'Not even himself. You should not have brought him here. You could both hang for this.'

Romford shuddered. On the floor, Shaw moaned again. Millstone regarded him. He thought for a moment. His eyes flicked around the wrecked shop.

He walked across the floor to where Shaw lay, and crouched down beside him.

Shaw was shaking. Millstone bent down and used a finger to gently open one of his eyelids.

Romford watched uneasily.

'Where are his men?' said Millstone, without looking up.

'They fled,' said Romford.

Millstone nodded. He spoke to Shaw in a low voice. 'Did you stand in the way of our men?'

Shaw groaned in agony. 'He bit off my nose,' he croaked, his voice thick and distorted. 'He bit off my fucking nose.'

Millstone moved his finger to Shaw's lips. 'Did you stand in the way of our men?' he asked again. 'You can nod your head if you did.'

Shaw opened both of his eyes, and stared at Millstone's hard face. It seemed to Romford that the East Anglian saw something terrifying there. Something worse even than what lived in Father.

Shaw nodded his head fearfully. 'I'm sorry.' Blood continued to froth from where his nose had been. The tiny bubbles reminded Romford of the air crabs puffed out when they scuttled below the sands on the beach. 'I'm sorry.'

Millstone said: 'I told you not to do that.'

Shaw began crying, his sobs sucking the bubbling blood-snot back through the hole in his face. 'I'm sorry,' he said again. 'Please.'

'You should have listened to me,' said Millstone.

Shaw continued to sob, shaking his head back and forth. Millstone watched him with pity. Then he looked back at Romford. His eyes met the boy's. Locked on to them. Romford felt them grip him. He felt safe. He felt as though nothing could ever hurt him again.

Millstone gave him the faintest of nods. Then without breaking his gaze, he raised his hammer and smashed it into Shaw's forehead.

Shaw's skull exploded. A mess of grey and red and white chunks of bone spattered outwards.

Romford turned away and vomited. He retched until his stomach gave up only thin yellow acid. Tears streamed out of his eyes. After a minute he could heave no more, and he crouched, exhausted, his palms on the floor.

Shaw's legs were twitching. Then they stopped.

Millstone stood up and wiped his face with his sleeve. He walked over and placed a gentle hand on Romford's shoulder.

'I didn't want to do that,' he said. 'But it had to be done. Find what it is you require here. Attend to Father's needs. Then burn this shop. We will see you back at the camp.' He patted Romford gently on the shoulder.

Millstone walked out of the door. Romford vomited again. The effort hurt his ribs and filled his eyes with more tears.

He spat and blinked. Looked around the silent shop. The apothecary's wife was curled up around her dead husband. Father was slumped against a wall, Shaw's blood congealed on his lips and in the heavy stubble of his beard. He seemed to be asleep.

Romford began methodically to search the shelves on the walls for what he needed. After a short while he understood how the potions and powders had been arranged, and found a large stone jar half-full of the powder. He filled his pouch to the brim.

Then he crossed the room to Father, tilted his chin up, peeled back the crusted, bloody upper lip, and rubbed a powdered finger on the old priest's gums.

His finger came away red. He used the other hand to feed himself his own portion. He lifted Father gently from the floor and propped him upright by dragging his arm over his own shoulder. Then he guided him out of the shop, and settled him against a wall.

Leaving Father in the alley, Romford went back into the shop. He pulled the apothecary's body outside, dumping the corpse in the alley as well. The man's wife followed, insulting him in French, and beating weakly at his back.

Romford pushed her off and she let him be.

He went inside again and built a fire-pile from everything he could find that would burn. He found some oil, which stank, and poured it around the base of the pile. He took one last look at Shaw's grotesquely broken carcass.

When he touched the flame of a candle to the fuel, his hands were shaking so much he could barely light the fire.

13

The noble prince [Edward] of whom I speak, never, from the day of his birth, thought of anything but loyalty, noble deeds, valour and goodness.

Life of the Black Prince by Chandos Herald

At the half-dismantled camp, Loveday stared at the woman from Valognes. She quickly hunkered on her haunches, keeping her profile low. She scrambled a few paces sideways, tucking herself tight into the shadow of an empty tent.

She motioned for Loveday to come closer to her. She put her finger to her lips, and bade him be quiet. Then she looked around nervously, and listened hard. Loveday watched her in astonishment.

'What are you—' he began.

'Shut up,' she hissed. 'Give me your knife.'

Close up Loveday could see she was filthy. Her face was marked on one side with a grazed bruise a day or two old. She wore a simple shift, which had torn at one shoulder, exposing the upper arm stained with round purple finger marks.

Her hair was knotted and tangled. The grubby curls he had seen in Valognes were now the colour of the dirt under their feet. 'My knife?' he said. He wondered if the woman was mad, or a witch. Then her bright eyes flashed at him, and he felt strangely unable to resist.

'Hurry!' she whispered, and held out her hand. She rolled her eyes. 'I'm not going to stab you with your own blade. If I wanted you dead, I would have broken your head open already. Before you had even seen me coming.' She laughed, quickly and sharply. 'Like I did to your friend.'

The woman motioned to him. Demanding. She kept glancing around, with the diligence of an experienced soldier. Surveying the field around her. Keeping her guard up.

Loveday reached to his belt and unhooked his little blade. He flipped it around so the handle pointed towards the woman. She grabbed it roughly, and as she did so the sharp edge nicked his palm. Loveday winced.

The woman sneered at him. 'You English. You are so easy to hurt.'

She gave the knife a cursory glance to assess it. She flipped it so that it spun in the air, and balanced the blade-point momentarily on her index finger. Flipped it again, and caught it by the white bone handle. She grunted approval.

'It'll do,' she said.

'It's my oldest possession,' he said. 'It's travelled with me a long time.'

'Has it killed a man?'

Loveday nodded. 'More than one. But now mostly I use it for eating. And carving.'

She snorted, mocking him. Then she grabbed a clump of her own hair and with her free, right hand, she used Loveday's knife to start sawing at it, cutting it off close to her head. She worked fast, ignoring Loveday as she focused on her task, biting her lower lip gently in concentration.

After a while she spoke to him again. 'So how is your friend?' She hacked at another clump and dropped the handful of dirty, knotted hair at his feet.

'You hurt him,' said Loveday. 'He's very sick.'

'He was very sick *before* I hurt him.' She cut another clump. Then another. Then another.

'Maybe,' Loveday said. He glanced in the direction of the royal pavilions. 'Are you not supposed to be...'

'With your prince?' she sneered. 'The boy thinks he is a man. He thinks that because he will be a great king one day, he must show his power through his cruelty. He did what he wished with me. When I fought him, he beat me. But he did not hurt me.'

She stared straight at Loveday, and briefly paused cutting her hair.

'Your prince talks of knights and romance and love. He speaks of round tables, and green giants. He thinks war is a game. But he does not know what it means.'

She went back to her cutting, swiftly and determinedly, until almost her whole head was shorn short, like a boy's.

'Where are your men?' she asked. 'You are always with your men.'

'They are...' began Loveday. But she did not wait for his answer, and he was not keen to give it. So far as he knew, the Dogs were helping bring misery to the lives of the folk of Saint-Lô. He did not reckon the woman would be sympathetic.

She had nearly finished. 'Have I missed some?' she asked. Loveday nodded, and pointed to a last tuft.

She took his hand, and pulled it towards the left side of her head. 'Help me,' she said.

Against his will, Loveday closed his hand around the

remaining long hank of her hair, and the woman moved the blade, close to her scalp. She kept her hand on his as she worked, staring straight into his eyes. Her hand was warm. Her hair was soft. It made Loveday shiver.

Then, with one last slip of the blade, it was done. As the hair came loose in Loveday's hand, she let him go. She sighed in relief. She ran her own hands over her head, brushing off loose strands.

She looked very different. The ragged crop now emphasized her high cheekbones and determined jaw. Her eyes looked much wider than before.

'Thank you,' she said. 'You are a good man. I know you do not want to be here.'

Loveday swallowed hard. 'How—'

But once more she was not listening. She was looking carefully around, preparing to dart through the camp in the direction of the hillside and the town.

Loveday reached out caught her upper arm. 'Where are you going? You must be careful. It is dangerous here.'

She laughed bitterly. 'It is dangerous everywhere. I am going to Caen. Or Rouen. Or Paris. Or to hell. Perhaps I will see you in one of those places, when your prince and his father lead you there. Or perhaps I will never see you again.'

Loveday held on to her arm for a moment longer. Suddenly he did not want her to leave. 'Stop,' he said. 'Wait. Don't go now.' He pointed to her torn shift. 'You will need different clothes.'

The woman looked at him as though he were an idiot. 'I will find them,' she said, impatiently. Then her voice softened. 'You should leave too. You should go back to England and stay there with your wife. And grow fat and old. You are not a killer any more.'

Loveday swallowed. 'My wife is dead.'

'Well. Then you should find another.'

Loveday tried one last time to delay her. 'Please. What is your name? Tell me that at least. Mine is Loveday.'

She looked at him, as though he understood nothing at all of the world. She ran her hand over her head again.

'I have no name now,' she said. 'Nor ever will again. But you will know me if you ever see me again, won't you?'

Loveday nodded quietly. 'I shall,' he said. Then he had a thought. He took his pack from his back and rummaged quickly in it. Found what he was looking for, and thrust it at her, hard. 'Take this. And take care.'

She took what he had given her, and briefly inspected it. It was the small bone figure of St Martha.

'It's not finished,' he said apologetically. 'But it may bring you protection.'

She nodded and closed her hand around it.

'Godspeed,' said Loveday. He felt tears in his eyes again.

'God,' said the woman. 'I remember him.'

Then without another word, she wriggled free of his grip, and in an instant she was gone, scampering low between the tents, her knees bent and her thin chest close to the ground.

Loveday squatted down on his haunches. His heart was hammering. For the first time since they had landed he felt afraid.

At his feet was the matted pile of the woman's filthy golden hair. He realized he no longer had his old knife. She had taken it. And left him holding the last tress of her matted curls.

Loveday was not angry, though he wondered, stupidly, how he would stir his stew at the next meal they took. He did not want to drop the hair, so he curled it around his finger and put it into the purse on his belt. Then he looked in the direction the woman had run. She was nowhere to be seen.

Loveday picked up the sack of knights' heads and stood. As he did so he heard men's voices ringing across the camp. Bellowing loud curses.

Two of them he did not recognize. One of them he did.

The Earl of Northampton stormed towards his tent, flanked by a pair of knights. Both of them were a head taller than Loveday – in their armour, they looked to be the size of the Scotsman. They wore helms on their heads, with the visors pulled up above their eyes. Their square jaws were set. Northampton was railing alternately at them and the world.

'The woman,' he fumed. 'Where's the fucking woman?' He placed his hands on his hips and looked around the deserted camp. Loveday hurried a few paces forwards, away from the pile of hair.

Northampton paced in a small circle and kicked out at the closest thing he could see: a half-burned log on a dead fire. It flew a few feet and coughed black cinders in the damp grass.

Loveday considered trying to slink away, but Northampton had spotted him. He marched over, the sword by his side clattering against the metal cuisses he wore over his thighs.

The two knights clanked alongside him.

'You,' barked the earl, pointing a finger accusingly at Loveday. He wore thick leather gloves, their outsides rough and hardworn.

'My lord,' said Loveday, half bowing.

'My lord fuck off and bollocks,' said Northampton. 'John the Baptist's head on a butcher's block, I haven't got time for this. Have you seen the fucking wench anywhere?'

Loveday flushed. He straightened his back. 'Sire,' he said. 'The wench?'

Northampton blew through his nose. 'A French wench,' he said. 'You know. French. Fucking wench-like. About so high.' He motioned with his hand, the approximate height of the woman Loveday had seen so recently. 'No tits on her. Hair like a haystack after the whole village has finished fucking on it.'

Flustered, Loveday opened his mouth, found he had nothing to say and closed it again.

'Christ's holy stinking shitting loincloth,' exploded Northampton. 'What are you? A fucking fish? The carp in my lakes don't gawp as much as this when I'm throwing them maggots in the morning.'

Northampton squeezed the bridge of his nose with his gloved fingers. He closed his eyes and seemed to be at prayer, or counting. He looked suddenly worn out.

The knights smirked.

'My lord,' said Loveday, wincing slightly in case he set the earl going once more.

Northampton sighed. 'What?'

'I have the heads,' said Loveday.

'The *what*?' This time the lord simply looked confused. 'The heads?'

Loveday held up the sack. He shook it gently.

A look of pure disbelief crossed Northampton's face. 'You're joking,' he said. 'You got them?'

'Of course,' said Loveday. 'My men may look rough, my

lord, but we take our orders seriously. Would you like to see?' He made to open the bag.

'By Christ, no,' said Northampton. 'I assume they're fucking rotten and belching out vapours. I've seen enough cut heads in my life. I don't need to see three more. Give them to Sir Big Bollocks here.' He hooked his thumb at the knight to the right. The man stepped a pace forwards and stretched out a large hand towards Loveday.

'Sir Denis,' he said. 'Of Moreton-on-the-Weald.' The knight had a huge, square jaw and sun-lines spreading away from the corners of his eyes, like bird's feet. A long mane of glossy brown hair extended down his back.

Loveday did not pass him the sack. 'Forgive me, sir,' he said. 'These need to be delivered to Sir Godefroi.'

Sir Denis smiled patiently. 'Old friends of his, are they, Sir…'

'… FitzTalbot. Men call me—'

'His name's fucking Loveday,' said Northampton. 'But by God, I don't give two farts from my mare's well-fed arse what anyone's fucking name is right now. Sir Denis, get that fucking bag off him. Take it to the traitor. See that Loveday and his men get some gold for their trouble – although why Loveday here isn't down in Saint-Lô taking it for himself Christ only knows. Did Sir Godefroi promise you the earth if you fetched him these, Loveday?'

'Well, he suggested that we might all be rewarded…'

Northampton laughed loud. 'Ha! You see, Loveday, that's the problem with the Normans, the French, the Bretons – the whole fucking lot of them. They're full of shit. You'll get some gold, don't worry.' A shadow crossed his face. 'But I tell you, you'll get a lot more if you happen to see a wench. The prince has been fucking her every which way, and now she's vanished, so he's sulking, and refusing to move on until she comes crawling back. And that's a problem for me. So if you see her... you'll tell me. Won't you?'

Loveday cringed inwardly. 'Of course, my lord,' he said. 'But I have not—'

Northampton waved a hand dismissively. 'You told me that already. And I told you, I don't have time for anything except finding wenches and trying to keep this fucking expedition on the road, before the king comes down here and heads start rolling. As soon as the prisoners down there have been sorted and marched off back to the rearguard, we're expected to start the *chevauchée*. You know what that means?'

'Aye, sir,' said Loveday, the sick feeling returning to his stomach. 'Aye, I do.'

'Hmmph,' said Northampton. 'Stuck-up French word for spreading out and destroying everything in sight and teaching the people a lesson: don't live in a shit country where there might be a war.'

Loveday said nothing. Sir Denis swung the bag of heads back and forth. The other knight stood impassive at Northampton's side. The earl nodded. As though the day's business had been mapped out.

'So, Sir Denis – the heads to the traitor. Loveday, keep your eyes out for a wench, and get your company in order as soon as you can for some wanton fucking violence. And one more thing.'

'Sir?'

'You've a priest in your company, am I right?'

Loveday's heart sank. 'Well, my lord, we do – I mean – he's a sort of priest,' he said.

'Grand,' said Northampton. 'I'll let Lord Warwick know. A

sort of a priest is exactly what we need. The less fucking godly the better. Come and see me tomorrow, and I'll tell you more. And in the meantime, Loveday...'

'Sir?'

Northampton grinned. 'Cheer up, you miserable cunt. It's a war. You're either going to die, get horribly maimed or have some fucking fun!'

Northampton marched off. His knights followed a pace behind him. As they went, Sir Denis opened the head-sack and showed the other knight what was in it. Both of them gagged, then burst into fits of laughter.

Loveday put his hand in the purse and let his fingers feel the woman's soft hair.

He wondered if she had made it to the bottom of the hill.

14

So was the good, fat land of Normandy ravaged and burnt, plundered and pillaged by the English.

Chronicles of Jean Froissart

'We've got a problem.'

Millstone's face was set firm, but Loveday knew he was troubled. The thickset Kentishman was not one to gabble or panic. He was last of the Dogs to take fright and the first to bring calm to chaos.

When he was worried, Loveday listened.

The two men were riding side by side, across open countryside west of Saint-Lô. The *chevauchée* was under way. Thousands of horsemen and footsoldiers trampled crops and burned anything that would catch. Grass drying for hay in the summer sun was aflame everywhere. The noon sky was a livid orange. Hot, wretched smoke stung Loveday's lungs. Pismire, Scotsman and the Welsh brothers were a few hundred yards distant, setting fire to a barn. Beyond them Englishmen hewed trees, felling an orchard with their axes. Killing trees ripe with fruit. Trees that had grown for fifty years.

Half a mile away, on one of the web of tiny sunken tracks that crisscrossed the Norman countryside, a subdued Romford was guiding the donkey and cart, laden with stacks of church plate, reams of cloth and two large wine barrels the Dogs had brought up the hill from Saint-Lô after the raid. Tebbe and Thorp balanced on the back of the cart, loosing off arrows at any livestock they saw: sending cows and sheep lurching miserably around until they fell to their forelegs, bellowing and dying.

Romford had Father with him. As Tebbe and Thorp shot and whooped, the old man sat with his knees tucked into his chest. Pismire had stolen a small cage with a songbird inside it. Father fed it grain and muttered to it, but he would say nothing to anyone else.

When Romford had dragged a dazed Father up the hill to the vanguard camp Loveday had seen his face, rusted with dry blood, and guessed, roughly, what might have happened. He cursed himself. He knew Father had become unpredictable and savage. He had brought him to the war anyway. Hoping perhaps that somehow he would become the old Father, the bullish but steadfast man of faith whom he had known years before. He had been a fool.

Loveday did not learn the details of what had happened in Saint-Lô immediately, for in the hurry to pack up the hilltop camp and ride out to blow death across the land, there had been no time to sit down and hear the story told.

Now, though, Millstone seemed ready to tell him.

'What kind of problem?' Loveday asked his broad-chested friend.

Loveday first met Millstone in the winter that his wife Alis died of the sweat. Seven years and more ago. The sickness had come for her at the end of autumn, while Loveday was away at work with the Dogs, robbing merchant ships as they lay at anchor in Thames-side wharves and estuary ports by night.

He had known something was wrong when he came home on a crisp November morning to find Alis had let their cottage run to filth and dirt, the door swinging unlatched on its hinge. She had smiled when he picked her up from her stool by the fire, saying she would mend once she rested. But in a few weeks the sweat reduced her from a broad-shouldered, happy-faced alewife to a clammy, coughing, delirious skeleton.

Then, like all three of the children she had borne him, she was gone. Stiff and cold one morning. Buried shallow in frozen ground the week before Christmas. A handful of earth shot through with flecks of ice was the last thing he had given her. Tossed on her reed-woven casket as he had once thrown handfuls of stolen coin into her skirts.

For weeks, Loveday had been sick at heart and mostly drunk. He had stewed in his cottage until the early spring, when the Dogs came and dragged him back to work.

Millstone had simply been there when they came to get him. A new face in the group. Men drifted through their company from time to time, and before Millstone joined there had been five of them: Loveday, Pismire, Father, Thorp. And the Captain, who before Loveday was their leader.

In the bleak days after Alis died Millstone made them six. And it was he, rather than the Captain, their talisman, who had dragged him out of his despair and made him see a cause to carry on. Millstone was with the Dogs because his other choice was to be hanged for killing the foreman in Rochester Cathedral. He had little love for the work they did, but he did it, and well.

As he had often said in those first months, he preferred to

be a robber and alive than a convicted killer and dead. That uncomplicated approach, preferring the earth he knew to the greater pains of purgatory, was what drove Millstone on. And, by his example, Loveday learned to carry on as well.

Millstone told him what had happened in Saint-Lô, with little emotion and no fear. Just a sense that their lives had grown complicated.

But Loveday felt his heart plummet as the tale unfolded.

When Millstone had finished they were both quiet for a few moments. They listened to the bleats of hurt sheep and the roars of cattle being butchered in the fields mingling with the crash of falling apple trees. The howls of families run down as they abandoned their wrecked homes. The war cries of the English army given its head and gone half-mad.

Then, as evenly as he could, Loveday said: 'This is bad.'

'I know.'

'Really bad.'

'I know that too.'

'It's not just the East Anglians. We could all be hanged.'

'You don't have to tell me, Loveday. I've done this before.'

Loveday took a deep breath and stared out into the distance. Into the chaos of a land on fire. 'I keep seeing her,' he said.

But before he could say any more, they heard a whistle. Three shrill blasts, low to high. Thorp's warning signal. The two men stood in their stirrups and looked in the direction of the archers.

The cart was stopped in the narrow sunken lane, at a gap in the hedgerows. Through the gap, Loveday and Millstone saw that Romford now stood in front, with Father alongside him, head bowed and staring at the ground. Tebbe and Thorp remained on the cart, but they had their bows slung over their shoulders.

In front of them were two knights. From the size of them, and their liveries, the bright blue slashed white, with red stars, Loveday knew exactly who they were. Sir Denis of Moreton-in-the-Weald and Northampton's other guard.

With them was another figure. Pot-bellied and proud, with a helmet strapped tightly on a fat head. A small roll of parchment in his hand.

Sir Robert le Straunge.

Loveday looked at Millstone. 'Trouble's found us already,' he said. 'Get out of here. Disappear into the *chevauchée*. We're heading to Caen. Find us there, but take no risks. If you must, get back to the coast. Get aboard a ship. Meet us at home at the end of the summer. We'll bring your portion and your pay. If we get any now.'

Millstone frowned. 'Thank you. Shaw crossed us. But I didn't mean for—'

Loveday waved him quiet. 'You know how we are. All and one.' He held out a hand. Millstone grasped it.

'*Desperta ferro*,' said Millstone, quietly. 'Try and save the boy.'

Then he kicked his horse and set off towards the burning barn where Scotsman and Pismire stood, his hammer hanging heavy by his side.

Sir Robert was in full flow when Loveday arrived, reading from his piece of parchment. Sir Denis and the other huge knight stood by his side and smirked. The two had evidently been sent by Northampton to accompany Sir Robert, and they were effective. Even on foot, they could use the vast bulk of their armoured bodies to block the lane. But it seemed they were unimpressed by their task. They exchanged glances over the top of Sir Robert's head.

Sir Robert continued: 'Item,' he said, savouring the word. 'No one should be so rash as to start a quarrel or dispute in the host on account of bad blood in the past or anticipated. And if anyone should die as a result of such a quarrel or dispute, he or they who have been the cause or supporter of it shall be hanged.'

He peered at Romford and Father. 'Do you know what those words are? What they mean?' Neither of them said anything. Father shuffled his feet in the dry dirt of the track.

Loveday, arriving at the hedge, wondered whether to interrupt. His hands were clammy. He kept seeing little green and yellow stars creeping into the edges of his vision.

'I have been informed that yesterday in Saint-Lô these two men, in flagrant breach of the said royal ordinances, did with callous and cold aforethought most treasonably, ah, most execrably and woefully cause the death of William Shaw,' said Sir Robert. 'Shaw was a subject and servant of the lord king, and a captain in my employ, thereby under the protection of these said ordinances.'

He glared around the group. Tebbe and Thorp said nothing. Loveday opened his mouth. Yet as he did, he realized anything he said was likely to rile Sir Robert further. His mind raced. He considered, madly, whether he could grab Father and run. Hope that Romford had the wit to follow them. Then he glanced at Sir Denis and thought better of it.

Father grunted. He looked around for the little bird in its cage. Romford looked white and sick.

Sir Robert continued. 'This is, I say, an outrage. I am told by Shaw's associates that he suffered a most grievous death, at the hands of men of this company. For which they will now come with me to be tried for their crimes by a court martial over which I shall of course preside, in my capacity as a lord officer of the royal army.'

Sir Robert craned his neck and looked up at Sir Denis. 'Take these men,' he commanded.

Sir Denis smiled beatifically, the lines by his eyes creasing. 'Take these men, if it please you, Sir Denis? Was that what you meant, Sir Robert?'

Sir Robert puffed his cheeks and reddened. 'Sir Denis, I have given my order,' he said.

'As you please,' said Sir Denis. 'I merely made a suggestion. You make the decisions.'

He stepped forwards to lay his hands on Romford and Father. As he did, Loveday dismounted. 'Sir Denis,' he said. 'Wait.'

Sir Denis stopped. 'Is there a problem? Sir Robert has asked me most chivalrously to take these men away. I can bring you back their heads in a sack, if you desire.'

He said this with the same smirk on his face as he had worn during Sir Robert's harangue. But Loveday detected the hint of a wink as he spoke.

Sir Robert was not amused. He rounded on Loveday. 'Are you presuming to countermand my quite clear instruction to Sir Denis, FitzTalbot?' he puffed. 'In case you were out of earshot when I read our dread lord king's ordinances of war, these men are responsible for the death of one of our company captains. Unless you know otherwise, FitzTalbot?'

'Respectfully, my lord, I think there has been some mistake,' said Loveday.

Sir Robert raised an eyebrow, bunching up rolls of fat on his damp forehead. 'Indeed? Might there be some others of your men I should also arrest?'

Loveday thought of Millstone, and hoped he was heading for either the woods or the sea. 'No, sir.'

'Quite so,' continued Sir Robert. 'Now, Sir Denis is going to take these criminals away to face justice. I am happy to ask Sir Adrian here to take you too, Loveday. Since you have been harbouring evildoers in your company, I might well decide to have you hanged as well. Or your archers here.'

He nodded towards Tebbe and Thorp, who stood looking defiant, staring as insolently as they dared at the knight.

Loveday kept quiet, but his fear was turning to anger. Sir Robert sneered. Sir Denis shook Romford by the shoulder, and pushed Father over to Sir Adrian to march away. Sir Robert strode off ahead of them, down the road. Loveday looked after them in despair.

Behind him Scotsman and Pismire appeared, laughing together. Their faces were blackened by soot and streaked with sweat. Scotsman's undershirt hung open to his navel and he had scratches that looked to have come from human nails crisscrossing his chest.

When they came through the gap in the hedgerow and saw Father and Romford disappearing under the guard of Northampton's knights, Scotsman called out angrily: 'Hey! Where in the name of Christ's holy foreskin are you taking our men?'

Sir Robert stopped and glared at him. 'To be hanged like the contumacious filth they are,' he yelled.

The Scot made to storm towards Sir Robert. Pismire and Loveday grabbed one of his arms each and hauled him back.

Sir Robert catcalled: 'Finally FitzTalbot keeps his men in order!'

Scotsman bristled with rage, but did not tear himself free from Pismire and Loveday's grip; he simply watched as the two Dogs were marched away.

'The fuck are we going to do?' said Pismire.

'I don't know,' said Loveday weakly.

But as he spoke, Sir Denis paused, his hand still on Romford's shoulder. He turned his face back in the Dogs' direction and motioned quickly with his head towards Sir Robert, rolling his eyes. He mouthed a single word. Loveday lip-read. Sir Denis cocked his head towards Sir Robert again, mouthed a second word, then kept on walking.

'What was he saying?' said Pismire.

'Northampton,' said Loveday. 'Quick.'

15

In an army such as the King of England was leading, it was impossible that there should not be plenty of bad characters and criminals without conscience.

Chronicles of Jean Froissart

They tracked down Northampton in the woods outside a place they heard men call Torigny. Loveday rode there with Pismire and Scotsman.

They left the archers taking the cart moodily towards Caen. Although the Welshmen continued to enjoy themselves in the *chevauchée*, Tebbe and Thorp seemed to have had their spirit knocked out of them. They drove the donkey listlessly along the sunken lanes. Tebbe waved flies away from his face. Thorp did not even bother to do that.

Loveday knew that, like him, they were anxious.

He wondered where Millstone might be – whether he was riding ahead of them, or had turned back for the coast. He knew Millstone could look after himself under even the most dire circumstances, but he hated his crew to be broken up. And he knew that in war, fortune's wheel turned fast.

We are all survivors. Until we are not.

Just before Torigny they came off the road into the woods where Northampton had pitched camp to take his midday meal in the cool. Beeches interspersed with ancient yews provided a leafy canopy above and a springy carpet of fallen needles underfoot. As they led their horses through the trees, Loveday spoke firmly to his men.

'We haven't come to bicker or argue. We're here to plead for mercy,' he said. 'Be prepared to grovel.'

Scotsman growled. Yew straw crunched under his boots. 'Kissing noble arse so we can get back a pair of fiends who've caused us nothing but trouble?' he said. 'Forgive me if I don't whoop with joy.'

Pismire also griped. 'I don't want to lose anyone, but they brought this on themselves. The boy was good when he joined us – he's strong and he can shoot – but he's been a halfwit lately. Eating that fucking powder. And as for Father…'

Loveday flinched. 'What about him? He's been one of us as long as we've *been* us.'

Pismire swallowed whatever he had been about to say. 'Aye, he has,' he said. 'And we've done much together too. But tell me honestly—'

Loveday cut him off. 'I tell you honestly, both of you, that I'd never let any one of you hang if there was a chance of saving your worthless skins,' he snapped. 'We are who we are. We do what we do. We look after each other.'

Pismire and Scotsman frowned, but did not argue. They approached a clearing in the woods, where pavilions had been hastily slung up among the trees. Members of Northampton's retinue lounged, some with their back to beech trunks, others washing their feet in a small stream. Loveday also saw men wearing Warwick's livery of red with gold crosses.

And they heard, before they saw him, the shrill voice of Prince Edward.

★ ★ ★

The two earls were sitting either side of the prince, eating their meal at a trestle table hung with a finely embroidered cloth. They dined on plunder: a stew of what smelled like cockerel, flavoured with wild garlic and wine. The earls sipped from cups made of pewter or silver. The prince swilled wine from a large gold chalice set with jewels. Pages and squires buzzed around the table. Knights, including Sir Denis and Sir Adrian, stood behind it. A gaggle of petitioners stood in front.

The Scotsman, a head taller than the small crowd, surveyed the scene. 'That fat cunt Sir Robert is up there at the front,' he said. As he spoke, two knights controlling the flow of petitioners to the nobles' dining table motioned the portly Sir Robert forwards.

'Can you see Father or Romford?' asked Pismire.

'Nowhere,' said the big man.

'Let's get forwards,' said Loveday. And using Scotsman as a battering ram, they pushed to the front of the crowd and listened to Sir Robert address the prince and the earls.

As usual, he droned like a wheezy bagpipe. The prince did not even pretend to listen, but leaned back in his chair and whispered and laughed with one of his own knights, who was squatting on his haunches behind. He appeared to have forgotten the woman from Valognes. Northampton rolled his eyes and shifted in his seat, bored, picking meat from between his teeth with the tip of a dagger. Warwick alone attempted to follow the drift of Sir Robert's protestation. At length he interrupted.

'Gentle Sir Robert, if I follow your speech correctly, you

complain of a dispute between your own men which has ended in the death of one of them – this, ah, Shaw?'

Sir Robert nodded enthusiastically. 'Quite so, my lord,' he said. 'To repeat: the ordinances of war handed down by our dread lord and sovereign, the most noble prince's father, by the grace of God King Edw—'

Warwick winced. 'I know all about the ordinances,' he said. 'Where are the men accused?'

Sir Robert puffed out his chest. 'By St Anthony's holy jawbone, my lord, they are already apprehended. And by my own hand, no less. No doubt it would have been a quieter matter for me to let squabbles between my men pass, but I pride myself as a man of integrity and honour and—'

Again Warwick interrupted. 'Yes, Sir Robert, you pride yourself very well indeed. But I, and my lord prince, and my worshipful friend Lord Northampton here, pride *ourselves* on the speedy dispensation of justice. Or if I may put it another way, good Sir Robert, pray silence. Please.'

Having quietened Sir Robert at last, Warwick leaned across the prince and muttered quietly to Northampton, who in turn motioned with his head to Sir Denis.

Warwick turned back to the huge knight. 'Sir Denis, go and fetch these men and let us see what we may do with them. There is no shortage of trees here, should a quick struggle from a high branch prove the most suitable remedy.'

Sir Denis immediately strode off among the pavilions in the wood.

Meanwhile, Sir Robert was nodding his head vigorously. 'Indeed, Lord Warwick,' he said. 'The ultimate penalty as prescribed in our dread and sovereign lord king's commands at the outset of this campaign...' But Warwick flashed him such a glare that he petered out.

Sir Denis returned promptly with Father and Romford in tow and brought them to stand off to the side of the prince and earls' dining table. The two Dogs had their hands bound behind their backs. Father still looked dazed, but Romford had recovered some of his wits.

His gaze flickered around the men in the crowd. He seemed surprised to see Loveday, Pismire and the Scot at the front of it. Loveday gave him what he hoped was a reassuring nod.

Romford's eyes were wide. Perhaps he had heard the talk of hanging. He seemed frightened.

Warwick massaged the bridge of his nose with his forefingers and then addressed Sir Robert once more. 'Sir Robert. Could you in no more than one breath tell me what you believe we should do with these men of yours?'

Sir Robert inhaled deeply – so deeply his eyes bulged – and began again his whole account of Romford and Father's misdeeds. Northampton threw his head back in frustration and groaned loudly. Warwick closed one eye and ground his teeth. But they allowed Sir Robert to continue, until he had run so low on breath that he was croaking like a bullfrog, finally ending with the words '... hang them until they be dead'.

Warwick did his best to remain calm. 'So be it,' he said. 'This case sounds straightforward. Let them hang. Unless anyone here has any objection?' He scanned the crowd.

Loveday raised his hand and stepped forwards. 'Aye, sir,' he said. 'I have an objection.'

The crowd fell quiet. Loveday felt every pair of eyes on him. Even Prince Edward momentarily stopped bantering with his knightly companion and looked around. Seeing little to interest him in Loveday, he turned away again.

Warwick tried hard to suppress a smile. 'FitzTalbot! You seem to be everywhere I go. So be it. What irks you so much that you would speak up for such a pair of miserable felons?'

'If it please you, these are my men,' said Loveday. 'And though they are not perfect, they are good men of mine, and have been good servants of the king so far, before this, ah, this incident.'

Warwick continued to half smile, and held up a hand to Sir Robert, instructing him to hold his peace. 'Good servants, eh?' he said. 'Well, good enough for you, but as you can see, your lord Sir Robert here is most aggrieved. He says they've mutilated and killed one of his best men. What can you tell me in mitigation, FitzTalbot?'

Loveday's hands felt clammy. 'I am no lawyer, sir. But they were provoked. I was not there, but I have heard from one who was, and I say on good authority that this was no callous deed, but the settlement of a score pursued by the dead man. It was self-defence.'

Sir Robert harrumphed. 'Self-defence! Nonsense and lies!' he cried out. But again Warwick held up a hand.

'Please, sir,' Loveday said. 'These are valuable men of my company. They would not have done this unless sorely baited. And I will vouch personally for their good conduct from here on.'

Warwick looked uncertain.

Loveday continued, a hint of desperation now in his voice: 'The boy here is an archer of rare skill and accuracy. As good as any Englishman, and even some of the Welsh. And the priest is... well, he is our priest. He gives us... ah... he provides us spiritual comfort. As we require it. If I may, Lord Northampton said to me he might need such a man.'

Loveday felt his face flush, and dared not look left or right to see Pismire or Scotsman's reaction to this unlikely description of Father. He barely believed it himself. An image flashed through his mind of Father and Romford's legs kicking, spastic, as they throttled in the lynch-ropes.

Warwick leaned his elbows on the table and tented his fingers. 'Good character and straight shooting is all very well, FitzTalbot. But Sir Robert here is your lord in the field. It would be provocative of me to overrule him, would it not? It might risk his men taking revenge on yours. Worse, it might risk Sir Robert himself speaking once more, and I'm not sure I can tolerate another sermon.'

Warwick looked at Sir Robert. 'I do not mean to offend you, sir. But you never shut your mouth.'

Sir Robert glowered. Loveday's throat was tight. 'Please, my lord,' he said. 'If there is any way you can find it in your heart… if there is any way my men can serve you…'

Warwick sighed again. 'I have many archers,' he said. 'And I care little for priests.' He looked across the table at Northampton. 'Unless my lord disagrees…' He nudged the prince with his elbow. 'Or perhaps your grace…?'

The prince ignored Warwick, still deep in a gossipy conversation with his knight. Northampton opened his mouth and seemed about to reply in the negative.

Yet just as Northampton was about to speak, Sir Robert piped up once more. 'If I may just restate, sirs, the importance of discipline on this campaign. Notwithstanding our need to chastise the false French king and disabuse his subjects of their unfortunate loyalty to so base a traitor…'

A look passed over Northampton's face. He seemed to change his mind. 'You know, my lord Warwick,' he said, although he fixed his eyes on Sir Robert's face, 'perhaps we *can* use these men.'

He leaned across the prince and muttered to Warwick. Warwick shrugged. He looked quizzical. Northampton said a few more words. Warwick shrugged again, but now a brief smile crossed his lips. Just for a moment the smile became a laugh. His whole body seemed to relax and, leaning back in his chair, he gestured with his ungloved hand and allowed Northampton to speak.

'Thank you, my lord,' barked Northampton. 'Now. Sir Robert. My lord Warwick and I here have discussed your complaint. And it is our considered judgement that you're an annoying boil on the arse of this campaign and you can go and piss up one of these fine beech trees if you think we're going to stand for it.'

Sir Robert's mouth hung open. There were guffaws from the other soldiers gathered around. 'Sir – I – This is—' he began, but Northampton was now in full flow.

'I mean it. I'm fucking sick of men like you, telling me what my job should be. You do know I'm Constable of the whole fucking Army, don't you?'

Sir Robert gibbered.

Northampton mimicked him. 'What?' he said. 'What now?'

Sir Robert stood still with his mouth open.

Northampton turned to Loveday. 'FitzTalbot. You're a fuck-up. You look like a fuck-up and your men are clearly a pack of fuck-ups. You've spoiled my meal, and I'm not grateful to you. But your luck must be in. Because right now you're less offensive to me than this prick. So here's what I've decided.

If your men keep killing the wrong people, I'll cut your legs off and I'll have your crew nailed upside-down to barn doors every ten leagues between here and Paris, so the crows can nibble on your pintles. Got it?'

Loveday felt like weeping. 'Thank you, my lo—'

'Stick your thank yous up your bollocks,' said Northampton. 'There's more. You're right about the priest. I do need one. Preferably one we can live without. I have an unpleasant job that requires a churchman who doesn't mind dicing with having his tongue pulled out, and I don't want to send mine, because I like them. So I'm going to have yours.'

Loveday felt Scotsman nudge him hard in the ribs. This did not strike him as entirely good news. 'My lord,' he said. 'This priest is a good man, but he is not quite himself. There was an accident...'

Northampton banged the table with his fist. 'There'll be a bigger fucking accident if you don't keep quiet,' he said. 'This isn't a negotiation. It's what's going to fucking happen.' He took a breath. 'Now,' he said. 'The boy. I have absolutely no use for him at all. But I'm not going to give him back to you, because you obviously can't control him, and that has led, indirectly or otherwise, to Sir Robert spoiling my enjoyment of this very fine cock soup.'

The earl was now playing to the crowd. Sensing it, the troops tittered. Sir Robert, unable to take any more humiliation, stormed off through the crowd of soldiers.

Loveday just nodded, reckoning silence was the safest response.

'So,' said Northampton. 'What shall I do with him, do you think?' He turned theatrically to Warwick. 'My lord Warwick, have you any use for a dopey yet possibly murderous archer, whose mates say he can shoot well, but who can't be trusted not to kill Englishmen instead of the dirty fucking French?'

Warwick, playing his own part in the show, shook his head. 'My lord, alas, I have no use for such a boy.'

Northampton turned around to the knights behind him. 'Good sirs, do any of you cunts want a squire who might kill you in your sleep?'

There was a rumble of laughter from the knights. Sir Denis spoke up. 'My lord Northampton, we are not desirous of squires who might serve us so poorly,' he said.

'Wonderful,' said Northampton. 'In that case we have but one option.' And saying that he turned in his seat and used his forefinger to flick Prince Edward on the ear.

The Prince, shocked out of his discussion, rounded on him. 'Lord Northampton, how dare you! What is the meaning of this?'

Northampton laughed. 'The meaning is that you've got a new squire. He's almost as much of a pain in the arse as you are.'

Prince Edward looked confused and angry. 'What?'

'You heard me,' said Northampton. 'A new squire.'

He winked to the troops. There was open laughter at the idea of an archer promoted to the position of a squire – even more so a squire to the heir to the throne. And there was great amusement at the humiliation being heaped on the prince.

'I don't want a new squire,' the prince squeaked. 'I don't want—'

'Listen, I don't want to babysit you, my little lordling,' barked Northampton. 'But war makes for strange bedfellows.' He turned to Sir Denis. 'Take the boy away, untie his hands, and get him cleaned up a bit. Stick him in royal livery if you can find one. In mine if you can't. Take him to John Chandos and give him the good news.'

Sir Denis nodded, grabbed Romford by the wrists, and marched him off towards one of the pavilions.

The prince stood in fury, pushed back his chair and stormed from the table. 'My father will hear of this!' he shouted.

'Your father hears of everything, you dozy whelp,' called Northampton. 'He gets a daily report and is very pleased with how things are going.' But the prince did not respond.

Northampton now seemed to be quite delighted. He bowed to the laughing troops. Then he looked Father up and down. Father was staring at the yew needles on the floor, muttering incomprehensibly to himself.

'Is this completely mad?' Northampton said, turning to Warwick.

Warwick shrugged.

'Ah well,' said Northampton. 'Who cares?' He beckoned Loveday. 'FitzTalbot. Approach.'

Loveday walked to the front of the earls at the table. He tried to catch Father's eye, but he could not. Father was scratching his balls and shaking his head furiously from side to side.

Warwick tried to adopt a serious tone. 'Tell me frankly, Loveday. Is this priest of yours even vaguely sane or competent to perform a simple task?'

'That depends what it is,' said Loveday. 'If it is dangerous, he may be better with us.'

Warwick broke into a laugh. 'That is not part of the deal. He's alive. Now he must do his penance.'

Loveday looked blank. 'I'm afraid I don't follow, my lord,' he said.

Northampton fixed him with a hard stare. 'FitzTalbot. Have you ever heard of the mad Bishop of Bayeux?'

Loveday shook his head ruefully. He hadn't seen Sir Godefroi for several days, and although Northampton had mentioned being paid for fetching the knights' heads from the walls of Saint-Lô, no pay had actually yet been forthcoming. 'I suppose we will have it at the campaign's end,' he said, realizing how pathetic his words sounded.

Pismire snorted. 'Campaign's end my bollocks. Twenty-six days from now I'm going to whichever of them owes us, showing them my sword, taking what's mine and fucking off home.'

'Me too,' agreed the Scot. 'Fucking lords. All they do is talk, and send men like us to do their shitwork and risk our skins. It's always been the same.'

Loveday let them grumble. He could not disagree, although he did not care much either. The Captain had been fond of saying that a lord was a lord, whether he had you at the plough or in his army.

He looked at Father, ridiculous in his friar's garb. 'Come on,' he said to the others. 'We've groused about this a thousand times before now. It'll do us no more good today than it ever did in the past. We have the letters, and we have our orders. Archers, you stay here. Scotsman, Pismire, we take Father to Caen. With luck, Millstone will meet us there. Let's do our best not to get ourselves killed.'

They came on Caen from the north, riding out from thick woodland towards fields of ripening wheat and barley. It was the largest city they had seen so far.

Two small rivers, low in the heat of the summer, ran north and south of the old city centre. The streams and dried-up stream-beds linking them cut out little islands in the land, where rich suburbs stood. Two large abbeys rose behind high walls on the outskirts of the city. Their gates were closed and barred.

On the side of Caen nearest them was a castle, square-keeped and defended at its corners by four round towers. Briefing them the previous night, the Earl of Warwick had told them it was once held by William, the bastard duke who had invaded England many hundreds of years ago.

'And there's another bastard in it now,' he had laughed, describing the Bishop of Bayeux who was commanding the garrison. Bishop Guillaume Bertrand was, he had told them, the younger brother of Robert Bertrand: the Marshal of France and the man, as Warwick put it, 'who has been masterminding the ingenious French tactic of fleeing at the first sight of trouble'.

'The Green Lion Knight is hiding behind his brother,' Warwick told them. 'And well he might. Once upon a time men here feared him more than every other French knight alive. But while the Green Lion has grown ancient and feeble, his brother Bishop Guillaume is as wild as a leopard.

'He's going to reject our lord king's gracious offer to grant him peace if he yields the city. But we have to make the offer all the same. Which makes your job a simple one, gentlemen. Present him with the king's letters, and then get out of there any way you can. As soon as he formally rejects the offer, we will attack.'

When Warwick had laid out the plan, recounting tales of old knights as though he were reciting the ballads of Arthur, it had seemed simple. But now Loveday contemplated the size of Caen, the formidable defences of its castle, and the shambolic state of Father, he had not the slightest idea how they were going to make it past sunset that evening.

From the woodline, Sir Denis appeared, wearing plate armour on his shoulders. He brought horses, each escorted by one of Warwick's squires. There was a fine, strong mare each for Loveday, Pismire and Scotsman. A donkey for Father.

Pismire dug Father in the ribs and pointed at the donkey. 'Hey, St Francis, are you fit to ride?' Father glared at him and muttered. '*Say that the lord needs them,*' he said.

Pismire looked baffled. 'What?'

'*The lord needs them and will send it back shortly,*' said Father.

Pismire shook his head in disbelief. Scotsman stepped in. He picked Father up under the armpits and dumped him on the donkey's back. It was tacked with a lead-rein. 'I'll look after him,' he said.

The three Dogs saddled up, and Sir Denis addressed them. 'You know what to do?'

'Aye,' said Loveday. 'We do. Shout up to the battlements that Brother Geoffrey here has come with peace terms. Get in, get out and signal that the peace has been rejected.'

'Good,' said Sir Denis. He handed Loveday a pennon bearing King Edward's arms, and Pismire a plain white flag. 'These should stop you being shot before you get within yelling distance of the castle,' he said. 'Have you got helmets?'

Loveday and Pismire pulled up their headgear. The Scot reached back and patted the wide-brimmed iron hat which hung around the leather cord at his neck.

Sir Denis looked them up and down. He seemed amused by their ragged hair-stuffed jackets. He pointed back towards the woodline. 'The whole army is assembling in the trees,' he said.

'They've been marching here since dawn. And not only the vanguard. The king is with the prince and my lords Warwick and Northampton now. The baggage train is in place. They say that the rearguard is joining, too. There will be nigh-on ten thousand bloodthirsty Englishmen behind you. If that helps.'

He handed Loveday a piece of vellum, folded in quarters and sealed with a huge lump of wax, bearing the impression of the king on horseback with a sword in his hand. 'Don't fucking open it – not that I expect you can read.' He clapped Loveday on the back, nearly knocking him over his mare's neck. 'God speed you, Essex Dogs,' Sir Denis said.

Then he added: 'Rather you than me.'

They rode forwards in silence, trampling crops for the better part of a mile as they crossed the open field towards the castle. Loveday, Pismire and the Scot all looked anxiously at the soaring towers, expecting a volley of crossbow bolts at any moment. Pismire kept the white flag waving high as they went. Scotsman tugged the donkey along and Father bobbed back and forth on its back, saying nothing, but darting his eyes around all the while.

They drew up and dismounted some fifty paces from the bridge that led through to the castle gatehouse. It was a large, squat, square-based building that reached up three storeys to a tiled roof. Its corners were rounded, and arrow slits were cut into them at various heights. The walls were unpainted, yet they gleamed a brilliant white as the sun bounced from it. The hewn stone itself appeared to radiate light.

However, it seemed abandoned. They tethered the horses loosely at a row of posts at the end of the bridge. Scotsman hauled Father off the donkey. Loveday placed the royal standard carefully next to his horse, but Pismire kept hold of the white flag.

Slowly, gingerly, they began to walk across the bridge towards the gatehouse. There was still no sign of life.

'No fucker here,' said the Scot as they came to the great arch, where the giant doors stood closed. But as he did so, a voice rang out from a tiny window high on the leftmost tower. '*Présentez-vous! Parlez, par Dieu!*'

Loveday looked at Pismire and Scotsman. 'Either of you want to answer?' he whispered.

Scotsman nodded. '*Alors!*' he shouted. '*Bonjour!* We've got a friar here to see you, and he has a message from King Edward.'

There was no response from the tower.

Scotsman shrugged. 'I said we have a message,' he yelled. 'Or rather, we have a friar. With a message. You hear me?'

Again, no one shouted back. The Scotsman puffed air through his nose angrily.

'Christ's twitching arsehole,' he said. 'We've got you a fucking message! Now *ouvrez* the gate, you French cunts!'

Loveday winced. But Scotsman's profanity and the baseness of his roar seemed to overcome any barriers of language. The voice rang back down from the tower.

'*D'accord. Posez vos armes, s'il vous plait, messieurs.*'

The Dogs looked at each other. The voice called again, heavily accented but now in English. 'Your swords, misters. Throw them at the ground. Or... we come down and make you dead.'

Loveday pulled his short sword and laid it down at his feet. Pismire and Scotsman did the same. They all pushed back their helmets.

There was a short silence inside the tower. Then: '*Merci, messieurs*. What is you wanting?'

Scotsman shrugged at Pismire and Loveday. 'I've already told you. We've got a messenger for you. He's a very esteemed holy man. He's read a lot of fucking books. And he's got a message for your master. The bishop. How does that sound?'

Another long pause. Then another voice rang out. It was deep and resonant. The voice of an older man, but one who was used to speaking in public. It boomed, in more accomplished English: 'Speak, cleric! Let me hear this message aloud.'

Scotsman looked at Father. Father shook his head violently.

'He's taken a vow of silence,' yelled the Scot. 'He's contemplating the mysteries of the fucking faith. Just come down and get his message, will you?'

This time the silence went on for a very long time, and Loveday was beginning to wonder if they should simply leave and call in the attack, when from within the tower rang out the stomp of boots, hammering down a staircase. Then, a scraping of metal – keys turning in locks – and finally, a thick wooden door at the base of the tower swung open, and from the gloom inside emerged a loaded crossbow. Then another. Then another, until there were ten weapons, all loaded, all pointing at the Dogs.

Each was held by a heavily armoured crossbowman, their upper arms covered in polished steel, mail covering their chests and throats, and tough leather tunics underneath. Loveday stepped instinctively back, and Pismire and Scotsman did likewise. The Scot pulled Father back with him. The French soldiers were all grim-faced.

Loveday's heart pounded. He had handled crossbows before, and knew well how light their trigger mechanisms could be to the touch. It would only take the wobble of a hand for one of the Dogs to be lying on his back with his heart speared by a thick iron bolt.

He raised his palms slowly in front of him. 'We're here in peace,' he said. 'We're unarmed. You can see our blades on the ground.' He had no idea if his words meant anything to the soldiers. But before any of them could reply, out from the small door in the tower stepped another figure.

It was an old man, his skin papery and sallow. Thin yellow-white hair hung long and lank around his ears. His shoulders were a little stooped and rounded. His eyebrows were enormous and bushy, and his nose long and curved at the end. There was something cruel in the puckered pinch of his mouth. But he walked more strongly than his aged body had any right to do.

Although he wore no mitre, nor carried a crozier, and his clothes were simple and black, Loveday knew that this must be Guillaume Bertrand. The mad bishop.

He stepped between the crossbowmen, who were arranged in a semi-circle, the Dogs within their sights. He eyed them steadily. 'Who are you?' he asked. His voice rang with a clear, true timbre. It was the same voice they had heard floating down from the tower minutes before.

Loveday kept his palms raised. 'We're messengers, from King Edward,' he said. 'And the English marshal Lord Warwick.' He paused. 'And the Prince Edward.'

The mad bishop stared. His breath rattled softly in his chest. He nodded softly. 'The King of England sent you,' he said. It was a statement, not a question. Loveday nodded.

'Actually, he sent Brother Geoffrey here,' he said, gesturing deliberately with his head to Father, who stood sullen and morose, looking at the ground. 'Of Maldon. He's a famous friar. In England.'

The bishop looked at Father incredulously. 'This is not Brother Geoffrey of Maldon,' he said. 'This is not a famous friar. This is some ape you have dressed up.' He glared at the Dogs. 'Have you been sent here to mock me?' he asked.

Pismire, the Scot and Loveday shook their heads vigorously. Loveday looked around the crossbowmen nervously. 'No, my lord. Not in the least. We have been sent to—'

The bishop interrupted him. 'You have been sent in bad faith. This is not a peace delegation. It is a bauble. A joke, by God.' He pointed at Father. 'Who is this man? Do not deceive me, or I shall order these men to shoot. They will shoot accurately, but they will not kill you. Instead, they will hobble you all with a bolt through each knee. I shall then have you tied to a post in the market square here in Caen, and flayed, one by one. Believe me, this will hurt.'

Loveday's mouth was suddenly dry. As though he had bitten an unripe apple. Pismire and the Scot said nothing.

Father mumbled: '*After me cometh a man who cometh before me.*'

The bishop looked curiously at Father. To Loveday he said, 'What did he say?'

Loveday broke out into a sweat. 'He – he is somewhat not himself,' he said.

Father mumbled again: '*Behold, an Israelite, in whom is no guile.*'

The mad bishop frowned. 'Silence, ape!' he commanded. He returned his attention to Loveday. 'Where is this letter? The ape's hands are empty.'

'I have it,' said Loveday. 'I was holding it for him.'

The bishop nudged the crossbowman closest to him. Loveday flinched instinctively. But the crossbowman lowered his weapon and stepped forwards, holding the weapon in his right hand and stretching out his left. Loveday handed the letter over, and the crossbowman took it to the bishop.

Bertrand split the wax seal roughly with a crooked finger, then scanned the page. Loveday, who had never learned to read anything beyond the most rudimentary signs and his own name, was always fascinated to observe those who could decipher the scratchings of quill and ink on parchment. As though they were divining the future from the stars.

What the bishop saw on the parchment displeased him greatly. In the short time it took him to read the words, his face darkened and his rasping breath became noisier and more rapid. He began to jabber in French – words that Loveday could only assume were great oaths and curses unbecoming a man of the Church.

Finally, he raised his chin and fixed Loveday and the other Dogs with a murderous stare. Without saying a word, he raised the royal letter in front of him, and slowly and deliberately tore the vellum in half. Placing the pieces together, he tore them again. Then, with some effort, he tore them a third time.

He threw the small squares to the ground and, his angry gaze still on the Dogs, ground them under the heel of his leather shoe.

'Take this message back to your king,' he said to Loveday in English. 'Or whoever it is that really sent you.

'The city of Caen is under my command. My brother, the Lord Marshal of France, represents our king, Philippe. We have under our protection not only eight thousand townsmen and an innumerable crowd of refugees but the right reputation of France herself.

'Inform your lord king that his peace terms are like the rest of his invasion: a foolish play, as would befit peasants at a midsummer feast, but not real men. Your king is welcome to try his luck at taking this city by whatever dismal means he likes. But we will never surrender it to him. He may do his worst.'

With effort Loveday swallowed. Although his mouth and throat were parched, sweat was pooling in the small of his back and he felt the urgent need to piss. 'My lord,' he began. But as he did, the bishop hobbled rapidly and aggressively towards him. He came so close Loveday could smell the sourness of his breath, heavy with stale wine and meat rotting between his yellow teeth.

'Tell your king,' said Bertrand, 'that he will rue the day he ever set his feet in France. And tell him that the pains of hell which await him will soon be foreshadowed here on earth by the grace of God and the mighty hand of our lord king of France. Do you think you can remember that, messenger boy?'

Loveday nodded slowly.

'Good. Now go, before I have my men shoot.' And he turned back to the crossbowmen and the tower door behind him.

Loveday looked around. Pismire and Scotsman seemed ready to run. Loveday spoke to Father. 'Fath— I mean, Brother Geoffrey. Let us withdraw.'

But at this the bishop suddenly spun on his heel. 'No,' he said. 'You may go. Your two companions here may go. But leave your weapons. And the ape stays with me.'

Loveday shook his head. 'My lord. He is – he cannot—'

Bertrand cut him off. 'The ape stays with me. Men – take him.'

Three of the crossbowmen lowered their weapons and stepped forwards. Father shrank back. Scotsman instinctively made a move towards Father, but as he did so one of the crossbowmen standing by the bishop loosed off a bolt, which juddered into the ground a mere handspan from Scotsman's feet. The Scot froze.

'For the final time,' said the bishop, his voice oozing quiet menace, 'the ape stays with me.'

The three crossbowmen grabbed Father, one of them on each arm and another grabbing the hood of his friar's robes. Father began to howl. Over his anguished cries, the Bishop of Bayeux started laughing. 'Now,' he called out to Loveday, 'I will give you to my count of thirteen to leave this gatehouse, before we kill you all. One...'

Helpless, Loveday, Pismire and Scotsman backed away. 'Father,' called Loveday. 'Don't panic. We'll return for you.'

'Two...' cried the Bishop of Bayeux. 'If you come back for him, I'll try and remember to have all the pieces of him piled in the same spot.'

Father screeched. The bishop stepped forwards and slapped him. 'Three...'

Loveday, Pismire and Scotsman turned and broke into a run towards their horses at the far side of the bridge. They were barely halfway when the first crossbow bolt split the air above their heads.

'Warning shot,' panted Pismire.

'Fucking mad bastard,' shouted the Scotsman.

They ducked their heads and sprinted for their lives.

Their horses were snorting and stamping where they had been tethered. The Dogs scrambled into their saddles and kicked them hard, back towards the crop-fields and the woods. As they galloped, more crossbow bolts started landing around them.

Loveday flattened himself against his horse's neck. He saw Pismire and Scotsman doing the same. His heart was thumping so hard he wondered if it was about to burst.

As the horses charged into the wheat and barley, he remembered what he was supposed to do.

He was holding the king's flag in his left hand as he gripped his horse's reins in the right. Leaning rightwards slightly, so that he was still tight to his horse, sighting his direction of travel through the gap between beast's ears, he raised the flag, emblazoned with fleurs-de-lis and lions.

The mare galloped strongly forwards. Loveday closed his eyes briefly. He put his left hand as high as he could in the air above him, and waved the royal standard back and forth for all that he was worth.

Over the sound of his heart and the beat of the hooves beneath him, he made out a blast of trumpets, the bang of drums and, above it all, a great human roar.

When he opened his eyes he saw the woodline in front of him start to move. And from between the trees poured a wave of bodies with weapons raised above their heads.

Knights charged with lances couched. Pikemen and footsoldiers carrying short swords and clubs ran on foot. Archers advanced with bows slung across their chests and daggers at their belts.

Flags and standards waved above the mob. The late-morning air was torn with bloodthirsty yells and screams.

The English army was on the charge.

17

The King of England became master of Caen, though at a
heavy price...

Chronicles of Jean Froissart

The body of the army flowed round them like the rush of
a tide. Loveday's horse reared and pulled, but she did not
throw him.

By the time Loveday had his mare under control, the line had
passed them, leaving only straggling runners: the fat, lazy and
lame, jogging to join the roaring thousands who were rushing
to Caen's crumbling walls, and the riverbanks that protected
the island suburbs.

Loveday threw down his flag and looked for Pismire.

He saw him with Scotsman, scanning the field. They had
already wheeled their horses. Loveday knew what they would
be thinking.

Find the Dogs. Get into the city. Find Father.

He guessed Tebbe, Thorp and the Welshmen would by now
be somewhere among Warwick's host. Loveday knew they
would be keeping their distance from Sir Robert. Romford
would be with the prince – although what that meant for the
lad, Loveday did not dare imagine. He tried not to wonder
where Millstone might be.

He drew his steaming mare alongside those of Pismire and Scotsman. 'Weapons first,' he said. 'Let's find the baggage train. Then we'll get back there and rescue Father. But we can't run towards a fight without arms.'

'Aye. Let's be quick,' said the Scotsman.

They kicked their mares and cantered to the woodline. It took them no time at all to find an armourer with a selection of swords, axes and short pikes. Rough weapons, but sharp and serviceable.

They picked the weapons they liked best. Loveday and Pismire selected short swords and daggers. Scotsman grabbed a large, long-handled axe, with a double head and a leather strap, so he could sling it on his back. They took Warwick's horses back to a corral where grooms had water and fodder.

Then they set out at a jog, back towards Caen, to join the siege.

The army had gathered in large mobs at various points around Caen's uneven walls. One large group swarmed outside the castle gatehouse, where Loveday, Pismire and Scotsman had encountered the bishop. But the castle was huge and by far the strongest point in Caen's defences. It was the least likely place to enter the city: the men who loitered outside were simply hoping to stop Bishop Bertrand from escaping.

Larger groups were assembled by the two abbeys to the east and west of the castle. 'That's the prince's flag,' said Pismire, pointing towards a green banner emblazoned with a red dragon. It fluttered near the larger of the two monasteries, which lay ahead and slightly to their left, perched on a hill that was separated from the old city by a few hundred yards of open ground. 'And Northampton's with it.' The abbey was protected by the hill and a low wall. But it was undefended. A battering ram was crashing into its gates, to loud cheers from the prince's retainers.

Loveday thought of Romford. He wondered how the lad was coping with his elevation from archer to royal squire. Let alone what horror the events in Saint-Lô had left in his mind. Then he shook the thought away. The boy was alive. That would do – for now.

Scotsman pointed right. 'And that's Warwick's,' he said. A smaller group, of perhaps a dozen knights and men-at-arms, clanking in plate armour, and about half as many archers wearing mail shirts and leather, were skirting around the western perimeter of the city. The knights were surveying the trenches and palisades that had been added to the defences – a mixture of stone and timber fencing. The archers moved slowly along with them, keeping their bows trained at the tops of the walls, lest any crossbowmen should pop up above the high crenellations.

Loveday could make out Warwick himself at their heart, his burnished helmet gleaming in the sun. He also saw a wiry archer on the edge of the group, with a long thin plait hanging down his back. 'That's Tebbe,' he called. 'Let's get over there.'

The three set out at a half-jog. As they ran, Loveday's legs felt stiff. But his hands prickled urgently, too. The strain of the morning's activity was fighting against the excitement and the fear of what lay ahead.

As they neared Warwick, a loud bellowing high up to their left told them that the prince's men had broken through the gates of the abbey. The Dogs looked, momentarily distracted by the noise. Up the hill they saw Englishmen tripping over broken wood and one another as they hurtled through the smashed gates. Loveday glimpsed a beautifully kept garden beyond.

He wondered if any monks had been foolish enough to remain in their cloisters.

Or worse, nuns.

But there was no time to dwell. They were now just paces away from Warwick's small band of knights, men-at-arms and archers. In contrast to the prince's men at the abbey, this crew was moving carefully and deliberately, the knights around Warwick deep in discussion about how best to advance.

Scotsman strode forwards and clapped Tebbe on the shoulder. The archer swung round, surprised, then beamed and hit Scotsman on the back. Thorp, standing with Darys and Lyntyn, also broke into a huge smile.

'You're here!' Tebbe said. Then his face fell. 'Where's Father?'

Before they could answer, Warwick himself turned, irritated. But when he saw Loveday, Pismire and Scotsman his face brightened. 'The Dogs of Essex!' he said. 'Well, well. Did you bring back your fake friar?'

Loveday shook his head, sadly.

Warwick made a face. 'I am sorry,' he said. 'Did the bishop skin him on the spot or save him for later?'

'He was—' began Loveday, but Warwick seemed to lose interest immediately.

'If he's alive, we'll find him,' he said briskly. 'Meanwhile, you men join us. Your captain Sir Robert is on the far side of the city, attempting to get close enough to the king's arse to give it a kiss.'

He laughed, his white teeth flashing. Then he turned to one of the knights in the group – a handsome man of medium build with sandy hair, a scar running down one cheek and his left eye socket covered by a leather patch. 'Sir Thomas,' he said. 'Be good enough to explain to these friends of mine what we're looking at, and what we're going to do.'

As the knight spoke, it dawned on Loveday who he was: Sir Thomas Holand, a man widely famed for his military prowess and chivalrous reputation. The tabard he wore over his breastplate was forget-me-not blue, and decorated with tiny silver lions. He also wore a crusader's cross, and – most curiously – what seemed to be a woman's garter around his leg.

Sir Thomas caught Loveday glancing at it. 'My wife,' he said. 'Joan. You've never seen anything like her.'

But he said no more about her. Instead, Pismire, Scotsman and Loveday listened intently as the knight explained the military situation around Caen. He spoke plainly and rapidly, but there was a light in his one remaining eye and the laughter lines that crinkled in the sun-browned skin around it told Loveday he was at his happiest here, where stone and wood met metal and flesh, and the air rang with bellows of triumph and pain.

Against the din of the siege Sir Thomas's voice, accentless and strangely hard to locate, was smooth and persuasive. 'Sirs,' he said, 'welcome to Caen. There's no bigger city we'll see in this land other than Rouen and Paris. No one has taken this city by storm in one hundred and fifty years, since the days when the French kings fought our valiant ancestors – old Henry and his son the Lionheart. Before the sun sets today, that's going to change.'

Scotsman looked at the western wall of the city. It was

broken with a small gatehouse, some hundred paces distant from where they now stood. 'How many inside?' he asked.

Sir Thomas shrugged. 'Troops? Between the castle garrison and the regular French troops who have been falling back these past two weeks, maybe fifteen hundred. Perhaps two hundred crossbowmen. Genoese.'

Pismire nodded. 'We met a few crossbowmen earlier,' he said. 'But they weren't Genoese.'

'How could you tell?' asked Sir Thomas.

'When they shot at us, they missed,' said Pismire.

Sir Thomas laughed. 'Very good. But Italians are rated too highly. They have the best crossbows, no doubt. But it's not about what you've got, men.' He winked, a strange gesture for a man with an eyepatch, which Loveday felt he must have clung to out of habit from the days when he had two eyes. 'It's about what you do with it.'

Scotsman and Pismire laughed. Loveday felt them warming to this handsome, charming knight. He felt a small twinge of jealousy. But he pushed the thought to the back of his mind. 'How many civilians?' he asked.

Sir Thomas looked surprised that anyone would care. 'I have no idea,' he said. 'Thousands, I would reckon. Every town that has emptied before us on our march has sent its refugees here. But they will cause us no more difficulty than the citizens of Saint-Lô.'

The Earl of Warwick broke away from his discussion with the other knights and strode over. 'Sir Thomas. Have you finished outlining to my friends from Essex here what we plan to do?'

'A thousand apologies, my lord,' said Sir Thomas. 'Not entirely.' He put a hand on Loveday's shoulder, and with the other pointed a metal-gauntleted finger towards the gatehouse. 'As you can see, the good folk of Caen have had enough sense to keep us from easily scaling their walls.' He gestured to recently dug ditches in front of the western wall, which bristled with sharpened stakes driven into the ground. 'As you also know, the castle defends the north-eastern approach.'

'What of the south?' asked the Scot. 'The river doesn't look large. Can we wade it?' He was looking beyond the western gatehouse to the point where the old walls of the city curved around and followed the bank of the first of the two rivers that cut around Caen and its island suburbs.

At this, Warwick took over from Sir Thomas. 'Indeed. The south of the walled part of the city relies on the water for protection. There is a single bridge that crosses it between the walled town and the islands. But if we can see it, so can they. The marshal Bertrand has filled the river around the bridge with every barge and boat available. That's where we will find most of the crossbowmen. It is the most obvious point of attack, and the one that they will fight to the last man to hold.'

'So we are heading there for the assault?' asked Loveday.

Warwick smiled slyly. 'Yes. But not quite by the route you imagine.'

As he spoke a whistle rang out from the gatehouse ahead of them. Warwick, Sir Thomas and the rest of the knights looked at one another. 'Are you ready, boys?' Warwick asked the Dogs.

'We were born ready,' growled the Scot.

Warwick drew his sword. 'Then let's move.'

The small gatehouse Warwick's small group ran towards had been built into the old city walls a very long time ago. Unlike the castle entrance the Dogs had seen earlier, however, this place was in shabby repair. Its stonework was failing. Clumps of grass had invaded the mortar, sprouting in dry, green and tan patches all the way up to the ramparts. And unlike the castle's entrance, it was barred not by thick oaken doors, but by a portcullis: an iron grille, rusty in places, that could be winched open from the inside by a thick rope which wound around a drum turned by a handle.

They did not run all the way up to the gatehouse, but sheltered fifty paces short of it, where a long tethering point and drinking trough for horses stood at an angle. The men crouched low, pressed tight together. Loveday was next to Sir Thomas. The one-eyed knight's hair flowed out from beneath his helmet. It smelled of meat grease.

A few bodies away, Warwick leaned across and spoke in a low tone to Sir Thomas. 'You're sure?' he said.

'You heard the call,' said Sir Thomas. 'They're on the move. Now is the time.'

Warwick looked satisfied, though Loveday could see the muscle in the side of his jaw balled tight.

'Archers,' said Warwick. 'To the sides of this stall. Cover the ramparts. Cover the portcullis. Shoot anyone I tell you to.'

Then he beckoned Pismire and the Scot. 'I need one big bastard and one small one. We have a man inside the town. He's given us the signal. The gatehouse is clear. The troops are falling back to defend the bridge in the south, towards the island. Our man is going to give the portcullis a winch, but if he's spotted, either the citizens will lynch him or the bishop's men will butcher him as a traitor. So he'll start you off, then he'll run for his life.'

'Aye,' said the Scotsman. 'So what are we to do?'

'Once he gives the handle a turn, that portcullis will move up. You're going to hold it. Your mate here is going to squeeze under it, get in there and carry on with the winching. As soon as he's under, we'll rush up and get in there too.' He gave the Scot a hard stare. 'You feeling strong, Scotsman?'

The Scot bridled. 'Stronger than any Englishman I see here.'

'Good,' said Warwick. 'Because if you drop that gate while your friend is rolling under it, he's going to have a hole in his side like the Holy Lance went through it.' He glanced at Loveday. 'Your men up to this?'

Loveday regarded them. His heart was booming in his chest. 'Yes, my lord.'

Darys and Thorp took up position on one side of the horse stalls. Lyntyn stood with an archer Loveday did not know. Tebbe ran to a small shack a few yards away and placed himself next to it. All trained their bows on the gatehouse, waiting for word from Warwick to start loosing off arrows.

Pismire and Scotsman pulled their helmets down tight on their heads, and yanked on the leather cords that laced their coats. 'You trust me?' the Scot said to Pismire.

Pismire eyed him sceptically. 'Not a bit, you hairy, godless cunthound. But I don't see a better option.' He took a deep breath. Then he and the Scot set out at a run towards the gatehouse.

It took them a bare few heartbeats to cover the ground, but for Loveday it seemed like a month.

They reached the gate and pinned their backs against the stone arch that surrounded the portcullis.

Then they waited, glancing nervously through the bars. Very

soon, a short figure appeared, moving daintily. Like a bird. They exchanged a few words. After a couple of seconds the figure skipped away and the portcullis slowly began to move. Loveday had a strange flutter of recognition. But he dismissed it.

The portcullis crept upwards at a painfully slow rate. Loveday wondered whether the birdlike man was trying to open it silently, or was just not strong enough to turn the winch any faster.

The men around Loveday were breathing heavily. Sweaty and impatient. All around Caen, cries and crashes rang out. Loveday could sense Scotsman's frustration from across the fifty paces that separated them.

Loveday scanned behind the portcullis. On top of the gatehouse.

Looked at his archers: Tebbe, Thorp and the Welshmen.

Each of them was taut and focused. Strings drawn and arrows nocked. Waiting for a flash of movement ahead. Or a word from Warwick.

None came.

Loveday watched the grille edge up, and then, when there was barely a finger's space between its iron teeth and the dips in the ground they were leaving, he saw Scotsman put his back to the iron grille, and clamp two great hands on one of its horizontal metal beams. The Scot puffed his cheeks, and prepared to take the strain.

Pismire hopped from foot to foot, waiting his moment. Loveday could see him chattering to the Scot, and turning to hiss instructions through the grille to the invisible figure winching.

Still the portcullis inched upwards, and now Loveday could see the sharp spikes fully emerged from their holes. Slowly, very slowly they rose. Then, when they were less than a single arm's distance from the ground, the winching abruptly stopped.

And Scotsman's face changed colour.

His skin had been well reddened by many days' march in the sun. His cheekbones and forehead had turned tight and pink. But now, as the weight of the portcullis bit into his hands, and every fibre of every muscle in his body engaged at once, his head, face and neck turned purple. Veins sprang out all over him. The huge man let out a roar like a baited bear.

As he did so, Pismire threw himself to the ground, shuffling on his belly sideways through the tiny gap beneath the portcullis's wicked teeth.

'Go!' screamed Warwick, louder than Loveday had ever heard him shout before.

And as one, Loveday, the knights and the other men-at-arms in the little company burst from behind the horse stall, hurtling flat out to the portcullis.

As he ran, Loveday felt his heart leap into his mouth.

Pismire was stuck. His leather overcoat had caught on one of the spikes, and he was wriggling desperately to get free.

Loveday could hear the Scotsman screaming at his friend to move. But Pismire could not. The Scotsman threw back his head and howled.

Loveday's feet pounded across grit and dried mud. Pismire continued to squirm. The Scotsman's forearms looked as though the blood was going to burst out of them.

Then they were there, and each man laid his hands on the portcullis and heaved as though his own life were at stake. The Scotsman alone let go, falling forwards on to his knees and gasping as the dozen or so men behind him wrestled the gate upwards a handspan. Enough for Pismire to be free of its teeth.

Enough for him to scramble to his feet and run to the handle and the winch drum.

He eyed it quickly, then began cranking the handle around. And with a whine and a groan that sounded as if the walls of Caen were being wrenched apart, the portcullis began to move up again.

The archers – Tebbe, Thorp and the Welshmen among them – broke from their covering positions and hurtled forwards to join the company at the portcullis. As they arrived, Warwick's men were dropping, one by one, to the ground, and rolling under the grille.

Loveday was among the first of them. He scrambled on his belly beneath the portcullis, little stones finding their way into his clothing. Dust getting up his nose and into his mouth.

Quickly he was through and back on his feet. He ran over to Pismire to take the other end of the handle on the winch.

But when he was just yards from Pismire, he saw movement flicker from a street to the side of the gatehouse.

A crossbowman stepped out. In a smooth, unhurried motion he trained his weapon on the small Essex man.

Loveday opened his mouth. The crossbowman – dark-haired and clean-shaven, with bushy eyebrows and large nose that bent at a hump in the middle – had an unworried look on his face. The butt-end of the crossbow was pressed into his right shoulder. He wore the same armour as Loveday had seen on the bishops' men earlier.

The round metal stirrup at the front of his bow caught the sun and for a fleeting instant it gleamed.

The crossbowman closed his left eye and sighted. And before Loveday could even yell, he had pulled the trigger.

The man was no more than five paces away from Pismire when he shot.

Pismire had half turned when he sensed the man appear. But in doing so, he presented the crossbowman with a perfect target: his body, front on, protected only by cloth and horsehair.

The crossbowman couldn't miss.

Loveday heard a sound like the click of a key in a lock. The string was released. The bolt, as thick as a man's thumb and tipped with sharp steel, slammed through Pismire's chest.

It knocked him backwards, as though he had been butted by a bull. He hit the ground hard. Where he had let go of the winch handle, the portcullis reversed its upward motion and slammed noisily shut once more.

Everyone froze.

The crossbowman ran.

For an instant, Loveday stood rooted to the spot and stared. Then he dropped to where Pismire lay and held his friend by his shoulders.

'Pismire...' he said. 'Don't—'

But Pismire could not hear him. Loveday had seen this many times before. Too many times to hope that his words would make any difference.

He put his face to his friend's ear and frantically began whispering his paternoster – the only prayer he knew by heart. The gurgling of Pismire's breath told Loveday he was hit through the lung. He was drowning in his own blood.

Before he was even halfway through his prayer, Pismire died in his arms.

18

With Our Lord's help our men won the bridge and thus entered the town... So far our affairs have gone as well as possible, praise be the Lord!

Letter to the Archbishop of Canterbury, 29 July 1346

For a moment he could hear nothing but a sound like the roaring of the sea. From somewhere far away he felt a dragging, as though the saints were lifting his soul from his body through the back of his neck.

As though they were shaking him loose from his earthly self.

But he saw nothing, save grey shapes, drained of colour. Ringed by a pure white light. A light that somehow roared. He knew Pismire had been shot. He thought perhaps that he had been too. That he too was dead.

But then the shape of the light and the roaring sound changed, and his vision grew edges and tones.

And the roaring became a voice he knew.

Up, it was saying. Up. Up.

Up.

It was not angels pulling his soul, but knights and men-at-arms dragging at his clothes. And then he felt a hard blow to the side of his face. The slap of a hand encased in metal, which seemed to loosen a few of his teeth.

He closed his eyes and opened them again. The Earl of Warwick's face was in his. 'He's gone,' he was shouting. 'He's gone. We need you with us. Can you run?'

'Run,' Loveday mumbled numbly.

Warwick shook him, then pushed him roughly in the direction of Sir Thomas Holand, who passed him on to two other pairs of hands. 'Keep him moving,' the earl shouted. 'And for Christ's sake, someone keep an eye on the big fucker.'

Then arms on each of Loveday's started dragging him, forcing his legs into a run. And as he was bundled through the streets of Caen, his senses came back to him. He saw that it was Tebbe and Thorp on either side of him. They pulled him left as they ran. He realized they were helping him to avoid tripping on the body of the crossbowman, which lay face down in the dirt of the street. Five arrow shafts stuck out of his back.

'We got him,' said Thorp, a grim look on his face. 'Are you with us now?'

Loveday swallowed and nodded. He felt as though he might vomit. 'Pismire,' he said. 'I didn't—'

'Come on,' said Thorp, avoiding the subject. 'Let's just try not to lose any more of us.'

Warwick's group stopped at the end of the empty street, where it ran into another that crossed it at right angles. They flattened themselves against the wall of a housefront and waited for instructions.

Sir Thomas looked carefully around the corner. Then, moving stealthily, he disappeared. After a few moments, he came back and reported what he had seen to the rest of the group. He spoke in a low voice.

'This road leads down to the river. It opens into a square. There's a church on the opposite side of it, and beyond that a bridge. They're mobbing it. It's the only way across to the island.'

Warwick quizzed him: 'Who's going over?'

'Everyone,' said Sir Thomas. 'Rich folk, poor folk. Troops, citizens. It's exactly as we thought. They're abandoning the old city. Making a stand on the suburb.'

'Defences?' called Warwick.

'Barricades going up now. Carts, grainsacks. Stuff from the church by the bridge. Whatever they can find.'

'Can we take it?' Warwick asked.

Sir Thomas gave him a mirthless grin. 'Not if you want us all to get out of here alive,' he said. He looked at Loveday. 'Sorry. About your man.' Then he turned back to Warwick. 'We'd be better waiting for reinforcements.'

But as Warwick was considering this, from the back of the group a large figure barged forwards, trailed by two smaller ones.

Scotsman's face was sweat-streaked and filthy. His matted beard and hair were as wild as Loveday had ever seen them. Darys and Lyntyn each hung off one of his arms. He looked mad with exhaustion, rage and grief.

The Scot pushed his way up to Warwick and took hold of a handful of the earl's tabard with his right hand. Warwick's knights, hands on sword hilts, stepped forwards but Warwick – unfazed by the Scot, despite his enormous size – warned them back.

'We've just lost one of our best men,' he growled at Warwick. 'I'm not waiting for any fucking reinforcements. The cunt who killed my friend is behind those barricades—'

Warwick shook his head. 'The cunt who killed your friend, my man, is already dead.'

Scotsman eyeballed the earl. He nodded, conceding the point. Then he said: 'But his friends aren't.' He breathed heavily through his nose. 'With your permission, *my lord*, I'm going to storm that bridge my fucking self and take down every French bastard I can before they get me. I'd be glad of some support. But Christ be my witness, I don't give a wet fuck at Whitsun whether you're behind me or not.'

He let go of Warwick's tabard, but did not take a step back. Warwick smiled. He looked at the Scot for what felt like a very long time. Then he spoke quietly. 'That's the spirit. The devil take the reinforcements.' He glanced at the group of knights, who seemed uncertain at this turn of events. 'We've been in this godless country a long while, men. Shining our helmets and burning down undefended villages. This man thinks we should finally roll the dice and attack.'

He looked around his men again. Held Loveday's gaze briefly. 'We can wait here until word and men arrive from the king, telling us our young prince is coming down here to command the siege of the barricades. Or we can break them down before they're finished. But we must all agree.'

A smile was creeping over a few of his knights' faces. Loveday saw now why these men had been chosen as Warwick's closest comrades. Sir Thomas spoke up: 'Let's do it, my lord. Let's give the chroniclers something to write about.'

Warwick nodded, pleased. Then he said, 'Archers, get ready to cause havoc. We're going to need cover. And perhaps a miracle.'

★ ★ ★

Loveday peered around the corner and down the street that led to the square. He squinted hard. He could see the bridge across the river that Sir Thomas had mentioned. It was narrow, and had caused a jam of bodies, with the last groups of panicked civilians trying to press over it while garrison troops dragged what they could to barricade it. A large, pretty church at the near end of the bridge had clearly been stripped of anything useful. Ornate wooden chairs were upended on top of other pieces of debris.

A few crossbowmen were in position behind the barricades, scanning the streets of the old town. But the lack of attention paid by the knights and ordinary troops who were building the barricade told Loveday that the presence of Englishmen in the town was not yet known.

Warwick gave the archers their instructions. He divided them into two groups. The Welshmen were in one, Tebbe and Thorp were in another.

To the first group, Warwick said: 'Find buildings with windows or rooftops overlooking the square. Get high and shoot down. Aim for civilians around the bridge. Shoot fast, but don't kill if you can help it. We want panic, not a pile of bodies.'

Then the earl turned to the other group of archers: 'Spread out. Once the civilians start falling, pick off the crossbowmen. We need them all down. Kill if you can. Don't stop shooting until there's nothing coming back.'

He looked around the rest of the men. 'We hold our position here, until the crossbowmen are dealt with,' he said. 'Then we attack the barricades. We don't go before it's clear. You got that, big fellow?' The Scot grimaced.

Loveday saw Pismire flying backwards. Felt the breath rattling out of him. He blinked hard.

timbers and sacks, all stacked as high as a man's head. In front of this makeshift defence, a crossbowman was slumped as if sitting to rest. An arrow was buried halfway to the fletchings in his left eye socket. A few paces away a woman lay writhing and whimpering. Her long skirts were black with blood, and her hair was plastered to her face. Two arrows were buried in her left hip.

When they were twenty paces away from the barricade, a head popped up behind it. A young man, perhaps a squire. Loveday saw him rise, and was about to drop to the ground. In case he raised a crossbow.

But if he had a weapon, he never had a chance to raise it. From somewhere high, behind Loveday's right shoulder, two arrows flashed through the air. The first grazed the young man's ear. The second lodged in his throat.

It could only have been Darys and Lyntyn. He felt a surge of pride.

Loveday did not turn to see where the Welshmen were shooting from. Nor did he check his run. He heard Sir Thomas yell behind him: 'Keep going!'

He saw Warwick take the lead of the group. The earl, running as fast as Loveday had ever seen anyone move in heavy armour, threw himself right down to the base of the barricade. He called the rest of the men to do the same.

They all scrambled there, sitting with their backs to the pile of detritus, breathing hard. They were now just a few paces from whatever troops were in place on the other side.

Loveday guessed that, on that side, Frenchmen were sitting just like him. Hearts racing. Knowing that the next hour would bring the agony and horror of wounding or death, or the exhilaration of living. He looked at Scotsman's dirt-streaked face. 'What now?' he mouthed.

Sir Thomas caught the silent words. He leaned over and whispered. 'We wait for them to do the wrong thing. It won't be long. They won't be able to help themselves.' He glanced to Warwick, who put a leather-and-metal-covered finger to his lips. Then he craned his neck and looked up, above himself and backwards, to the top of the barricade.

Loveday wiped his damp palms on his thighs and glanced right. He saw the door to the church, which was slightly ajar, move fractionally. It was such a small movement that he wondered if he had imagined it. But he knew he had not. He nudged Sir Thomas, and gestured with his two forefingers over to the church.

Someone. In there. Do we go to them?

Sir Thomas acknowledged the signal, but he shook his head. With his own fingers, he pointed out three buildings across the square from them.

The archers. Up there. Trust them to cover us.

So Loveday did not move. But he kept his eyes on the church door. Concern was tightening in his chest.

Just as he was about to implore Sir Thomas for a second time to take action, there was a loud creak behind their heads. And another. And a third. Loveday realized what was happening.

French troops were climbing the barricade. They were trying to do it stealthily. But they were making a poor job of it.

Warwick had moved from a seated position into a crouch on his heels. He adjusted his grip on his sword. Loveday did likewise. The Scot turned his axe in his hands.

Behind them the creaking stopped. There was a moment's

silence. And then, with bloodcurdling yells of *Saint Denis!* from over the barricade leapt about half a dozen French troops.

And then half a dozen more.

And then half a dozen *more*.

And Loveday could have laughed, because to a man, the troops all ran instinctively forwards, not thinking to turn and look behind them, at the barricade where the English knights now stood.

He could have laughed even harder as the archers, still embedded in their sniping posts, began sending well-placed shots aimed at groins and chests, and all the soft, undefended parts of the French troops, who wore metal helmets and breastplates, but leather on their limbs.

But Loveday did not laugh. For, within a few heartbeats, the storm of arrows had turned the French around, and they saw to their surprise where Warwick's company was.

Loveday gripped his sword handle with both hands, so tightly he thought the knuckles would pop through his skin.

The Scotsman lofted his great axe above his huge ginger head and bellowed.

And the two groups charged at one another.

The French had lost three or four men to arrow shot. But they still outnumbered the English.

A man half a head shorter than Loveday, with a long drooping moustache that wobbled at the sides of his lips like a carp's barbels, picked Loveday out and strode towards him, swinging a sword longer than Loveday's.

Loveday braced. Instinct kicked in. He watched the man's sword, and the man's eyes. And when the man attacked, Loveday took a half-step left, dropped his left shoulder, then rolled under the swing of the man's blade.

As he moved up, he transferred his weight to his right, pivoting off the ball of his right foot, and drove his sword upwards in an arc from his hip to his shoulder, aiming the tip at the man's left armpit, undefended by armour and which the man had left exposed.

His opponent was a brave fighter. But not a smart one. Loveday felt the blade sink in a few inches. Not a lethal wound, but painful. The man howled. Loveday pulled the sword back out, then bent his knees and powered forwards with his left shoulder, aiming squarely for the man's midriff. He hit him hard. Felt all the air blow out of his lungs.

He dropped him to the floor, knelt on his chest, yanked his head back by his long moustaches and cut his throat.

He rolled off, stood up, and backed away to the barricade to catch his breath. He had blood in his eyes. He did not know if it was his or not. He looked again at the church door. It now hung wide open. Whoever had been there was gone.

He wiped his eyes on his sleeve, feeling the blood sticky across his cheeks. Before he knew it the next man was on him.

This one was bigger. He came at Loveday with a short pike, the shaft about Loveday's own height, and the wicked point protruding another arm's length or so.

He was a more talented fighter than the man Loveday had just killed. And he knew how to use a pike. He kept his body side-on, the pike held in two hands. He moved his feet like a maypole dancer. Small movements, but they kept the stabbing motion of the pike's head unpredictable. It prodded forwards at Loveday's gut. Loveday too adopted a sideways stance, trying to present as small a target as possible.

Yet he was aware that he was no waif. And as the pikeman advanced, Loveday found himself wrongfooted and edged backwards. He tried to move left and right, but the pikeman was pushing him towards the barricade, where he would have no more room for evasion.

Loveday kept his sword shouldered. He had not tested it, save in the first man's armpit and throat. He did not entirely trust it. And he had no wish to see the blade shattered on the pike shaft. He continued to weave backwards. The pikeman continued to stab. He had a crooked leer on his face and taunted Loveday in French. Loveday did not understand the words, but he could guess what they meant.

He was just a couple of paces from the barricade.

Out of the corner of his eye he saw the Scot. The big man was fighting with the axe in his weaker left hand, and using the raw strength of his right arm as a second weapon. Loveday kept watching the pike-head, but he glimpsed the Scot shatter a squire's nose with a forwards blow from his elbow.

The Scot turned to another opponent: a knight. He aimed the axe left-handed at the knight's chest, using the flat of the blade and the power of his weight transferred from foot to axe-head to knock the man to his arse. He kicked the knight hard in the head, knocking his helmet crooked so he could not see.

Then, momentarily putting both hands on the axe handle, he raised it high and swung it down, severing the knight's left leg halfway up the thigh.

The crunch was sickening, and the scream from within the French knight's twisted helmet was horrifying. Loveday momentarily imagined what he was suffering – a world of suffocating blackness, smelling and tasting only of leather and iron. And the indescribable pain of a leg cleaved like a log.

But Loveday could not dwell on this. The pikeman jabbed

again. And now Loveday was fully backed up against the barricade.

He shouted, as loud as he could: 'Scotsman!'

The pikeman thrust, and Loveday swerved backwards, only just avoiding being speared in the gut. He banged the back of his head on a chair leg poking out from the barrier.

He winced. He saw himself dead. He smelled very intensely the stink of his own sweat and the blood that smeared his face. He watched the pike-head and waited for it to pierce him.

Then the pikeman made a mistake.

Too excited by having nearly gored Loveday, he tried the same thrust again.

Had their roles been reversed, Loveday knew what he would have done. He would have aimed for the feet, sent his trapped opponent off balance, then gone back up for a fatal dig through the stomach.

But the pikeman did not do that. So as the second thrust came towards him, Loveday dropped his sword, stepped towards the pikeman, and in the same movement clamped both his hands around the shaft of the pike and pulled as though he were in a tug-of-war. The yank he gave the pike doubled the power of the pikeman's thrust. It drove the heavy metal tip of the weapon into the barricade behind him, and with enough force that the spearhead lodged firmly in the wood of an old door.

The pikeman stumbled forwards but stayed on his feet. He looked startled, as though he had not thought this possible. Loveday did not delay. Using the momentum of the pull he had given the spear, Loveday freed his hands, and took two paces forwards, so he was close enough to smell the pikeman's breath. Then he brought his right fist in a scything, looping punch over his shoulder and as hard as he could into the Frenchman's face.

He felt the man's nose shatter.

He felt bones break in his right hand.

He felt alive, as he had not felt in many years.

And he watched as the pikeman released his grip on the weapon and staggered backwards, stunned by the blow. His nose was smeared all over his face, split at the bridge and pumping out blood, which already stained his teeth.

The pikeman grunted in pain.

Loveday jumped as hard and fast as he could away from him. For as the man staggered backwards, he saw the Scot stepping up behind him, axe primed to swing above his right shoulder.

Loveday tripped and, on the ground, rolled away in the dirt, so that he was on his back as the Scot swung the axe through a perfect semi-circle, landing one of its sharp edges at the nape of the pikeman's neck. The blade went through the neckbone, the flesh and the throat. And it came all the way out the other side. The head flew off, tumbled once in the air and landed by Loveday's face, so that they were almost nose to nose.

Its eyes seemed to widen hugely, then the eyelids fluttered closed.

Loveday scrambled back, and stared at the Scotsman.

'I've never seen that before,' said the Scot. Gouts of blood from the pikeman's neck had covered him from chest to shin.

Loveday sucked in air and nodded. 'I thought we'd seen enough of severed heads,' he said.

He picked up his sword, and he and the Scot stood shoulder to shoulder, scanning the melee for the next fight.

Three of Warwick's knights and men-at-arms lay dead or dying in the dirt. But far more of the French had fallen, felled by the snipers as they struggled with the English.

'Let's help finish this,' said Loveday. He pointed to Sir Thomas, who was fighting a man-at-arms around his own size, the two men exchanging sword blows that glanced off their plate armour. The Scot launched himself towards the French knight, swung his axe at his ankle, shattering the bone so that the man-at-arms collapsed sideways, screaming in pain.

Sir Thomas, fighting with the visor of his helmet pulled up, looked surprised to see them. 'Thank you, sirs,' he said. He kicked the man-at-arms in the head, and spat on him. Then he looked sharply to his left. 'Saints' bones,' he said.

The barricade was creaking again. Sir Thomas squinted towards the buildings on the other side of the square. Smoke was billowing from the windows where the archers had been. They were burning their sniping houses.

'They've run out of arrows,' he said. He looked back at the barricade. Another wave of French knights was coming over it. 'Time to get out of here.'

The Scot shook his head. 'I came to take that fucking barricade,' he said. 'We do it, or we die trying.'

Sir Thomas shook his head. 'You can die trying,' he said. 'I'm going to die in bed with my wife. God bless you, men.' He looked down at the man-at-arms with the shattered ankle. 'That was most Christian of you.'

But as he started to leave, from the direction of the old town there came a blast from a trumpet. Into the square rode the Earl of Northampton, with Prince Edward alongside him.

Romford was riding just behind the prince.

And at their backs, emerging from every street in the old town, came hundreds of English troops, brandishing clubs, scythes, swords, pikes, burning torches and every other conceivable weapon, and chanting war songs.

As they pressed into the square, they began to run, pelting towards the barricade, and sending the French who had begun to clamber over it scrambling into retreat back across the bridge. The few French who remained in combat with Warwick's knights were grabbed and butchered where they stood.

Sir Thomas, Scotsman and Loveday were pushed aside as hundreds of hands began to pull at the barricade, tugging it to pieces in a frenzy.

Northampton, sitting on a huge piebald destrier, wore a grin as wide as his ears. 'My noble friend Lord Warwick,' he called above the din of the troops. 'We bring you a message from the king, to be delivered by his son.'

He leaned over in his saddle and clapped the prince on the shoulder. 'Go on then, you little fucker,' he said.

Prince Edward sat up straight in his saddle. 'My father says we must halt this premature attack forthwith,' he called, his voice squeaking. 'He has massed our forces on the south side of the island, and insists we co-ordinate our attack from both sides at once.'

Northampton patted him on the shoulder. 'Very good,' he said. 'Delivered with a lot of gravitas.' He winked at Warwick. 'How do you reckon our chances of calling off this band of fucking ne'er-do-wells and waiting for our official invitation to join a carefully planned assault from both ends of the suburb?' He gestured with his head towards the barricade, where English troops were already halfway through the barrier, the mob passing the debris backwards over their heads, and leaping up to swipe with their weapons at any French hands or faces that appeared over the top of it.

Warwick tried to wipe sweat from his face with an armoured hand. 'Not good, my lord.' He smiled back.

'Aye,' said Northampton. 'Not fucking good at all.'

He turned once more to the prince. 'Go and find a drink somewhere. Leave this to the men. We'll pass on your apologies to your father.'

He rode forwards, and leaned in to Warwick. Loveday was standing close enough to hear what he said. 'What in the name of St Beatrice's fucking nipple-rings has been going on here?'

Warwick shrugged. 'The heat of battle,' he said. 'We took a chance.'

Northampton eyed him sideways. Screams at the bridge told them the barricade had fallen, and the English troops were about to breach the island's defences. On the far side of the city, something heavy fell from the castle tower.

'A chance?' he said to Warwick. 'A chance is letting out a fart at the king's table while the chaplain is saying grace.'

He took a look around the streets, littered with French bodies and thronging with marauding Englishmen.

'I'd say you boys just got very fucking lucky.'

PART 3

BLOOD

31 July–26 August 1346

19

The army stayed in Caen for six days, and the spoils which had been seized up to then from the towns and the countryside... were sold to or through the sailors, who had been following the king off-shore and destroying all the naval defences of the French.

The Chronicle of Geoffrey le Baker

Five Days Later

'Throw it in.'

Loveday met Scotsman's sombre gaze. He looked at the chaplain, who nodded gently.

He bent slowly, painfully, and picked up a handful of the warm soil, flecked with sand and gravel, which the Dogs had spent the day digging from the corner of the little churchyard.

He used his left hand. After the battle at the bridge, his right was a swollen, throbbing mess. Merely bending his fingers brought tears to his eyes. The flesh from his forearm to his knuckles was mottled violet and black. A hard lump bulged in the back of the hand. One of Warwick's physicians, a sober man called Jordan, had confirmed what Loveday knew. The bones were broken and would take weeks to heal.

Using his left hand felt awkward. Some of the dirt slipped

through his fingers. But he tossed what he could into the hole. The Scot threw in a handful. Tebbe and Thorp did likewise. None of them had seen the Welshmen for days.

The soil dusted the linen cloth in which Pismire's body lay wrapped.

The chaplain cleared his throat. 'He is with God.'

Scotsman snorted. 'No he fucking isn't. Nor will any of us ever be. Save your pieties for halfwits and the bairns.'

The chaplain cleared his throat again. 'Would anyone like to speak for this man?'

Loveday looked around the little group. Tried to catch each of their eyes. Neither of the archers had anything to say.

He took a deep breath. 'He was one of us, and he chose this life,' he said. 'He wanted the same thing as we all want. To fight, to earn, to survive, to go home. I wish to God that—' He stopped himself. 'You all know Pismire was our friend and our brother. We rode with him. And now we mourn him.'

There were a few moments of studied silence. The chaplain bowed his head respectfully, although Loveday realized he had probably heard more eloquent eulogies in his time.

Then Scotsman used his boot to shift a larger pile of sandy soil into the grave. Tebbe and Thorp joined in, and soon Pismire's shroud was covered. Before long there was nothing to see of him at all, save dim contours in loose, scattered earth.

The chaplain watched them work, but Loveday felt him growing impatient. He walked up beside his archers and murmured to them. 'We'll finish later.'

Then he nodded to the chaplain, who led the four Dogs in a tiny procession to the second hole that they had dug that morning.

It had the same dimensions as Pismire's grave: a man's height long and a man's height deep. Beside it was the pile of cut turf and spoil they had removed. They all stared to the bottom of the hole, at the second corpse, bound tight in stolen linen.

The chaplain crossed himself, and began to sing in reedy Latin.

The Dogs lowered their eyes and listened.

It was time to say goodbye to Father.

When it was done, and the sun was going down, they found a tavern beside the river at the northern side of the island, looking back at the old town.

The tavern's Norman owner had survived the sack – or else fled but quickly returned to take advantage of the army's passing trade.

The old man served wine and ale from a wall-hatch, while English troops lounged outside at wooden tables, or sat on the ground. Three young girls, all with the same high foreheads and jet-black hair as the owner, flitted nervously around the groups, refilling mugs and extracting what payment they could from the drinkers.

Order was kept by a pair of large men-at-arms wearing royal livery. They leaned lazily against the side of the tavern, but their eyes flicked constantly around the drinkers.

The royal proclamation that ended the sack had been clear. Military law was back in force. Those who disturbed the king's peace would face flogging, amputation or hanging. Those citizens who were still alive and prepared to work did so under royal protection. That protection was especially extended to bakers, innkeepers, alewives and whores.

An army at rest needed certain tradespeople to keep it happy.

The four Dogs sat in silence on stools at a table outside the tavern, and Tebbe poured wine from a blue-glazed pitcher. They could see the towers of the castle in the distance: the last part of Caen that was holding out against the English troops. Each was thinking the same thing.

Finally, Thorp spoke. 'Do you think he was—'

'Who knows?' snapped the Scot. 'He was either dead when he hit the ground, or straight after. What difference does it make?'

Thorp looked wounded. 'Christ on the Cross, Scotsman. I don't like thinking about it either.'

'So why are we talking about it?' said the Scot. 'It's done. And it's simple. It's our fault. Loveday and I walked Father into the arms of that depraved French fucker up in the castle. The bishop locked him up, he most likely tortured the poor old fucker, and when he got sick of him, and he realized our army was burning this shithole down, he threw him off the top of that tower.'

Scotsman jabbed a finger at the corner of the castle. 'Off there. Top to bottom, with a big fucking thud at the end. If Warwick's men hadn't recognised him, we wouldn't even have been able to bury the bastard.'

He picked up his cup angrily, drained it in one, and slammed it down. Tebbe, Thorp and Loveday stared at the table. The Scotsman refilled his cup, then topped the others' until they were brimming over.

'Pismire,' he said. 'Dead. Father. Dead. The lad – up to God knows what with that little fool of a prince. Millstone? Probably dead, since we've seen nothing of him for a week, and he's now a fucking outlaw. No sign of those Welsh fuckers, although they're likely up to their balls in one of the brothels. Good luck getting Sir Robert to stump up their forty days.'

He stared at Loveday, accusation suddenly burning in his eyes. 'How many times did you blab to us about sticking together, staying alive, getting paid, doing what the fucking Captain always taught us?'

Loveday nodded. 'I know,' he said, quietly. 'It wasn't meant to be this way.'

The Scotsman looked off, back towards the castle. 'Ah, Christ's bones,' he said. 'It's a war. What did we expect? I just wish they'd hurry up and take that castle. I want to see that fucking bishop ripped apart by dogs.'

'We all do,' said Loveday. 'But it'll take time. It's the only bit of the city that didn't fall. The Bertrand brothers and however many crossbowmen they have in there could sit behind those walls for two months. And we'll probably be marching out of here tomorrow. All we can do is try and keep the rest of us alive. Find Millstone. Get Romford back. Track down the Welshmen, if they're even still here.'

He raised his cup, and motioned for the others to do the same. They all drained them. The pitcher on the table was empty.

'I'll go,' said Loveday, and stood up to take it to be refilled by the old man at the hatch.

A warmth was spreading out from his stomach. It dulled a little of his sadness. It eased the throbbing in his right hand.

The English army had been camped in Caen for five days, since the town fell. The sack, as always, had been evil.

Loveday, Scotsman and the archers had gone over the bridge

into the suburb with the first wave. They had arrived in time to see King Edward's huge force – thousands of spearmen and archers, driven forwards by knights and men-at-arms – wading waist-deep into the river, overwhelming the line of French and Genoese crossbowmen stationed on barges. Many of the French had their throats slit on deck. Even more were dragged into the river and drowned in the shallow water.

After that, the thousands of citizens and refugees crammed on to the island were as helpless as newborn mice. Some fought, throwing rocks and timbers from the upper storeys of the higher houses until they were smoked out or shot by sharp-eyed archers. Others were robbed of all they owned. And, of course, Loveday had seen hundreds slaughtered. A single image burned in his mind: a pregnant mother with a babe-in-arms, gored by a wild northern pikeman and her baby tossed in the river to drown. When order had eventually been restored, royal engineers dug long trenches in the fields outside the city. Bodies were stacked in them like fire-logs, with no religious rites and no difference made between rich and poor.

They were only buried to get rid of their stink.

Loveday drummed the fingers of his left hand on the table, as Thorp went to fill yet another wine pitcher. Why was it, he thought, that he found it so hard to remember clearly the good things that he had seen in his life? His children's faces, when they had been happy and living? The scent of his wife's hair in spring after she had washed it for the first time in weeks?

Now he would never know those things again, they were fading from his mind. Yet war and robbery had given him memories that he would keep until the Day of Judgement.

What was it the woman from Valognes had said to him? That she was going to Caen, or Rouen, or Paris...

Or to hell. Perhaps I will see you in one of those places, when your prince and his father lead you there.

Perhaps, he thought, I am in hell already.

The wine was softening the lines and edges of his vision. He scanned the crowds spilling out around the tavern, wondering if he would see her face, with the ragged hair cropped by his knife.

He saw no one who even remotely resembled her.

He drained another cup. Tebbe, Thorp and Scotsman were laughing and joking now. Tebbe was telling a long, bawdy joke concerning a greedy bishop who found a magic ring that gave him a permanent erection. Loveday had heard it before, but he laughed along at the right moments. Scotsman went for more wine. Loveday wasn't sure if it was their fourth or fifth. Tebbe finished the joke. Scotsman came back to the table with tears of mirth running down his dirty cheeks.

As he did so, he almost bumped into a stocky, thickly bearded sailor, who was approaching their table out of the crowd. Some of the wine sloshed out of the jug and Scotsman bridled. But the sailor raised his hands in apology.

'No offence meant,' he said. And Scotsman, soft with drink, sat down heavily on his stool. The sailor remained standing, and placed his hands on the table. He had thick black hair on forearms nearly twice the size of Loveday's.

'Name's Gombert.' He nodded a greeting around the table.

Loveday raised his glass. 'To you, Gombert.' He drank half his cup. 'What do you want with us?'

Gombert crouched beside them. 'I'm with the fleet. We've had our orders from the earls. We've burned every port along the coast, and all their ships too. The only way a Frenchman is getting to England in the next twelve-month is if he fucking swims. We're done. So we're going back to England this week. Tomorrow, with the afternoon tide, most like.'

Thorp eyeballed him, swaying slightly. 'And?'

'And,' said Gombert, 'I'll pay you for anything you want to sell. You boys look like you must have done well out of the last few weeks.'

Loveday nodded. 'We took our share.'

'Well,' said Gombert. 'You know how it works. I'll pay silver for your share tonight. You bring it down to the dock. We'll ferry it by moonlight to the seaport at Ouistreham. No need for you to cart it all around any further. You'll have coin in your purses for more of this...' He picked up the wine jug, which was already half-empty. '... and you won't be peasant-broke until the end of your forty days, or whenever it is your tightwad commander reaches into his hose and pulls your wages out of his arsehole.'

Gombert winked at the archers. But Loveday felt his stomach twist. He realised he could not remember how many of their forty days had now gone by. Only Pismire had been able to keep count. Gombert went on: 'I can't promise to make you as rich as Old One-Eye Tommy Holand just became.' He smiled around the table. 'But we can strike a fair bargain.'

The four Dogs looked at each other and shrugged. The sailor's offer made sense. They had heard a rumour that the admiral of the fleet, Lord Huntingdon, was preparing to leave whenever the army turned inland. And it was usual in war that when the fleet left, the sailors bought up plunder to trade back in the English markets.

Trying to put Pismire out of his mind, Loveday turned to Thorp. 'We can bring the cart up from the baggage train tonight, can't we?'

Thorp drained his wine, and belched. 'How hard can it be?' he slurred. He stood up and wandered off to piss at the waterfront.

But as he went, a puzzled look crossed Scotsman's face. 'What did you say about Holand?'

Gombert laughed. 'You didn't hear? Old Tom Holand struck gold. He *captured* his old crusading mates. A couple of the French commanders – their constable and some other fucker, I forget the name. Tankard-ville or something.' He raised his eyebrows archly as he said the word 'captured'.

'Tancarville,' said Loveday. 'Chamberlain of Normandy.'

'Aye.' Gombert laughed again. 'Sounds about right. Well, Tankard and his mates were up a tower shitting their breeches, and spotted their pal Holand down below. Sly fucker was trying to get away from the fighting as fast as they were, as I heard it. Anyway, these French cunts call down to him; he recognizes them from some battle they all fought cutting the bollocks off the heathen and rutting with the wives of the Christ-killers down in Spain. They figure they can all come out alive and get paid while they're at it.'

'Alive and paid, eh?' said the Scot. He stared hard at Loveday.

Gombert ignored the beat that passed between them. 'Well, the short of it is, the king has bought Holand's prisoners off him for something like twelve thousand pounds.'

The Dogs' mouths hung open. Thorp returned from his piss. 'What?' he said.

'Crown of Thorns on a dead fucking donkey,' said Scotsman. 'Twelve thousand?' He shook his head, the matted ropes of ginger hair swinging across his face. 'Fucking noblemen. We put our friends in the ground, and they barter theirs for a king's ransom. I wish we'd left that Holand cunt to fend for himself outside the barricade now.'

Thorp looked no wiser for this explanation, but he caught the general drift of the conversation and shrugged. 'Of course. What's new? We do the work, the lords have the fun, and the chroniclers write it up as history. Tell us something we don't know.'

He clapped the sailor on the shoulder. 'Bollocks to it. Gombert, stay here and get drunk. I'll go and get the cart.'

The Dogs sold Gombert everything they had. Rolls of thick, soft red velvet they had taken from a clothmaker. A box of church plate stamped with images of the apostles. Gold brooches set with coloured glass. An incomplete set of carpenter's tools. Five fine silver candlesticks. Father's crucifix. The little songbird Pismire had stolen, which Father had fed grain.

The sun was setting by the time they had unloaded it all beside the flat barge at the docks. The sky away towards the west was slashed orange, pink and dark blue. The barge was just one of dozens that had come upriver to take away the possessions of Caen's citizens and merchants, and the plunder seized before in Valognes, Carentan and Saint-Lô. All around sailors were haggling with troops over the price of loot.

Gombert underpaid them. They didn't care. They didn't sell him their barrels of wine. They filled their purses to bursting with silver coins, some English, others French.

As Gombert was bidding them farewell, Loveday grabbed his arm. 'Take us too,' he said, hearing his words come out thick and slurred, as though he were talking through a mouthful of porridge. 'Help us find Father. Take us home.' But as he spoke he remembered Father was dead, and half his crew was missing. He had lost track of how long he had been in France, and how long he had left. All he knew was that he could not go home.

Gombert didn't seem to mind. 'They all ask that,' he said. And after that, he left. The four Dogs went back to the tavern and drank until it was fully dark, and the owner slammed the hatch and the men-at-arms called curfew.

Then they unrolled their blankets and slept on the ground.

The night was hot and humid. Towards midnight, thunder began rumbling somewhere, a long way to the north.

Loveday tossed and sweated on the warm ground. He dreamed he was walking through a thick wood, painfully thirsty and searching for a drink.

A rain was falling, yet when he put out his hands to catch the water as it dripped from the canopy of leaves and branches above him, his hands began to pool with blood.

He half woke, breathing hard. He was soaked through with sweat. His right hand was throbbing. His head was pounding, too.

He opened his eyes fully, and saw that the stars above lit a few fat clouds. They hung, almost motionless, in the sky. He was desperate for them to open and drench him. To cool him. To wash off everything that clung to him, and everything that had happened.

To make him young again and bring back all the people he had lost.

But no rain fell. And before long, it was morning.

20

Caen is a very large and fine town, and at one end is a very noble abbey where William the Conqueror lies...

Campaign newsletter by Michael Northburgh

The prince rubbed his eyes and yawned loudly. The yawn echoed up into the high vaulted ceiling of a huge abbey church, half lit by candles and thin windows that admitted the breaking dawn. His father, walking several paces in front of him, turned and frowned.

Romford, a few paces behind the prince, locked his gaze on the floor. He knew that, as a squire, he was not allowed to catch the king's eye, even accidentally. To avoid it, he shrank back slightly into the group of squires, knights and other royal attendants. In doing so, he almost trod on the toes of Sir John Chandos, the prince's steward. Chandos hissed and nudged him in the small of his back, to keep him moving. Romford raised his hand quietly in apology. Chandos looked annoyed, but said nothing more. Romford felt, not for the first time, a long way out of his depth.

It had been about a week since he was saved from the rope and sent to follow the Prince. But though he was glad to be alive, nothing that followed had been easy. For one thing, there was just so much to be done to satisfy the needs and the pride of a single young man of his own age. Romford slept on the ground inside a great red-and-green pavilion, with a dozen or so other squires. But they seldom slept for long. They were shaken awake long before dawn each day to start their tasks – many of which were just as menial as Romford had been used to with the Dogs. The squires scrubbed at dirt baked into the cracks and joints of armour. They cleaned and polished anything that would shine – from eating dishes to blood-caked swords. They helped grooms feed and brush impatient horses, and hitched donkeys to carts that carried tools, kit and food. They broke down and put up tents. They made fires and stamped them out. They took turns to dig and fill in the pit that the prince alone was allowed to shit in.

All these things Romford could do. He could even do them while enduring the itch of unfamiliar clothes and the gnawing for powder, which he had been enduring since Sir Robert's men arrested him and took it all away.

But what he found most perplexing – and exhausting – was the subtler side of his new life. The things that looked easy, but were very hard. Things like trying to know where and how he should stand, whom he could and could not look at or speak to. Like working out whether he ought to bow, kneel or walk backwards when some great lord approached the royal presence. No one had ever shown him how to do this, and he knew it was evident in his every move. The other squires were pointedly unhelpful, and Romford felt many of them were outright hostile to him, as an archer among the sons of the well-born. They used French around him, knowing he could not keep up with that strange language, which they all seemed to speak fluently. And they often let him fail and be embarrassed or scolded rather than helping him blend in.

Only the steward, Chandos, treated him with anything like kindness, though Chandos was generally too busy to teach Romford the things he did not know. So Romford felt his life had become a ceaseless dance, in which he was the only one in a group of skilled performers who did not know the steps. He thought from time to time of running away. But that would mean being caught. And being caught would mean the noose.

All he could do was try to survive. One day after the next.

The dance that morning led the prince and his squires along the nave of this huge abbey church on the outskirts of Caen. When they had attacked the city, the prince's troops had smashed the abbey's gates, but found no one inside. Yet as it transpired, there *was* someone inside – a dead man whom the king wanted to visit. Whom he wanted the prince to meet. It was to be their last task before they raised the camp and set off – wherever they might be going next.

The small group was approaching a glossy black marble tombstone sunk into the smooth pavement of the church. When they got there, the king turned, and faced his companions. Then he dropped to his knees dramatically, bent and softly kissed the stone.

To a man, the whole royal entourage fell to their knees too. As usual, Romford was a heartbeat off the pace. But on this occasion, Chandos let him be. They all knelt in silence, watching and listening as the king spoke, his breath misting faintly in the church's early-morning cool.

'My ancestor.' Edward spoke to the tombstone. Though his voice was soft, he was able to project it so the words rose clearly. 'William. Nearly three hundred years ago you fought for your right. Born a bastard, you rose to become a king. You were disparaged and overlooked by your enemies, who thought they could deny you what was yours by right of law and of blood.

'By the purity of faith and believing in the ferocity of your sword and those of your loyal men, you put your trust in God, and put your men on board ships. And you claimed the crown – our crown – the crown of England – on the battlefield.'

There was silence. The king paused. He bent and kissed the tomb for a second time.

'William. You joined Normandy and England as one realm. You gave generously to your friends, and you harried your enemies without mercy. May God grant me the power to do the same.'

He looked briefly at the prince. The young man's eyes were closed.

King Edward raised his voice deliberately. 'May God grant *my son* the strength and wisdom to play his part too.'

The prince opened his eyes and stifled another yawn. 'Amen, Father,' he said. 'Well spoken. Might we now go and eat? We have a long march, and I believe the cooks have been awake all night roasting mutton and beef for us to break our fast on.'

King Edward pursed his lips and studied his son for a moment. No one else dared say a word.

'My son,' said the king, although he was addressing the whole group. 'Do you know what happened when our ancestor was buried beneath this marble slab, here in this church of St Stephen, which he himself had founded?'

'No, Father.' The prince's voice was flat and listless. He sighed.

King Edward nodded his head quietly. 'Then let me educate you. King William had been fighting here in Normandy, when he was thrown from his horse and killed. It happens. This is the way of war. In the time it took for his burial to be arranged, his body bloated. It began to fill with the death vapours. And when he was lowered into this tomb, the hole had been dug too small. His guts ruptured and they burst, releasing clouds of stinking gas and foul liquid. I gather it was quite unpleasant for all concerned.'

The prince screwed up his nose. His father continued.

'Do not look sick. That is the way of all flesh. What matters is that you did not know the story. And the reason you did not, despite my best efforts to have you schooled in history and the arts, as well as trained for combat, is that our ancestor William – through his deeds of arms, his force of personality and his vast conquests – had achieved so much by the time his belly exploded that even this undignified end was soon forgotten by all but the most diligent annalists...

'Do you understand what I am saying?'

The prince nodded, though it seemed to Romford that he was lost.

'You and I,' continued the king, 'have achieved nothing yet. Nothing. We have landed an army and burned some towns. We have taken some prisoners and our men have some trinkets to show their wives. But this is nothing new. The French king is gathering an army at Rouen. His allies – other kings, hundreds of knights, crossbowmen, men-at-arms from across Christendom – are riding to meet him. We face grave danger. You may die here in Normandy, like our ancestor. But unlike our ancestor, should your dead belly burst and release poisonous miasmas that sicken all who smell them, then that, my son, will be the story of you.'

He released the prince from the vice of his gaze and looked around the whole group. 'We are here to make stories that will be told for hundreds of years. What those stories are depends on how we now conduct ourselves. The French pretender Philippe knows we are coming to take what is ours by right and blood.

'He and his men cannot run and hide in towers much longer. A reckoning is coming. God will decide if it is for him or for us. And men will tell one another what happened here long after we are all cold beneath marble tombs like this.

'Anyone who yearns for mutton may leave my presence now and enjoy it. But I intend to saddle my horse and ride. We go next to Rouen. The greatest city in Normandy. The false French king is heading there too.' Edward bent and kissed William the Conqueror's tombstone one last time. 'It is time to show him who we really are.'

The army began the march out of Caen at mid-morning. Romford rode among the prince's entourage. And as they left Caen behind, his mood finally started to brighten a little. True, he was still alone and often confused. But while they moved he could at least enjoy the new sensation of a horse and a soft saddle underneath him.

What was more, he looked fine – finer than he had ever done before. His legs were clad in tight hose, and though they itched, the colourful stripes that ran down them were undeniably handsome. He admired the way they hugged the muscular curve of his thighs. Likewise, though his boots pinched at the toe and chafed at the heel, the leather was expensive and his feet were dry. And his tunic, dyed bright green and red, trimmed with squirrel fur, was the finest garment he had ever worn.

Around him, the other squires in the company were identically dressed. A newcomer would not have seen anything to mark him out from them. There was nothing different, he thought, but what was in his head.

As his horse trotted, Romford listened to the prince chattering away to Chandos and the other knights beside him. He spoke boldly, gleefully aware that there was no one close by to check him. The road that led east away towards Rouen took them inland on to a wide plain, and the open countryside had given the army a chance to spread out. That meant the king, Warwick and Northampton were all far away, out of earshot.

'Of course, when we have taken Rouen and Normandy falls, my father will give me the duchy for my own. And then the simpletons here will find out what discipline really looks like. When I put a noose around a rebel's neck, it doesn't come off until they're cut down from the scaffold.'

Romford's toes curled inside his boots.

The prince carried on, tossing his hair as he spoke. 'I told my father we should have hanged every one of those rebels in Valognes – especially that scrawny bitch. But of course Father imagines these peasants respect *mercy* – tell me, Chandos, when has mercy ever won a man a war?'

Sir John Chandos pursed his lips, but did not disagree.

'In any case, I think even Father now accepts the time for lenience is past. You heard about the papers they discovered in the royal lodge in Caen?' He did not wait for a response. 'The Normans have been committed by treaty for the last eight years to supporting a full invasion of England, with the Duke of Normandy to be crowned king! You might have thought Sir Godefroi would have mentioned that, though what does one expect when we are in league with a traitor?

'Meanwhile we're expected to piss around on our knees watching Father slobber all over the tomb of a man who managed exactly that! I think if he could have lifted the tombstone, he would have stuck his tongue down the Bastard's throat.

'Between you and me, Chandos, I wonder if Father is losing his grip – he is not yet ancient, of course, but he surrounds himself with men like that horrible Northampton – and of course the traitor... Let us hope it is true that Hugh Hastings has landed with our second army in Flanders – I know his family has not always been highly favoured, but Hugh has been...'

Romford's attention wandered at the mention of so many names he did not know and places he had not been. He looked around the countryside. Something was moving far away to his left. He strained his eyes and made it out. Away from the road, on the northern edge of the plain, a lone rider was galloping bareback, head close to the neck of his horse, arms wrapped around the beast's neck.

Heading away from Caen. Across the open countryside.

The rider was about a mile away. Yet something about him looked familiar.

Romford squinted. At distance, he could make out little. All the same, he felt certain he had seen this person before.

No one else in the group seemed to have noticed. They were all listening dutifully to Prince Edward's monologue.

'Sir John...' Romford called forwards to Chandos. The knight turned to him, surprised. He narrowed his eyes. Chandos was around ten years older than Romford and the prince. He was immaculately dressed and straight-backed in his saddle. His exceptionally wide jaw was covered in a long and densely curled brown beard, which began high up his face, right at the top of his cheekbones. His mouth rested naturally in a slight grimace, yet there was something light and lively in his gaze.

Chandos turned and raised a hand to the prince, who momentarily stopped talking to draw breath. 'Yes, squire, what is it?'

Romford looked again at the rider, who was now overtaking them. 'Sir, that horseman,' he said. 'I...'

Chandos tilted his head quizzically. Then he shielded his eyes against the high sun and looked into the distance, where the rider was galloping steadily. He then looked over his left shoulder.

Romford and several of the other squires around him did likewise. They saw a group of four or five mounted English troops, lightly armoured, giving chase from the direction of Caen.

The prince was now irritated at having lost his audience. He leaned in his saddle and slapped Chandos on the arm.

Chandos ignored him, and kept watching the rider. He was outpacing his pursuers. Barring a fall, there was no hope of him being caught. As Chandos watched, he spoke to Romford. 'Well sighted, boy. You want to give chase too?' He smiled. The other squires laughed. One or two of them made what Romford assumed were sly comments, in French.

Romford felt his face redden. 'No sir. I just thought... Something about the rider.'

Chandos shrugged. 'Don't worry. An escapee from the castle, perhaps. Or a messenger. He will be riding to Rouen to warn the French king that we are coming.'

The Prince puckered up his face. 'The *false king*,' he pouted.

Chandos smiled indulgently at him. 'Quite so, my lord. Forgive me.'

He turned back and addressed Romford. 'It happens. But our march is no secret. The *false* king' – he glanced at the prince – 'may be disheartened to hear we are moving. He will not be surprised. But well spotted, boy. You have a sharp eye.'

Romford flushed again, this time with pride. Yet inside, he was nagged by the sense that he knew the rider. Something about his bearing. It made him think of Loveday, though he could not think why.

Romford wondered if he would ever see the Dogs and their thickset leader again. They had made him one of their own. Drawn him into their group. Fed him and protected him.

Now he did not even know if they were alive.

Ahead the prince had taken up his chattering once again. He was talking of a second English army arriving from the north, of commands sent to England for the common folk to pray for the success of their campaign, of the immense number of people who would be hanged and beheaded and sent to the fire once he was in personal command of Normandy.

Of the days when he would take his father's place as king.

He spoke of some difficult legal case concerning the legality of a marriage between his cousin, a girl he called Joanie, and a knight Romford had heard of before, by the name of Holand. The prince made lewd remarks about Joanie's figure and her chastity. Compared her breasts at length with those of the woman from Valognes.

Chandos and the other knights and squires in the little company half listened and made respectful noises at the right moments, glossing over the vulgarities as they could.

Effortlessly, they performed the dance Romford was struggling so hopelessly to learn.

And so they whiled away the time as the English army crossed the plain east of Caen, then followed the road down into salt marshes, and traversed a boggy river called the Dives.

By the time they got there, the sun was low, and Romford was saddle-sore and very tired. Yet he could not rest. Chandos set him to work with the other squires. He did everything without complaint, even when he had to guess what he was meant to do.

Finally, at nightfall, the camp was made and they stopped. The squires ate only once the lords were finished, served what was left over from the prince's table. Yet the fare was spectacularly good: mutton and beef, and a young deer served with its heart roasted and its liver fried, and sweet egg custards. It was rich and delicious. Far better than the stews Millstone and the Scotsman cooked, Romford thought, although he immediately felt guilty and disloyal.

After they ate, they drank young French wine, which was sweet on the tongue and warmed Romford's body from his toes to the roots of his hair.

And while they drank, sitting around the campfire outside the pavilions, some of the squires played a game of cross and pile. It was the same game Tebbe and Thorp had taught him the night he had first found the powder. The only difference was that the squires flipped coins instead of scallop shells.

For the whole week that he had been with the prince, Romford had always been excluded from activities like this. Yet tonight – whether it was the novelty of a new camping spot, or simply a sign that he was beginning to show that he might one day learn the steps of the dance – one group of squires invited Romford to join them.

When they asked, he tried to be gracious and calm, although inside he was so glad he almost wept. However, he also remembered that it was dangerous for him to play games of chance with strange men. So when he joined the group he tried to lose as often as he could. Yet by the time they all curled up in their blankets to sleep, his purse was full of silver pennies and he had made himself known among the prince's retinue as a gambler.

This was a mixed blessing. As he played, and won, and impressed his fellow squires, he felt happy. He was at home with his new companions at last, and they seemed to treat him with acceptance, and put him at his ease.

But there would be many days in the remainder of his life when he wondered if ingratiating himself with Prince Edward's retinue had really been a good idea.

21

When [Edward] came to the city of Lisieux, he met two
cardinals of the Lord Pope, who had been robbed of twenty
horses by Welshmen.

Eulogium chronicle, by the anonymous monk of Malmesbury

The day's march across the plain outside Caen was painful.
All four Dogs had woken cold and hungover from their
night on the ground. Stiffness stayed in their legs all day.

They found Sir Robert in spiteful mood. They had avoided
him in Caen, but he had not forgotten the humiliation Loveday
had earned him from Warwick and Northampton. Briefing the
company leaders, he let them know that the army was heading
to hunt down the French pretender at Rouen, via a town called
Lisieux. But as he spoke, Sir Robert refused to acknowledge
the red-eyed Loveday.

Nor had he looked at him since.

But the two men Sir Robert had added to his personal staff
paid the Dogs close attention. Shaw's deputies. The no-eared
East Anglian and the man with the M brand on his face stood
by Sir Robert's side, their faces curled in sneers.

They eyeballed Loveday at the briefing. The man with no
ears kept popping his knuckles.

When the army moved out, Sir Robert leading his men

among the vanguard, the East Anglians regularly stole backward glances towards the Dogs. Scotsman and the archers noticed, and it unsettled them.

'Inbred English streak of piss,' snorted the Scotsman, glaring at the no-eared man's back as the line moved slowly along. 'Let them try what they want. There'll be another two bodies missing their heads.'

'And four of us swinging from trees,' replied Loveday. All day his mouth tasted of metal and shit. He hawked and spat. 'That wine must have been sour.'

Thorp grunted. 'Aye, all eight jugs of it.'

The rutted tracks that led across the plain away from Caen had been baked hard by the sun, and were covered in stones. Loveday felt each hard lump in the soles of his feet. His boots were wearing thin. Since the landing on the beaches, he had put up with them, sparing the leather as he spent his days in the saddle. Now, however, the Dogs were all on foot. Sir Robert, vengeful, had refused to assign them horses. And it seemed to Loveday that every step brought him closer to the point where his bare feet were touching hard ground. He knew that when his boots finally wore through, the road would cut and scrape them to the point of agony within two days.

'I'll soon be leaving bloody footprints behind us,' he said, to no one in particular.

Tebbe grunted. He was tired and thirsty. ' What's that?'

'Nothing.' There was no point complaining. Loveday knew if he was feeling sore, so would the others. So he kept walking, head down, looking out for sharp pebbles.

Ahead, the earless man and the branded man rode abreast

with Sir Robert, listening attentively as the fat knight held forth about the countryside and the iniquities of its people.

He spouted. They nodded, obsequious.

And they kept it up after the day's march was over. When the company stopped to eat they sat near Sir Robert, slurping thick pottage as he rattled on.

That night, when the fires were lit, rugs and blankets unfurled and tents put up for the knights and lords, the East Anglians slept in Sir Robert's pavilion porch.

The longer it continued, the more nervous Loveday felt. 'Something's brewing,' he said as the Dogs sat around their fire, watching the sun disappear.

Scotsman muttered agreement.

'Better organize a watch,' he said. 'And I guess it'll have to be one by one.' So the four slept in rotation, taking short shifts through the night. When it was Loveday's turn, he stoked the fire high. He liked the way the heat and the smoke made the black of the night shimmer.

The Dogs watched. And the East Anglians did nothing. They bided their time.

In the morning, they all rose, and the march east continued.

They crossed the marshy valley of a river called Dives, where the dry sharp terrain gave way to wet and sticky mud. This spoiled Loveday's boots even further, for the leather first soaked through, and later dried hard in the sun. It became inflexible and brittle, and now pinched his heels. He knew he would have to steal replacements at the next place he could.

Scotsman eyed him as he winced. 'You need a new pair,' he said. 'You'll be riding on a litter if you don't. I'm not fucking carrying you, and I doubt they will either.' He nodded at Tebbe and Thorp. Both shook their heads.

'You should have found some back there,' said Thorp, jabbing a thumb in the direction of Caen.

Loveday sighed. 'I had other things on my mind.'

Thorp shrugged. They all had.

That afternoon, the countryside became hilly and the march slowed. The track narrowed, with hedgerows once again closing in on both sides. The day became humid, the air thick and close. Though the sun no longer roasted them, they could feel its glare through high grey clouds. Sweat stang their eyes and dripped from their noses.

Ahead of them the no-eared man's horse dropped a fat pile of shit. The East Anglians sniggered to themselves. Loveday pretended not to hear them, and stepped around the ripe mound. He wondered if this march would ever end. He looked at his men, and felt a pang of sorrow.

They had started as ten. He had vowed to follow the Captain's example and keep them alive and together. Now they were down to just four.

Or perhaps three and a half. His right hand throbbed. He frowned at it, suddenly angry. And in doing so, he missed a jagged rock on the path in front of him. He put his left foot on it, and the leather in his boot-sole finally gave in. The rock stabbed the tender skin between the heel and ball of his foot, splitting the leather of his boot along its full length.

He let out a yelp of pain. 'Christ's bollocks!' Everyone in the company turned and stared at him.

Sir Roberts smirked nastily. 'Really, FitzTalbot, these blasphemies do not become you, nor do they enhance the dignity of our sovereign king's armies.'

Loveday looked murderously at the knight. The branded man, riding beside Sir Robert, leered. 'You scratched your toe, Essex boy?'

Scotsman bristled and clenched his huge fists, taking a pace towards the East Anglian's horse.

Sir Robert barked: 'Back, savage, or you hang!'

The Scotsman nodded. Then he took another step forwards. Sir Robert paled and the two East Anglians put their hands to their swords.

Tebbe and Thorp went for their bows.

And then, riding hastily down the hill in the wrong direction, against the slow-moving march, came a red, puffy-faced youth Loveday recognized as the Earl of Warwick's herald.

'FitzTalbot,' he was calling as he went along the line. 'Has anyone seen FitzTalbot of Essex?'

Distracted, the East Anglians and the Scot all looked at the brightly dressed young man. Loveday stepped back in surprise. 'It's me. I'm here,' he called to the herald.

The herald looked relieved. But not happy. 'FitzTalbot, you are summoned to the presence of his worshipful grace, my lord the earl—'

Scotsman broke in. 'Fucking Warwick wants him. What for now?'

The herald reddened. 'An urgent situation. You have a pair of Welshmen who answer to your command, I believe, FitzTalbot.'

'I wouldn't say they answer to anyone,' said Loveday. 'And I haven't seen them for days. To be honest, I was not sure they were even alive.'

'Well, they are,' the herald replied. 'Rather too alive. But unless you come fast they may soon not be. I'm afraid your Welsh friends have decided to rob a pair of churchmen.'

Loveday shrugged his shoulders. 'And? What else have we been doing since we landed here?' he asked.

The herald grimaced. 'I'm afraid these are not ordinary churchmen. They are...' He paused, apparently wondering if he had said more than he had been bid. Then he looked at Loveday's feet with a confused expression. 'Can you ride? You and your large friend here had better come quickly and see for yourselves.'

Loveday barely stifled a laugh when the herald commanded Sir Robert to give him and Scotsman horses, for it meant the East Anglians had to dismount and hand over their reins.

He took the no-eared man's mount. Scotsman took the other.

The branded man stepped aggressively towards the giant Scot when he approached and threw the reins at him. Scotsman smiled like a saint. The branded man glowered.

Loveday mounted his horse – a pot-bellied mare, greasy for lack of brushing. The East Anglians did not groom their animals. And with the grease and his broken hand, mounting was not easy. Tebbe helped shove him aboard.

'You and Thorp look after one another,' Loveday said as he settled in the saddle.

Tebbe smiled. 'Same to you two.'

Loveday took a deep breath. 'We'll be back soon. With Darys and Lyntyn, I hope. Christ only knows what they've done.'

Then he and Scotsman kicked their horses and headed off up the hill behind the herald. Companies grumbled and moved out of their way as they trotted along the line. But the herald did not care. Nor did Loveday.

★ ★ ★

Sir Robert had been leading his company near the rear of the vanguard, which snaked for nearly a mile up the hill. But eventually the herald took them close to the line's front. As they crested the slope, the hedgerows widened out, and the Dogs found themselves riding between recently erected pavilions bearing royal and noble flags.

Loveday saw the prince's dragon banner flying over one of them, and scanned urgently for Romford. But the boy was nowhere to be seen.

There was no time to stop and ask after him. Warwick's herald pointed ahead. Loveday and Scotsman looked out over a wide valley, in the middle of which sat the town Loveday assumed must be Lisieux. It was smaller than Caen, though it had in its centre a large cathedral built in the fiddly modern style. All spires and thin stone pillars on the outside, which stuck out from its tall walls like spiders' legs.

The two Dogs were not the only ones taking in the scene.

Sitting beside one another in the saddle, also gazing towards the settlement below, were the Earls of Warwick and Northampton, and the traitor, Sir Godefroi.

Warwick turned as Loveday and Scotsman approached. 'Don't dismount,' he said. 'No need to grovel. We know each other well enough.'

Loveday gave a half-bow in his saddle anyway. Warwick ignored it as he looked back down towards Lisieux. In the fields outside the city, several men were driving a herd of around two dozen horses.

'Have you ever been to Wales, FitzTalbot?' Warwick asked.

Loveday shook his head slowly. 'No, sir. I've been to Scotland and—'

Warwick interrupted. 'Well, I shall tell you about the place another time. For now, let us speak of the Welsh. Look ahead. What do you see?'

Loveday looked. The horses and the men behind them were tracking steadily away across the rolling plain outside Lisieux.

'I see men... driving horses,' said Loveday, knowing he sounded a fool.

'Yes,' said Warwick. 'Stolen horses. And Welshmen. Your Welshmen, I think. Not for the first time, your fellows have disrupted the smooth progress of our campaign.'

'My lord,' began Loveday, 'these Welshmen—'

Warwick spoke over him once more. 'Let me come to the point. The town below is known here as Lisieux. We will occupy it shortly, and the usual entertainments will be indulged. Arson, robbery and mayhem allowed. Rape and murder officially prohibited – I need not rehearse this further, need I, FitzTalbot?'

'No, sir.'

'Good. Now, what is to make the torment of Lisieux different is the fact that our merciful King Edward is to receive a peace delegation in the form of two cardinals of the Church.'

Loveday said nothing.

'The good tidings, FitzTalbot, are that the cardinals have arrived promptly, and are currently ensconced inside Lisieux, with their various attendants, awaiting King Edward's arrival.' Warwick paused. 'The bad news is that on their way in they were set upon by a gang of Welshmen. Seven or eight in all, led – rather ably – by a pair of brigands whom I have been told are companions of yours.

'The cardinals are unharmed. But they have been relieved of all their horses. And as you have observed, the horses are being driven off.'

Loveday squinted. The horses were now far away. He tried one more time.

'Sir,' he said. 'It's possible these were men attached to our company. We had two Welsh join us on the cog... But if I may, my lord...'

Warwick raised an eyebrow.

'They do not speak our language or obey commands. And lately they have been missing from our company altogether. I am not sure I could bring them back if I wanted to.'

'And do you want to?'

'Sir?'

Northampton, who had been pacing as Warwick spoke, puffed, exasperated. 'My lord, don't trouble this man with riddles. FitzTalbot, can you get those fucking horses back or not?'

Loveday thought for a moment. He decided to speak truly. 'No.'

'Christ's nails,' said Northampton.

'On my faith, my lord,' said Loveday. 'If I could do it, I would. But I am hurt. I have lost half of my men. Aside from my companion here, I have two archers, who are on foot, and we are already being treated hard by Sir Robert. I do not mean to speak ill of Sir Robert, but...'

Northampton sighed. 'I know, FitzTalbot. I am well aware of Sir Robert's deficiencies of fucking character.'

'Aye,' said Loveday. 'What's more, my lord, the Welshmen you see – their names are Darys and Lyntyn – are as wild as cats. They are some of the best with a bow I have ever known.'

He glanced at Warwick. 'God knows we might have been killed in Caen without them. But they are their own men. They do not speak our language and even if they did—'

Warwick now cut him short. 'You have said so already.' The earl looked down to the valley once more. The horses and the Welshmen riding them were vanishing into the horizon. He peered at Loveday's bruised and swollen hand, and at his ruined boots. He studied the Scotsman, his beard hanging in greasy ropes of matted hair, his face burned and his body stinking.

'You men fought bravely at our side in Caen,' he said. 'How much does Sir Robert vex you?'

'A good deal, my lord,' said Loveday.

Warwick considered this. 'So be it. Then let us make a deal. I will help you with Sir Robert. But I need to tell the king that we tried our damnedest to retrieve those horses. And since I am both marshal of this army and his sworn man, I cannot tell him a lie.'

Loveday's bowels tightened as he listened. The last bargain he had struck with the earl had cost Father his life.

Yet he was in no position to argue. So he just said: 'No, sir.'

Warwick nodded. 'Good. So what I need, FitzTalbot, is for one of your men to chase those Welshmen, shouting dire threats about the punishment that awaits horse thieves. He must do his best to apprehend them, which I know he will be quite unable to do. Then he must return to me and tell me that he has failed. I will turn him over to the constable of the army' – Warwick smiled courteously at Northampton – 'who will berate him. I will report all of this to the king. And then we shall say no more of it.'

Loveday mopped his brow with his left hand. 'I'm sorry,

my lord, but just so I understand. You want one of my men to chase the Welshmen—'

Northampton interjected. 'You heard him, and you understand him. Chase after the bastards, give up, come back and I'll call you every kind of cunt under God's heavens. Now get on with it.'

Loveday's mind swam. He looked at his injured hand. He looked at the earls, both of whom wore stern expressions on their faces. 'Sirs, if I may,' he said.

Northampton's face began to turn red.

But Loveday persisted. 'With respect to your lords' dignity, when I gave you one of my men before, it ended poorly indeed for him. He was thrown—'

'I remember,' said Warwick, stepping in before Northampton could explode. He held up a hand. 'It was most unfortunate. But this is quite another matter. I am asking nothing more than for you to send a man down to that valley, in order to come back. If you cannot do it, of course, I shall send for any one of my men-at-arms, and you may go back to Sir Robert.'

Loveday opened his mouth and shut it again.

'Fuck it,' said the Scot, before he could say anything more. 'We'll both go.'

Loveday was not sure if it was the pain in his foot and hand, or the tangled strangeness of the situation, but he felt as dizzy as if he were drunk as he sat in his saddle beside Scotsman and they picked their way down towards the outskirts of Lisieux, in the direction that Darys, Lyntyn and the rest of the horse thieves had disappeared.

The Scot shook his head repeatedly to himself, and Loveday

could hear him muttering curses into his rank beard. When he checked behind them, Warwick and Northampton were sitting in their saddles at the top of the hill, looking on expectantly, as though they were watching a play.

Northampton shouted after them. 'Hurry along, lads! The faster you fucking go, the sooner you're fucking back!'

'How far do you reckon we should go?' Loveday said to Scotsman.

'Until we can't hear them fucking shouting at us,' said the Scot. 'Christ in his tomb, this is the last time.'

'For what?'

'For anything.'

It was not long before they reached the bottom of the valley, and kicked their horses into an easy canter. Loveday had to bunch his reins tight in his left hand, and keep them short in order to control his dirty and poorly broken horse's head. The effort made the muscles of his thumb and palm ache. But it was all he could do. His right hand was useless, and if it even brushed against the leather of his saddle, it made him gasp. They covered a mile or so, keeping the town and its suburbs at a safe distance. The hill slowly receded behind them. Ahead, they could no longer see the Welshmen or their stolen horses at all.

They kept riding in this way, over rolling pastureland where the grass grew to a man's knee-height, until the lords on the hill were completely out of sight. Still they sighted no horses and no Welshmen. But, Loveday thought, they were not meant to.

Eventually their own horses tired. So when they came to a small pool surrounded by trees they stopped to water them. To let the animals drink, Scotsman dismounted, and helped

Loveday scramble down. They let the horses loose. Once their mounts had finished drinking, the Scot bent down at the water's edge, and he too drank from the pool, filling his cupped hands and slurping thirstily from them. Loveday stood and watched, envious.

After a few gulps, with water coursing off his greasy beard, Scotsman suddenly looked up at Loveday hovering behind him. The big man's face was full of guilt. 'Shite, Loveday. What was I thinking? You must be gasping. Here, pass me your flask.'

Loveday's old skin pouch was in the pack on his back. He started to fumble with the strap that held it. But, one-handed, that too was a hard task.

The Scot watched him for a few moments. Then he stopped him. 'Ah, give up,' he said. 'Come here.'

Loveday hobbled over to the water's edge. The pool was half-dried by the sun, and where the water had shrunk, its banks were uneven and dusty.

The Scotsman watched him approach. 'Can you kneel down?'

'Aye.' Loveday knelt, though even that was not easy with one hand. Eventually, though, he was down. And Scotsman, as tenderly as Loveday had ever known him do anything, filled his hands from the water in the pool, and raised them to Loveday's mouth.

Loveday realized how thirsty he was. Putting his left hand on the back of Scotsman's, he took deep draughts from his friend's dirty hands. The water was tepid and gritty, and it tasted of Scotsman's reins. But it was the best Loveday had ever drunk.

'Thank you,' he said.

'The blood of fucking Christ,' said the Scotsman.

Loveday laughed.

And then an arrow split the air between them.

They spun in shock, and Loveday felt the Scot's huge hand on his back, pushing him prone on the ground. He fell on his right hand, and pain shot through his arm as though he had thrust it in a furnace. He tried to swallow a howl. He rolled off his arm and lay on his back. He was looking up at the sky – fat white clouds against a brilliant blue. Then he peered over his feet, which were towards the water. He saw that the arrow had cut the air between their faces and lodged on the far side of the pond at the base of a tree. He spread his arms and tried to flatten himself against the dried-up pool-bank. His belly stood up like a molehill.

Scotsman was lying on his front beside Loveday. They looked at each other urgently. 'God's name did that come from?' Scotsman hissed.

Loveday looked at him, eyes wide. He had no idea. He tried to wriggle his head back into the hard dirt of the pool-bank, to look back in the direction of the grass. But it was impossible. He adjusted his head once more. Looked helplessly at his friend.

'There was no one here,' he whispered.

'Well, there fucking is now,' the Scot said. 'Christ. Fucking, fucking Christ. Where the fuck did they come from?' Trying to keep himself pressed as tight as he could to the ground, he wriggled his axe free of his back, and rested it in front of him. He pushed his hair out of his eyes.

Lying helpless, like an upturned beetle, Loveday tried to do something useful. Keeping his burning right hand pressed to his chest, he used his left to feel around on his beltline for his short sword.

Nothing.

He cursed himself. His sword was where he had left it: rolled in his blanket behind the saddle of his horse, which was twenty paces away, oblivious to their peril. Grazing the yellow grass.

Another arrow fizzed over their heads. 'Shit,' said the Scot. 'We're going to have to run.'

'Don't think about it,' said Loveday. 'If we get up, we're dead.'

'Virgin's tits, Loveday, if we lie here, we're fucking dead.'

An arrow thudded into the dirt no more than five paces in front of them.

Then another, which splashed in the water behind them.

'I'm sorry,' said Loveday. The sky was a perfect blue. It seemed such a beautiful day to be killed. 'Scotsman, I'm sorry.'

Scotsman buried his face in the ground for a second. 'Ah, fuck it,' he said. 'So am I.'

And he put both hands on the axe, filled his lungs with air, jumped to his feet, raised the axe above his head and screamed.

He screamed like a man possessed by demons.

As though he were about to smash through the gates of hell and harrow it again.

And then he ran.

For a moment Loveday froze, not knowing whether to scramble up and follow him, armed with nothing more than his own yells and his yearning to die in the way he chose.

But before he could choose, Scotsman's screams changed.

They were still loud. Still wild. Still full of all the furious spirit the huge man could summon in a fight.

Yet there was something else in them.

Not pain. Not rage. But shock. Astonishment.

And then laughter.

Manic, deranged laughter. Laughter like no laughter Loveday had ever heard. Laughter like it might never stop. Like they said men used to sound in the old times when the cackling sickness came.

Scared, but no longer for his life, Loveday rolled to his side and pushed at the dusty ground with his left hand, trying as best he could to hold his broken right against his chest to protect it.

Had another arrow flown he would have been dead. But none did.

Instead, Loveday levered himself up to his knees. And when he did, he was soon laughing too.

Scotsman had made it just twenty paces before he had seen who was shooting at them.

Darys. And Lyntyn.

They were both sitting astride large, glossy, finely groomed horses, their manes and tails plaited, tacked in fine leather, with gold-plated bits between their teeth and the pink and white caparisons of some churchman Loveday did not know.

They were both holding their bows and grinning from ear to ear.

And standing facing them, caught between laughs and coughs and tears of relief, Scotsman was calling them every foul name he knew. The more he abused them, the more they all laughed. And the more Loveday laughed.

He laughed until he thought he was going to vomit.

'Savage godless bastards,' Scotsman was shouting. 'Sheepdog fucking arseholes of the fucking devil.'

But after a while, he cursed himself out. He sunk to his

hands and knees, and Loveday walked over and put a hand on his shoulder. 'Maybe God wants us alive,' he said. 'Though He alone knows why.'

Then Loveday shook his head at Darys and Lyntyn, who were watching them. There was an expression on their faces Loveday recognized but had never understood before now. They looked at the two Dogs as though they were observing children learning things of the world that had been hidden from them.

Lyntyn said something to Darys, and the shorter Welshman nodded. He spoke rapidly in Welsh to Loveday, and made a circling motion with his hands. Loveday looked at him blankly.

Darys made the motion again. He pointed to the Dogs' mangy horses. And then to the fine beasts all decked out in ecclesiastical pink.

And then Loveday understood. 'You want to swap.'

'You – want – to – swap!' said Darys, mimicking Loveday's voice. He puffed out his cheeks and boggled his eyes, and now the two Welshmen laughed loudly together.

Lyntyn jumped off his horse, and clicked and whistled, so that Loveday's and Scotsman's trotted over to him. Darys slid down from his. They checked over the Dogs' poor mounts and muttered to each other. They stripped off Loveday's blanket with his sword inside and threw it in Loveday's direction. They pulled off Scotsman's pack and tossed it as well.

Then they jumped nimbly into the saddles. Darys waved at Loveday and spoke again, quickly and in Welsh. He motioned to Loveday's broken right hand. Mimed binding his arm to his body.

'A sling,' said Scotsman. 'Yeah. Wouldn't be a bad fucking idea.'

Without another word, or anything like a farewell, the Welshmen kicked their new horses and galloped off across the grassland.

They left Loveday and Scotsman staring at the fine animals they had traded. Scotsman shook his head. 'Fit for cardinals, right enough. It isn't the whole fucking lot of them,' he said. 'But I reckon this will do.'

And they too mounted up, and set off back towards the hillside, to tell Warwick and Northampton what had happened.

22

Two cardinals came and tried to open peace negotiations at Lisieux. They were received in courteous enough fashion... they were told that our lord the king, always anxious for peace, would seek it by all reasonable ways and means... if a reasonable offer was forthcoming...

Campaign newsletter by Richard Wynkeley

The food at the banquet in the abbey hall they took over was the richest Romford had ever eaten.

He inhaled the fine smells of the tables. The main dish, served on large oval platters, was a white fish, whose name he did not know, smothered in a creamy sauce that tasted like sweet nuts. Large bowls held green peas swimming in butter and eggs boiled so their outsides were hard and the yolks sticky like honey.

At the king's high table the lords tore chunks out of roasted chickens and some other bird, thinner and darker in colour. After they had taken the best, the carcasses were sent down the longer tables where Romford and the other squires sat. Romford ripped off legs and wing-tips. He swallowed juicy flesh and crunched up thin bones. He stuffed food into his mouth as greedily as he dared, until it made his belly hurt.

The squires on either side of him poured wine. Romford

had drunk a great deal the previous day, and it made his head heavy. But it took just a cup to fill him with life and cheer again. So he drank and ate, and listened to the sounds and conversations around him. A pair of musicians were tuning lutes. Men were talking about the plans for the next stage of the campaign.

During his time with the Dogs, Romford had not known talk like this. With the Dogs, he had done what Loveday and Pismire and Millstone and the others said he should. He knew that they in turn were doing what someone else had told them they should.

Now he understood where those demands and commands came from. They tumbled out of the mouths of kings and princes, and the great lords who gorged each night on fat birds and tender fish, and gambled for silver, knowing that what they lost today, they would win back tomorrow.

Carefully, he observed King Edward, in the centre of his high table, facing out towards the hall. In a crowded space like the hall, he had learned that it was safe to steal the occasional look. In a closer, sparser setting it was not. The dance, he thought, was beginning to make sense. The king sat straight-backed. Around him were his son, the prince, and the earls who had saved Romford from the noose. A handsome knight with an eyepatch sat there too, with a grin on his face.

The king was proud, but not prideful, thought Romford. The way he sat made it clear he was certain of himself. His hair was glossy and beard neatly trimmed. His clothes were plain but costly: dark silk trimmed with thread that glittered when it caught the light. His face was a mask of steel and calm. He was a man. And yet much more than that.

Two churchmen sat at the king's table. They were also

richly dressed. Both wore red. One, slightly larger and older than the other, had a fine white beard, with moustaches grown so long they fell in curls around the corners of his mouth. The other was clean shaven and dark. They were mighty men – cardinals. The closest servants of the Pope. Yet Romford sensed they were not comfortable in their power. For while Edward looked at his ease, strain seemed to rise from these men like steam.

The squire on Romford's right nudged him and gestured towards the high table with his knife. 'Poor fuckers got their horses robbed on the way in. Did you hear?'

Romford shook his head. The squire shoved a chunk of bread soaked in sauce in his mouth and chewed as he spoke. 'Done over by Welshmen. What do you expect? Still, better to have the animals on our side than against us.'

Romford smiled. He thought about the brothers who had ridden with the Dogs. He had liked them. The squire chattered on. 'Waste of time them being here, in any case. There's as much chance of us agreeing a peace deal as there is of them taking my wife back down to Avignon and making her pope. We're going to hit Rouen, we'll cross the river, and then Paris is fucked. Everyone knows that wild bastard Hugh Hastings has landed his army in Flanders. He's already marching down from Ypres. France is done. Peace now? Forget it…'

Romford nodded along. He had heard the name Hugh Hastings a lot. It seemed that there was a second English army somewhere not far away, though where Flanders was in relation to where they now sat, he had no idea.

He was about to ask the squire beside him where Ypres was, and how long it would take to march from there, when the musicians finished tuning their lutes and began to pick the first notes of a song.

The chatter around the tables fell to a murmur, and the men listened as the taller of the lutenists – a bright-eyed fellow with tousled blond hair and sharp cheekbones – began to sing.

It was a tune Romford recognized. But the words were new. The musicians seemed to have made them up to entertain the crowd – and as they sang chuckles began to rumble around the hall.

Their words poured scorn on the French king. They hailed the English as scourging conquerors.

> The piggy's head in hand bring we,
> Roasted in his piggery,
> Squealing oink for clemency!
> Fleeing scared back to Par-ee!
> A-feared of his adversary!
> King Edward in his majesty!
> The very flower of chivalry!
> Hurrah! Halloo! Hurray!

At the mention of his name, the king smiled indulgently and raised a hand. And with each hurrah, the men on the lower tables banged their mugs and fists, stomped their feet and cheered. Romford joined in. The singers went on.

> Our prince was on the beach made knight,
> Girded with the sword to smite
> The heretics and Moabites,
> The fornicating sodomites,
> The sceptre-stealing parasite

King Philippe – who presumes the right
To wear the fleurs-de-lis!
Hurrah! Halloo! Hurray!

This time it was Prince Edward's turn to acknowledge the
crowd. And once more a great thumping erupted, echoing
up into the high vaulted ceiling of the hall. Romford glanced
at the cardinals. Their faces were like stone. The white-
bearded cardinal had both his hands on the table before
him, fingers splayed, inspecting each of the fat rings on his
fingers.

Occasionally the earl with the scar on his face and grey
hair – Northampton – leaned across and spoke into the ear of
the smaller, clean-shaven cardinal. He seemed to be taunting
him, for with each comment, the cardinal shook his head, and
occasionally returned angry words.

Pleased with his game, Northampton also leaned over to
whisper to the Earl of Warwick, who threw back his head to
laugh. Romford watched them. And the song went on.

At Barfleur ships we set afire;
Valognes we made a funeral pyre.
At Carentan the flames licked higher;
Saint-Lô became a great bonfire.
At Caen Lord Tancarville retired,
Abandoning the liv'ried liar
Who calls himself Philippe!
Hurrah! Halloo! Hurray!

The tables were growing wet and sticky with spilled drink.
But the men along them did not care. The squire beside

Romford threw his arm around his shoulder as they joined in with the chorus of cheers.

Then, from the high table, the prince caught Romford's eye. He tilted his chin back. At first Romford could not think what the gesture meant. He merely felt a cold panic at having caught the prince's eye at all. But then the prince repeated it. And Romford realized that he was being summoned. He untucked himself from the arm of the squire beside him. The boy's bleary eyes looked confused for a moment, but he soon lost himself back in the singing and the drink.

Romford rose from the bench. When he did, he found the wine had made his own knees soft too. Walking felt awkward, as though he could not trust his own body. And once more he was dancing, unsure of the steps.

Doing his best not to show it, he squeezed between the rows of revellers. No one paid him any mind. Another verse of the song had begun.

France, your daughters' legs we spread.
Your widows' wails lament your dead...

Romford stopped listening to the words. He came to the lords' table and stood before the prince. The handsome man with the eyepatch motioned to him to kneel. Romford put his knees on the floor and looked down. The reeds and straw strewn there were black and damp.

Prince Edward eyed him for a few moments. 'Rise,' he said. Romford stood. The prince seemed to have drunk a good deal of wine. His velvet hat, embroidered with tiny silver roses, sat at a crooked angle on his head. 'I have heard you play dice well.'

'I have learned a few games,' said Romford. 'But I have little experience.'

The prince nodded. 'Well, boy, let's get you some more.'

For the first time, Romford found it strange that the prince called him boy. They were born in the same summer. Why were they not both boys? But he knew better than to betray his feelings in his face. 'It would be my honour, my lord.'

The prince beamed. He turned in his seat and shouted to a servant loitering in the shadows by the far wall of the hall. 'Dice! And hurry up.' The servant seemed prepared for this, and was quickly over to the table. He shook from a small, soft black bag two sets of dice cut from white bone. The prince picked them up and inspected them. He took one set, three little cubes with tiny gold buttons for the numbers. He gave the other set, pipped with silver dots, to Romford, whom the servant brought a stool. Romford stood by it, unsure if he should sit down.

The one-eyed knight watched all this with an amused smile on his lips. 'My lord Edward, you don't care to dice with lords this evening?'

The prince stared at Romford as he answered. 'I have heard this boy is the best game-player among my squires, Sir Thomas. Maybe he will give me a better challenge than I would have taking your money all night.'

Sir Thomas laughed. 'I doubt this lad has much to lose to you, save the shirt on his back – which is yours in any case. He's a squire. A week ago he was an archer. Lad, do you have anything to stake on your game?'

Romford felt deeply uncertain. 'In truth, my lords, I have nothing at all. My pay for this campaign was to be given me by my captain, Loveday, and—'

Romford's words seemed to spark something in Sir Thomas's memory. 'Loveday?'

'Aye,' said Romford.

'An older man? From Essex? Always looking mournful?' Sir Thomas pulled a face, remarkably like the worried expression Romford associated with Loveday.

'I think so, sir...'

Sir Thomas looked satisfied. 'I know him. He fought at the bridge. He was hurt, though, and he lost some men.'

Romford's neck prickled. 'My lord?'

But Sir Thomas could say no more, for the prince was now impatient to play. He swilled wine and shook his dice peevishly. 'Sir Thomas, I pray you in the name of the Virgin, shut up,' he said. 'No one cares about yokels lost at the bridge.' He looked unsteadily at Romford. 'Sit, boy. We will play. I do not care to take Sir Thomas's money, though I am aware he has plenty, thanks to my father's generosity.

'You must look after your new wealth, Sir Thomas,' he added, nastily. 'Heaven knows proving to the courts that your marriage to my cousin Joanie is valid will prove expensive. And we all know how demanding little Joanie can be... in all ways.'

Sir Thomas opened his mouth, but thought better of responding. 'Yes, my lord,' he said, his words clipped and precise. Then he said no more, turning his one eye instead to studying the silver goblet in which his wine was served.

The Prince turned back to Romford. He shook his head rapidly, as if trying to clear it. 'Sit down. I will give you money,' he said. He called again to the servant. 'Money for the boy.'

The servant bustled over, now with a purse, cleared a space on the table and dumped a large pile of silver pennies between him and the Prince. The Prince divided it sloppily between the two of them. Romford sat down. He stacked his coins neatly into piles. The Prince left his in a heap. Then he cupped his dice in his hands, rattled them and rolled them out.

The total on the faces was sixteen: two sixes and a four.

Romford did likewise. The total on his faces was nine: a one, a five and a three.

'I begin!' cried the prince, as though he had been expecting the result before he had even thrown.

Romford sighed inside. His brother had told him about dice like these. He looked at the pile of pennies and counted them quickly in his head. It would take him barely any time to lose them, though he felt the prince might try and prolong the game a little to pretend he was not cheating.

But one – or perhaps two – of his three dice was weighted to land high, whereas Romford's were either unweighted or – more likely – loaded to land low. The game was fixed for the prince. The only thing Romford did not know was whether the prince realized it. Either way, Romford knew he was just there for the prince's entertainment.

Yet the thought did not make Romford angry or even sad. Since he knew he had been summoned to the prince's table to lose, there was no point gnashing his teeth about the outcome. In any case, he was a good deal more interested in what Sir Thomas had said about Loveday. *He was hurt. He lost some men.*

Who was lost? Romford ran through the faces of the Dogs in his mind. Scotsman and Pismire. Father and Millstone. Tebbe and Thorp. The Welshmen. He found he could not bear the idea that anything had happened to any one of them.

The Prince wagered a stack of pennies and rolled his dice.

He landed fifteen: three fives. Only one score beat that: three sixes.

Loaded as they were, Romford knew his dice could not land that score. He shook them anyway and threw. Four, three and one. Eight. Useless.

Another round of the minstrels' songs had started up.

In Rouen, Caen and Saint-Denis,
In Orléans and sweet Paris,
The Frenchmen choose: to die or flee,
Unless Philippe will bend his knee,
To Edward of our own country...

A servant brought Romford a fine silver goblet and the prince filled it with wine, spilling some on Romford's hand and giggling as he did so. Romford caught the Earl of Northampton sending a contemptuous look down the table at the young man. He kept his own eyes lowered, and sipped the wine.

The prince threw his dice again. Sixteen: two fives and a six. Almost as strong a throw as his last.

By now, Romford had lost all interest in the game. He focused only on the dance.

Make no mistakes. Draw no attention to yourself. Stay alert.

He threw his dice. Eleven: two fives and a one. A good throw, but he still lost. He guessed that perhaps only one of his three dice was loaded. But one was enough.

The minstrels' song went on. The men at the long tables, now very drunk, cheered the chorus:

Hurrah! Halloo! Hurray!

'I win again!' cried the prince. 'Why, we could play this game all night.'

And so they played on until the end of the meal, the Prince redividing the pile of coins between them each time he reduced Romford to nothing.

They only stopped when the banquet drew to its close, when it was quite dark outside, and the peacemaking cardinals had tired of being taunted in song and needled by remarks from Northampton.

When the two stood to leave, and bowed goodnight to the king, each English lord at the table wore a smirk on his face.

Romford was close enough to hear King Edward bid the men goodnight.

In a steady voice, he said: 'God rest you in peace tonight, my lords. I am sorry we cannot agree your terms. But wish my cousin Philippe well in putting down the riots in the streets of Paris. I hear the smoke in the air has driven our subjects quite mad there. We shall soon see for ourselves which of our claims to the crown they prefer.'

The cardinals walked out of the hall, faces grim.

The lords around the table grinned to one another and raised their goblets in a quiet toast.

The prince, realizing the meal and the game were over, abandoned all interest in both, and in Romford, and leaned back in his chair, his head lolling around as he stared into the black depth of the roof above.

With a shiver, Romford felt the king's gaze pass over him. He held his breath until he was sure it had come to rest on the prince. Through the very corner of his eye, Romford thought he caught a grimace of distaste crossing King Edward's face before he looked away.

Needing somewhere to look besides the table, Romford braved eye contact with Sir Thomas.

'Off you go, lad,' said the knight in a soft voice. 'I am sorry about this.'

'Sir. Thank you, sir,' said Romford. He stood up from his stool. He did not touch the silver coins that lay scattered before the prince. He bowed deeply to the lords.

Not one of them so much as looked at him.

Romford backed away towards the lower tables, where men were now standing up and stretching. Some were making their beds on the dirty reeds of the floor.

Before he was out of earshot, Sir Thomas called to him again: 'Lad. One thing. Your friend Loveday. The Essex men. You were one of their number?'

'Aye, sir,' said Romford. 'I was.'

Sir Thomas nodded, considering this. 'I will send Loveday your greetings. And let you know how he fares.'

Romford's heart leapt. 'Thank you, sir. Please tell them I am... I have...'

But as he spoke, he realized he had no idea what to say.

23

Sir Godefroi rode out towards Rouen to assess the state of
the city... They passed a [leper colony] and found a mad
woman begging for alms from passers-by...

Norman chronicle of Pierre Cochon

In the days after they returned the cardinals' horses,
Loveday, Scotsman, Tebbe and Thorp galloped with a
company of outriders led by Sir Godefroi. Loveday reflected
to himself on how dramatically the Dogs' luck had changed.
Warwick had been true to his word, and sent curt word to
Sir Robert that the Essex Dogs were henceforth removed
altogether from his command, and were to join the retinue
of the Norman turncoat. Tebbe had laughed when he told
how puce with rage the fat knight's face had turned when
Warwick's herald gave him the order. Though they had no
idea who would now pay them at the end of their forty days,
at that moment none of them felt even the faintest pang of
sorrow.

Riding with Sir Godefroi, of course, was not easier work. If
anything, it was the hardest posting they had been given since
they landed. Sir Godefroi's company rode far ahead of the
vanguard and the main mob of the *chevauchée*, scouting the
landscape as Sir Godefroi – who knew it intimately – directed.

Sir Godefroi rode them hard, and they were often in the saddle from dawn to the day's last light.

Yet to be away from Sir Robert and the glowering East Anglians was a fine thing. The Dogs made sure not to grumble to one another or anyone else.

That day there were around sixty of them in all – a mixed group of knights, men-at-arms, mounted archers and footsoldiers, like Loveday and Scotsman, who could ride – striking out as usual, miles ahead of the rest of the army.

It was hot and waterless country, and though Sir Godefroi steered a course that doglegged between little half-dried streams and villages with wells, the heat and the pace of the ride made it hard going. The air was unbearably humid, and when the sun cut through the hazy cloud, it burned their faces. Some of the men-at-arms rode shirtless, slinging their padded mail coats, iron breastplates and leather arm protection over the backs of their saddles, going unarmoured above the waist. They preferred to risk probable death in an ambush to being roasted alive inside mail or plate. Yet still they sweated, and their sweat dried, leaving white salt streaks on their clothes and skin. No sooner had they watered their horses and filled their flasks than they were running dry again.

Sir Godefroi was particular about which villages they burned and which they left alone. As they rode he named the local lords, calling out to the senior knights who accompanied him, instructing them either to torch or spare farms, crops and homes according to his opinion of the landowner.

One of the local lords was a man called Robin de Lombelon. He was nowhere to be seen, but it was clear to Loveday he was one of Sir Godefroi's friends. Nothing under de Lombelon's lordship was touched, and the few villagers who had not fled were treated brusquely but not harmed. Yet when they came to villages in territory held by other lords – especially the Green Lion Knight, Robert Bertrand – Sir Godefroi demanded total devastation: crops and barns put to the fire, animals set loose or killed, people not fast enough to run and hide struck or kicked or whipped.

The knights Sir Godefroi had chosen to ride with him were happy to indulge in all this. One of them was Sir John Dawney, a round-shouldered but energetic knight with a strong West Country accent, who wore his black hair long on top of his head and shaved down to the skin above his ears. A second was an energetic younger knight called Sir James Basden, who wore a feather tucked in his helmet. Another, with a pockmarked face and long greasy hair, was called Sir Richard de la Marsh. Then there was the one-eyed lord Sir Thomas Holand.

Loveday and Scotsman remembered Sir Thomas well from the fighting at the bridge. And he remembered them.

He greeted them heartily when the outriders assembled at daybreak. And throughout the hot ride that followed, they found him often nearby, encouraging them with his curious one-eyed wink.

'Cunt looks too pleased with himself,' grumbled Scotsman when the Dogs stopped for water at a small brook that trickled along the edge of a village they had burned.

Thorp mopped his forehead, squeezing sweat out of his eyebrows. The ash and fire grime on his hands left dirty streaks across his face. Loveday noticed that the archer's ring on Thorp's right thumb had slithered round to sit the wrong way.

'Wouldn't you be?' Thorp said. 'This war has made him rich.'

'Aye,' said Tebbe. 'We should stick by him. Hope that some

of that good fortune rubs off. Christ knows we need it.' He hawked and spat. They had all breathed in plenty of smoke that morning, and their phlegm was flecked grey and black.

Loveday glanced at Tebbe. He could not quite tell if the archer was needling him. But he decided against rising to the comment, and bent down to fill his flask from the brook. It was a painful task even to work the stopper out of the flask's neck.

Scotsman helped him, as he had before. But in place of gratitude, Loveday was beginning to feel embarrassment.

And sheer pain.

This was not the first time he had broken bones. But in the days that had passed since the battle at the bridge, his hand seemed to be worsening. To help him ride he had fashioned a sling from a discarded blanket he found when they camped at Lisieux, and he found a way to bind his good left hand into the reins so that it would not ache and chafe too much. Yet the livid bruise and the swelling on his damaged right hand had not gone down, and his arm throbbed from the back of his hand to just below his elbow. He was able to set fires and hold a sword in his left hand, but he had no idea how he would defend himself if he were thrown into another serious fight.

Fifty paces away, at the roadside, Sir Godefroi was calling directions and commands. The general thrust was clear: they needed to mount up and move. But quite where, Loveday could not tell. He tried to make out where the traitor was pointing. When he shielded his eyes against the sun he saw. A mile or so from where they had stopped, the road ran into a long line of woodland. Some of the half-naked men were already heading towards it, waving burning torches above their heads, leaving traces of smoke in the air.

'La Forêt de Moulineaux,' Sir Godefroi was calling. 'We go

through this wood. We find more to burn on the other side. And then, my friends – Rouen!'

The traitor seemed to be at the greatest ease, as though nothing made him happier than wrecking the homes and lives of people from his home country. He beamed and swept a sword around his head, carving the hot, heavy air.

Loveday thought back to their first encounter with Sir Godefroi, sitting in Northampton's tent outside Saint-Lô. Hearing him spin stories of his rivalries with his neighbours and peers. Telling them to fetch his friend's rotten heads. Of the promises he had made: they would have gold and ride at the front of the king's army.

There had been no gold, and it was clear that they were here now by chance, not Sir Godefroi's good lordship. Loveday wondered what invisible whim of God or man had raised such a feckless lord to a position of such immense power in an army that was not his own.

He would likely never know. So he stopped trying to ponder it.

'Come on,' Loveday said to the rest of the Dogs. 'Let's make for the woods. At least it'll be cooler among the trees.'

When they neared the far side of the woods later in the afternoon, almost all the men were fully clothed again. The sun's heat was blunted by a high canopy of beech and oak leaves, and in the dappled shade flitted hundreds of biting insects. They tormented Scotsman in particular, and he slapped and scratched at his neck and forearms as the gnats landed on him and drew blood.

Tebbe said he knew a trick to keep the pests at bay. He lit a torch and waved it around, so its smoke formed a cloud like incense in a church. The smoke made them sneeze and splutter but had a less potent effect on the insects. The horses swished their tails and snorted. And every man in the company ended up with clusters of tiny raised red dots on their skin, which itched and made them curse.

When the trees finally thinned and the track ahead of them wound towards clear countryside once more, Sir Godefroi called the company to halt. They looked out from the shade of the woodland's edge. Although it was hard on the eyes to peer into the bright of the open land, Loveday could see why the traitor had led them to this point.

They were gazing over a lush and rich area. It seemed to be almost an island, contained inside the wide loop of a significant river – larger than any the Dogs had encountered in Normandy so far. A long way in the distance, Loveday could see the suburbs of a major city – at least as big as Caen. Closer at hand were several clusters of well-appointed buildings. Closest of all were the outhouses and walls of a monastery.

Sir Godefroi conferred quietly with the knights around him, including Sir Thomas, John Dawney and the greasy-haired Richard de la Marsh. They gestured to the features of the near-island ahead. They seemed to be debating the order of assault.

After a time, Sir Godefroi addressed the company.

'My good men, ahead lies a very great place,' he said. 'The River Seine you see. This flows all the way from Paris and beyond. The edge of the city in the distance, this is Rouen. We have a chance to be the first of this army to go there. Who wishes to come with me?'

A cheer went up. Sir Godefroi seemed pleased. 'Good,' he said. 'Then we go. And we do not make this a secret.

'Men, I wish you will form up into four groups. Some with me, the rest with Sir Thomas, Sir John and Sir Richard. We advance. We burn everything in our way, so that the people of Rouen know we come. We meet at the south of the bridge and we see how fear grips the hearts of the people. We tell them how many more English come behind us, so they know they must surrender or die.'

The Dogs looked at one another. Scotsman could not stay his tongue. 'That's a pretty big city for five dozen tired, gnat-bitten fuckers to attack on our own,' he called out.

Sir Godefroi seemed bemused. He looked the Scotsman up and down, as though it was the first time he had seen him. 'My friend, this is the stuff of war. This is prowess. This is *noblesse*. Have you ever read the great histories of war?'

Scotsman raised one eyebrow. 'I'm still working my way through my bible, Sir Godefroi,' he said.

Sir Godefroi snorted. He was about to begin dividing the men when another voice called out. This time it was Sir Thomas.

'I will take these Essex men,' he said. 'We will head to the abbey.' He pointed towards the monastery. 'I doubt it will prove the most rich or spectacular prize of the day, but we are happy to leave the best of the fun to the rest of you. Aren't we, Essex men?' He stared at Loveday.

'More than happy, Sir Thomas,' Loveday answered. He looked around at the archers and Scotsman and made sure they fell in with him.

Sir Thomas nodded gracefully. 'No time to waste, then,' he said. He kicked his horse and set off. Loveday led the

Dogs close behind him. As they left, Sir Godefroi tossed his hair. He began showing the remaining men which houses to destroy. He was saying something as Loveday galloped out of earshot.

'No prisoners.'

As the Dogs and Sir Thomas rode towards the abbey gates, an old woman walked out. She was small and so stooped that her shoulder blades rose up above the crown of her head. Her hair was covered in a rough red shawl. The rest of her body was wrapped in a shapeless shift, torn and ragged at the hem, which barely covered her knees. She shuffled along slowly, moving as though every step were painful. To look where she was going she had to crane her neck around and up, like a chicken pecking for grain in a farmyard.

'Fuck's wrong with her?' said Scotsman. 'And what's she doing hanging round here?'

Loveday shrugged. But when they were ten paces away from her, he understood.

The woman's eyes bulged wildly in their sockets, and almost all the colour had gone from them. The whites seemed to have grown over everything in the eyeballs, so that where once they might have been green or blue, now there was just a milky blob in the centre.

And her eyes were not the worst of it. The woman's face was scored with rough and deep lines, so close together that the skin resembled tree bark. The end of her nose was gone, leaving just a swollen stump. Her lips were puffy and covered in sores and blisters. Her hands, which held a simple wooden begging bowl and a gnarled stick to help her walk, had only

three fingers on each, and these digits were fat as sausages. Her
bare feet were in the same way.

It was leprosy. Loveday instinctively wriggled his own sore
toes in the fresh boots Warwick's men had given him. He felt
for his own tender hand. Although he was in pain, he realized
his own sufferings were nothing compared to what this woman
must be experiencing.

The five men drew up their horses. 'Don't get too near,'
muttered Tebbe. 'It spreads on the breath.'

Sir Thomas looked amused. 'It does no such thing.'

'Aye,' called Scotsman. 'You'd have to be fucking her for a
month to catch it.'

'Tebbe's had worse, by Christ,' said Thorp. 'But his pintle
hasn't dropped off yet – and it certainly hasn't swollen up.'

Tebbe chuckled nervously. Yet Sir Thomas appeared to have
no qualms. He dismounted his horse, clearing his throat noisily
so that the leper woman could sense where he was. She moved
her head around, then adjusted her path towards him.

As she approached, he spoke to her in French, his voice soft
and melodious. Loveday tried to follow, but Sir Thomas spoke
quickly. The woman listened. She nodded her head and uttered
a few words, her voice hoarse and scratchy. She shook her
wooden bowl.

Sir Thomas looked around. 'Her name is Marie. She asks for
alms,' he said.

'So give her some,' said Scotsman.

Sir Thomas smiled. 'I'm sure you men could spare this poor
woman a coin or two.'

Scotsman looked at Sir Thomas in disbelief. 'St Lazarus's
stinking toe-rags, I thought the king just made you the richest
man on the campaign,' he said.

Sir Thomas seemed to find this funny. He slapped his thigh. 'Ha! The king rewarded me well. But not in coin, nor in wealth I can easily pull from my sleeve. I am a knight. If I want food or wine, I call for it. If I want anything else, I take it. I *do not* carry a purse of coin around with me.' He shook his head, as though this were the most obvious thing in the world.

Scotsman's mouth dropped open. Tebbe and Thorp rolled their eyes.

'Lord save us all,' said Loveday. 'I'll help her.' With his left hand he felt in the purse at his belt and pulled out a silver coin. He threw it underarm to Sir Thomas, who bowed theatrically, then held it out between his forefinger and thumb and dropped it into Marie's begging bowl.

'*Merci, monsieur,*' she croaked. Then she rattled off another burst of French. Her cloudy eyes swam as she spoke. The effect made Loveday uneasy. Sir Thomas affected not to notice she was a leper at all, and listened intently as she spoke.

Eventually he said, '*Très bien,*' and, '*Merci, madame.*'

Then he clicked his fingers at Loveday and pointed once more at her bowl.

The Scot growled. Loveday ignored him. He threw another coin to Sir Thomas, who gave it to Marie. She thanked him again, and waved her stick in greeting in the vague direction of the Dogs. Then she shuffled off, back inside the abbey gates.

Sir Thomas watched her go, nodding in silent satisfaction. He called after her, some good wish Loveday did not understand. Then, softly, to himself: 'A remarkable woman.'

'Do the monks have a hospital?' Loveday asked him.

'Not quite,' said Sir Thomas. 'There is a leper ward in a corner of their grounds. They attend the poor wretches' needs and pray for their healing. But this woman says they and all the lepers have fled. Just like everyone else in this unfortunate land.'

He paused, now wistful and distracted. Loveday looked towards the horizon. Fires rose everywhere between the woods and the distant river.

'Aren't we supposed to be burning this fucking monastery down?' called Thorp impatiently.

Sir Thomas, stirred from his thoughts, shrugged. 'If you feel so inclined, archer, be my guest. But perhaps just light up a grain shed or the stables. There are bigger things afoot and we need to be quick.'

'What things?' asked Loveday. 'And where are we heading?'

Sir Thomas's eye twinkled as he spoke. 'Well, good Loveday, since you paid for the information, I see no harm in telling you first. King Philippe is in Rouen. He has arrived in haste. And his guard is no bigger than our company.'

He grinned.

'Shall we go and see if we can catch a king?'

They dug their heels hard into their horses' sides, and rode towards the smoke. It took them no time to find Sir Godefroi.

Word spread of the exciting news. The rest of the English outriders began to reassemble, and they cantered towards Rouen, pulling on helmets and strapping armour over their stiff and sweat-salted clothes as they went. As they drew close, Loveday realized that what the leper woman had said was true.

On their side of the river, a few groups of buildings formed the small southern suburbs of the city. The rest of the place, substantially bigger and encircled by thick stone walls, sat on the north bank of the Seine.

In the middle of the river was a small, grassy island, with a couple of boathouses on it. A short distance downstream an arched stone bridge crossed the Seine. One of its central arches had been deliberately broken. Rubble piled in the water. The strong flow of the river created eddies around the stones, where the water frothed and foamed.

Above the walls fluttered two sets of flags. A few bore alternating horizontal stripes of red and gold. But at least twice as many more were blue, with gold fleurs-de-lis embroidered on them. The gilt lilies caught the light of the fading sun.

They drew their horses up two hundred paces from the southern suburb. The traitor's face lit up with excitement. He pointed at the flags with their fleurs-de-lis.

'Your crone was right,' he murmured. 'Philippe is here.'

'Aye,' said Sir Thomas, a satisfied smile playing at the corners of his mouth. 'And if I'm not mistaken, so is...'

Sir Godefroi nodded. 'Jean. My brother.' He curled his lip, then leaned over and spat on the ground.

Sir Thomas narrowed his eye. 'But look at the bridge. Broken. Barricaded too, I'd guess. We will not be able to go beyond those tiny suburbs on the south bank of the river.'

Sir Godefroi nodded. 'This is true.' He shrugged. He pointed his sword towards Scotsman. 'And what this man said earlier today was true also. We are...' He searched for the Scot's rough words. '... five dozen tired, gnat-bitten fuckers. But we may show the false king, my false brother and the false Rouennais what lies in their future.'

Sir Thomas thought about this for a moment. As he did, Loveday looked around at the assembled company. The men were tired, dirty and thirsty. Their horses were in much the same way. They were at least twenty miles from where they had begun their ride that morning, and from the rest of the English army.

He caught Sir Thomas's eye. 'If I may, sir?'

Sir Thomas nodded. 'FitzTalbot?'

'Should we not wait for reinforcements? At Caen, we—'

At the mention of Caen, Sir Thomas looked vexed. He cut Loveday off abruptly. 'Saints be, FitzTalbot, have you any spine at all? Or does your poor hand ail you?'

Loveday was taken aback by the spite in Sir Thomas's response. 'Sir Thomas, I only—'

'Only what?'

'I only thought that in the situation, we risk losing men to no advantage. Is it not better to—'

But Sir Thomas turned away from him, and Loveday realized that he had blundered. As though in questioning the prudence of an assault, he had questioned the one-eyed knight's honour.

Yet what was done could not be undone. From wavering, Sir Thomas now seemed to puff up with a sense of immense urgency and pride. He addressed the traitor. 'Sir Godefroi, you're right. We do not have the men to take this great city. But we have our honour to prove, as we always shall.

'It seems there are those among us who would prefer not to risk their skins. So be it. I am no fool. But I will be damned to the devil if we do not announce ourselves to the false king in that city with more than a show of burning haybarns.

'Any man who wishes to ride with me may do so. Any man who wishes to be judged a coward by man and God alike, stay here and sip your flask and scratch your arse.'

A silent moment passed. Then, one by one, men started to walk their horses forwards.

A beam crept across Sir Thomas's face. He nodded around the group of men in satisfaction. Then he smiled at Loveday, as though he were proving a point. 'FitzTalbot, what do you say?'

Loveday said nothing.

Sir Thomas nodded again. 'Watch this,' he said. 'We shall return with a tale for the chroniclers to embellish!' He tugged hard on his horse's reins, making the great animal rear and whinny. 'Men, we ride!'

Then he rode towards the bottom of the broken bridge, half a mile distant, leaning forwards, low in his saddle. Close on his heels went the greasy-haired knight Sir Richard de la Marsh and the West Country knight Sir John Dawney.

And once he'd set off, the whole company, almost to a man, seemed to be possessed by a common urge to throw themselves towards the suburb.

Loveday looked helplessly at the Scot and his archers. They looked just as helplessly back at him. Then Tebbe jutted out his chin. 'I'm no coward,' he said, and took his bow around his shoulder.

Thorp followed. 'Nor me.'

Loveday and Scotsman exchanged a glance. 'Ah, Christ,' said the Scot. 'Here we go again.' And they kicked their horses, and joined the rear of the charge.

Ahead of them, Sir Thomas was screaming, 'St George! King Edward!' as he flew towards the suburb and the bridge.

Behind them, Sir Godefroi was slowing, so that he would not be too near the front of the assault – although the Dogs had been among the last men to join the charge, they overtook him before they were halfway to their target.

And when they were within fifty yards of the suburb, Loveday understood why. From the shuttered windows in the top storeys of the dozen or so houses there, crossbows emerged and began to shoot bolts towards the forwardmost English outriders, from both left and right.

They had ridden right into a fully defended enemy position.

It wasn't even a trap. Just blind stupidity, dressed up as prowess.

Loveday's heart boomed. As he looked around in panic, the shapes of buildings and the movements of people seemed to leave traces across his gaze. He saw crossbow bolts move at the pace of birds, swooping gracefully, almost beautifully, through the air.

But at the same time he heard his own voice, screaming to the other Dogs to stop, to retreat, to get out alive. He tugged with all the strength he had in his left hand on his horse's reins, trying to get his beast to wheel.

A crossbow bolt sheared the air no more than two feet from his ear. He ducked. Another sliced just above his back.

Loveday yelled again, so hard he felt blood in his throat.

He saw a knight ahead fall from his mount as two bolts penetrated his light armour at the neck and in the back of his thigh. He heard war cries transform into animal howls of pain.

Then he heard the familiar roar of the Scot. Bellowing the same thing as Loveday.

Retreat.

Fucking retreat.

And mingled with that, in his head Loveday heard the Captain's voice, repeating what the Captain had told him so many times. Not screaming, but speaking calmly and coolly, as the Captain always did.

Bury your dead. Leave no living man behind.

Loveday's body was shaking in the saddle. But he realized he was alive. And as he fought to turn his horse back from the Rouen suburb, two men-at-arms from the outrider company raced past him. Then another.

The whole company was retreating.

Loveday's horse was whinnying in confusion, but he managed finally to wrestle her around and kick her back along the road towards the monastery.

The Scotsman was ahead of him. He turned back and saw Tebbe and Thorp riding hard behind him.

He felt a wave of relief. He ducked his head low and prayed that he would make it out of range of the crossbows. For a brief second he closed his eyes.

When he opened them, he saw the old leper woman standing by the side of the road, her head bowed low to the ground and her upper body hunched over her stick.

He rode on, meaning to nod to her as he went.

But as he neared the leper, she raised her head, and stood up straight, as though all the disease had suddenly been drawn out from her body.

Loveday's eyes widened in shock.

The woman pulled back her hood and smiled at him.

From a face that was not her own.

Her nose had grown back. Her eyes were no longer white and swollen, but small and dark and lively.

Her hair was cropped roughly all over, as though it had been hacked off with a knife.

Loveday's gaze locked on her in terror as his horse thundered past.

The woman from Valognes.

She smiled at him again and mouthed a silent sentence: *Perhaps I will see you in hell,* and he turned his face away from her in fear.

When he looked back at the road, there was no one there at all.

24

We found all the bridges broken or strengthened or defended, so that we were in no way able to cross to our enemy.

Letter to Thomas Lucy from Edward III

King Edward sat on a high-backed wooden throne and pursed his lips. The prince lounged sideways in a smaller seat next to his father's. He rolled his eyes.

Romford, in the group of squires and attendants who stood around the makeshift dais, kept his gaze firmly on the floor.

The Norman traitor Sir Godefroi and Sir Thomas, the one-eyed knight who knew Loveday and had been kind to Romford at the banquet, stood before the king. Sir Thomas looked impassive. Sir Godefroi squirmed.

'Richard de la Marsh was an excellent knight,' said King Edward.

Sir Godefroi looked pained. He gave a small nod.

'So too was Sir James Basden.'

'Yes, your grace.'

'Good knights die in war.'

'They do.'

'But I prefer them to die for a purpose. Sir Godefroi. I have this week sent a demand to England for two thousand more archers, since – as we have discussed on many occasions – the time will come when we will draw the false king to battle and, God willing, defeat him.' The king pursed his lips once more. 'But archers are easy to come by. I cannot so easily summon up good knights.'

Sir Godefroi looked sullen.

'Were Sir James and Sir Richard's bodies retrieved?'

'They were,' said Sir Thomas.

'Then see that they are buried with the appropriate honour.'

Sir Thomas performed an elaborate bow. Sir Godefroi, beside him, did the same. The king dismissed Sir Thomas. He bade Sir Godefroi stay.

Then he looked around the huge pavilion. They were now pitched on the outskirts of a town called Elbeuf, which the army had been pillaging all day. The tent buzzed with royal servants and attendants. 'And someone find my friend Lord Northampton.'

The king directed this order at no one in particular. But it did not matter, because at that moment, the grey-haired earl strode through the canvas flaps of the pavilion door.

Northampton looked cheerful. He marched towards the dais, bowing quickly without breaking his stride. At the sight of him, King Edward visibly brightened.

But the prince tensed. Romford noticed him swivel on his small throne, so his legs were no longer slung over the arm, and sit up. Yet his attentiveness did not seem to spring from any delight in seeing Northampton, or some desire to impress. He seemed to hate him.

Out of nowhere, Romford felt a sudden strong pang for his powder. He did not know what brought it on. He swallowed hard, scratched his thigh with his nails and tried to focus his mind on the business of the court.

Northampton hardly acknowledged the prince. But he clapped his hands together with delight as he told the king his story.

'I've said it before on this campaign, my lord, and I'll say it again. Rouen is a waste of fucking time.' He looked at Sir Godefroi. 'With respect, sir, you and fucking Cyclops found out the hard way what I could have told you the easy way.

'If we want to cross the Seine – and unless Philippe is as stupid as he looks, which he surely can't be, we're going to need to – the way to do it is not by trying to storm through the town with the biggest fucking walls in Normandy.'

Sir Godefroi pouted. 'My lord, we had intelligence—'

'Aye, I heard about your intelligence,' said Northampton. 'A leprous wench with her tits hanging off and no more toes than a fucking camel told you the king was at home, so your little pecker got hard, and all the blood rushed out of your brain and into your balls. Intelligence might not be the right fucking word for it.'

At the side of the dais, a priest waiting to attend the king winced. Romford struggled to suppress a laugh. He looked out of the very corner of his eye at the king, in the manner he was beginning to learn well. It seemed Edward was also restraining his mirth. In the days he had spent around the royal commanders, Romford had heard no one speak to or around the king like Northampton. But Edward did not merely allow it – he seemed to revel in the earl's earthy manner.

'Be that as it may, my lord,' Northampton continued, calming his tone somewhat, 'let me tell you what has happened in the grown-up world since we last spoke.

'I'll start with some bad tidings. We've lost Caen. The garrison there fought their way out yesterday. There's no point whining about it. If we wanted to hold it we had to stay there or at best split our army to leave ten times as many troops there than we did. But we decided long ago: we don't garrison. We move forwards. You said it yourself, my lord.'

Edward nodded his head slowly. 'I did. Deaths?'

Northampton narrowed his eyes. 'Lots. Most of ours. But a handful escaped. They made contact with the rearguard. My lord the Bishop of Durham passed their report to me.'

The king was quiet as he absorbed this information. 'Where does this leave us?'

'Right where we are,' replied Northampton. 'In Elbeuf, on a fucking clifftop above the River Seine, with Rouen downriver, Paris upriver, and Philippe scuttling back and forth between them, filling his boots with his own piss. We're on the south bank, and he's on the north, breaking all the bridges to keep us from getting to him. So be it. He doesn't have enough men behind us to trap us for at least two weeks, probably more like three. His son is five hundred miles away in Gascony. And we have our friend Hugh Hastings marching from Flanders. So Caen can go to hell for the time being. It served its purpose. We're no better, no worse without it.'

Edward nodded. 'Very good. I agree. But there is an important question that we must answer.'

Northampton jigged from one foot to the other. 'And your grace need not remind me what it is. If we wish to draw Philippe into the battle he does not wish to fight, we need to cross the river. All of us. Then Rouen comes into play. Paris comes into play. Every juicy fucking merchant town between here and the far side of the marshes of the Somme comes into play, by Christ. The question is how we cross. Or where. Our men are working on it. But we'll find a place. God's bones, if I have to lay a beam across the river and walk along it myself, we'll do it.

The king pursed his lips. 'I'm sure it will not come to that. He may even come to us. I have issued him the challenge, after all.'

Northampton laughed. 'What did you offer?'

'Battle,' replied the king. 'If you cast your mind back six summers, you may remember that my Valois cousin declined the opportunity to fight me man to man. This time I have offered him combat between our armies.'

Northampton kept laughing. 'I do remember,' he said. 'And I fancy the answer now will be exactly the fucking same as it was then. This is Philippe. He won't fight. You have to force his hand.'

'*I'll fight him.*'

The whole crowd around the dais, including Romford, had been hanging on this discussion between the king and his old friend. Suddenly they turned to look at the Prince.

'What was that?' said Northampton. The king raised his eyebrows at the earl. Northampton caught the gesture and corrected himself. 'What was that, *my lord*?'

'I'll fight him,' repeated the Prince. 'How hard can it be? How old is he? More than fifty. He's an old man. I'm young and strong. I will take my best knights and we will ride to Paris — disguised as knights from the crusading lands. We'll visit him in his palace. Then I shall reveal myself, throw down my gauntlet and tell him that he may fight me in single combat or be considered the worst coward in Christendom, and no knight at all.'

Northampton was silent for a moment. He just stared at the prince. A smile briefly played on his lips. He tried to restrain it. But the prince saw. He turned bright red. He jumped to his feet.

'You mock me, sir!' he squeaked. He turned to his father, who was maintaining his dignity. 'Father – this man makes jest of me. I am sick of him. He mocks me and he mistreats me. He has no respect for my station. I demand you have him punished.'

King Edward nodded indulgently. 'My son, sit down. Calm your temper. Lord Northampton was, I think, greatly moved by your bravery. Am I right, William?'

Northampton took a deep breath, wiped his eyes and straightened his back. 'My apologies, my lord,' he said to the prince. 'And bravo. Your courage cannot, indeed, be gainsaid. I'm sorry. It's just... there are realities to warfare that are not the same as whatever you've read in your romances, where Sir Lancelot does nothing but fuck queens and chop the heads off anyone who offends his honour. You are still learning.'

The prince sat back in his little throne. He was white with rage. 'Do not treat me as a child, *William*,' he said, icily. 'One day I shall be your king. And then we shall see who laughs at whom.'

And with that, he stood, bowed jerkily to his father and stalked from the dais, pushing attendants roughly out of his way as he half ran from the pavilion. As he left, Romford saw tears welling in his eyes.

Once he was gone, King Edward cocked his head and looked, half reprovingly, at Northampton. 'Must you do this?' he said.

Northampton raised his hands in apology. 'I am sorry, sire,' he said. 'You asked me to teach him. He must learn. And he will, in time. Now, may I return to the business of war? I said I had some good tidings to go with the bad.'

Edward waved his hand in assent and the earl went on.

'This morning, we found the bridge here at Elbeuf broken. No big surprise. But we also encountered across the river a gang of clever Norman youths who thought we'd like to inspect the whiteness of their buttocks and the filthiness of their arseholes. I'm very fucking pleased to say that they were punished for their cheek.

'A gang of Welsh – possibly the same unruly fuckers who stole the cardinals' horses – pilfered some rowing boats, got down to the bottom of the cliff, rowed across and slaughtered the lot of them. Surprisingly accurate bowmanship, even for the Welsh. I hear most of their victims were left with fletchings and arrow shafts sticking out of their arses. Their countrymen might think twice before showing us such soft fucking targets again.'

He turned to Sir Godefroi. 'Next time you decide to go rogue, sir, you might want to take a few of the sheep-fuckers with you.'

And so he went on. Romford listened to it all. He wondered how the prince was faring, having been so roundly humiliated by the earl once more.

But more than that he itched for powder. The feeling was coming back. He was not sure how long he could hold it at bay.

Romford did not see Sir Thomas again for all that day, nor the two that followed. Instead, he rode among the group attending the prince and his steward, Sir John Chandos, as the army began a fast march south-east, along the southern side of the Seine valley. Romford watched as hundreds of English companies spread out and burned everything around them as they went. Most of the villages they fired had long been evacuated. But after the marauding English swept through, they were nothing but scattered, smoking shells.

The river twisted and turned through huge U-shaped bends, and they did not always follow its course, for to do so would have added many days to their journey. There were times when the riverbank was out of sight altogether, and others where it was hidden behind large lakes and marshes that sat in the sweep of its bows. But more often than not they could see it, either because it was near, or because the ground rose up high and gave them a commanding view north over steep riverside cliffs to the Seine's course below.

As they marched they saw, for the first time since Caen, French forces gathering against them. Romford was more intrigued by them than he was afraid. At first they were a few score men, mostly mounted warriors – knights and men-at-arms. But as the hours and days passed their numbers swelled with hundreds of footsoldiers and crossbowmen. They stayed level with the English, tracking their progress upriver, and making sure there was no prospect of taking any town that might yield a crossing-point. Sometimes, when the smoke from torched buildings blew thick over the river, they disappeared. But when the air cleared, they were always back. Watching. Waiting. Their numbers growing by the hour.

The prince was in a foul temper after his argument with Northampton, and his mood did not lift. He rode listlessly, and snapped at his attendants, finding fault in all they did. When

Romford heard him converse with his knights, he uttered only complaint and criticism of his father's strategy.

'We're riding to our doom,' he told Chandos one afternoon, his voice shrill. 'All the French have to do is stay opposite. In under a week we'll be outside Paris – but why? We shall be a hundred miles from the coast, with no reinforcements and no siege towers. They'll keep us there, starve us, then take us from behind when the duke arrives from the south. It's pathetic. But Father listens only to that brute Northampton. When I am king...'

Chandos never argued with his master, although he never quite agreed, either. He listened, and made soothing noises, until the prince grew bored of grumbling and fell back to brooding again.

Romford, meanwhile, carried out his duties obediently and passed the time on the road making idle talk with the other squires. Every so often, usually when he was tired towards the end of the day, he would feel a sudden yearning for powder. But they stopped at no towns or cities where he might slip away and find some. The large settlements they did pass – called Pont-de-l'Arche and Le Vaudreuil – were walled and strongly guarded. Rather than spend time on sieges, the army burned what suburbs lay outside the walls, then pressed onwards. This, too, irked the prince. 'We should leave nothing of them,' he said. 'Besiege them all, slaughter every man, woman and child and throw their bodies in the river. Then we shall see how long the French king stays on his own side...'

And so they went on. Romford endured the itch, and put his mind to other matters.

He did not see the Essex Dogs.

★ ★ ★

He was rolling dice with two other squires, camped for a midday meal on high ground a little way outside a town called Gaillon, when the one-eyed Thomas Holand came to find him. The knight seemed to have recovered from his dressing-down by the King. His eye glinted, and when he pulled Romford away from his game, there was excitement in his voice.

He leaned in close. Romford smelled wine on his breath.

'Are you winning?'

Romford shrugged. 'More than I am losing.'

Sir Thomas patted him on the back. 'Good lad. You know the prince plays with loaded dice?'

Romford nodded. 'Yes. And I have seen it done before. My father knew taverns where it would get you killed.'

The knight nodded. 'I meant to tell you about your friends,' he said. 'They rode with us at Rouen.'

Romford felt his heart flutter. 'How did they fare?'

'Alive,' said Sir Thomas. 'All four of them. But the old one is in a sore way. His hand is badly broken. He winces a lot.'

'Four?' said Romford, confused.

'Two archers, the old one and a giant Scot,' confirmed Sir Thomas. 'They lost a man at Caen. I forget his name. Shorter than you. Crossbow wound. Straight through his heart. Nasty. But I have seen men die worse.'

Romford felt sick. 'Pismire.'

'If you say so,' said Sir Thomas.

One of the squires called from the dice game. Romford gestured with his hand, forfeiting. 'What of their priest, and the other footsoldier?' he asked. 'His name is Millstone. And two Welshmen...'

'Never heard of them, never seen them.' Sir Thomas was now impatient. 'The Welsh seem to be looking after their own. Enough. You asked; I've told you. Now I need something in return.'

The sick feeling did not leave Romford. 'Did you mention me to them?' he said. But the knight ignored him.

'It is said that you can shoot a bow even better than you roll dice. Is that so?'

Romford shook his head. Then he nodded it. 'I – I can shoot. I have not shot since we landed. But I can...' He tailed off. He felt dizzy. He could only think of the Dogs. Millstone's arm around his shoulders.

'Splendid,' Sir Thomas said, ignoring Romford's daze. 'We're going to have some fun. Show the French across the river what we can do. All you'll need is a bow, a pair of bollocks and an appetite for a bit of quick looting. Have you got those?'

Romford opened his mouth to answer, but Sir Thomas spoke over him. 'Thought so. We're going to hit Gaillon.' When Romford looked blank, he pointed towards the next hill between them and the riverbank. From where they stood, the land dropped away into a small valley, then rose again. A castle sat perched on a steep slope above a walled town.

The squires at the dice game called for him again. Their game was spoiled. Romford again waved them away. 'Why?' he asked Sir Thomas.

'Why what?'

'I thought we were to march quickly in search of bridges. The king...'

'We are marching quickly.' Sir Thomas smiled. 'And the king has given this small diversion his blessing. He wearies of his

Castle, beyond the range of the crossbows, and simply shoot as fast as he could towards its defences.

Perhaps one or more of his arrows would hit, wound and kill. He would probably never know. Because several dozen more archers like him would be doing the same. They would make the sky rain arrows. And the defenders would eventually either die or run.

The prince finished his speech. He looked happily around the crowd. 'Sir Thomas Holand will lead the assault,' he announced. 'Follow this man as you would myself.' Then he wheeled his horse on the spot, to face the castle, drew his sword and pointed towards it. 'Sir Thomas, ride on!'

And Sir Thomas, with a smirk to Sir John Chandos, and another man from the king's entourage, whom Romford recognized but did not know, rode out, ordering the troops and archers into their proper positions.

They rode down their hill, paused in the valley and ordered the men into their positions. The hill on which the castle stood was very steep. Romford saw nerves on the faces of many of the spearmen. Some of them were closing their eyes and muttering prayers. Others were beating themselves on the chests and crying out blasphemies.

Romford thought of a phrase Loveday had shouted on the boat that tipped them on to the beach.

Desperta ferro!

He did not know what it meant. But he liked the way it sounded. He glanced left and right at the bowmen lined up beside him, spaced an armspan apart. He nocked an arrow and drew it back halfway, feeling the familiar tug in his shoulder muscles, pulling against the bow's heavy draw-weight.

He looked along the arrow at the battlements. There were

half a dozen or more heads to be seen. He sensed the drift of the breeze on his face. Blowing from west to east. Gently. But enough to move the arrow's arc over three hundred paces. He slowed his breathing deliberately. Beside him, an archer let out a loud fart.

A few of the group sniggered. Romford stayed focused on his breathing. He tuned his ears only to hear the call from Sir Thomas. It seemed as though it would never come.

On the battlements, the French heads moved back and forth, unhurried. Romford wondered if they could see what was being assembled below them.

They had to.

They had to believe they were out of range.

His shoulder began to ache. But he did not take his eye off the battlement. Then, eventually, he heard Sir Thomas's voice, true and clear.

'Go on then,' he cried. 'Shoot them, by Christ.'

Romford drew. Then he let fly.

25

And so our lord king came to Poissy, where he found the bridge broken... When three or four beams had been put across the broken bridge, some archers crossed, though only few in number. They killed an estimated thousand men or thereabouts of the enemy...

Campaign newsletter by Sir Richard Wynkeley

Tebbe spotted a familiar figure running out of the apothecary shop.

The four Dogs had stood on the hillside and watched the slaughter of Gaillon's fleeing garrison. Men forced out of their defensive posts under the weight of arrow shot and a cruel assault behind a battering ram were chased down and trampled, or gored with lances and spears.

Now they were in the town, joining in the plunder. They stood in a street with a church at either end and a row of craftsmen's shops, stripped bare and starting to burn.

Tebbe was stuffing candles into the satchel he carried at his side.

'Shit,' the lean archer said. He peered through the smoke and the crowd. He pointed. 'I'm sure that's...'

Scotsman, a head taller, looked over the top of a scrum of jostling looters, joking and shoving, filling the street from gutter to filthy gutter. He finished the sentence for him:

'... fucking Romford.'

Loveday only half heard. He was sweating. He was clammy much of the time now. He felt the sweat mostly in his head and in the small of his back. Sometimes hot and sometimes cold. He knew his hand was causing it.

He was also getting used to seeing things and people who weren't there.

He blinked at Tebbe and Scotsman. Their words seemed to echo inside his head. 'Who?' he asked. 'Where?' He wondered if they had seen the woman from Valognes.

The two men ignored him. They tried to push their way forwards amid the mass of bodies in the narrow street. But there was no way through the crowd, and they gave up.

Scotsman turned back to Loveday. 'It was the lad,' he said. 'Bow on his back. Stupid black helmet on his head. Stripes down his trousers and the Prince of Wales's colours on his back. He's going up in the world.'

Loveday digested this information. 'At least he's alive,' he said. 'Where was he going?'

Tebbe shook his head. 'No idea. He must have been in the fight somewhere. But he was stepping out of an apothecary. Nothing good has ever happened when he's been in one of those.'

Loveday grunted. His head spun. He was sweating hard. His hand throbbed again.

Tebbe's face twisted, dissolved, and formed itself again. 'Come on,' it said. 'We're supposed to be riding with Northampton.'

Loveday nodded weakly. He tried to remember who Northampton was.

★ ★ ★

The days that followed seemed to swim, as though time were moving past him, rather than he through it.

There were periods when it all seemed clear. He was in the saddle, Scotsman on his right and Tebbe and Thorp behind. They were among a thrown-together company riding beyond the vanguard, hunting for a river crossing that was not yet broken. Depending on the day, the group was given its orders by the traitor Sir Godefroi, Northampton, or Sir Thomas with the one eye, who now wore a thick grey linen bandage around his left forearm – a wound he had suffered in the attack on Gaillon. The company rode up and down the undulating landscape, between woodland and open hillsides, tracking the S-bends of the river.

But at other times the sweat would come on strong, and he would forget where he was. Who he was. His dreams leaked out of the night, so that the boundary crumbled between the terrors of sleep and horrors of day. Then it was all he could do simply to stay in the saddle, following the route set by the lords, drinking what ale and water he could, yet always thirsty.

When they stopped to eat, and the other Dogs swallowed thick, lumpy stew or potage, Loveday slept, exhausted by the heat and the pain. And when he slept his visions grabbed him by the throat and squeezed at his chest. They took all his breath away.

He saw the men he had lost. Pismire's dying eyes. Father's terrified face as they handed him to the mad bishop. Millstone, clasping his hand before he rode away into the wild.

He saw the Captain, the last time they had been together. When they had spoken such bitter words.

He saw Alis, standing in the doorway of their home, combing her hair and singing the old lullabies she used to soothe the children. Calling him by his name and smiling. But when he looked again the flesh was fallen from her hands and the comb she used was no comb at all, but just her raw yellow fingerbones, crusted in dirt from the grave.

And there was always the woman from Valognes. Her blank eyes when the prince dragged her off with the noose around her neck. Her determined face as she cut away her hair with his knife.

All these faces haunted him as he sat slumped forwards, with his back against tree-stumps and hut walls, and his head and broken hand between his knees, while his men slurped tasteless field food and slept on the ground by fires made from green and stinking wood. As they spent their days in the saddle on worn-out horses, while the sun beat down on them, mocking them as they chased the course of the endless river, looking for a bridge that never came.

After four days, Loveday's fever broke. It was a Sunday morning. He knew this because when Scotsman shook him gently awake, he heard the low chunter of priests celebrating Mass at one of the lords' pavilions.

He sat up beside the fire's cold embers and tried to remember where they were.

He saw they were on high ground. There was thick forest on one side. The river was on the other, sweeping around in a huge arc, left to right. And beyond, shimmering in the early-morning haze, he saw spires upon spires.

The outline of a city bigger than any Loveday had seen before.

He could not remember lying down to sleep. He felt very hungry. 'Where are we?' he asked Scotsman.

'Daft fucker,' said the Scot. He growled, but there was kindness and relief in his voice. 'See that great shithole in the distance?'

'Aye.'

'Paris,' said the Scot, tugging one of the matted ropes of his beard. 'Full of fat churches and beautiful women.'

'We're going there?' asked Loveday.

'Maybe. There's about ten thousand French soldiers down there getting ready to fight us. Can you stand?'

'I think so.'

'Then you can come with me.'

They walked to the captains' briefing. Loveday's hand still ached, and he couldn't close or open the fingers, which were now set in an ugly claw. But the bruising was changing colour. Alongside the grape-like purple and black now were shades of yellow, orange and green. Like a sunrise.

He flexed his arm at the elbow as Scotsman led him through the camp to the earls' pavilions. Scotsman eyed him.

'You never learned how to punch a man properly, did you?' he said.

Loveday smiled. He still felt weak. 'I suppose not. Do you want to tell me the secret?'

'Stab him in the guts first,' said the Scot.

Northampton was waiting when they arrived, tapping his foot and glaring at the small group of crew leaders. His grey stubble had grown out into a full beard. His hair ran thick with grease. There were dark smudges under his eyes. But the eyes themselves still burned with intensity.

The earl began speaking before the whole group was assembled. As though he could not bear to wait a heartbeat longer.

'Gentlemen,' he said, 'and those of you who are not gentlemen, I'm not going to dip it in honey for you. If we don't cross that fucking river before sunset tomorrow, a lot of you are going to die. That's not a threat. It's a fucking promise.'

He paused and looked around, making sure to catch every man's eye.

'I know most of you are sick of hearing the names of the bridge towns along this stinking river. Rouen, Elbeuf, Pont-de-l'Arche and all the rest of them. We've come close a few times.'

He turned to Sir Thomas Holand, who had sidled up next to him, massaging his wounded arm.

'This fucker tried his hand at Rouen and Gaillon. And as you can see he wears the scars to prove it.

'Lord Warwick and myself thought we had taken the crossing at Meulan yesterday. I'm happy to say we don't bear any scars. But as those of you who were with us know, we lost some good men. Friends.' Northampton stared around the group. 'Brothers.'

Loveday felt a chill.

Northampton continued. 'I'm not going to lie to you. We're going to lose more friends. More brothers. But if I have to lay a fucking tree trunk across that river and crawl across it on my belly, we are going to get there.

'Our comrade Hugh Hastings is a week to the north with a gang of blood-crazed Flemings and a thousand English murderers and rapists. Most of them were in the Marshalsea until two weeks ago. Now they have bows in their hands and daggers in their belts. All we have to do to win this fucking war is meet them. Cross the river. Join our armies. Hit the French king before his army has had time to reach full strength.

'Do that and we crush these French fuckers. Boil their bones for soup.

'But if we don't do it, we'll sit outside the walls of Paris until the French join their forces and strike at us. My lord Warwick and I will be captured and ransomed. You lot will be butchered like sheep. There is no other strategy. We cross the river. Today. However we can. Does everyone understand?'

Northampton paused and let his words sink in. As he did so, Warwick strolled up to the little gathering. Like the constable, he was showing the strain of many weeks living in the field. But Loveday understood that he, too, was as hungry for the fight as he had been the day he stepped ashore.

Northampton glanced at Warwick, offering him the floor. Warwick nodded, accepting. He looked slowly around the dozen men assembled, making eye contact with each.

'This is our last chance,' he said. 'The town below us is called Poissy. It's empty. Evacuated. Of course, the bridge is broken. But we have a chance to rebuild it. We've sent scouts down to the town. They say there is not yet a single Frenchman on the opposite bank. Philippe has taken his army to Paris, where he is organizing his defences. Whatever reinforcements he has ordered to guard the bridge have not yet arrived.

'They will arrive – have no doubt of that. But now is our chance.'

He looked every man in the eye again.

'Does anyone want to say anything, or ask anything?'

No one said a word. 'Then by God and St George,' said Warwick, 'strap on your armour. Let's finish what we've begun.'

The path wound down into Poissy and led them past the grounds of a massive priory. Its church soared higher than anything Loveday had seen since they landed. It was decorated with finely carved statues of saints, and hideous stone imps, contorting their faces, sticking out their tongues and pulling apart their arse cheeks.

As they rode past it, Sir Godefroi drew alongside the four Dogs. He nodded courteously at Loveday and pointed to the priory church. 'St Louis, King of the French, was baptized there,' he said.

Loveday nodded.

Sir Godefroi persisted. 'You know of St Louis?'

Scotsman stepped in. 'He was the one who shat himself to death in Saracen country, wasn't he?'

Sir Godefroi crinkled his nose. 'St Louis brought Christ's Crown of Thorns itself to France,' he said. He crossed himself. 'It is kept in its own chapel in Paris,' he said. 'One of the finest chapels in the world.'

'Aye,' said the Scot. 'Well, when we get to Paris, fucking Loveday here can try it on. He's suffered about as much as Christ on the Cross this past month.'

Sir Godefroi gave the Scot a hard look, then kicked his dappled grey horse forwards, leaving the Dogs and heading towards Warwick and Northampton at the front of the group.

The Dogs passed the priory, following its high outer walls around two sides, coming into the small town beyond it. Dust swirled. The streets were sunbaked and silent.

It was as though no one had ever lived there.

A doglegged street brought them to the river-front, where the earls and half the company had already pulled up and dismounted. All were staring at a familiar sight.

The bridge, which on their side of the river was approached through a small toll house, was wrecked. The beams that lay over its central two arches had been roughly broken at either end, and thrown into the water, which eddied viciously below. Four of the beams were visible, half their lengths sticking out of the water's surface.

Thorp snorted. 'Fucking hopeless. If any man crosses the river here today, I'll grow tits and a halo and you can call me the Virgin Mary.'

A small crew of half a dozen thickset men Loveday had never seen before marched up, pushing their way urgently through the company. Engineers. They wore the king's livery. But instead of armour they had hardworn working dress.

As they passed, one of them, a stout middle-aged man with a dense and bristly black beard heard Thorp speak. He grinned. 'I reckon you'll look good with tits,' he said. 'Watch this.'

They all stood back and let the engineers work.

The half-dozen men set to work putting up a wooden frame with winches and pulleys, hooks and ropes. Shortly, more arrived. Another half-dozen. Then another. They moved together like ants, as though guided by nature. Barely speaking, yet knowing perfectly what to do.

Warwick and Sir Godefroi watched, arms folded. Thomas Holand slouched at the edge of the group, rubbing his bandaged arm. He looked dull and tired. Northampton paced among the company, muttering to himself. Knights and men-at-arms sat on the ground and dozed. Most were close to fully armed, and sweltering in the sun.

Loveday gazed across the river. The midday heat made the air shimmer. The far bank seemed to wobble. Beyond it, a track wound its way away through a dry marsh, formed in the crook of the river-bend. About a mile distant, the land rose gently and the track disappeared into woodland.

He thought he sensed something moving at the edge of the woods.

'You see that?' he said, turning to his left. Tebbe stood beside him. He shielded his eyes against the sun.

The archer shook his head. 'You're seeing things again. Have a drink. No one's coming.'

The engineers were hauling a rope like a tug o' war team. The rope fed through a pulley on a wooden frame, and it was attached to the longest of the beams in the river with sharp, barbed iron hooks. As they heaved, the beam moved from the riverbed. It made a sick, sucking sound.

Northampton walked up to the Earl of Warwick. He looked uncommonly subdued. The Dogs were close enough that Loveday could hear what he said.

'We're not going to make it.'

Warwick half turned to him, but he did not speak and his face gave nothing away.

Loveday looked back across the river. His stomach churned. He was sure there was something in the heat haze shimmering at the woodline. His eyes itched and burned as he tried to make it out.

He glanced around the company. Every man was either distracted by the bridge work, or bored. He turned his attention back over the river, past the engineers, grunting and cursing as they dragged the beam slowly upwards. Something was there.

Loveday could stand it no longer. He jerked away from Tebbe and set off, holding his injured hand, but moving at almost a run, down to the toll house at the entry to the bridge.

He crouched there on his haunches, gazing as hard as he could, trying to work out what it was. As he did, he felt a hand clap him on the back.

He flinched, turned and saw Northampton standing over him. He stood up.

'St Patrick and all his fucking snakes, you look like shit,' said Northampton. But he sensed something in Loveday's face. 'What is it?'

Loveday shook his head. 'I don't know.'

Northampton squinted across the river. 'I don't see anything.'

Loveday felt like crying. 'I know,' he said. 'But they're there. I feel them. I can't explain.'

Just ahead of the two men, at the bridge, the engineers cheered. The first beam was clear of the water, and swinging free on ropes, bouncing off the stone arches as it rose. It was moving, but not fast enough.

Northampton let out a long sigh. Then he opened his arms, and pulled Loveday into an embrace. Loveday did not know what to do with himself. Besides the deep discomfort of being touched in so familiar a fashion by a nobleman, the earl was also crushing Loveday's right hand between their chests.

As he stood stiffly in the embrace, Northampton spoke softly into Loveday's ear. He was so close, and his beard so thick, that Loveday was not completely sure of what he said.

But it sounded like: 'It's time.'

★ ★ ★

When the French company finally came into view, there were fifty or so of them. They emerged slowly out of the haze – just shapes at first, but as they came down from the woodline towards the far riverside, the shapes became distinct figures. Perhaps twelve knights and men-at-arms, the same number of crossbowmen, and the rest ordinary footsoldiers. They brought carts. They flew familiar flags: Philippe's blue-and-gold fleurs-de-lis, and the red-and-gold stripes of the traitor's brother.

They stopped around one hundred yards from their side of the bridge. They came no nearer. For a few moments they just stood there. At first Loveday could not think why.

Then he understood. They were standing out of range.

And they were going to build something.

The knights dismounted, and seemed to be gesturing to a group of the ordinary men. Shortly afterwards the men ran to the carts and started dragging timbers and ropes from them. Soon it was clear what they were doing.

They were assembling two wooden frames, each with a long arm, which bore a heavy weight at one end. They were the same contraptions the Dogs had seen the day they landed on the beach.

Catapults.

Loveday looked at Scotsman, Tebbe and Thorp. They all knew what it meant.

It was a race between the English engineers and the French. Scotsman said what they were all thinking. 'They get that fucking thing set up, they'll destroy the bridge for good. Then we're dead.'

They looked helplessly at one another. Around the English company, most of the men were doing the same thing.

The earls, the traitor and Sir Thomas were huddled in urgent conversation.

As they spoke, the English engineers finally heaved the first beam into place. They let it down on to the arches with a creak and a groan. But then, instead of continuing their work, they detached their hooks and ropes, ran back and took cover in the town.

They knew what was coming.

As they left, Northampton broke away from the huddle with the lords. He did not bother to berate the engineers. He just yelled to the whole company to gather round. The Dogs fell in with the rest of them. All the men stood in silence, facing the river. Northampton stood in front of the toll house, his back to the bridge. Warwick moved to stand beside him, staring over the heads of the company, a hard expression on his face.

Northampton cleared his throat. There was another moment of silence. Then he spoke. 'I don't need to tell you what's happening over there. And I don't need to tell you what will happen if they get those fucking things working.'

He was quiet for what felt like an age. The whole group was silent.

'We need to get across that river. And we need to use that beam.'

They all looked at it. The beam was no more than two handspans wide and at least fifty paces long.

Completely untested.

And balanced across the fast-flowing waters of the Seine.

Northampton took another look around the group. 'I don't like the look of it either, boys,' he said. 'But someone needs to go first.' He looked at Sir Thomas. At Sir Denis. At Sir Godefroi.

At Warwick.

None of them stepped forwards. Northampton puffed out his cheeks and ran his hand through his grey hair, stiff with sweat and dust.

On the other side of the river, the French catapults were almost complete.

The earl took a deep breath. 'God's fangs,' he said. He looked back at the beam. 'I suppose it's better than a fucking tree trunk.'

Then he puffed out his chest. 'Archers,' he barked. 'Cover me. Shoot anything that moves. Get across when you can.

'The rest of you: if you're coming with me, keep your fucking distance when we're crossing. I don't want to fall in, and nor do you.

'If you're not coming with me...' He paused. 'You can go and hang in hell.'

When Loveday had been a young man, a fair had toured the villages of Essex in the summer months, when there was harvesting and holidays, and men and women got drunk and danced late in the long evenings.

The fair had come every year, with the same cast of performers, always going through the same tricks: some juggling fire and conjuring coins from the air; others telling jokes before the whole crew performed a bawdy play.

There had been one display Loveday had always made sure to watch. A young woman with a large gap between her teeth, her limbs wiry and lithe and her hair wrapped tight in a scarf on top of her head, would tie a rope tight between two apple trees, clamber nimbly into the branches of one and walk the rope backwards and forwards, balancing on her feet, then finishing the trick by proceeding along it upside down, standing on her hands.

It was this trick Loveday remembered as he watched the Earl of Northampton, wearing armour that must have weighed as much as that young woman, his sword strapped to his side, and a helmet on his head, with the pointed visor opened to the sky, step through the toll gate towards the beam.

This trick he remembered as the earl tested the beam with his foot. As he checked the straps on his armour. Squatted and straightened his legs three or four times, as though he were checking they were fit to walk. From where Loveday stood, his guts twisting agonizingly, Northampton's legs looked strong and the beam looked solid. Yet the span from one bank of the river to the other now looked like it was more than fifty paces. Sixty, perhaps. The drop from beam to water was at least twenty.

Tebbe and Thorp went with the other archers to the riverbank. They stood, bows nocked, covering the far bank.

Northampton called down to them: 'Are you sure you can shoot across this fucking river?'

Tebbe and several others nodded. They did not take their eyes off the far side.

The French catapult-men were testing their counterweights.

Northampton called down to the archers again. 'Once I'm across, follow me. We don't need to destroy the stone-thrower, but we do need to kill every fucker who can work them.'

Then he looked back at Warwick and Sir Thomas. 'If I fall...' he began. But he didn't finish the thought. He just set off across the beam. One foot in front of the other. His arms out at his sides. Painfully slowly.

Loveday held his breath. Then he felt something stirring next to him. He twisted around. Scotsman was pulling his helmet on to his head. Loveday looked at him in disbelief. 'No...'

Scotsman nodded. 'Yes. We've taken out catapults. No other cunt here has.'

When Loveday turned back to the river, Northampton was already halfway across the beam. An alert French crossbowman was running towards the far bank, realizing what was happening and trying to get into range to shoot the earl. But as he ran, arrows flew swift and true from the English side. Two hit him and he collapsed, holding his side.

Seeing this, more of the French began to run to the bridge. Loveday could see their leaders, the knights, screaming at them to stay back, and wait for the catapults to be ready.

But their discipline was poor. Some ran forwards. Others hung back.

On the far side of the bridge, Northampton wobbled. He put both his arms out, and for a moment it looked as though he was going to pitch sideways into the Seine.

Yet somehow – by God's grace, or his own strength and nerve – he did not.

He righted himself. Then he raised a fist in the air and screamed from the bottom of his lungs: 'King Edward! St George! Come on, you fucking devils! Come here and fucking die!'

Then he jumped from the beam, rolled back down the bank towards the water and took cover under the first stone arch on the French side.

'Did he mean them or us?' murmured Sir Thomas.

Loveday ignored him. Instead he watched Thorp send an arrow straight into the throat of a Frenchman waving a scythe.

He watched Tebbe put another through the bowel of a huge, bald Norman villager brandishing a spear.

And he saw Scotsman setting off across the beam, with a line of knights, men-at-arms and footsoldiers forming around the toll booth.

Loveday put his left hand to his belt and felt his short sword hanging there.

Took a deep breath.

And joined the line.

When Loveday dropped from the beam to the riverbank and rolled, as Northampton had done, down to the covered spot below the stone arch, his hands were shaking and his ears were whining and his heart felt as though it was going to burst.

But he was there.

Scotsman was grinning manically at him.

Northampton was preparing to scramble back up the bank, shouting commands that he couldn't understand.

Sir Thomas Holand and Sir Denis were hunkered down too.

Then Tebbe dropped down from the bridge, and rolled down the bank to join them.

'Archers,' Northampton was saying. 'Finally some fucking archers. Spread out and keep shooting.' He winked at Loveday. 'Nice of you to join us,' he said. Then he drew his sword and bent his knees, ready to sprint.

'We all ready?' he called. 'For St George and King Edward?'

There were nods all around.

Behind them, there was a huge splash in the river, and spray fell around them like rain.

'I guess they've got the fucking catapults going,' muttered the Scot.

But there were no more splashes. For when Northampton gave the order to begin the assault up the steep riverbank, and they emerged screaming war cries into the line of sight and shot, all they saw was fifteen or so dying crossbowmen and peasants, lying with arrows in their chests and limbs, and two abandoned catapults.

One was in working condition. The other was missing its counterweight.

And in the distance the remainder of the French company was fleeing, abandoning their position, some of them sitting two and three together on a single horse.

Northampton sheathed his sword and looked around him. 'Christ preserve us all,' he said. He kicked at the dirt. 'Do these French cowards know how to do anything except fucking run away?'

The Earl of Warwick straightened and patted Northampton's back. He was wearing his big white grin again. He shook his head and then he and Northampton clattered breastplates in a great, armoured bear hug.

'Anyone fall in?' asked Northampton, looking back at the river.

'No one who mattered,' replied Warwick.

'Then let's tell those engineers to get busy making that bridge wide enough for a fucking cart,' Northampton said. 'I don't fancy tightrope walking back again. Meantime, let's get word to the king. And send riders north to track down Hugh Hastings and deliver him the good fucking news too.'

He beckoned Sir Denis over. 'Send runners to our lord Edward and that rum fucker Hastings.' He smiled. 'And tell every cunt who missed this that we cut down a thousand French, gave them a sharp battle, took a few casualties of our own, but sent them packing. It'll get cocks hard. We're going to need hard cocks from now on.'

Sir Denis laughed and marched off.

The earl looked around the group. He puffed out his cheeks. 'Never a moment of doubt,' he said. 'Right, men?'

There was a rumble of relieved laughter.

The Scotsman piped up. 'So what next?'

Northampton nodded his head, satisfied. 'Good question. Next, we secure this bridge and have a fucking drink. Then we get the rest of the army across it. Then we all ride as fast as we ever have, that way.' He pointed north, towards the treeline.

'What's there?' said the Scot.

'There,' said Northampton, 'is a hundred miles of virgin French countryside, an army twice as big as ours, another fucking river and the fight of our lives.

'In case you hadn't noticed, the game is fucking on.'

26

The king and his army approached a city in Picardy, which they were to pass by. The prince and his squadron stayed too long in front of the city, and he dearly wanted to obtain permission for his men to attack it... But he did not dare to carry it out, for the king told him that he was likely to meet the enemy shortly, and he did not want to lose any men...

The Acts of War of Edward III

'**B**ut Father—'
The prince was whining – again. His eyes were tinged pink. His skin was sallow and his cheeks puffy.

It was late in the morning, and they had stopped to eat in open-sided pavilions put up quickly by the squires. The prince was pushing his food around listlessly and complaining.

Like Romford, he was tired.

Romford guessed he was also sore in his guts.

Since crossing the repaired bridge at Poissy the army had been marching faster than ever before. Twenty-five, thirty, even thirty-five miles a day. Away from the sharp escarpments and woodland of the Seine valley, into rolling hills cut by streams and rivers long extinct.

The days were still hot and the pace of the march made men – even princes – dry and thirsty.

The quartermasters had run out of flour, which meant the men ate no bread, but only meat, salted cod and what half-ripe fruit they could raid from orchards.

The heat and the food clogged the guts and made it hard to shit. Each morning the foul-trenches the engineers dug rang with the groans and yelps of men straining to pass turds as sharp as stones. Like matins bells, sounding the hours of mens' suffering.

Powder made it even harder to shit.

And since the prince had discovered its pleasures, he had been taking it at every chance.

Romford knew how his secret had reached the prince. He had grown careless.

He had found more powder in the apothecary in Poissy than he had ever seen in his life. It was also the finest he had known: its smell not acrid like piss, but sweet as flowers. He had been dabbing it on his gums, little and often, as much as he dared. Eventually someone had seen him.

The one-eyed knight Sir Thomas.

Sir Thomas, rather than berating him or confiscating the powder, had started sharing Romford's supply.

Then, on the second night they spent in Poissy, sleeping in the hall of the French king's own hunting lodge there, waiting for the bridge to be made strong enough for carts, the knight had brought him to the prince. Smiled slyly at them both. Told Romford to drop a little of the powder in the prince's wine.

Romford had watched the prince sip the wine, his face drooping in pleasure and his eyes seeming to loosen.

In that moment he had remembered Father. The feel of the old priest's sticky spittle on his finger. The stink of his thin body.

The blood dripping from his teeth after he spat out Shaw's nose.

That vision had passed. But Romford's new obligation to feed his master's habit had not. The prince loved the powder as much as every man who tasted it. And once he had tasted it, he craved it. So each evening, after the lords dined, he summoned Romford to his private quarters, to spend long hours rolling loaded dice and licking powdered fingers, until oblivion came and they passed out on rugs and cushions on the floor.

Romford was as helpless to stop the prince as he was to stop himself.

During the days Romford could hide his mind's dullness and the ache from his hardbaked innards. He could go about his duties and keep quiet, melting into throng of servants and attendants.

The prince could not.

So every day, with his stomach pinched and his eyes bloodshot, the prince whinged anew at the king. 'But, Father—' he said, high-pitched and reedy.

The sound of his voice made Romford squirm, right down to his toes. So did the name he called.

That morning, the king's patience ran out. They were near a town called Beauvais. Romford could see it below the hilltop where they dined. It seemed a fine place – surrounded by high walls and strong gatehouses. The streets were planned around a gigantic cathedral, from which ornate towers and spires writhed higher than any building Romford had ever seen, or even imagined.

The prince wanted to take men to attack the city and rob the cathedral.

His father would not allow it.

'But, Father—'

Addressed this way for what seemed the hundredth time, King Edward put down the small, pearl-handled knife with which he was eating, and stared along the small table. 'In the name of the Virgin, my son, hold your peace,' he said. 'I have explained patiently to you what we are to do in the coming days, but since you seem as heedless of my advice as ever, let me repeat myself.'

A hush fell among the attendants at tableside. An old friar attending the king fiddled with the rope at his waist and looked away. Romford gazed at the floor.

'We are marching north, as fast as God permits. It is a simple strategy, which is its virtue. Yesterday I informed the French king that I am ready to meet him in battle at the time and place of his choosing. Naturally I meant nothing of the sort.

'What I wish him to do is chase us. To exhaust his men harrying us until we cross the River Somme, where we may rest, restock, swell our numbers and then destroy him.

'As I say, it is a simple strategy. But it relies on one tactic. We keep moving.'

He paused.

'Let me say it again: we keep moving. We do not stop. We have no time to waste besieging cities. Our men have plenty of plunder. I need them fit and alive. Not fat on the profits of theft and either drunk or dead. Do you understand? We keep—'

'But, Father—' The prince's face looked grey. Like wet clay.

King Edward banged the table, rattling plates. 'But nothing! Philippe has reinforced his armies. They are equal now in number to ours. They are still growing. And they have good men. Our cousin the King of Bohemia is leading his vanguard. Other divisions are led by—'

Now the prince, petulant and tired, interrupted. His voice was tense and high-pitched. 'The King of Bohemia is a hundred years old and blind. He is a dribbling cripple. Philippe is a coward. And the French are soft. What is there to fear?'

King Edward looked at his son. Romford dared a glance out of the corner of his eye. He saw something terrible in the king's face. Scorn.

'King Johann of Bohemia is one of the greatest warriors in the world. His bravery is legendary. He has survived half a century in a part of Christendom where you, my boy, would last half a day and no more. He lost his sight fighting pagans in the ice-fields of Lithuania. He is fifteen winters older than I am and has spent every one of them – and the summers too – doing battle with someone. By God, he may be blind, but he is a worthy adversary, and he is riding with his son Charles, who will one day soon be crowned German emperor.

'If we stop here, they will catch us before we reach the Somme. A part of me wishes this might happen, so that you could be taught a lesson in what battle really looks like. But I should prefer you to learn from the advantage of the winning side, rather than seeing our knights and archers lying dead in their thousands at the end of French and German lances.'

With this, Edward pushed back his seat and stood from the table. 'We have already wasted precious moments with this conversation. Think well on what I have said to you, and pray to Christ for guidance.' His voice was cold. He walked from the pavilion.

The prince sat, sullen, at his place. Then he picked up his plate and without saying anything tipped his food on to the ground. Mutton knuckles and muddy gravy spattered at his feet. He looked around the silent squires who stood at the edges of the pavilion.

'Boy,' he said to Romford. 'I need you.'

All afternoon, Romford sat in the gloom of the prince's tent and watched him drink wine laced with powder. The tent was stifling as the midday sun blazed on it. But the heat softened as evening approached.

The steward Sir John Chandos placed two men-at-arms at the tent's entrance. They allowed only Sir John to enter, though he never came in far. He only put his head through the flaps of the entrance from time to time, to see what state the prince was in.

Romford took a little of the powder. But mostly he watched the prince, and listened to him rant against his father. At first the prince was wounded and close to tears, and cursed the king for treating him like an infant, 'like my baby brothers Lionel and John'.

Then he grew bitter, complaining of courtly slights Romford could not understand. Later, as powder and wine gripped him, he became wild and incoherent, babbling in French and English, singing snatches of song to himself over and over.

Then he passed out for a time.

Through all of this Romford found he was not expected to say anything, but only to make sympathetic sounds, measuring out the powder dose.

He did not mind.

In England he had spent his life around men who drank or took powder. Some of them were boring. Others were violent. Yet others were gripped with a manic urge to fuck – an urge they sometimes tried to act out on him.

Compared to this, the prince was good company. So he listened, and kept his senses soft by dabbing powder, and then watched the prince sleep. Each time Sir John's head appeared through the tent-flaps he bowed softly to him, which seemed to satisfy Sir John.

This went on until the evening set in, the prince awoke, and Chandos came back, this time with Sir Henry de Burghersh and another knight Romford recognized but did not know. They dragged Prince Edward on to a horse, seating him in front of Sir Henry, like a little boy, and took him away.

Then Romford found his own horse, being tended by a groom, who gave it to him, along with his bow and the black helmet he liked, and told him which road to follow to catch up with the rest of the prince's division, who had set off late and gone past Beauvais, but burned the suburbs outside its walls to vent their anger.

Romford followed the groom's advice, taking a road that looped wide around the city, away from its armed gatehouses. He rode five or six miles, passing occasional small, straggling companies of English soldiers, slowed down by carts with broken wheels or men or horses with injured legs.

He arrived at the new camp, a long way to the other side of Beauvais, just as the stars were coming out. The king, he learned, had gone yet further ahead, and was camped near the vanguard, with the Earl of Northampton and Sir Godefroi, the traitor knight.

There was no sign of the prince, though there was excitement among many of the squires, who spoke of a night-raid that was to take place on two monasteries which they said stood nearby.

Romford had no urge to burn a monastery that night. Nor any other night. He found a space on the ground to sleep. He dreamed his mouth was full of fingers, choking him. Yanking at his tongue.

He woke up before the dawn, gasping for air.

He found the prince's tent at first light, before the trumpets sounded to rouse the sleepers. He guessed the prince would need powder and wine to help him move.

But when he approached the pavilion, the two men-at-arms posted outside moved together to bar his way.

He stopped and looked from one to the other. They did not seem hostile. Just certain that he would not pass inside.

He knew they must recognize him.

'Can I—' he began.

The man-at-arms on the left, who wore plate armour on his shoulders and had cropped his blond hair almost to the skin around his ears, chuckled. 'Forget it,' he said. 'Someone's in there already.'

Romford stood uncertainly, poised between leaving and staying. 'Sir Thomas?' he asked. 'One of the other squires?'

The blond man-at-arms began to answer, but as he did so, the tent-flaps opened behind him and the question was resolved.

The Earl of Warwick walked out, scowling. He seemed a little thinner than when Romford had seen him just a few days previously. He swept a hand through his hair and closed his eyes, as if trying to keep his composure.

The two men-at-arms hopped aside – nimbly, thought

Romford, considering their size. Warwick turned briefly to each and gave them a faint nod.

'Be sure he is ready when I return,' he said. 'It will not be long. He needs to be dressed. Get someone to help. Beyond that, allow no one in. By Christ, he is fortunate that the king sent me, and not my lord Northampton.'

Saying this, Warwick saw Romford. A look of faint recognition passed across his face, but evidently he had either forgotten saving Romford's life or had nothing to say about the matter. 'You – you're one of his attendants.'

Romford looked down at his striped hose, now grimy from a week and more of wear. 'I think so, my lord.'

Warwick knit his brows. 'Well, either you are or you aren't. If you're not, get out of here. If you are, get in there. Make him fit for public sight as fast as you are able,' he said. 'We have not much time before we break this fetid camp. The French are on to us. We march. All of us – vanguard, middle and rear together. But before we go, there is something that young man needs to see.'

With that, Warwick swept off. The men-at-arms grinned at Romford. Then they stood apart and let him in.

As he passed, the blond one said, 'God help you.' The other one said, 'Good luck.'

He found the prince slumped on a pile of rugs on the floor. He was face down, with his belly on the rugs and his arse sticking in the air.

He was dressed, but in the previous night's clothes. Thin, smooth hose dyed red covered his legs. Above he wore a short-cropped surcoat, in a thin and incredibly soft material, somewhere between black and blue. He had kicked off his boots. As he lay, his long hair spread untidily around his head.

Romford crossed the tent. The air inside was still chilled by the night. Romford smelled damp grass and mud, and male sweat. He could hear the prince snoring softly, his breathing muffled. He stood over him a second, not quite sure what he ought to do. Then he gently reached down and placed his hand on the small of the Prince's back. The soft pile of the fabric was like the fur of some newborn beast.

The Prince said something in his sleep and shifted around a little, then continued snoring. Romford stood back up and wondered what he should do. He knew he had no place laying his hands on a king's son. Yet he knew also that if Warwick returned and found he had not at least roused the prince, he would be in serious trouble.

He cleared his throat. Once. Then louder. Then louder still.

The prince mumbled again in his sleep. It sounded to Romford as though he said the name 'Joanie'.

But still he did not wake.

Romford looked at his body, and tried to decide which was the next-least offensive part for him to touch. He decided on the left foot.

He bent down and, as lightly as he could, tickled the sole. The prince stirred a little more. And now he spoke distinctly. 'Joanie, it's just us.'

Then, very abruptly, he rolled over and opened his eyes. He looked at Romford in confusion. 'Did you burn them both?'

Romford knelt down. 'I didn't burn anything,' he said.

'No,' said the prince, rubbing his eyes and looking around the tent, as though he sensed something was missing. 'Of course. What hour is it?'

Then his face drained of colour. He rolled over on to his hands and knees and retched on to the ground beside him. Romford stood back and let him puke. He walked to the corner of the pavilion, where, on a small portable altar, a wine jug stood beside a thin cup. He sniffed the wine, poured a measure into the cup, took out the powder pouch from the bag at his side and dropped a small pinch into the wine. He swirled the cup and watched the grains vanish into the glossy red liquid.

He took it to the prince, who was wiping his mouth on one of the rugs. 'Drink this,' he said gently.

The prince drained it in one gulp. He shuddered, then his whole body seemed to relax and he smiled comfortably. He wiped his mouth with the back of his hand. His gaze swam to meet Romford's.

'We need to dress you,' said Romford. 'The Earl of Warwick is coming.'

'Hmm?' said the Prince. He hugged himself and smiled blissfully. 'Warwick? What does he want?'

'I'm not sure,' said Romford. 'He said you had to see something.'

'Then he can bring it to me,' said the prince. He tried to smooth down his hair with his hands, but much of it still stuck up in unruly strands.

'Would you like me to change your clothes?' asked Romford.

The prince shook his head. He smiled again. 'It will be night again before long.'

Before Romford could answer this, trumpets began to sound all around the camp. The two men-at-arms walked into the tent. They looked at the prince, then at each other. The one who was not blond – he had black hair, receding far back from his forehead, and a cruel look in his eyes – addressed Romford. 'This the best you could do?'

Romford shrugged. 'He is awake.'

'He has nothing on his feet.'

Romford looked around. He saw a pair of boots thrown at the edge of the tent. 'He has boots.'

'Then get them on him.'

Romford walked slowly across the tent and picked them up. The prince sat on his rugs and looked ready to vomit again. But when Romford gave him the boots, he put them on.

The cruel-faced man tapped his foot as he waited for the prince to pull the laces tight and stand up. 'This way, my lord,' he said. 'You're wanted. Very badly, I gather.'

The prince pouted. The blissful look drained from his face. He stood on wobbly legs. The blond man-at-arms offered a hand, and the prince took it for a moment as he grew used to being upright. Together they tottered towards the tent-flaps which led outside.

Romford did not know whether he was meant to follow too. But he was not bid to stay. So as the other three men left the tent, he went behind them.

Outside the dew was almost dry on the ground, and men were hurrying everywhere, dressing and rolling up mats, swilling out their mouths from their flasks and spitting. The camp was busy – busier than Romford had known any camp before. It seemed the army had swelled in size. That all of the uncountable number of men under King Edward's command were pressing into one space. Romford heard knives being sharpened and the clatter of a blacksmith's hammer. Moans came from the shitting trenches. He tried to count the days since he had visited one. He reckoned it at four.

The men-at-arms walked fast through the thronging camp, weaving in and out of tents and pavilions, hopping over ropes and pegs and pushing through companies of soldiers and servants. Romford had to hurry to keep up as they guided the prince along. They were not dragging him, but nudging him to make sure he moved at their pace rather than his own. Some of the troops they passed recognized the prince and stepped respectfully out of the way. But others smirked and averted their eyes.

After a short while they came to the edge of the camp, where the crowd thinned out. At last Romford saw what sort of countryside they were now in. The land had flattened out, and a long and very straight track stretched away north through open fields, unbounded by hedgerows, as far as the horizon. Many of these fields had been recently harvested, and were covered in dusty stubble. But others were still to be cut, and they rippled gently as the morning breeze moved golden stalks, heavy at their heads with ripe ears of grain.

A small group of ordinary troops were standing around, looking at something beside the road. The men-at-arms pushed through them, and guided the prince to the front. Romford tucked in at the rear of the group. As he did so he saw what they were looking at.

Next to the road the king's carpenters had built a gallows.

It was a simple three-sided wooden frame, made of the same sort of hewn timber the engineers had used to remake the bridge at Poissy. Into its cross-beam were screwed four strong iron rings. Through each of the rings was threaded a thick rope, which ended in a noose. Against this structure slouched two unshaven priests. Romford heard one of them make some joke, and the other snort.

He thought of his father.

Then he saw what lay beyond the gallows. The sight made his stomach turn. Sitting on the ground were around twenty ordinary soldiers, guarded by five or six men-at-arms.

Romford recognized several of the men. They were of the prince's company.

The prisoners sat in pairs, tied back to back, with their hands behind them. Some looked glassy-eyed. A few sat with their heads slumped forwards. Sleeping – or trying to.

He knew one of them. It was the squire who had been next to him at the banquet, on the night the prince had first called him forwards to play dice. The young man looked pale and frightened. He was shaking his head, and seemed to be talking to himself.

Romford felt a strong urge to go over to him and say something. But he did not know what. And he knew he would be stopped by the men-at-arms.

Then he thought he might go – turn away from the scene altogether and wander away alone. Walk back, every step of the way they had come. Back across the river, back past all the bad places: Caen, Saint-Lô and Valognes. To the beach. To the boat. To the cog. To the beginning.

But before he could do any of that, a shadow fell on the ground beside him.

The Earl of Warwick strode past.

Earlier Romford had seen Warwick part-dressed, with his thick padded gambeson cinched at the waist. Now the earl was heavily armoured with a breastplate, covered with his arms of the bear and ragged staff, and his thighs protected by mail chausses and gleaming metal plates.

In his armour Warwick walked with a slight stiffness to his gait. But he marched briskly. So briskly that when he passed by Romford the air moved.

Then it moved again, as half a dozen of Warwick's men-at-arms clanked up. They did not pass, but came to a halt beside Romford, where they looked carefully at the gallows, exchanging a few words in low voices. One of them glanced in Romford's direction, but paid him no mind.

Warwick had gone on. He stopped in front of the gallows, turned to face the small crowd, and spoke quickly.

Romford watched him. But he also craned his neck so that he could watch the back of the prince's head.

'We have no time to dally here,' said Warwick. 'These men are condemned by the king's own hand to die. They were ordered to refrain from damaging Church property and to obey our lord king's command to march with all haste, since we are pursued by the enemy.

'They disobeyed this command, despoiled and burned two monasteries.'

He looked briefly around the crowd. Then he raised his right hand, and the six men-at-arms beside Romford marched around the group and took up positions behind the gallows. Warwick waited for them. He looked at the prisoners. Then he stared directly at the prince. 'This is the penalty for disobedience,' he said.

And once he had said that, he walked away, past the crowd, without a second glance back. When he swept past Romford, the air moved again. Then it was still.

Back at the gallows, the men-at-arms knew what to do. Two of them grabbed the nearest pair of prisoners. They cut them free from one another, but did not unbind their hands. They bundled them towards the gallows, and tightened a noose around each of their necks.

Then they did the same with another pair.

The sun was climbing in the sky behind the gallows. As Romford stared into the light he felt tears welling in his eyes. But he could not look away.

Neither could he look away as the four other men-at-arms, their faces shadowed as the sunlight grew strong at their backs, took up the loose ends of the ropes.

Three of the condemned men stayed silent. One began to sob and wail.

The priests passed along the line, placing a hand on each man's head and murmuring words Romford could not hear. The wailing man kept making his noise.

Romford glanced at the back of the prince's head. He was motionless, glaring straight ahead, as though daring Warwick's men to go through with the hanging.

But if the prince thought he could stop them through the power of defiance alone, he was wrong. The four men-at-arms holding the ropes took up the slack, and at a signal from one of the others, they stepped back and heaved.

The ropes creaked as they tightened. It reminded Romford of the ship.

Together the four prisoners were hiked into the air. Their eyes bulged and their tongues poked out of their mouths, quickly filling with blood so they became huge and grotesque. Like blood-sausages. The one who was wailing choked loudly for a few heartbeats, then made no more sounds. All four men thrashed their legs silently, kicking one another, pissing themselves and spinning around on the ropes.

As they spun, the prince stared at them. Romford stared at the back of the prince's head. All the while the sun continued to creep higher in the sky, so that Romford's eyes burned more and more and his skin began to prickle.

It took the men a long time to die. But when the priests decided they were gone, the men-at-arms released the ropes and the bodies thudded on the ground, where they crumpled. The rope-pulling men-at-arms rested on their haunches, flexing their hands and shaking out their arms. The other two dragged the corpses to one side of the gallows, and laid them out roughly, head to toe alongside one another.

By the time this was done, the crowd was losing interest and moving away, back to the camp to join the noisy preparations for the march. But Romford stayed as the next four of the twenty men were hauled forwards. Having watched their companions die, they were all very frightened. They dug their heels in, struggled and shouted. The men-at-arms hit them, backhanded, with metal gauntlets and arm-guards. By the time the men were tied to the gallows, three of the four had blood from split eyebrows running down their faces.

One of this four was the squire from the banquet. He sobbed and spat, and shook his head violently, so blood was streaked all down it.

It did him no good.

As before, the priests gave their quick blessings. Then the four men-at-arms pulled the ropes again. And the four prisoners choked slowly and agonizingly to death.

Halfway through this, the prince lost his nerve. He tried to turn away. But the two men-at-arms who were guarding him – the blond one with the short-cropped hair, and the cruel-faced one – placed their hands on his shoulders and kept him in place. Romford knew that he was being forced to watch every one of the men die.

This was his punishment.

Twenty lives lost, to show him the error of his.

Yet as he understood this, Romford realized that he himself was not being made to stay. So as the squire from the banquet and the three men beside him jerked and pissed their last, he summoned energy into his legs.

He stepped backwards at first, his eyes still fixed on the prince.

Then, after a few steps, he swivelled on his heel and stumbled in a daze, back towards the camp.

He could barely see. His vision was stamped with a green and black silhouette of four corpses dangling on ropes, and the prince's head, motionless, staring towards them.

As he tried to clear his eyes, he weaved between tents being taken down and rolled up by servants, catching his feet on pegs.

He tripped past horses being shod and tacked, and donkeys being hitched to carts.

He almost blundered into two huge-shouldered cooks in greasy aprons, pushing one another and snarling, face to face, locked in some disagreement he would never know.

He staggered. Yet as he did, he began to understand clearly where he was going.

Home.

Home.

And if not home, then to a quiet place where he would eat

all the powder he had left in the pouch. Eat so much he would sleep and never wake.

Warwick had said that burning monasteries was a sin. He was not sure if eating powder to die was too.

He did not care.

And that was how he was when he walked directly into Loveday and the Scotsman, and Tebbe and Thorp, who were coming towards him, part of the vast crowd now making their way towards the straight road north, the gallows and the track to another river.

Where the road away from home lay.

Where each step would take them closer to hell.

It was Loveday Romford stumbled into.

It was the giant Scotsman who caught him when he fainted.

And it was Tebbe who stood over him when he woke up. So that the first sight he saw when his vision returned was the sunburned face of the lean and long-haired archer he had known since the cog and the beach.

And that sight made him want to cry with happiness, even though Tebbe was shaking his head and calling him a silly cunt, and asking him what he thought he looked like, wearing those fucking stripy hose.

27

[The King of England's] men on a *chevauchée* were very pensive and melancholic, and each spoke to the other how in no part would they be able to cross the Somme... and at this time a squire... came and said to the king and all with him, 'Sire, if you wish to cross, I have found a good crossing...'

Accounts of a citizen of Valenciennes

Loveday watched over the boy as he slept.

He felt Scotsman's eyes boring into him from his right side. But he resisted turning to look at his old friend. He knew what the Scot wanted to say.

It was the same thing he had been saying for the past three days.

Loveday concentrated on Romford's chest, rising and falling as he lay beside the campfire. The light flickering on his face. He waited for the Scotsman to crack and speak.

It did not take long.

'We need to send him back to the prince.'

'No.'

'Loveday.'

'No.'

'He's no use with us. He's been asleep, or as good as, for

almost three days. We can't keep carrying him at this pace. We're almost at the Somme. There'll be fighting tomorrow. Probably for us all. Do you see him opening his eyes long enough to use that bow?'

Loveday said nothing.

'Anyway, he's supposed to be one of the prince's squires now. He's not one of us any more.'

Loveday shook his head. 'If they want him, they'll come and find him.'

Scotsman snorted. 'And you think they'll be happy with us when they do? He's absconded. Saints' bones, we're harbouring a fucking fugitive. ' He shook his head and stared at the flames.

Loveday finally looked at him. 'I don't care. We're not taking him back. Whatever has been happening to him there, it's killing him. I've thrown away that powder. But he'll find more if he's with them. We've just got him back. I'm not losing another man.' Millstone's steady face flashed into his mind.

They sat silent for a time. Tebbe and Thorp were playing cross and pile. Scotsman brooded. Loveday waited for him to speak again.

'He told us he was going home. Maybe he's right.'

'No.'

But Scotsman persisted. 'What are we still here for? Our forty days must be up. We got enough pay in Caen. That fat cunt Sir Robert would rather see us dead than pay us what we're owed. You can forget Sir Godefroi. And Northampton and the rest of them won't miss us. Not really.'

A glowing branch fell out of the fire, scattering embers like stars. Loveday kicked it back into the blaze. 'We can't go back. You know that. The French are a day behind us now. Not even. As you say, they're close enough that tomorrow we'll be fighting them.

'If we leave, we'll never get through their lines. And if we did, what then? The king's left no English garrisons behind. Just angry villagers coming out of the woods to find their homes burned, their animals gone, their women raped, their sons dead, their lives ruined.'

The Scot just grunted.

'The only way out of this is forwards,' Loveday said. 'Together.'

Then he too fell quiet, and both men listened to the noises of the night. Insects chirping. The fire crackling. Romford's soft breathing.

They sat and thought about the reckoning ahead. About all the times they had gone to war before.

Never knowing which time would be their last.

They moved out with Sir Godefroi before the trumpets woke the rest of the camp. Their company was small. Loveday reckoned it was no more than a hundred men, all on horseback. Half were knights and men-at-arms, and the rest a mixture of archers and footsoldiers. They all rode. Thousands of horses had been stolen on the march north from the Seine. Mounts were easy to come by. But in their saddles, all the men were tired and tense. Irritable on account of their empty bellies and blistered feet and sunburned faces.

The Dogs were now five, for Loveday had managed to coax Romford from his sleep and persuade him to come out with them. Thorp, ever resourceful, had found the boy a pony. They had stripped off the prince's livery and bartered with a couple of young archers for less striking clothes. All he retained was his bow and a blackened helmet he'd picked up from somewhere.

Yet he sat in the saddle with an empty look in his eyes. It was a look of purest melancholy. As though something inside him were broken.

Of course, Loveday's own problem was that something outside him was broken: his right hand. But he had become used to riding left-handed, and he found Romford's distress a salve for his own. He could not worry about himself and the boy at the same time. So he chose to forget his own woes and fret about the boy. To wonder what had brought him to the state he was now in.

War was hard on people. Was it harder on boys than older men? He was not sure. Perhaps it was hard in a different way.

He shook the thought away. Sir Godefroi was calling the company to a halt, to give them orders. The track they were following had led them to high ground from which they could survey the landscape in front of them.

It was dominated by the course of a huge river. The Somme. But this was not a river like the Seine, which they had crossed at Poissy. That river was deep and fast, and tightly constrained by its steep banks; the Somme was wide and marshy. As it flowed west, it broadened massively, expanding so that its waters seemed to go where they pleased, as if they were in permanent flood. And it gave off a rough tang that Loveday had not smelled for several weeks: not since they marched inland from the beach.

Salt.

This huge, marshy river, Loveday realized, must be tidal. He had no idea what the shape of France was, but he understood that if he could smell saltwater, then their long march east and then north had brought them back to the coast. The sea was near. And England across it.

For some reason that made him glad.

Sir Godefroi stayed in his saddle to give his orders. His lame left leg turned sharply inwards in its stirrup, yet Loveday knew he had ridden as hard as any man in the army. He was strange and slippery, a liar and a turncoat. But deceptively strong.

'Look out there.' The traitor swept his hand in an arc, pointing to the huge expanse of river marsh below and ahead of them. 'What do we see?'

Scotsman called out: 'A fat river and about a hundred miles of fucking quicksand. A shitty place to die.'

Sir Godefroi nodded. For once, he did not seem annoyed by the Scot's rough insolence. 'True,' he said. 'But that is not all. If we sit here until noon, we will see much more that is dangerous. The false king and his allies are close enough to smell us. If we sit still, they will fall upon us from every direction. Like...' He paused a moment, reaching for the word in English. 'Like wolves.'

He looked at Scotsman. 'So there are many shitty ways to die. Some of them we see. Some we do not.' He paused. 'We have to cross the river.'

Behind Loveday an archer groaned. 'We've heard that before.'

'Yes, and if God is gracious, perchance you will hear it again. There are many rivers in France.' Sir Godefroi shrugged. 'If you do not like this, you should have stayed at home with your mother.'

There was a hubbub of bleak laughter. Loveday glanced at Romford, who sat in the saddle to his left. The boy still looked dazed. He reached across to him and patted him gently on his arm. Romford gave him a weak smile.

Sir Godefroi continued: 'There are five bridges to cross this river. Pont-Remy, Fontaine, Longpré... I can tell you their names, but you will forget. And we cannot waste time. So I tell you just this. The king orders us to try them all at once. The Earl of Warwick, he goes to one. Northampton, another. The Bishop of Durham – and so on.

'Us, we are going there. Abbeville.' And he pointed off to the left, where Loveday could see, a few miles distant, a city that straddled both sides of the water, built at the point where the river began to widen into its tidal marshes. Most of the city lay on the river's far, northern bank, in front of what seemed to be a huge forest. But a curve of thick walls and towers protected the part that lay on the southern side. Within the walls, Loveday assumed, there must lie a bridge.

Yet getting beyond the walls seemed an impossible task.

The city was almost as big as Saint-Lô, which had only fallen after the whole vanguard had assaulted it with battering rams. It was as powerfully defended as Caen, where they had lost Pismire at the gate.

But Sir Godefroi seemed unworried by the odds. He looked around the group and forced a grin. 'What? You think we are going to climb up the walls like monkeys? No. All we need to do is take one of the gatehouses. We do this, Edward will know the city can be taken. He will send the full force of the army behind us.'

Then he explained what they were going to do.

★ ★ ★

They wheeled their horses, snorting and stamping, into formation.

'Christ's hairy arse cheeks roasting on a fucking campfire, this is insanity,' muttered the Scot.

Loveday set his jaw tight.

The Scotsman went on. 'Well? Did we learn nothing at Rouen?'

Loveday had no answer. He just tugged at the strap on his battered helmet. Watched Tebbe and Thorp adjust their own basic armour. He tapped Romford on the arm. The lad had his black helmet slung on its strap around his neck.

'Put it on,' he said. 'It could save your life.'

Romford did not move.

The Scotsman overheard. He prodded his horse so it walked crabbily towards Romford's. Then he leaned sideways in his saddle, grabbed Romford's black open-faced helmet, and, with one huge hand, jammed it down tight on the boy's head. 'Listen to the old fucker,' he said. 'You might not care about your life. But he does.'

Romford made no attempt to adjust the helmet, which now sat lopsided and low over his eyebrows. But he did not take it off. Scotsman moved back towards Loveday. 'What about you?' he said.

'What about me?'

'Can you gallop one-handed?'

'We're about to find out.'

'Can you fight? At all?'

'We'll see.'

'This is madness.'

'You've already said that.'

Scotsman puffed out his cheeks and yanked hard at the

tangled ropes of his beard. He started to say something else. But before he could, Sir Godefroi began shouting.

'Ride hard! Stay out of range! Return here! St George! And the devil take a coward!'

Then they all kicked their horses and set off, riding as fast as they could, towards the walls of Abbeville.

A few times, when he was a younger man, Loveday had seen horses raced at fairs. Their riders were usually little men as thin as girls, who spent their lives moving from town to town: paid by merchants who sold horses to gallop their animals as fast as they could go, to show them off to would-be buyers.

There was always a reward – a ring, a purse of coins, a fat ram – for the winner of the race. But most of them, Loveday had sensed, rode not for the prize but for the thrill. The glory of victory. The peril of a fall and a broken neck. The back and ribs trampled. An awful death – or worse, a lifetime as a cripple.

Likewise, he had known men who were entranced by these races. The Captain had been. Tebbe and Thorp were, too. They would bet heavily on the outcome of races, and yell at the riders at full tilt, as though their words could put air in the beasts' lungs. Or wings at their backs.

Loveday had never felt what they felt. Had never been a man for gambling. Yet now, as he braced his legs in his stirrups, trying to keep his balance as he controlled his horse one-handed, feeling the thunder of hundreds of other hooves close around him, he understood it better than he ever had.

His helmet jumped and shifted on his head. He smelled horse sweat. Heard the maddened yells of the men around him. He knew one of the voices was his own, but he could not hear what he was shouting. As though he were underwater. Or screaming in his sleep.

The one voice he did pick out was Sir Godefroi's. As the company hurtled down the slope towards Abbeville, he was screaming at them to keep going. 'Heads low!' he bellowed. 'Don't stop! Don't turn!'

It was good advice. As they neared Abbeville, their horses' strides lengthening, they passed outcrops of trees. From the edge of his vision, Loveday saw men and women stepping from behind them try to pelt the charging company. He did not know what they were throwing. He guessed it was stones. Fruit. Shit. He kept galloping. They all kept galloping. The gates were three hundred paces away. Then two hundred. Then one hundred.

Crossbow range.

'Don't stop!' screamed Sir Godefroi. The company was spreading out. Loveday knew this was the moment of maximum danger. He tensed himself. Expected at any moment to feel the burning sensation of a bolt burying itself in his flesh.

Seventy-five paces. Fifty.

No bolt came.

And then, finally, Loveday heard Sir Godefroi screaming: 'Split! Split!' And he pulled as hard as he had ever pulled on his reins, and his horse, grateful, and as tense as he was, went left. Half the company did the same. The other half went right. And then they were galloping away – the way they had come back up the hill, dodging lumps of mortar and dung and other foul things thrown at them by angry people.

Hoping to hear behind them what Sir Godefroi had promised they would. A clatter and thunder of hooves as loud as their own, as the mayor of Abbeville sent out his men to give chase. The war howls of enraged men defending their city's honour.

The start of a chase, which would end, Sir Godefroi had promised, with a skirmish, and victory, and a sweep down the hill once more, their faces smeared with French blood, to take the now-undefended gate.

But as they galloped up the hill, their horses' legs starting to give out after nearly four miles, Loveday heard only their own mounts' hooves, rumbling a little more softly. And their own voices, which had changed from bawling to the heavy breathing of men exhausted. They came back to their starting point, and Sir Godefroi called for them all to halt.

They wheeled and sat in their saddles, dripping sweat. Patting their panting horses in thanks and passing around flasks of ale and water. Loveday saw Tebbe had shit and fruit pulp smeared on his back. The Scotsman was leaning over his horse's neck, blowing hard. Romford had some colour in his cheeks, though he still looked as though his mind were somewhere else. At least he had kept up with the ride, thought Loveday.

They all looked down to Abbeville.

The gates remained barred. There was no sign of any pursuit. No interest at all.

'What the fuck was that?' breathed the Scotsman.

'Quiet,' snapped Sir Godefroi. 'Wait.' His eyes were fixed on the gates. 'They will come.' He stared at them, as though willing them open with his prayers.

But the gates did not open. And no one sallied out.

And what they did see, after they had sat there for some time, watching Sir Godefroi gaze at the barricaded city, was a column of armed men in bright liveries, with pennons and flags above them, riding along the far bank of the River Somme towards the large, northern half of the city.

'Holy Christ,' said Thorp.

There were thousands of them. They flew the blue-and-gold French standard, and the red-and-gold of Sir Godefroi's brother. And other flags of blue-and-white stripes with red lions, which Loveday had not seen until now.

'Germans,' muttered one of the knights close by.

Sir Godefroi, the Dogs and the rest of the company could only watch from afar, as the soldiers, as small as insects at such great distance, filed in through some other, distant gate at Abbeville.

Their hearts sank.

Eventually Sir Godefroi spoke. 'So be it,' he said. 'We return to the king. We hope some other company has better luck.

'If they don't, there is only one hope left.'

Gloom hung over the English camp that night like fog. Gloom and fear. Every company had come back with the same report. The bridges were either broken, or defended by thousands of men. Or both.

They had been racing north. They now knew they had lost the race. The blue-and-white striped banners of the blind warrior-king Johann of Bohemia were everywhere on the far side of the river, and German knights patrolled the shore, their units mingling with an ever-swelling French royal host. There were wild reports of its size: fifteen thousand men. Forty thousand. One hundred thousand.

And in the south, men said, the French king's son was on his way. It was just a matter of time before they were caught between the French forces. Slowly but surely, they would be pushed into the marshes of the Somme. And when they got there, they would be cut down or drowned in mud.

The whole English army was now together. It was the biggest camp since the beach, sprawled out like a city. Tents and pavilions, their bright colours now faded after weeks under the sun, were pitched together in districts. Men no longer gathered around little campfires, but by bonfires built by companies combining and pooling the last of their fuel.

Within the tent city, food was scarce. Good cheer was even scarcer. The Dogs sat with Sir Godefroi's men, although the traitor was nowhere to be seen. They kept to themselves and ate. All had been supplied with tough salt cod and beans, which was rationed out by a pair of men-at-arms. Scotsman sniffed the fish with disdain, but he mashed everything together, loosened it with ale and boiled it, to make a salty, bitter slop. The food was rank. But they were famished after the exertions of their hapless tilt at Abbeville. Even Romford ate his fill.

As the sun sunk, staining the sky a dirty orange, Loveday felt a shiver. The first pinch of autumn was in the air. The Dogs felt it too. Thorp pulled his blanket, now ragged and stinking, from his satchel and draped it around his shoulders. Tebbe wrapped his thin arms around his body, and rubbed himself to warm his skin. Together they watched the bonfire dance. Scotsman, meanwhile, sat sullen. With a stick he dug a small trough in the dry earth between his legs. Romford hunched over his knees with his back to the fire, staring into the blackness.

Loveday reached over and patted the boy on his shoulder. 'Don't think about tomorrow. It will be what it will be.'

Scotsman snorted. 'What it's been so far has been a long ride on the hunt for a slow death,' he said. 'And I reckon we're getting close to our reward.'

Romford just shook his head sadly.

'What have you seen?' Loveday asked. 'What happened to you?'

'Nothing worse than has happened to others,' said Romford, his voice barely more than a whisper.

'We'll be home soon,' said Loveday.

But even he didn't believe it.

He woke with a start in the darkest part of the night.

For once it was not a dream that jolted him awake.

Something was moving. He knew it. He felt it.

Without turning his head, Loveday opened his eyes as wide as he could and looked around. It was not easy. The light was dim. At the centre of the sleeping company the bonfire was still warm, tiny flames licking up now and then from its embers. But their glow was red and low, and above, the moon and stars were hidden by high cloud.

Without standing up, he could not see very much at all.

So instead of straining his eyes, Loveday closed them. He lay in the dark and listened.

He listened long and intensely, trying to block out the other night noises of the camp: the tramp and low chatter of the guards on the western perimeter, maybe three hundred paces away. The farts and moans of men who had dined on nothing but bean paste and warm ale. The heavy breath of sleeping horses and the yapping of the stray dogs that trailed the army, scavenging scraps.

Loveday tried to listen for the sound of men at watch around their fire, as there ought to have been. He heard nothing. The Dogs had not been chosen for duty that night. From what Loveday could hear, whoever had been selected was asleep at their post.

A serious failure, thought Loveday. But given the exertions of the march, an understandable one. So instead of fuming, he did the watchmen's job for them: he kept his eyes shut and carried on listening. He wriggled his shoulder blades against the ground, trying to alter his position and coax some of the stiffness out of his back without giving away the fact that he was awake. And in his mind he teased apart what he could hear.

To one side of him, Scotsman. There was no mistaking the depth and growl of the man's breath. On the other, Thorp, a light sleeper who frequently muttered and yelped. To the other side of Thorp—

Then he stopped. He heard again whatever it was that had woken him. A tiny scuffing, scraping sound. Coming from somewhere behind his head.

His heart started thumping, and he cursed it, for the pounding of the blood in his ears made it harder to hear.

He strained his ears over it.

He waited for the scuffing to come again.

But before he did, he felt something cold at his throat. Cold and very sharp.

And then he heard a voice in his ear – breathy and soft, yet so close that it almost deafened him.

The voice said: 'Don't move.'

It said: 'Don't open your eyes.'

It said: 'Don't shout.'

And in an instant Loveday knew who it was. Which

meant he knew very definitely that he had to do as the voice said.

He kept his eyes shut. And he kept listening.

The voice was fast and certain. It said: 'Tell your master: ask Gobin Agace for the way. He knows the white crossing. Blink twice if you understand me.'

Very carefully, without opening his eyes, Loveday scrunched them. Twice.

The voice breathed thanks.

Then it said: 'I'm sorry about your friend.'

The owner of the voice took the blade away from his throat, and felt about for Loveday's left hand on the ground. He felt something small, ridged with contours, pressed into his palm.

The voice came back to his ear. 'You need this more than me now.'

Then it was gone, and Loveday was once more on his own in the dark. His heart was still hammering. His eyes were burning beneath their lids. And he felt a fury such as he had never known before building in his chest.

The woman from Valognes's voice was ringing in his ear.

He counted to ten, trying to control his building rage. He only partly succeeded. He opened his eyes and sat up. He saw the dark cut by ember-glow. The sleeping men. The clutter and filth of the camp.

He thought: Gobin Agace.

He thought: Northampton.

He thought: Pismire.

He saw his friend dying again.

He opened his left hand and in the blood-light of the fire he saw his own oxbone carving of St Martha.

He closed his fist around it, and crushed it into dust.

28

The battle at the ford of La Blanchetaque was hard and fierce, for the ford was well defended by the French. Many fine feats of arms were performed on that day by both sides.

Chronicles of Jean Froissart

'He's asleep.'

'Then wake him up.'

'Have you met him?'

Loveday stared at the tired, squat man-at-arms standing in the dark outside Northampton's pavilion. 'Let me in. I have to speak with him. Urgently. Now.'

'That's what everyone who comes here says. It's my job to tell you to fuck off. Urgently. Now. His lordship sleeps less than a fish. You ever seen a fish sleep?' The man at arms spoke in an exaggerated whisper.

Loveday felt anger rising from his gut like bile. 'If you don't let me in, we're all dead tomorrow.' He looked at the sky. The moon was briefly visible through the clouds. It was high. 'Today.'

'You might be planning on dying. I'm—'

From within the pavilion came a familiar voice. 'By the first hairs on St Agnes's cunt, can a man not fucking rest?'

The man-at-arms glared at Loveday as though he wanted

to throttle him. 'You fool,' he said. But he stood aside and let him in.

Northampton wore nothing but a nightshirt, which covered his knees, and a sword belt. He stood. A single torch lit the tent. By its faint orange glow Loveday saw a sword lying next to the earl's bed and a hard cot piled with rough woollen rugs. There was nothing else in the pavilion save a portable altar, its hinged doors unopened.

'Gobin Agace?' Northampton said. 'What the fuck do you know about Gobin fucking Agace?'

'I was told. By an... by an informant.'

Northampton studied Loveday in the torchlight. 'You don't have any informants. What happened to your hand?'

'I hurt it, sir. It has been this way since—'

'Tell me another time. Who told you about Gobin Agace?'

'My lord, I—'

'Don't fucking lord me. Who?'

'A woman, sir. A woman I met a long time ago. At Valognes. She came back. Here. Tonight. She told me. But I don't know who he is, or...'

Northampton shook his head. 'A fucking wench of the night told you about Gobin Agace. A prisoner we picked up less than a day ago. Christ on the tree at midnight. Did she bring you the Holy Grail as well?'

He buried his face in his hands for a moment. Then pushed them up and through his hair. He looked very hard into Loveday's eyes. 'What else did this night-wench say?'

'She just said someone called Gobin Agace knows about the white crossing.'

'I'd say he fucking does.'

'My lord?'

'We got it out of him a couple of hours ago. He didn't hold out long. Who the fuck was this wench?'

Loveday looked at his feet. 'I don't know, sir. She was in Valognes. She was a prisoner of ours for a time. Of the prince...'

Northampton nodded. As though he understood at last. 'Ah. Christ.' He put his face in his hands briefly once more. Then he looked up. 'Thank you, FitzTalbot. For telling me. You can go.'

'Sir, do you need me to do anything?' said Loveday. 'This white path—'

'They don't call it the white path. They call it the Blanchetaque. It means white stain. Would you like to see it?'

'Sir, I—'

'No point answering. The trumpets will sound shortly. And you'll be getting a very close look at it. Whether you like it or not.' He rubbed his eyes. Stifled a yawn. 'Go on, fuck off.'

Loveday thought about bowing. He nodded instead. Northampton nodded back.

For the briefest moment he even smiled.

Just as Northampton had promised, the trumpets blasted across the camp before Loveday had even made it back to the Dogs.

The discordant sound made him jump.

And by the time he arrived at the dead bonfire, the Dogs and the rest of Sir Godefroi's company were already scrambling up, rolling their blankets, pissing on the circle of ashes and fetching their horses so they could mount up.

All around them thousands of bleary troops were doing the same thing.

Men-at-arms and company leaders were calling orders for the men to abandon the tents and leave anything they could not carry. 'If you can live without it, dump it,' shouted one. 'We're not coming back.'

The Dogs shouldered their packs. They had little to leave behind. Thorp rounded up the horses. They all mounted. And as they did, Loveday told them what had happened in the night.

The Dogs listened intently. The Scot furrowed his bushy brows. 'Who's Gobin Agace?'

'I don't know. A prisoner, apparently. Someone who knows the river, I suppose.'

'And you're sure it was her? Who was here?'

Loveday nodded. 'It couldn't have been anyone else. She knew about Pismire. She said she was there – as though it was her who did it.'

Tebbe was shaking his head. 'You've been seeing a lot in your sleep,' he said. 'We killed the man who shot Pismire.'

'By God,' said Loveday. 'I wish this had been a dream.'

Out of the dark behind them Sir Godefroi rode up, wearing full armour. 'What do you wish was a dream?' he said.

'Everything,' said Loveday.

Scotsman snorted. In the black in front of them, the line began to move.

The whole army, a vast snake of men, marched and rode out of the camp, finding their way by torchlight until the grey came before the dawn. They skirted far around Abbeville, descending into a dry valley then following it a mile or so north.

Finally, as the sun rose on their right, they came to the vast marshes of the Somme. The Dogs followed Sir Godefroi's company, turning left as they reached the fringes of the marsh. As the terrain changed, their horses' hooves began to sink into grey mud that stank of salt from the sea and shit washed down from the towns upriver. No more grass grew. Slimy weeds, submerged for half of each day, lay on their sides. And in front of them, a hundred paces away across the sludgy flat, the grey mud became the brown river.

The water looked shallow. Knee height. Perhaps waist-high in the middle. But from the way it was lapping at the mud, Loveday could see it would not stay that way for long. It was low tide and this was an estuary. Soon enough the water would start rising.

There was no sign of any French or German troops on the far bank. Loveday felt prickles along the back of his neck.

They went another half-mile along the marsh-edge before the troops around them drew to a halt. Still there was nothing ahead of them but mud and water.

'Stay here,' said Sir Godefroi. Then he rode off back the way they had come.

Loveday looked left and right. As far as they could see, Englishmen were lined up at the river's edge. Silent. Nervous. Awaiting a command.

'What happens now?'

Loveday looked round in surprise. It was Romford. He adjusted his battered black helmet. It was the first time he had spoken since he woke.

The Scotsman answered for him. 'Now we find a way to get across that fucking swamp without sinking in the filth or drowning when the tide comes in. Loveday's heard there's a way. The white path.'

'The white stain,' said Loveday. 'It must be some sort of rock. A ford we can use.'

'The white whatever it is,' said the Scot. 'Someone has to find it, and we all have to get across it.'

Romford nodded. 'Where is it?'

Scotsman laughed, grimly. 'That's what we're waiting to find out.'

Loveday peered along the line, hoping to see some sign that whatever it was Gobin Agace had told Northampton was correct. That the ford had been located. But he could barely see fifty paces. The sun was now above the horizon, and the night's clouds were breaking up. The glare of first light reflecting from the wet estuary mud was dazzling. He used his left hand to shield his eyes. It was no good. 'I can't see anything,' he said, without turning round.

'That's because you're looking in the wrong direction,' said Tebbe, his voice grim.

'What?' Loveday turned away from the light, his eyes stinging and briefly half-blind.

The tall archer pointed to the far side of the river. The first French companies, rank upon rank of men-at-arms flying banners showing gold stags against a bright blue background, were moving into place.

It was not long then before Sir Godefroi came back, his face pinched. He stopped his horse before his company. The Dogs were in the middle of the men.

'I need archers,' he said in a strained voice.

'What's the job?' called an archer with a London accent.

Sir Godefroi pursed his lips. 'To wade into that river, cover our knights and kill anyone that comes towards us.'

'Sounds like a good way to get drowned,' said the London archer.

The traitor shrugged. 'Probably it is.'

There was a long silence as Sir Godefroi looked back and forth along his line of tired, hungry troops. Behind him the French force on the far bank of the river continued to grow. Loveday could see what looked like crossbowmen among the lines of men-at-arms and knights. Sir Godefroi began to look impatient. He opened his mouth to say something else.

But before he could speak, Romford got down from his horse and stepped forwards. 'I'll go,' he said.

Loveday turned to the boy in shock. Romford's eyes were dull. As though he had lost all care for himself. As though to go into the river or stay on its bank were all the same thing.

'No,' said Loveday. He tried to dismount too, to pull the boy back. But one-handed, he was not fast enough. 'Scotsman,' Loveday said. 'Stop him. Tebbe – Thorp—' But even as he said it, Romford was standing by Sir Godefroi's side, unslinging his bow. He was looking carefully at the string, checking its draw and inspecting it for weak points as though he had volunteered for target practice at some village butts.

Loveday finally untangled himself from his reins and stirrups. But once he was standing on the ground, he realized he could hardly pull Romford away from Sir Godefroi without looking ridiculous, and angering the knight. He looked back helplessly at the other three Dogs.

'Saints on fire,' said Thorp, staring at Romford. 'What's he doing? He doesn't even have arrows.'

Loveday was frantically trying to catch Romford's eye. To dissuade him.

But Thorp and Tebbe were looking at each other. A thought was passing between them. And Scotsman was hanging his head back, as though accepting the inevitable.

'We can't let him go alone,' said Thorp.

Loveday closed his eyes. He kept them closed for a few seconds. But before he opened them, he was nodding. And then they were open, and he was looking at the river again.

'I know,' said Loveday. He felt for the short sword at his belt. 'I know.' They all stepped forwards.

'One for all,' said Loveday, forlornly. '*Desperta ferro.*'

'You can leave your horses here,' said Sir Godefroi. 'These cowards will bring them to you later, when it's done.'

Then he turned his horse and trotted off along the edge of the estuary marsh. 'Follow me,' he called back to the Dogs, who were jogging on foot behind him. 'It isn't very far.'

Sir Godefroi led them along the line to where around one hundred men-at-arms and knights were assembled on horseback, with Northampton at the heart of them, flanked by another high-ranking lord with a long nose and a deadly serious look in his eyes. They all wore plate armour on their upper bodies. Some were in the process of unbuckling it from their legs and throwing it behind them. Around thirty other archers had also arrived, all on foot.

Loveday saw at once that they were at the Blanchetaque. Beneath their feet the pungent mud of the estuary marsh hardened, and here and there they could see patches of a chalk-white hard rock poking through. It made a faint trail which ran north into the water. Loveday stared down at it, fascinated.

'The white stain,' called Northampton, seeing Loveday across the group. 'Couldn't resist a look, eh?'

Before he could answer, Northampton called the group to order. 'We don't have much time,' he said. 'The tide is already turning. There's only one way across. And we only have one chance.'

He turned to the long-nosed knight, who was trying to calm his skittish horse. 'You all know Sir Reginald Cobham. He and I will lead the charge. We don't stop. If we're not all killed, firstly it'll be a fucking miracle and secondly there'll be more men behind us.

'But let me say it one more time. We don't fucking stop.'

He looked at the archers in the group. 'You lot have one job. Create mayhem. Shoot over our heads. Don't stop shooting for anything. Do I need to say anything more?'

There were cries of, 'No, sir'.

Northampton sought out Loveday and Scotsman, standing awkwardly on foot between the archers and the knights. 'You two fuckers, I have no idea what you're doing here, but if you get in our way, I'll kill you myself.' He grinned, wild. 'Stay back. This fight isn't for you.'

Loveday and Scotsman looked at each other, uncertain what to do.

'Archers, get forwards,' cried Northampton. And as though they had been there a thousand times before, the thirty archers, including Tebbe and Thorp, with Romford between them, set out at a jog towards the water's edge. Northampton called after them: 'And leave us some fucking room to get by.'

Loveday and Scotsman watched the archers jog into mud that sucked at their boots and tripped them. Saw them hold their bows up. Find positions either side of the Blanchetaque where they could stand, up to their ankles in river slime, and aim.

Across the water, at the fringe of the north side of the river marsh, an uncountable line of French men-at-arms and crossbowmen was now lined up. Waiting. Bristling. Watching every move the English made.

The river was wider than a crossbow's range. But it was well within longbow range.

As Northampton had commanded, Loveday and Scotsman stood well back from the knights, who were wheeling their horses into ranks of four and five abreast – as wide as the tongue of white rock beneath the mud.

They kept their eyes on Tebbe, Thorp and Romford.

They heard Northampton shouting to his knights to hold until his command. Heard metallic clunks as some pulled down the visors on their helms. Glanced over and saw them swinging swords and axes, spike-headed maces and hammers. Instinctively, though they had been told to stay back, Loveday felt again for his short sword at his belt. He saw the Scot check the axe slung on his back.

Then they felt the hard white tongue of the Blanchetaque quake as Northampton screamed 'St George' and, rank by rank, the English horsemen began to kick sharp spurs into their horses' flanks and set out at a gallop along the rock which stretched along the riverbed and into the slowly rising tidal waters of the Somme.

They saw water spring high, catching the light as it sprayed, while mud spattered in all directions, caking horses and the men's armour.

In the distance, on the far side of the river, they saw the first wave of French knights kick their own horses, charging into the river to defend the crossing.

Between the two closing lines of armoured knights Loveday watched the English bowmen nock and draw, and begin to shoot volley after volley into the onrushing French.

All the English bowmen except for Romford.

The boy was holding his bow, but he was not shooting. He was starting to walk out into the river, towards the onrushing French.

Loveday knew what he was saying to himself.

I'm going home.

He put his left hand out to grab Scotsman and show him what the lad was trying to do. But his hand just swept the air.

Scotsman was already gone. Running, as he had never run before, at the side of the Blanchetaque. To grab the boy himself.

Running one-handed was harder than riding. Holding his iron hat with his good hand, Loveday used his damaged right to try and keep his balance. He was more than ten paces behind Scotsman as they both blundered into the water, their legs slowing under them. The water was cold, and it swirled – the flow of freshwater from upstream meeting the sea-tide coming in from the estuary.

The fighting in the river was like nothing he had ever seen before. The first wave of English and French knights had crashed into each other. All around them, horses were rearing and biting and screaming and kicking, their legs half-submerged and their bright caparisons made dark and heavy by the wet. Above Loveday's head, knights in their saddles were wheeling and swinging weapons at one another with vicious force. They struggled to keep hold of sword handles that slipped as they soaked. The hard stone of the ford kept the fighters from sinking into the riverbed, but it was uneven and slimy. Horses and men were starting to lose their balance and fall.

Beside Loveday, the long-nosed knight, Sir Reginald, commanding the company with Northampton, whirled a long sword about his head and smashed it at the shoulder of a French man-at-arms, putting a huge dent in the plate of the Frenchman's upper arm. Loveday heard the man scream inside his helmet, as the crushed metal was driven into his flesh. But he flailed back at the long-nosed knight, fighting with his visor raised. He swayed back in his saddle and missed a slashing sweep of the French knight's sword, which, had it landed, would have cleaved his face in two.

Loveday looked around desperately for Romford. Scotsman was doing the same. The big man had run into the melee with a clear sight of the boy, but now Romford was nowhere to be seen. And the press of the fight was becoming thicker as every new wave of English and French knights rushed into the river.

As the Scot scanned the foaming water, a French man-at-arms who had lost his horse splashed towards him. Loveday shouted a warning, but the Scot had already sensed him coming. As the man-at-arms raised his sword, two-handed, to strike, Scotsman pivoted and drove his right shoulder into his heavy metal chest-plate. The Scot half lost his footing as he did, but managed to regain his balance and, with a great heave, pushed the man over backwards, sending him past the edge of the ford into the sucking mud of the riverbed.

The Scot was standing. The man-at-arms was not. He had been wearing armour that weighed around as much as a small squire. For a few moments huge bubbles rose to the surface of the water at the place he had gone down. Then there was nothing.

Scotsman pushed his soaking hair off his face. He took his axe, which was still slung on his back, and held it in one hand. But still there was no sign of Romford.

Loveday felt his stomach burning. He tried to wade towards the Scot. But as he did, two knights fighting with short axes crashed in between them, their horses pushing their flanks against one another and snapping with crooked yellow teeth. Loveday stumbled backwards to avoid being trampled. He tripped and fell backwards, landing sitting down on the ford-rock. The water was up to his neck. In panic, he flapped with his left hand at the water surface and tried to push himself up. But he slipped again and this time he went all the way under. His padded coat became sodden and heavy; his iron hat came off. He sucked in a lungful of water. For a moment, under the water, everything seemed very quiet and calm.

But he knew it was not. And with one great effort he pushed again with his left hand, found his feet under him and stood up. He rubbed water from his eyes. He thought he could taste blood in it. He could see nothing but spray and the flesh and iron of horses and men. He did not even know which way he was looking.

From somewhere, something heavy hit him in his right shoulder. It did not catch him cleanly, but he staggered forwards, pulling at his short sword as he did. Regaining his balance, he turned, bracing for a second blow and preparing to deliver his own. Yet none came. He could not even see who had hit him.

But he could see Scotsman. Two knights, both fallen from their horses, neither with heavy weapons left, their helmets lost, were grappling like wrestlers, trying to push one another under the water. Loveday could not tell which was English and which French. He wondered if they were even certain they were enemies, or whether the fighting itself was all that mattered. The knights rolled, slipped and both fell – one sitting with his head above water, the other on his knees, trying to push his opponent's head down.

And as they did, Loveday saw Scotsman behind them, holding his huge axe near its head in his left hand and with his right sweeping something from the water. Something large, and limp. Like a soaking bundle of rags, topped with a black metal tip.

The boy.

A surge of something so powerful it made his legs burn went through Loveday's whole body and he powered through the water, now close to waist-height, towards the Scot. He was with him in what seemed no time at all.

He screamed so Scotsman could hear him: 'Is he...?'

But as the Scot opened his mouth to reply a shadow fell on them both. The Scot's eyes widened, and, holding Romford's still, white body under his right arm, tried to juggle his axe into a striking position in his left.

Loveday had no time to think. Only to rely on a lifetime of experience moving his body as though it were under the command of some being from the heavens. Or from hell. He whipped round, holding his short sword in front of him, and saw what his instinct had known was there – a French knight on a towering destrier, with a thick-shafted mace tipped with wicked, curved spikes raised and ready to strike at the three of them.

As a younger man, Loveday's instinct might have told him

to duck, to lean back, or just to tuck his arms around his head. To try and avoid or deflect the swing of the mace, or the hooves of the horse.

But he was not a young man.

With every scrap of power left in his body, Loveday stepped towards the knight and his horse and, using the strength in his left arm, what spring remained in his legs and the weight of his body, drove his sword forwards as hard as he could.

Just above the horse's shoulders. Into a patch of soft flesh at the base of its throat.

He was lucky. The horse had either lost its armour, or the rider had not wanted to weigh the beast down for a fight in the water.

He was lucky. The knight's arms and the handle of the mace were not long enough to swing around the front of the horse's neck and into Loveday's unarmoured back.

He was lucky. His sword did not hit bone, and the blade did not bend or break. It sliced deep into the animal, almost to the hilt.

The horse reared in shock and pain. And Loveday knew what to do. He did not let go of his sword, but clung on to it, jamming his right forearm across the crook of his elbow to add weight, so that as the horse went up, Loveday was lifted briefly off his feet, then returned to them as the blade cut downwards towards the horse's breastbone, opening a massive wound.

When the horse came down, its own weight forced the blade upwards, in the opposite direction, towards its lower jaw. Then Loveday braced his legs against the slippery rock under his feet, managing to stay upright, and keeping the sword driving into the horse. He felt it carve through muscle and skin, opening the windpipe and all the blood vessels in the beast's neck. Hot blood sprayed from the wound, filling Loveday's eyes and mouth. Blind with gore but sure he had done what he needed to do, he pulled his sword out. The horse tried to scream in terror, but could only blow more blood, pink and foaming as it mixed with its spit. It fell sideways, and it took the knight with it. They crashed together into the water, the horse's legs thrashing as it died. The knight was trapped with his leg beneath it.

Loveday left the knight to drown. He used his right hand to splash water on his face. The roar of the battle and the immense thudding of his heart had stopped it from hurting altogether. He blinked blood out of his eyes as best he could.

The whole world was stained pink.

He looked for Scotsman, but felt him before he saw him. The big man had reslung his axe and grabbed Loveday by the back of the coat with one hand, while using the other arm to hold Romford.

'We're fucking going,' he bellowed into Loveday's ear. 'Now.'

Loveday nodded. Beside him, he heard Romford cough up water.

Then the Scot began to run, holding them both, back towards the English lines on the south of the River Somme. As he ran, more and more English knights and men-at-arms were charging into the river, now rising above Loveday's waist. Some were on horseback, but many had dismounted and were going in on foot.

Archers were also starting to run into the water, going as far as they could while still able to use their bows, some of them shooting with the bows sideways. Loveday looked for Tebbe and Thorp. Sensibly, they had held their positions, standing where the water was no higher than their knees, and they were shooting deliberately into the melee. Loveday could not see where they were aiming, but he could imagine they were targeting knights' visorless faces and horses' flanks.

As they ran past, Tebbe noticed them. For a moment, he lowered his bow, and with his right arm, pumped a fist holding an arrow in the air.

Moments later, they were out of the water. They ran to a patch of the bank away from the charging knights, where the ground was damp but firm. Scotsman dropped Loveday. He put Romford over his shoulder and began hammering the boy on the back. After a few blows, Loveday heard Romford vomit up more of the river.

Scotsman put him down, gently, on the ground and rolled him on to his side. Loveday sat up. He tried again to wipe blood from his eyes, but only managed to replace it with mud. He gave up for a moment, and just listened to the sounds of the battle in the river, still loud yet also eerily far away. From the yells of 'St George' and 'King Edward' he guessed the English knights were winning the day.

Suddenly exhausted, he lay on his back. He heard Scotsman whispering to Romford: 'You'll be fine, you daft fucker. You'll be fine. We'll get you home.'

He heard Romford murmuring, as though he were agreeing.

And then he heard another voice. One he had not heard before, but would later know to be that of Sir John Chandos, the Prince of Wales's steward.

Chandos was not angry – he seemed almost amused. But there was an edge to his voice that Loveday did not like. It made Loveday sit up again, and with his right eye, which was less full of blood and mud than the left, look at the steward.

Chandos was standing over Scotsman, who in turn was

kneeling over Romford. The steward was wearing armour, so clean and polished that it was clear he had played no part in the battle for the Blanchetaque, and did not intend to. He had his head cocked. He was looking at Romford as though he were a creature the Scot had pulled from the river.

Chandos did not seem troubled that Romford was half-dead, though he knelt and helped Scotsman unbuckle Romford's black helmet. However, he did seem intensely interested in the fact that Romford was still present in the army.

Loveday and Scotsman kept quiet and let the steward look him up and down.

He said: 'So this is where the lad got to. I think we'll have him back.'

29

On that day there was a battle so horrible that... there never was a man so hardy that he would not have been astounded by it...

Life of the Black Prince by Chandos Herald

Romford lay on the cushions behind the curtain in the prince's pavilion and pretended to sleep while the lords assembled there talked.

'Hastings has abandoned his campaign.' That was the earl with the white teeth: Warwick.

'Of course he has. Fucking piss-hose little cunt.' That was Northampton, the one with the grey hair, whom the prince feared most.

'In fairness to Sir Hugh, our Flemish allies abandoned him.'

A grunt. 'That's Flemings for you.' A silence. 'Food?'

'Not good. We sent riders to the port at Le Crotoy. Our ships were due there five days ago. Nothing. They came back with a herd of stolen cattle. That is as much as we have for now. The men will have to go hungry.'

'Why? Let us ride out and burn every town for fifty miles and take their food!' The prince was sitting nearest Romford, in a chair in the middle of the pavilions, and his high voice was louder than the other lords'.

There was an exasperated sigh, which Romford thought came from Northampton. 'Have I not told you—' the earl began.

He was cut off by Sir John Chandos, the one who had brought Romford back to the prince and put him back in his squire's clothes. Who had told him he was to rest and recover in the prince's quarters – on the express wishes of the prince himself. 'My lord, thank you.'

The prince did not say anything more. Warwick spoke again. 'There's nothing we can do now until the king makes his decision. The men are hungry, yes. But we crossed the Blanchetaque. We remain ahead of the main French army. Half a day perhaps. But ahead. We may still see a few of Hastings's men make it here. Either way, in the morning, we will see which direction the king wishes to continue.'

Romford rolled on to his back and stared up into the roof of the pavilion. A little bird was perched in the space where the wooden poles met the canvas. Occasionally it darted out and circled the tent, looking for an escape. But it never found one, and each time it came back to the same place.

'What would you do?" Warwick again.

The Earl of Northampton was quiet for a moment. 'Christ knows,' he said. 'We're camping at the edge of the biggest forest between here and fucking Germany. So we either go round the forest or we go through it until we find some ground that looks good for fighting. And then we have another fucking fight.'

When the lords had left the pavilion, the prince pushed the curtain aside and came to the back of the pavilion where Romford lay. He was already dressed for sleep, and he climbed on to his own comfortable pile of cushions and rugs, arranged beside Romford's. He did not look at Romford or acknowledge him.

Romford said nothing either.

Outside, it began to rain very hard, and the rain drummed loudly on the canvas of the pavilion. Romford tried to listen to the sound of it to help him drift off to sleep. But he kept thinking about the river. How much he had wanted to die. Yet how relieved he had been when the big Scotsman rescued him. It all seemed like a dream now. As though he had always been lying on cushions in a prince's tent, and everything in between was just a story he had been told.

'Did you fight in the battle, boy?'

Romford had thought the prince was asleep. He glanced briefly across at him. Trying to remember how much he was allowed to look when it was only the two of them. Trying to remember the steps of the dance. The prince was staring up into the darkness of the pavilion roof too.

'I would not say fought,' said Romford. 'I was in the water, that's all.'

The prince was quiet again. Romford knew he was not supposed to demand things of the prince, but only respond to his questions. But he asked anyway. 'Have you been in one? A battle, I mean.'

For some reason he had an idea that the prince was crying. But when he spoke his voice did not give it away. 'I have taken part in many melees,' he said. He paused. 'For training. And of course at Caen...'

Romford thought about Caen, when the prince had watched his men-at-arms break down the doors of an abandoned monastery. He was not sure what to say.

'It seemed very loud,' he said.

'Yes,' said the prince. 'Very loud.'

He was quiet again. They listened to the rain drum the canvas. It grew louder and louder. Romford thought of the men outside. Loveday and the others. Wet from the river, and now wet again.

When the prince spoke again, his voice only just carried over the din of the rain.

'Boy,' he said. 'Come and lie beside me.'

Romford was not sure what to do. The prince did not repeat his question, but it seemed to float in the air all the same, haunting the tent until it was answered. Neither of them moved. But Romford's heart was beating hard.

Then he realized he could not refuse. He also realized this was what he wanted. So he climbed stiffly up from his own cushions. It was not easy. His ribs ached where the Scot had gripped him to haul him from the Somme.

He walked softly across to the prince's cushions. It was only a few steps there from his own, but through his bare feet he felt the cold of the earth. As though the summer heat was leaving it now. He knelt beside the prince's bed, then slid beneath the rug. It was the softest thing he had ever felt.

The prince was lying on his left side, both his hands beneath his ear, clasped as if in prayer. Romford worked his way gently across the cushions until his chest was pressed against the prince's back, and his knees were tucked behind the prince's. He put his right arm over the Prince's side and laid his hand on the prince's chest.

He pushed his face into the prince's hair. It smelled of the damp earth.

The prince said nothing, and he did not respond to Romford's touch. But so far as Romford could tell, he had done what was expected. So he stayed where he was, though his left arm was squashed awkwardly beneath him.

The rain grew so hard that the individual drops all seemed to become one roar of thunder. The prince still did not move.

So Romford just lay where he was until they both fell asleep. Holding the prince just as his brother had once held him, when he was small and lonely too, and yearning for a father.

Romford was woken by sunlight pouring into the pavilion. The prince was no longer there. He sat up. His ribs still hurt, and he was hungry, but he felt more rested than he had for many days.

He threw off the soft rug and stood up. He was still in his clothes, and he used his hands to try to smooth out his surcoat. He could hear no sound from behind the curtain in the pavilion, so he pulled at its edge and peeked around it.

Empty.

A basin of water stood near the entrance. Romford crouched beside it and drank, using his hands. The water tasted dirty, but he did not care. He dipped his finger in it and rubbed it over his teeth and gums on both sides, trying to rid his mouth of the night's bitter stink. Then he washed his face and splashed his hair to smooth it down. It was getting long. He could also feel that in the weeks they had been in France the soft hair on his face had grown dense and curly.

He looked around the pavilion. He remembered that his black helmet was back behind the curtain. He went back, found it, and tucked it under his arm. Then he walked out of the pavilion. The man-at-arms posted there barely glanced at him as he passed.

He picked his way through the campsite, looking for somewhere to piss. From the sun he could see that it was still early in the morning. As Northampton had said the previous night, they were on the edge of a forest. He had heard men call it Crécy. Romford headed for the trees. As he went, he noticed there were far fewer tents than at any other camp they had held. Many had been abandoned on the other side of the river. Instead, to keep the rain off, men had made makeshift shelters from torn-down branches, propped and loosely woven together. They did not look as though they had kept out the night's torrent. The campsite was full of cold, wet men wringing out their clothes.

By the time Romford got back to the pavilion, other squires had arrived and were taking it down. They ignored him, and it seemed clear that he was not expected to help them, nor wanted for his company. So he stood on the edge, half watching them work but avoiding eye contact with anyone, until Sir John Chandos arrived. The steward seemed anxious. He was short with the squires, and told them sternly to hurry.

Chandos was a little more gracious with Romford. 'Will you ride with the prince today?' he asked.

Romford nodded. 'If it pleases you, sir.'

Chandos nodded. 'We're going round the forest,' he said. He looked impatiently at the collapsing pavilion. 'We ought to be moving already. You have a horse?'

'No, sir.'

'We'll find you one,' said Chandos. 'Remind me. Do you fight?'

'I am a bowman, sir.'

Chandos winced. 'I know that. But can you swing a sword?'

'I can try. I am better with a bow.'

Chandos grunted. 'So be it. Go to the armourer and take what you will.' He turned to leave. Then he turned back. 'One more thing. Who were those men who pulled you out of the river? Your old company?'

Romford flushed. 'Yes, sir. They call themselves the Essex Dogs. They once rode with Sir Robert le Straunge, but now they are with Sir Godefroi, and sometimes with Lord Northampton.'

Chandos considered this for a moment. Then he nodded. 'In that case you may see them again today,' he said.

Chandos was right. Romford saw the Dogs almost as soon as the vanguard broke camp, for they were once more with Sir Godefroi.

Along with Warwick and Northampton, the traitor knight led the first division, with the prince between them all. Romford was riding just behind the prince, who was now dressed in gleaming, faultless and undented plate armour, with a beautifully crafted helm on his head. The young man said nothing of the night before.

When Romford turned in his saddle, he saw the Dogs, all four of them mounted, trotting fifty or so paces behind him. He was not sure if they had spotted him. But from what he could make out, they had recovered from the battle at the river and were now armoured with pieces scavenged from the Blanchetaque's dead.

Loveday wore a rough brown leather coat that extended to his thighs, and a helmet that looked to have been stripped from a dead crossbowman. Both Tebbe and Thorp had new iron caps on their heads. The Scot had pulled from some vast corpse a mail coat almost too big even for him. Its links were browned and rusty, and it had a split which ran from above the heart to the middle of the gut.

It did not seem much, and when Romford looked at the lords and squires in the line – himself included – the Dogs did not seem very well protected at all. But it was something, and he was glad to see them safer than before.

He looked down at his own armour. He still had his black helmet, and at the armoury he had found another dark-stained mail coat to match it. He had selected a new bow and forty arrows in two bags. Chandos insisted he kept a short sword at his belt, though he had no idea how best to use it, and in truth it rather scared him.

Yet it was better, he supposed, to have weapons than not. From what Romford could understand of what the lords around the prince said, the French could come at them at any time and their army was big. Twice as big as theirs. With nine divisions and four kings among its commanders.

Their king – Edward – was still commanding the middle of the army. He decided against trying to take all his men through the trees, for fear of being lost or stuck on the winding tracks that crisscrossed beneath the ancient oaks and beeches. So they marched in the open. For a long while they skirted east around the forest edge, keeping the trees on their left as the afternoon sun slowly arced behind them. Then they continued to track the treeline as it swept north, picking up a rough uncobbled track, deeply rutted by generations of hooves and wheels and boots.

Riding on this road was somewhat harder than going across

the countryside, for the track was dry and uneven, like the roads they had known many weeks ago at the start of their march, when he had ridden a cart pulled by a donkey. The horses had not liked it then and did not now, for they stumbled and occasionally lost their footing on its surface. And the men found it little easier.

When Romford looked back to check on the Dogs, he saw a dust cloud billowing high in the sky behind them, forming a haze in the sun. He wondered what it must be like to march with the rearguard, with legs weary and mouth and eyes always full of dust. But he did not wonder for very long, for shortly afterwards the track came to another, forming a crossroads, on the other side of which was a smaller wood – little more than a copse, in which the leaves of the trees were just starting to turn over from green into the rich yellow of autumn.

Just beyond the crossroads was a little windmill.

As they came towards the crossroads and the windmill, Romford saw the Earl of Warwick talking to the traitor Sir Godefroi. Then Warwick called to the other lords: 'This is it.'

And they all seemed to know exactly what was to be done. All the lords dismounted, summoning squires to take their horses to graze the grass around the crossroads.

Sir Godefroi strode off with a small group of men-at-arms to inspect the windmill.

Warwick sent runners along the line, shouting, 'Carts up! Engineers up!' and prompting a flurry of activity as every wooden wagon in the line was pulled forwards to the crossroads, with men and horses forced out of the way.

Northampton clanked off in his armour and paced out a line from the treeline of the large forest on their left to the road, then another from the other side of the road to the trees.

And the prince stood with arms crossed, watching it all unfold, with no duties and no role, save to puff out his chest and try to look as though he were in command. Romford climbed down from his horse. He badly wanted to catch the prince's eye and say some words that would comfort him. But he dared not. Instead he scanned the crowded field and picked out Loveday, who looked up from an intense discussion with Tebbe and Thorp and noticed him looking.

The leader of the Dogs nodded. He raised his dead man's helmet just a fraction from his head in salute.

Proudly.

Romford smiled. Then he felt someone by his side.

'It won't be long.' The prince was standing close to him, his back very straight and his hand already on the hilt of his sword.

'No, my lord,' said Romford, although he had no way of knowing if the prince was right or wrong.

'You'll fight beside me when it starts,' said the prince. It was not a question.

'Yes, my lord,' said Romford.

'Good boy,' said the prince. He pulled a stopper from a flask and drank deeply – long, deep gulps. Then he handed it to Romford. 'Drink.'

Romford dared a glance at the prince, who nodded encouragement. He put the flask-mouth to his lips and briefly tasted the young man's lips on it. He tasted nothing but fine grapes and the sweet fragrance of spiced wine.

It was good. It was strong. And it burned his throat. After two gulps Romford handed the flask back to the prince, who drank deeply once more, then exhaled with satisfaction.

'Good,' said the prince. 'Good.' He clapped Romford on the

back, with a rougher touch than Romford had known from him before.

Then he said it again. 'It won't be long.'

They heard the French before they saw them.

The sun was dipping low, throwing long shadows from the wall of trees that was the Forest of Crécy, to their right. Romford was tired. His legs were stiff from standing all afternoon in the group around the prince, now mostly composed of large, intimidating knights and men-at-arms, wearing plate armour and carrying heavy weapons. Romford's mouth was dry from drinking the prince's wine. And his heart was thudding, so the first sound of trumpets and drums banging, yells and songs – faint to begin with, mingling with birdsong from the trees on either side of them – was almost a relief. Something was about to happen.

Romford knew that many – perhaps all – the other men in the field felt the same. And as the sound of the French approaching reached them, a murmur went round, which became a cheer, and then a banging of anything that would make its own sound. The sound echoed and reverberated. It rose and crashed and rose again like a wave in the sea. It filled the early-evening air in the death-trap the English had built between the forest and the little wood and it struck Romford as horrifying.

But also thrilling.

Beside him, the prince was turning constantly around, looking at the defences that had been put up.

Every cart and wagon in the army was on its side in a great curved wall in front of them, stretching between forest and wood.

In the centre of this was a large gap, maybe a thousand paces in width. Romford realized now that this structure was exactly what he had seen the Earl of Northampton pacing out when they arrived. Here and there in front of the gap, the engineers Warwick had called up to the front had dug pits and holes deep enough to break a horse's leg and have it throw its rider.

To either side of the gap, in lines stretching diagonally away from it, stood thousands of archers. More archers, the boldest of them, had climbed on top of the wagons, facing out. And directly in front of the gap stood the vanguard, eight ranks deep, and all of them now dismounted, with the Prince of Wales, Northampton, Warwick and Sir Godefroi spaced out at its head, their positions marked by their flags and standards. The middle and the rearguard, commanded by King Edward, hung back by the windmill, ready to be deployed. The king himself was in the windmill tower.

Watching.

Romford looked up at the prince's bright red dragon, twisting and snaking gently in the light evening breeze above them. He wondered if the king could see it from his tower, and whether he thought of his son beneath it. Or if kings did not think such things. He wondered if there was a place on earth where dragons really roamed. Breathed fire and gobbled men alive.

The sound of the approaching French was growing louder. The words to their war songs becoming distinct. Romford wished he knew what the words meant. He knew the prince spoke French, but he did not dare ask him.

The thud of a single set of hooves within the English stronghold sounded from Romford's left. He peered and saw the Earl of Northampton, riding along the line and shouting encouragement to the thousands of men who stood in it. 'This is it, boys!' he shouted. 'This is fucking it, by Christ's own right arm! We're going to cut some bollocks off tonight!'

The prince curled his lip. He was more than half drunk. 'Very poetic,' he sneered as Northampton rode past.

But Romford could feel that Northampton's earthy crudeness was exactly what the nervous, hungry men needed to hear. Without thinking, he put his hand to the short sword at his waist.

For the first time, he felt he might use it well.

Northampton thundered all the way along the line; then he returned to his post, clambering out of his saddle and smacking his horse's behind so that it galloped away, riderless, to find its way back towards the windmill.

Then, just for a moment, absolute silence fell across the army.

On the left-hand wagon barricades, something moved. The archers standing on top of the carts suddenly began leaping backwards off them, and a tremendous hammering broke out on the far side.

Romford flinched. There was still no sign of the enemy through the large gap between the two wings of the wagon-barrier.

But something was coming.

Moments later, Romford saw what it was.

Crossbowmen. Hundreds of crossbowmen. They were running with only their bows in hand, scrambling to follow an order. They had shot at the archers on top of the wagon barricade. Now they were trying to find positions in front of the English vanguard to reload and fire again at the troops ranked there.

Even Romford could see this was a terrible mistake.

'Hold still, men!' The order was screamed along the line of the English vanguard, coming originally from Northampton's direction.

Above it, Romford could make out the voices of the crossbowmen, yelling back and forth to one another in some other language, which was not French.

He never knew what they said.

But he never forgot what he saw next. For as the crossbowmen stood and struggled to reload their weapons, from behind each of the wooden barricades the English longbowmen took a step forwards in unison.

They nocked. They waited for a command.

Then they shot.

At the call to nock, Romford put his hand on his own bow, before he remembered where he was. He removed it, and continued to stand and watch the bloody pageant that was unfolding in front of him as the crossbowmen were cut down by volley upon volley of arrows.

It was a massacre.

Some of the crossbowmen managed to load their bows and shoot. But for every one that did, another four were simply slaughtered where they stood. Romford looked over to the barricades, where the first, coordinated volley of crossbow shot had landed. Behind the barrier he saw one single English archer lying dead, a bolt sticking from his face.

He saw not a single other casualty on their side.

But opposite them, what had appeared as an organized first assault with crossbow bolts had failed utterly. Within almost no time, the crossbowmen had broken up, and those who were not dead or dying had begun to run away.

In the worst direction they could have chosen.

As they ran directly away from the English defences, there appeared from a dip in the ground the first sight of the men Romford had heard blowing their trumpets and banging their drums.

The French cavalry. Hundreds of knights and men-at-arms on horseback charging up from the direction towards which the crossbowmen were fleeing.

Romford put his hand to his mouth. He prayed with every fibre of his body that he would not see what he was about to see.

But no prayer could stop it.

The French knights must have seen the crossbowmen. But either they did not care or they were charging in such tightly packed ranks that they could not have stopped if they wished to. They simply barrelled over and through the fleeing men, as though they were not there. Hooves of heavy horses weighted down with large men in armour crushed their lightly protected fellow troops.

Romford saw bodies mangled and skulls crushed. He watched confused and terrified crossbowmen try everything to get out of the way – to dodge, run away, drop to the ground in a ball or wave their arms in hopeless protest. He heard them squeal like rabbits.

Beside Romford the prince took another swig from his flask of spiced wine. He offered it around the men-at-arms. He clapped Romford on the back and passed it to him. It was empty. Romford pretended to drink from it, then handed it back. The prince shook it. 'By God, there was not much in there,' he said, his words slightly slurring.

And then Romford heard him say nothing more. For the

French knights, having ridden down their own crossbowmen, were now gaining on the gap in the barricades.

The man-at-arms to the other side of the prince reached over and shut his visor for him. He took a look at Romford, in his black, open-faced helmet and mail vest, completely unprotected by any plate armour, and shook his head. 'Do you know what you're doing?' he said.

Romford shook his head.

'Christ's wounds,' said the man-at-arms. 'In that case, keep out of the fucking way.'

And then he said no more either. He pulled down his own visor, gripped his long sword in two hands and moved around so that he was directly in front of the prince. The first French horsemen were at the gap in the barricades. Romford saw the archers either side of it loose another volley, sending horses rearing and some of the knights aboard them flying from their saddles. His hands itched. He wished he were among them.

Then he saw just as many of the knights run the gauntlet of the archers, bearing down on the English lines. Towards the front. Towards him. And he realized suddenly that he might be about to die.

Unlike in the river, he wanted not to.

He put his hand on his short sword. Pulled it from his side. Saw a knight with a beautiful blue surcoat whipping a huge sword around his head as he galloped at full pelt towards exactly the spot where Romford stood. As the knight neared him, Romford heard a series of booms like thunder – louder and more startling than anything he had heard before.

He thought he could see smoke, although he was not sure if it was dust. And he could smell something that reminded him of powder.

But he had no time to think about what it was, for the knight was almost upon him. He heard the horse snort, and felt the air move.

Then the world around him went blurry, and he tasted grass and mud.

Behold the end, he thought.

A heartbeat later, everything was black.

Feet.

All he could see was feet. Some clad in leather. Some in iron or steel.

Shifting, stamping, slipping. Kicking.

Feet trod on him. Heels with sharp spurs dug into his sides. He tried to get away by crawling forwards. But wherever he went there were more feet.

He tried to clamber on to all fours so that he might get up and away from them. But feet kicked him back down. A stray heel caught him hard in the mouth. He tasted blood and knew his lip was split. He spat out a tooth.

Again he tried to scramble up.

Fell.

Two feet stepped on his hands. He yelped. Drooled blood. Another set of feet walked heavily across his gut, winding him.

He tried to roll left. He found himself face to face with a dead man-at-arms. The man had a dagger buried up to its hilt in his eye socket. The other eye was wide open in disbelief.

Romford yelled for help. Once more he struggled to get up, and this time in desperation he grabbed one of the legs near him. It was covered in plate armour, which was slick with sweat and mud and spit and puke and piss and blood. His hands slipped, but he found a joint in the armour and pulled himself harder upwards.

He was on his feet, bent over almost double. But as he rose he had smelled, just briefly, fresher air.

Then the leg stumbled backwards. Romford was jolted back with it, and then he was crushed between two sets of armour and the bodies heaving inside and all around them. He heard muffled screams and yelps of pain. He was not sure if they were his or someone else's.

The press became harder. And harder. The air was being emptied from his lungs.

The world started to go black again.

Then, suddenly, the bodies were wrenched apart. He was released. Gasping, Romford finally managed to stand up straight and stagger a few steps. He looked around and saw that he was in a vast crowd – hemmed in by men in every direction. All pushing one another and swaying. Arms above swinging weapons. The whole thing lurching as though it were one beast rolling from side to side, back and forth.

He knew no one around him. He could not see the prince. He looked up and tried to look over the sea of helmets, some lost or ripped off, revealing bruised and bloodied faces, with swollen eyes and broken noses and hair plastered across them. He was searching for the prince's dragon flag. Dusk was falling above the fighters. The light was fading fast. Yet there was enough for him to know the dragon flag was nowhere.

It had fallen.

Romford forced a hand to his belt, feeling for his short sword.

It was gone.

He felt his chest for his bowstring.

His bow was gone too.

He still had one of his arrow bags attached to his side. And the black helmet on his head.

That was something.

As the crowd heaved, Romford managed a few deep breaths. Then he began to push his way back in the direction of the only thing he recognized. The windmill. He knew he was heading away from the fighting. From the French and Germans with their horses, and the blood of their comrades on their hands.

He wondered if that made him a coward. He did not care. He just pushed on.

Then he walked into someone he knew. A handsome face looking straight into his. A bandage covering one eye.

Sir Thomas Holand.

He had not seen Sir Thomas since the night he had asked Romford to give the prince powder for the first time. But Sir Thomas recognized him. He grabbed him by the shoulder, leaned in to shout in his ear.

'The prince,' he yelled. 'Where is he?'

Romford shrugged.

Sir Thomas scanned above the crowd, just as Romford had. 'His banner is down,' he shouted. 'Why aren't you there?'

Romford showed Sir Thomas his hands. 'No weapons,' he yelled back. His split lip made him lisp.

Sir Thomas closed his eye briefly. The noise was now deafening. He leaned into Romford's ear once more and bellowed something that sounded like, 'Wool, string'.

Romford shook his head. Sir Thomas was now screaming as loud as he could. 'Word to the king! The prince! Tell him! You – now – go.'

Then he freed his arm from the press of the crowd, raising a sword above his head and barging men out of his path on his way back to the fight.

Romford stood on the tips of his toes and sighted a line to the windmill. Then he ducked his head down so he could burrow forwards.

It was easier to move among the feet. He took a deep breath and started using all the strength he had to tunnel back through the bodies towards the windmill.

Soon he found that with each body he squeezed past it became a little less difficult to move. He pushed, and pushed, and eventually he stumbled out of the back of the crowd, where the groaning wounded were being dragged, and where weary knights were taking on water and replacing broken weapons.

Romford passed a dead archer with a bow next to his white hand. He thought for a second. Remembered Loveday in his long brown crossbowman's coat. Picked up the bow and slung it on his back.

The windmill was thirty paces away. He set out at a run towards it. As he went he began to shout as loud as he could: 'The prince! The prince is in danger! The prince is in danger!'

The running and the shouting made his eyes water. And the light of the day was almost gone. So he did not see the big man coming towards him until it was too late.

He ran head first into his solid chest. It was not armoured, but still hard enough that it stopped Romford in his tracks and knocked him on to his backside.

He sat on the ground in a daze. Wiped tears from his eyes and blood from his chin.

Millstone stood over him. He had a giant hammer in his right hand. His thickly curled hair was tied at the back of his head, and his face was burned almost black by the sun. But his blue eyes sparkled in recognition.

He put a hand out, and Romford took it. Let him pull him to his feet.

'Millstone,' he said. 'I thought you were—'

'Not yet, lad,' said the big stonemason. 'And not today either.'

Millstone followed Romford to the squat stone tower of the windmill. The door was blocked by a squadron of men-at-arms. Romford looked up. There was a window at the top, behind the sails. He supposed that was where King Edward must be.

'I need to see the king,' said Romford. He still lisped. And he knew how ridiculous he sounded.

The men-at-arms glared at him. From the battlefield, somewhere near the cart-wall, there came another series of the booms Romford had heard before he fell. He jumped, startled.

'Cannon,' said the man-at-arms. 'Never heard them?'

Romford shook his head quickly. 'Please,' he said. 'I have a message for the king. From Sir Thomas Holand. It's his son. The prince. He—'

The biggest of the men-at-arms looked down at Romford. 'We know. He knows.'

Romford felt dazed. He finished his sentence anyway. 'He needs help.'

The man-at-arms laughed. He put his hand on Romford's shoulder. 'We saw the flag fall from here. Shall I tell you what the king said?'

Romford opened his mouth. Shut it.

The man-at-arms nodded. 'He said if the little prick wants to play at being a knight, then today he can earn his fucking spurs.' He smiled. 'If you want to save him so badly, go and save him.'

He folded his arms. He looked Millstone up and down, and said, 'One of Hastings's lot?'

Millstone nodded.

'At least you turned up,' he said.

Romford looked back round at the battlefield in panic. The sun was almost done. The sky was grey and a strange smoke was drifting over the melee. Exhausted men were fighting themselves to a standstill in the gloom.

He turned and looked at Millstone. 'Will you help me?' he said.

Millstone said, 'Of course.'

They half ran around the edge of the crowd, skirting the forest until they came to the wall of wagons. Where the ground sloped gently down towards it, blood was trickling in little streams. It made the ground squelch under their feet.

From the extreme right of the battlefield, they could see the English line of men-at-arms and knights on foot pushing the French steadily backwards towards the gap in the cart-wall. The noise was still deafening. And through the crowd, there was no way to see where the prince could be.

They were standing right up against the cart-wall. Romford shouted to Millstone: 'Lift me up.'

Millstone looked unsure, but he did it anyway, interlacing his fingers so Romford could use his hands as a step. Romford heaved himself on to a cart. Stood on its upturned side.

He took his bow from his back and nocked an arrow, and used it to sight his way around the melee.

The dark was settling in, but he strained his eye and could pick out pockets of action within the crowd.

At the far side of the field, he saw the Earl of Warwick's scarlet flag with gold crosses standing firm, huge knights giving no quarter and no ground around it. Near it, Sir Godefroi and Northampton's banners were close together and a similarly tight fight was under way. The archers still just about held their positions in the lines on either side of the gap in the cart-wall.

Romford shifted his sight and trained his bow to the centre of the field. There he saw something peculiar happening: an ancient knight with a gold crown fixed to the top of an old-fashioned helm in the shape of a tube, mounted with ostrich feathers, was being helped on to his horse by two others, whose horses were then lashed to either side of his.

Romford had no idea who this was, though he could see he was not French. From the man's movements it seemed as though he might be blind.

He remembered King Edward lecturing the prince about a blind King of Bohemia.

He watched for a moment as the blind man and the knights tethered alongside him began a charge. But they disappeared into the churn of the fight, and he saw no more of them.

He moved his bow around the French army further.

Then he saw him.

Perhaps two hundred paces away. Behind the main line between the armies. Being dragged, thrashing and screaming, by a man who looked no better prepared for battle than Romford.

Romford called down to Millstone. 'I've found him.'

Millstone shrugged. He could not hear.

Romford kept his arrow trained on the man dragging the prince.

The shot was hard.

But not impossible.

Two hundred paces. A moving target. Shooting high to low. In poor light. A breeze, left to right across the battlefield. A bow he did not know.

The risks were very high. And to lose the gamble could mean hitting the prince.

He steadied his feet on top of the cart, and pulled back on the bowstring, feeling the tension transfer from the string to his shoulder and the muscles of his back.

He had not shot a bow since Gaillon.

Another reason not to gamble.

But Romford loved to gamble. He pulled the arrow back until he could pull no more. Blew out through his nose until his lungs were empty. Told his heart to slow down.

Aimed for the biggest part of the man pulling the Prince.

And let go.

As he released the arrow another huge boom came from the cannon, which he could now see were placed with the archers: short, ugly tubes mounted on wooden carts. Men with their faces stained black from whatever made them boom scurried around them, making them fire.

The explosion from the cannon once more filled the air with drifting smoke. With his heart pounding, Romford knelt and tried to peer through it, looking for the prince.

He could see nothing but dark and grey. He willed the smoke to clear. It hung, stubborn, above the howl of the fight.

He looked down at Millstone. The stonemason was waiting patiently. Picking at something hard crusted on the head of his hammer.

Romford turned back to the battle. And now he could see.

In the middle of the English line, the blind king with the ostrich feathers lay, cut to pieces, on the earth. A circle had formed around him, and knights had stopped fighting, looking down on his corpse with awe.

On the opposite side of the field, where the small copse stood, a new wave of hundreds, maybe thousands of English knights were now running towards the battle from the direction of the windmill. The king's banner flew above them.

And back in the English lines, the dragon flag of the Prince of Wales, tattered and muddy and well trampled, was being hiked up on its pole. Two men-at-arms were hauling the prince back through the crowd. They stopped as they passed the ring of men who stood around the dead blind king, and Romford saw them point out the king's corpse to the prince.

The prince walked into the circle and removed the blind king's feathers from his helmet. Then the men-at-arms pushed him on backwards through the crowd.

Romford felt his whole body flood with happiness and relief. He jumped down from the cart and threw his arms around Millstone.

'He's safe!' he shouted into Millstone's ear.

Millstone nodded. 'That's good.'

'We have to go and see him!'

Millstone looked doubtful. 'Not me,' he shouted back. 'I'll see you by the windmill.' He put two hands on Romford's shoulders. 'Did you hit what you aimed at?'

Romford shrugged. 'I didn't see. But I think so.'

Then he scampered off, dodging weary knights staggering back from the front and leaping over the wounded and dying as he tried to intercept the prince.

He caught up with Prince Edward as he was emerging from the back of the crowd. He was no longer being dragged by the men-at-arms, but walking proudly, his chest out.

He had lost his helmet, and one of the shoulder plates from his armour hung loose. But he held his sword aloft in one hand, and the three ostrich feathers of the dead, blind king in his other.

He was shouting something in a harsh language Romford did not know. '*Ich dien! Ich dien!*'

He had a wild, triumphant grin on his face.

'Where's my father?' he cried. 'He needs to see this. The French are retreating! We have carried the day!'

The men-at-arms, now behind him, exchanged glances.

Romford stepped into the prince's path at exactly the same time as Sir John Chandos. Awkward, he stepped backwards. Chandos addressed the prince.

'A fine escape, my lord. One for the chronicles, I gather.'

The prince beamed wider. 'Where's my father?' he said again. 'I will show him my prize and tell him how we drove the French peasants away.'

Chandos smiled thinly. 'The king is presently leading the reserve knights of the middle and rearguard,' he said. 'They are...' He paused. 'Mopping things up.' He cleared his throat. 'I see you have the King of Bohemia's insignia. The whole of Christendom will weep for such a fine warrior.'

The prince snorted. 'Fine warrior? He died like a fool. I shall keep these as a reminder never to be so stupid. What other prizes have we taken?'

As the prince and Chandos spoke, Romford had been unbuckling his helmet. He stepped forwards. He knelt before the prince, then smiled shyly up to him.

'My lord,' he said. 'I am glad to see you safe.'

The prince looked at him impatiently. 'What is it, boy?'

Chandos was scanning the battlefield. Romford began to feel uncomfortable. But he pressed on.

'My lord, I wanted to present you with my helmet. It is a... gift. To give thanks that you survived. I was on the cart and I saw you and...'

He knew he was gabbling. He heard his voice, thick and lisping from his split lip.

The prince's face curled in contempt. He took Romford's helmet from him. 'It is black,' he said.

Romford nodded. 'It has brought me luck. I think it saved my life. I thought it might—'

The prince snorted. 'No prince wears black armour,' he said. He tossed it back to Romford. Then he swept away, towards the windmill, without a backward glance.

Once he had gone, Romford walked in a daze in the same direction, to the spot where he had said he would meet Millstone.

He felt as though every arrow he had ever shot was piercing his breast. Buried in his heart up to their fletchings.

A tear rolled down his cheek.

The salt stung his lip. He did not wipe it away.

Behind him, he could hear that the battle was over. Men were lighting fires on the battlefield, preparing to stay there that night. To sleep among their dead.

By the light of the flames, and the rising moon, he looked around for Millstone. He could not see him for a long time, but he waited and he wandered until he did. He took a skin flask half full of wine from the hand of a dying knight and drank it straight down.

Eventually he found the stonemason. Standing with a group of other men on the far side of the windmill, at the edge of the battlefield, where the grass was ripe with horseshit, but did not leak blood.

He did not recognize the men until he was close to them.

But then he saw it was the Essex Dogs. Or those who remained. The big Scotsman. The wiry archer Tebbe and his friend Thorp. The round and kind and dependable figure of Loveday, a silhouette of dark against dark. He held his right hand by his chest and leaned forwards on his short sword, looking as always as if he was trying to catch his breath.

Romford walked up to the group. They did not see him in the dark.

He did not say anything to alert them. Just stood and listened.

The Scotsman, blood matted in his hair and beard, was growling curses. The archers had their arms crossed. Loveday was shaking his head, but saying nothing.

Romford could tell that something was wrong. That

Millstone had brought them bad news. But he could not understand what it was. Another tear rolled down his face.

Loveday said: 'I can't understand it.'

The Scotsman said: 'I fucking can.'

And Millstone said, 'I'm telling you, I've seen him.

'The Captain. He's alive.'

Epilogue

Since the outcome of war is dubious, and since battle is harsh, and everyone fighting tends to conquer rather than be conquered, and those fighting cannot consider anything going on away from them, men are unable to judge well even those things that are happening to them. Yet afterwards, the events must be judged...

Gilles Li Muiset, Major Chronicle

She slept that night in the forest, but woke before dawn, and crept once more to the edge of the trees to watch the next day unfold. She watched the French attack once more, before being driven off by the English.

Easier, this time.

She stayed another night, too, so that she could see how they treated the dead. How they were piled up in stacks of three on three on three. Their fine things stripped. Hands cut off to take rings. Wagons of food and drink brought up from abandoned camps.

She could not decide whom she hated more.

But she knew she was not finished.

In the middle of the second afternoon she saw the kind man from Caen and his friends, stretched out exhausted in the sun.

She fingered his knife. She kept it sharp.

He had told her it had killed men.

She balanced it by the point on her fingertip. Flicked it in the air and caught it by the handle, as she had done now hundreds of times.

She thought about Valognes. And everywhere she had seen since.

She thought about the prince, who now strutted proudly about the camp, telling stories of the battle that was won to all who would hear him.

She flicked the knife in the air and caught it.

It had killed men.

It would kill men again.

Author's Note

Edward III's army and fleet, numbering around 15,000 men, invaded Normandy in the summer of 1346. Over the course of the next six-and-a-half weeks, they marched, burned and fought their way from the Normandy beaches to the edge of a forest beyond the Somme. This was one of the first and most dramatic major campaigns of the Hundred Years War, fought between the Kingdoms of England and France and their various allies between 1337 and 1453. Many of its events had become legendary even before the participants had arrived home.

This book, self-evidently, is a fictional portrayal of that campaign from the eyes of one small company, the Essex Dogs. True, many of the characters depicted in this book really were present on the Crécy campaign, and most of the major episodes described here really occurred – from the landing at Saint-Vaast-la-Hougue to the retrieval of the three knights' heads at Saint-Lô to the crossing of the Blanchetaque and the final battle itself. The source quotes that begin each chapter are drawn from original fourteenth-century chronicles. But the Dogs are purely imaginary characters, and all the real historical characters who are depicted – the Prince of Wales, the Earls of

Northampton and Warwick, and others – have been drawn as I pleased. I have written many history books. This one is fiction. Readers who want to see where I have followed the historical facts, and where I have taken liberties, can consult the basic reading list that follows this note.

I conceived this book in several stages. The idea of writing about a rogue band of freebooter-soldiers known as the Essex Dogs came to me while I was dozing on a flight from Prague to London in 2017. I began writing about them, but could not find the right adventure for them to have. So I shelved the project, and forgot about it until the winter of 2018/2019, when I rented a house in Normandy, quite near Saint-Lô. During a New Year's Day walk on Omaha Beach with friends, I began to think that having the Dogs take part in Edward III's 1346 landing a little further up the coast (on 'Utah Beach') might be viable, and fun.

Yet even then I dithered. It was not until that summer, after a wide-ranging conversation over dinner with George R. R. Martin, a history lover whose works of fiction I admire enormously, that something clicked. I went home and started work. George had nothing to do with the writing of this story. His contribution ended at being an inspiration and a personal hero. But it was an important contribution all the same.

A few people read parts of this book as I was writing, and offered suggestions, their encouragement or both. I am grateful in that respect to Natasha Bardon, Shane Batt, Honor Cargill-Martin, Julia Dietz, Walter Donohue, Elodie Harper, Wayne Garvie, Blake Gilbert, Duff McKagan, Oliver Morgan, Joel Wilson and Paul Wilson. I am grateful to Michael Livingston for sharing an advance manuscript of his superb and groundbreaking history of Crécy. My publishers Anthony

Cheetham and Nic Cheetham at Head of Zeus encouraged me to add fiction to my repertoire. Terezia Cicel and her colleagues at Viking Penguin brought it to a US audience. Laura Palmer and her team turned this from a manuscript into a book. My agent Georgina Capel had my back – again.

Extra special thanks go to two important companies. To the Dogs, for allowing me to bring them to life, and to my family, for putting up with me while I did.

Dan Jones
Staines-upon-Thames
Spring 2022

Reading List

Andrew Ayton and Sir Philip Preston: *The Battle of Crécy, 1346* (Boydell: 2005)

Richard Barber: *Life & Campaigns of the Black Prince* (Boydell: 1986)

Michael Livingston: *Crécy: Battle of Five Kings* (Osprey: 2022)

Michael Livingston and Kelly DeVries: *The Battle of Crécy: A Casebook* (Liverpool University Press: 2015)

Marilyn Livingstone and Morgen Witzel: *The Road to Crécy: The English Invasion of France, 1346* (Routledge: 2013)

Jonathan Sumption: *The Hundred Years War Volume I: Trial by Battle* (Faber: 1990)